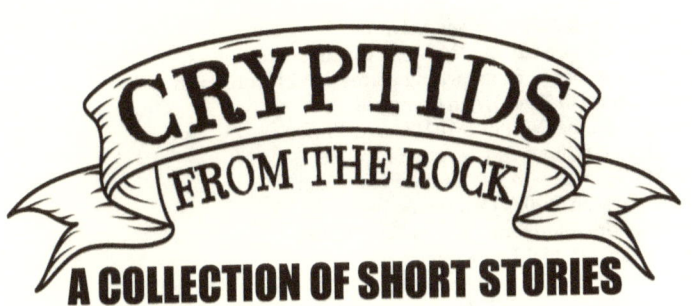

CRYPTIDS
FROM THE ROCK
A COLLECTION OF SHORT STORIES

Library and Archives Canada Cataloguing in Publication information is available upon request.

ISBN-13: 978-1-77478-164-7

Distributed by:
Engen Books
www.engenbooks.com
submissions@engenbooks.com
First mass market paperback printing: June 2024
Cover Image: © 2024 Graham Blair Designs

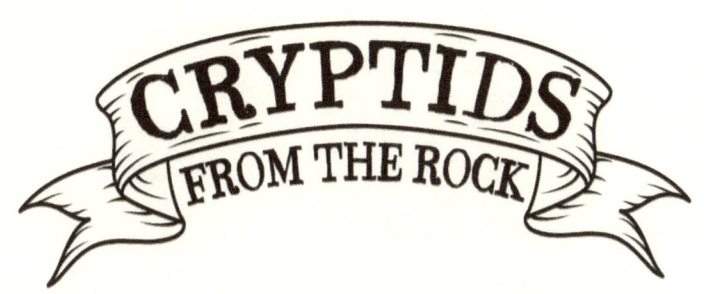

CRYPTIDS
FROM THE ROCK

EDITED BY ELLEN CURTIS AND ERIN VANCE

ENGEN
BOOKS

Introduction
Ellen Louise Curtis

There is something uniquely unsettling about driving some of Newfoundland's less travelled roads at night. In areas where the tree limbs reach out to touch your car, and the light of your headlights struggles to illuminate each bend in the road, a sense can steal over you that causes the hairs on the back of your neck to stand to attention. When you are schooled into hypervigilance watching for errant moose to cross your path, it's easy for the shadows to play tricks on you, for the wildlife stirring in the tree line to stir fear in your heart. A swooping bird can seem too large, shadows can seem to follow you too close, and the reflection in your rearview mirror can begin to play tricks on you. Woe to the person, arriving late at night to their isolated destination, who is not well stocked on spare batteries for their flashlight. A beam of light passing through trees could reveal a rabbit as the source of rustling branches, but what if the darkness conceals a bear? What if the night shrouds something worse?

The idea for this collection was fueled by such excursions, by childhood days spent searching for Sasquatch with cousins in the forest surrounding our family cabin, and by campy films about Mothman or Nessie. In these pages, you'll find stories that bring goose bumps out on your skin or a laugh to your lips, but all will leave you wondering what cryptids may lurk nearby.

Ellen Curtis
Editor

CONTENTS

Ali House

Ali House is an award-winning, bestselling author, originally from Newfoundland. She is a graduate of the Fine Arts program at Sir Wilfred Grenfell College (MUN), and currently resides in Halifax where she works in arts administration and spends more time than a person should in and around theaters. She is a master storyteller whose work has helped define the landscapes of science-fiction, fantasy, and horror writing in Atlantic Canada.

House's short fiction has appeared in the *From the Rock* anthology series, *Bluenose Paradox, Kit Sora Artobiography,* and *Terror Nova.* Her short fiction was collected in 2020 in *The Lightbulb Forest.*

Previous novels include *The Six Elemental* and *The Fifth Queen,* both a part of her creator-owned *Segment Delta Archives* series. Other works include the fantasy series *Choose Your Own Adventurer,* the *Santa Claus Protection Program,* and *The Island Adventure* as a part of the Slipstreamers series of novellas, and *Variety Show.*

In April 2024 she released her eigth novel, *The Hunters and the Hunted.*

Episode 43 - Transcript

[*theme music (spooky and upbeat)*]

Ricky: Hi everyone, I'm Ricky.

Alex: And I'm Alex.

Ricky: And welcome to *The Unexplainable World*, where we bring you the weirdest and spookiest tales from this big ol' planet that we call Earth. When Alex and I started this series, we had plenty of tales to choose from.

Alex: [*counting on fingers*] Bigfoot, Nessie, Mothman, Roanoke, Bermuda Triangle…

Ricky: Just to name a few. So imagine our surprise when we received an email from one of our listeners in Newfoundland–

Alex: –that's in Eastern Canada, for all of our non-Canadian listeners out there–

Ricky: –telling us about a creature we'd never heard of. In fact, when we asked our friends and family, none of them had heard of this creature either.

Alex: Normally, we'd think that this person was pretending to be a fan, and was telling us a tall tale in order to pull our legs. Trying to make fools out of us by getting us to report on a fake cryptid that didn't actually exist.

Ricky: Except that this listener brought receipts. Newspaper articles, eyewitness accounts...

Alex: [*nods*] It was surprisingly thorough.

Ricky: So why did this creature never make it into the mainstream consciousness?

Alex: I'd argue that it's because of *where* it happened. How many of you knew Newfoundland existed before we mentioned it? Be honest. I bet it's not a lot.

Ricky: I thought it was fictional, like Narnia or Middle Earth.

[*they both laugh*]

Alex: You weren't a good student in school, were you?

Ricky: And you were?

Alex: I was, as a matter of fact. I was a straight-A student. You seem like more of a C-plus.

Ricky: Well, it doesn't matter, because we both ended up here.

Alex: Valid point.

[*they both laugh*]

Ricky: Needless to say, our interest was piqued.

Alex: We love hearing about strange, spooky creatures.

Ricky: So we decided to do some more digging, and the more we discovered about this creature, the more we realized that we had to share our knowledge. And who better to share it with than you — our amazing listeners and supporters.

Alex: Our faithful Unexplainers.

Ricky: So, without further adieu, let's discover the unexplainable mystery of *The Newfoundland Harbinger*.

[*spooky music starts*]

Ricky: Our story starts in 2012. On August 14th, Terry and Emily – not their real names – were driving along Highway 430, on the northern coast of Newfoundland. Earlier that day, they had driven from their home in Daniel's Harbour to Norris Point, and as they were driving back, night was beginning to fall. Emily was an experienced driver who had travelled this highway many times before, and while she drove, both Terry and she kept a close eye out for moose.

[*spooky music stops*]

Alex: Moose?

Ricky: Moose. You know, moose. [*put hands up to his head to signify antlers*]

Alex: Hold on, let me look this up. [*takes phone out and starts typing*] Holy crap. Those things are huge.

Ricky: Just imagine one of those running in front of your car. You – and the car – would be toast.

Alex: Yikes. Wait, is this our creature? Is the creature a moose? Have I solved it?

Ricky: I'd say that it's unlikely, but we're getting ahead of ourselves.

[*spooky music starts*]

Ricky: All was well as Emily was driving, but as they neared home, Emily suddenly saw an animal about the size of a coyote dart across the road, towards the sea. There were no other cars on the road so she switched on her hazard lights and put on the brakes, worried that more animals might appear and cross her path. Nothing did, but as she looked over at the creature that had run in front of her car she noticed that it had made its way to the water's edge and was now staring back at her. It was unlike anything she had seen before. The body was similar in shape to a coyote, there were antlers on its head, and its face was weird. It was flat and almost looked human. But the thing that scared her the most was that its eyes were glowing bright red and it was staring right at her. Startled, she stepped on the gas and drove away from the creature.

Alex: Spooky.

Ricky: Indeed. Can you imagine something glaring at you with glowing red eyes?

Alex: Not many creatures out there with those.

Ricky: She was still spooked once Terry and she arrived home – unable to shake the memory of that strange creature. Terry hadn't gotten a good look at it, but he had no reason to doubt his wife. She wasn't the kind of person who made up stories like that, and he could see that she was genuinely unnerved.

Alex: That's nice of him to support his wife.

Ricky: The two of them wanted to ask around to see if anyone else had seen a creature like that, but they knew they'd have to be careful. In a small town, rumours spread quickly, and they didn't want to be labelled as crazy. So they decided to tell people that they'd seen an animal – probably a coyote – on the highway, and warned them all to keep an eye out.

Alex: That's a good way to get people watching for it without them thinking you're nuts. I applaud their plan.

Ricky: It was a good plan *and* it worked. Three nights after the incident, a friend of theirs, Chris – also not his real name – was driving along the same stretch of highway when he saw something run past. When he told Emily and Terry about the animal, he sounded quite strange, and Emily instantly knew something was up. It took quite a few beers to coax out the details, but Chris told them about the antlers, the strange human-like face, and the red eyes. Emily, who had never told anyone what she'd seen, was astonished that he'd seen the exact same creature as her.

[spooky music stops]

Alex: It's always a relief when you see something odd and then someone else sees that same thing. Like sharing a delusion. Makes you feel not so alone.

Ricky: *[pauses]* Does that happen to you a lot?

Alex: Not nearly enough.

Ricky: Anyway...

[spooky music starts]

Ricky: Now here's where things get really weird. One week after Emily had first seen the creature, there was an accident. It was a rainy day, but nothing remarkable. People in the area had seen rain like this many times before, and saw no reason to think that anything might be out of the ordinary. Chris was driving along the highway just as it was starting to get dark. He'd been trying to see the creature again, in the hopes of getting a picture or video of it, but so far had no luck. As he was driving past that same area, Chris noticed that the road ahead seemed to be moving in a wavy, shaking way. He wondered if it was a trick of the rain or wind, but something about it unnerved him, so he sped up in order to pass that section quicker. When he was on a part that was more stable, he slowed down and looked back just in time to see the road behind him suddenly shift and break away, sliding down towards the water.

Alex: What?

Ricky: If he hadn't sped up, his car would've been washed away with it.

[*spooky music stops*]

Alex: But how does that happen? The road just went [*Alex gestures as if pushing something to the side*] woosh?

Ricky: It's what's commonly referred to as a washout. When too much rain causes a portion of a road or highway to wash away.

Alex: Hold on – you said there was nothing strange about this rainy day.

Ricky: Exactly.

Alex: Woah.

Ricky: Nobody's sure how the highway washed out, especially since it was such a normal day, and the few days before had been sunny and without rain, but they assumed it was something to do with moisture gathering underground or years of accumulation building up.

Alex: What a load of phooey.

Ricky: That's what Emily, Terry, and Chris thought. They'd seen the creature right along that stretch of highway, and now that part of the highway was no more. So they got to thinking; wondering if maybe this kind of thing had happened before.

Alex: From the smile on your face, I sense a

scoop!

Ricky: Have you ever heard of a show called *Ghastly Varmints*?

Alex: You know I haven't.

Ricky: It aired in 2002 and didn't last very long; only about ten episodes. The few reviews I could find said it wasn't very good.

Alex: Some people would argue that our show isn't very good, but we've lasted four times as long.

Ricky: Their premise was that they wanted to research creatures that most people had never heard of and bring these legends into the mainstream. However, they had a hell of a time gathering proof and getting people to talk to them. Most of the locals they tried to interview thought they were crackpots, trying to make honest people look crazy for the sake of getting good ratings.

Alex: Fair enough. You've got to be careful around those kinds of people. Some creature hunters are super cool – like us – but there are some people out there who do hatchet jobs in the cutting room. And those people are jerks.

Ricky: The show reported on some pretty strange things, but episode eight of their ten-episode run was on The Newfoundland Highway Hell-Wolf.

Alex: Hmm. They probably could've workshopped that name a little more. It's a bit... [*waves hand in air*] ...wordy.

Ricky: I don't think the creature had been named before them. And, to their credit, their research is part of the reason it later came to be known as The Newfoundland Harbinger.

[*spooky music starts*]

Ricky: It was discovered that in 1999, a section of Highway 430 between Parson's Pond and Portland Creek had collapsed due to "irregularities in the ground," damaging two cars and sending the passengers to the hospital. However, in the week before the collapse there were rumours of people seeing a creature with glowing red eyes along the same stretch of highway. Some people said it was a coyote with odd ears or a very small caribou. There was even a rumour that it had the face of a man, but most people seemed to think that this part was made up – just local kids adding extra bits onto it, to make it more foolish. Anyway, the *Varmints* crew tried to talk to people in the area to get the rumours on record, but nobody wanted to speak to them, nor would they confirm anything about what had been seen.

Alex: And they still did a whole episode on it?

Ricky: Lucky for them, they had newspaper reports to help. In 1986, a similar incident happened along the same highway. Between Barr'd Harbour and Castor River South, a section of highway washed out due to rain, nearly taking a car with a family of five out to sea with it. Everyone survived unharmed, but they were shaken. Now, in the same newspaper that reported on the washout, buried in the Letters to the Editor section was an anonymous letter about how everyone should have known that something would happen, because there had been sightings of a red-eyed creature in the area. The letter said that this creature was from hell and had been sent by the devil to cause the accident.

[*spooky music stops*]

Alex: That person sounds fun. I'd like to hang out with whoever wrote that.

Ricky: Of course you would.

Alex: For someone who believes in this stuff, you're very judgmental at times. How do you know the creature wasn't sent by the devil? Huh? Do you have proof?

Ricky: Moving on...

[spooky music starts]

Ricky: The message was mostly discounted as some kind of crack-pot theory, but now we have three instances of people seeing a strange creature with red eyes just before a highway accident. And while three is pretty good, we've got a fourth sighting!

Alex: Whaaaat?

Ricky: In 1973. The tale wasn't in any of the newspapers, but was instead found in a book published in 2015. An author published a collection of stories about growing up in Newfoundland and tales about local folklore that her grandparents had told her when she was younger. One such story, which she'd discounted as a local legend, was about a couple seeing red eyes on the side of the highway just days before an incident on that same stretch of road. And if you look at newspapers from that time, it's true that in 1973 a section of Highway 430 washed out between Sandy Cove and Pines Cove, damaging two cars and sending three people to the hospital.

Alex: Okay, things are getting really weird now.

[spooky music stops]

Ricky: Have you done the math yet?

Alex: Never.

Ricky: 1973, 1986, 1999, 2012. Every thirteen years.

Alex: Woah. Maybe that person was right about the creature being sent by the devil. Thirteen's a pretty devil-ish number.

Ricky: That's why it became known as the New-foundland Harbinger. People who connected the dots thought that the creature was some kind of harbinger of doom, warning those in the area that it was time for another accident to happen. If you didn't heed the warning of the harbinger, then you might find yourself swept out to sea.

Alex: Spooky.

Ricky: It's a pretty long highway, too. Over 400 kilometres — or 250 miles, for the rest of us. It goes all the way up the north coast of Newfoundland.

Alex: Imagine knowing that every thirteen years something bad was going to happen to a part of the high-way, but never knowing which part it was. Maybe the harbinger's secretly good.

Ricky: From all reports, the creature doesn't do anything harmful. It just crosses the road and then sits by the water, staring at you.

Alex: With glowing red eyes.

Ricky: And the face of a man, but the body of a coyote, and the antlers of a moose.

Alex: What an odd assortment.

Ricky: But very regionally appropriate. Honestly, these are the easiest kind of creatures to discount — the ones that look like they might be something else. I mean, if Mothman dropped down in the middle of Newfoundland, people would notice, right? But something that might have been a coyote? Even with the red eyes, you might be able to convince yourself that maybe you'd imagined the antlers or the face.

Alex: Maybe the next time this creature comes a-calling someone will be able to get a photo or video. That would be cool. Heck, maybe we should go out and try to see it for ourselves. Let's see, every thirteen years...

Ricky: That'd be 2025.

Alex: Not too far off. Tell you what, listeners, if we're still doing this by 2025, we'll be sure to make a trip to Newfoundland to try and hunt for this harbinger. And we'll find it too!

Ricky: We can't guarantee that.

Alex: I can. And I do. [*points at the camera*] We'll find it.

Ricky: [*sighs*] Well that does it for this episode, fans. We hope you enjoyed this spooky, unexplained story just as much as Alex and I did. If you've heard any tales of the Newfoundland Harbinger or if you've seen it yourself, give us a shout. We love adding to our spooky creature files.

Alex: And if you're the person who wrote that Letter to the Editor and you wanna hang out, let me know.

Ricky: [*sighs again*] Thanks for listening, Unexplainers. We'll see you again next week.

Alex: Remember to keep your eyes on the road and your ears to the ground.

Ricky: Bye.

Alex: Bye!

[*musical outro plays*]

D. Thomas Minton

D. Thomas Minton was born in the deep south of the United States, but grew up around the world. In 2019, he settled in the mountains of British Columbia with his family. When not writing speculative fiction, he works to protect the B.C.'s lakes and rivers.

Minton's fiction has appeared in numerous science fiction magazines and anthologies, including *Asimov's*, *Lightspeed* and *Apex Magazines*, and has been translated into several other languages. His fiction has appeared on numerous year-end recommended reading lists, and his story "The Schrödinger War" was selected as a South Million Writers Award notable story in 2014.

Footprints in the Forest

Bowden Duclair's description of his older brother was entirely congruent with my expectations for Cortez Duclair, North America's foremost bigfoot hunter and cryptozoologist. Everything I had read about Cort portrayed him as larger-than-life, like he'd stepped out of a Paul Bunyan tall tale. He sounded as mythical as the purported creatures he had spent his life pursuing.

"Cort wasn't the type to go quiet," Bowden told me one hot July evening over a half-dozen Budweisers. Cort's brother was built like a cut stump and smelled of freshly turned loam. "He told me he was gettin' close, that he had a real lead. That's why he went up there."

With "there" being the town of Toulamine Creek, Cortez Duclair's last known whereabouts.

The bug lantern sizzled, its bluish glow lashing over the crevices that carved lines in Bowden's forehead. All the while we talked, his brow wore those furrows, growing deeper whenever our conversation turned to his brother.

Bowden shook his head. "Bet it was a sasquatch."

Toulamine Creek sits nestled in the high montane forests of British Columbia near the terminus of a winding ribbon of cracked asphalt north of the Crowsnest Highway. Its fate was inexorably linked to the economics of resource extraction, primarily virgin timber and zinc. When the ore and the trees were no longer easy to remove, the town's prosperity drained away, but unlike other towns that withered like unpicked salmon berries, Touley persevered, eventually reinventing itself as a haven for eco-adventurers from Vancouver and Seattle. After a day of revitalizing their ravaged souls on the forested trails and crystal mountain lakes, those affluent suburbanites could fortify their bodies with a vegan-friendly farm-to-table feast at the Silverleaf Cafe or a pint of pine-needle IPA from Touley's own Evergreen Brewery.

"Touley is the town everyone wishes they could live in." Peggy McIllith, owner of the Silverleaf, refreshed my cup of steaming chamomile tea and nudged a plate of fresh berry tartlets closer to my hand. We lounged beneath the spruce boughs on the back deck of her small cottage, bathed in dappled sunlight and birdsong. In the distance, the staccato report of a downy woodpecker broke up the serene afternoon.

After the death of her son in a car accident, Peggy's marriage had unraveled (it was no one's fault, she insisted, sometimes things just happen). She moved from Lethbridge to Touley eleven years ago, and in the process of resurrecting her own life, she did the same for her adopted town. While other Toulamites credit her for leading the town's reinvention, Peggy's modesty was as legendary as her kindness. "It takes a village to save a town or a person," she told me.

Peggy was known for putting up wayward souls in her spare room. When I met with her, she introduced me to her current resident, a recovering addict from up north — "the exact place isn't important," she said.

Last year, when Cort Duclair would have come to town, she had a person known only as Chuck living with her. "I never learned his actual name," she explained with a wistful glance into the forest. Peggy often gazed into the trees, as if longing to heed the call of the forest spirits. "I think Chuck might have been Norwegian," she continued after a moment. "Biggest fella I've ever seen, and lots of blond hair. Didn't speak any English, at least not to me, but responded when I called him Chuck, so Chuck he was."

Cortez Duclair had dedicated his adult life to proving sasquatches were flesh and blood.

"I don't know if I'd call it an obsession." Bowden finished his beer and cracked open another. I could not tell if he believed his words or not.

For over twenty years Cort had followed every lead that came his way. He examined every photograph, video, footprint, and tuft of hair. He interviewed hunters, farmers, hikers, even children, who claimed to have seen the elusive cryptid. Much of this "evidence" he had discredited as fake, some of it he found inconclusive, but a few pieces he was certain were real, even in the face of mainstream skepticism. He frequently published his findings in the Journal of Cryptozoology, and kept meticulous notes, which filled hundreds of handwritten notebooks that Bowden had recovered from his brother's one-bedroom cabin on the outskirts of Ellensburg, Washington.

"Bigfoot was his life," Bowden eventually conceded. Indeed, Cort had never married, and he appeared to have no friends outside other sasquatch enthusiasts. His childhood friends had drifted away because "Bigfoot became more important than hanging with us," one of them told me. For nearly six weeks, he dated a woman named Catherine, a fellow cryptozoologist, but their relationship ended after a "professional" disagreement over the legitimacy of a femur bone found by a rock climber in the shadow of Mt. Despair, Washington.

"No doubt Cort was a brilliant man," Catherine told me over the phone, "but he was obsessed with finding a live *Homo cascadensus*, even though all the evidence points to them being driven extinct soon after the arrival of white settlers to the Pacific Northwest. Don't get me wrong," Catherine continued, "I'm as obsessed as the next woman about proving the existence of *cascadensus*, but Cort? He was almost pathological, as if it was the only thing that mattered."

"It wasn't always like that," Bowden told me, with a sad shake of his head. In the distance a thunderstorm rolled across the Palouse prairie, but Bowden assured me we'd not "smell a drop of rain," and true to his word, our acre of grass never got wet.

The Duclair boys had grown up in a suburb of Kennewick, Washington, where their father owned a moderately successful auto body shop, and their mother scaled teeth for the family dentist. As with most of us, Cort's childhood was unspectacular: an above-average student but never one that excelled and a below-average baseballer who eventually gave up the game when a slow bat relegated him to the bench. He attended Sunday school, shot pick-up hoops at the local park, and rode bikes with his friends to the local Dairy Queen for Oreo Blizzards.

This undistinguished childhood changed the day after Cort's tenth birthday.

Reluctantly, Bowden related that day to me. "Dad was gone by the time Cort and me got up," he explained. "He'd gone flyfishing on the Yakima River. He'd go a few times a year, but I remember him going a lot that summer. Usually, he went with a buddy of his from high school, but not always, and not that time. He never came home."

Three days later, the Washington State Police found Jack Duclair's 1983 Ford F-150 on a logging road outside of Easton. A search of the forest with dogs and a dozen local volunteers never found Jack Duclair's body or any signs of foul play. A brief investigation concluded he had "most likely gone missing of his own accord," ostensibly to escape an unhappy marriage.

"Cort never believed that," Bowden said, shrugging his shoulders as if to indicate he didn't know what to believe. After all these years, I suspect the truth no longer mattered to him. Whatever that truth was had died with the Mrs. Duclair six years ago.

"When Dad disappeared, that's when Cort got interested in bigfoots. He read every book he could get his hands on. He would post on one those computer bulletin boards — you might be too young to remember those — called CryptiNet. He even started a bigfoot club at school."

Bowden clucked his tongue. "He got teased fierce for that, but he didn't care."

"Do you think Cort believed bigfoot was responsible for your father's disappearance?"

"I don't think he could accept that Dad would just leave us."

"What about you?"

Bowden sucked his teeth while he contemplated his response. "I think people are capable of believing just about anything if they're desperate or sad enough."

When my editor first assigned me to the Duclair story, I read everything the man had written — over a hundred articles and book chapters on cryptids. The vast majority of these "scientific" papers focused on humanoid cryptids, from Himalayan yeti to the orang pendek of Sumatra, but Cort Duclair's primary interest was clearly the North American sasquatch, which he had given the latin name *Homo cascadensus*. He had authored dozens of articles on different sasquatch "sub-species," of which he had identified at least four that he distinguished by the length and prevalence of hair and body morphology, which he had extrapolated from the size and shape of footprints. Admittedly, these papers suffered from suspect scientific methods, a dearth of credible data, and an abundance of wild conjecture, which only lent credence to the derision heaped on cryptozoologists like Cort Duclair by the credentialed scientific community.

"Mr. Duclair certainly considered himself a scientist," said Dr. Paul Popovich, Professor of Biology at Central

Washington University. "He may have been an observant man — perhaps even a competent naturalist — but he had no formal scientific training and it showed in his work." For forty years, Dr. Popovich has studied large mammals in the Pacific Northwest, and he's authored what many consider the seminal volume on the bears of North America. He has spent more years in the forests and mountains of Washington, Idaho, and British Columbia than I have on this Earth, so his response to my question about the possibility of sasquatches existing unseen in the Pacific Northwest carried considerable gravitas. "I do not doubt Mr. Duclair's conviction," he told me, "but I'm aware of no legitimate and compelling evidence to support a large, cryptozoic species of hominid living in North America."

And yet, that evidence was exactly what Bowden Duclair believed his brother went to Toulamine Creek to find. In support, he showed me Cort's last dozen entries in his final notebook. These detailed a series of conversations with a Seattle-based amateur cryptozoologist who used the handle "CryptoCroc." CryptoCroc had recently returned from Toulamine Creek with information about "*Homo cascadensus parvus*," Cort's subspecies of sasquatch that was the smallest in size, covered with the least amount of hair, and which Cort believed might credibly be able to pass as an unusually tall human.

"I don't know if that's possible, but it don't matter what I think," Bowden said. "My brother went up there looking for a sasquatch, and no one has seen him since."

# # #

The RCMP, the Royal Canadian Mounted Police, conducted a brief investigation after Bowden reported his brother missing. Over two months had passed since Cort had purportedly gone to Toulamine Creek (Bowden seldom saw his brother, and only grew concerned after Cort's landlord reached out to him about missed rent), so the lack of evidence was not surprising. No one in Touley could positively say they had seen Cort, and while the description of Cort's pickup truck matched one that had been towed from the Evergreen Brewery parking lot several months earlier, the vehicle had been recycled after no one had claimed it. With no other leads, the RCMP closed the case, pending new information.

Which brings us back to Chuck, Peggy McIllith's mysterious Norwegian boarder. According to Cort's notebook, CryptoCroc had sent a grainy photograph of the purported sasquatch, but it was nowhere to be found in Cort's belongings. Presumably Cort had taken it to Toulamine Creek to aid his search.

I had no idea what I would find in Touley, but after spending several days interviewing over a dozen of its residents, I'm convinced that Cort Duclair came to find Chuck. Unfortunately, by the time I arrived, Chuck was nothing more than a collective memory among the Toulamites. Chuck had vanished one Tuesday morning after failing to return from his daily walk in the woods.

"He was a forest spirit, no doubt," Peggy told me, her eyes growing misty. "He would spend hours in the woods. I don't know what he was looking for, but I assume he found it. When he did, his time here was done, and I believe he just kept walking."

"People come and go all the time," Adam Marborough, another long-time Toulamite, explained when I asked him if he was concerned about Chuck's disappearance. Indeed, a third of Touley's population was transient, arriving at the start of the summer when tourism peaked, with most moving on by mid-October to other locations, primarily to ski towns farther north and east. "To be honest, I'm more sad than concerned that he's gone," Adam said.

A transplant from Guelph, Ontario, Adam operated the Evergreen Brewery with his partner Travis. While in Touley, Chuck had frequented their brewery, and even pitched-in carrying kegs and mopping floors. "That man had an insane nose for beer," Adam said wistfully. He credited Chuck with perfecting Evergreen's Piney Knob IPA, their award-winning pine-needle beer. "No matter what we tried, Travis and I couldn't get the recipe right. Then, one afternoon, that big guy lumbered into the brewery with a handful of the greenest, softest pine tips I've ever seen and dropped them into the kettle." Adam mimed the scene, tossing imaginary pine tips into an invisible copper kettle like a flamboyant chef might add a large pinch of seasoning to a simmering gumbo. Adam settled back in his chair, wrapping his arms around himself. "Don't know what we're going to do without him," he said. "Chuck saved us from bankruptcy."

Adam wasn't the only Toulamite to speak fondly of Chuck. If I were to believe the stories — and I heard dozens of them during my brief time in Toulamine Creek — I could only conclude Chuck was a superhuman altruist. He rescued Bradley Donner's cat from a tree, changed a flat tire for Meghan Kilgor and her five-month-old son, and even helped Candice Wu stain her back deck. "Such a gentle soul," Candice told me, reminiscing about how Chuck would gently rescue the ants from the deck instead of staining over them.

"It's not what's on the outside that matters," Peggy told me when I asked her to describe Chuck's physical appearance. "A gentle and genuine soul," Adam offered when I posed the same question, and no amount of silence shook loose anything more except a serene smile.

Asking around town, I received similar evasive responses from other Toulamites, except for Summer Wilson. Eighteen years ago, Summer had followed her lumberjack boyfriend, Leaf, to Touley. The boyfriend eventually followed the company out of town, but Summer remained. After several years sampling endemic psilocybin mushrooms and living off a generous stipend from her estranged mother, she inherited a sizable fortune, and used the money to open Rock Stomping, Toulamine Creek's upscale bootery for men.

As we spoke, she insisted on fitting me with a pair of Saloman Ultras, which she insisted were the best boot into which any man could stuff his toes. When I inevitably brought our conversation around to Chuck, Summer sat back on her heels and chewed at her lower lip as the corners of her mouth rose mischievously. She fanned herself with a shoebox lid as a burst of nervous laughter shook loose from her. "Lordy, it's gotten hot in here." She tapped the hot pink nail of her index finger against her lips. "Chuck was . . . how should I put it? Let's just say he was a credit to his Viking heritage."

"So he was Scandinavian?"

"Oh, I don't know. Peggy said he was from Norway when she brought him in for a pair of boots. Poor man never spoke a word to me. He was the... sexy, silent type." Summer flashed a wicked smile.

I asked how the fitting went, but instead of answering, she complimented me on the shape of my toes. After some additional conversation, it became clear that Summer had more than a professional interest in feet — she handled mine with an almost sensual tenderness. "I can tell a lot about a man by his feet." She proceeded to "read my feet," producing a flattering, even if mostly inaccurate, personality profile.

I surreptitiously returned to my question of Chuck's fitting, and now sufficiently primed, Summer was more amenable to talking. "Chuck had most amazing feet. Big and square, which tells me he's principled, honest, and reliable. Someone with a big heart."

"How big?"

"Oh, he'd give you the clothes off his back, which is why I think he didn't have any shoes!"

"I mean his feet, not his heart. How big were his feet?"

"I stock up to a size thirteen for my popular boots, but I had nothing that came close to fitting him. He must have been a size twenty-three or more." She held up her hands with over a foot of space between them. "That's a custom-made shoe, so giving those away would be a real sacrifice, you know, but that would be consistent with who Chuck was."

The only problem with Summer's logic was that

Chuck's shoes would have fit almost no one. The largest feet in the world — wearing size twenty-six shoes — belonged to a man in Venezuela, and it seemed unlikely he and Chuck would have ever crossed paths.

This documented fact also indicated that Chuck's feet, while extremely large, were within the size range of humans. Was Chuck a *Homo cascadensus parvus* — a bigfoot — or simply a *Homo sapiens* with abnormally large feet? I left Toulamine Creek without a concrete answer, but then, did the truth really matter? Or was Bowden correct in that the only thing that truly mattered was what Cort Duclair believed?

The forests around Toulamine were once dominated by giant cedars, spruce, and Douglas fir, with a smattering of leggy lodgepole pines. Over the past half-century, most of these giants have been removed and processed into homes and furniture and particle board or split and burnt to roast marshmallows or warm our homes through long dark winters. But there is a path that starts at the edge of Touley, about a hundred yards past the T-mart, that winds its way up the mountain, through hectare after hectare of scrubby secondary growth. It crosses several small creeks, whose waters still do not run crystal clear, and eventually up a ridge, where it stops abruptly at a drop too treacherous to navigate without ropes and pitons. There, you can gaze down into a secluded valley wreathed almost perpetually in clouds, but if lucky, through the perforations in the mist, you will see a patch of mossy old growth forest nestled between the imposing granite cliffs.

Peggy told me that a path winds down into that valley, but it wasn't for the faint at heart or even the sane. Once, when Peggy was younger and in better shape and a little less wise, she had clawed her way down it into the shade of those giant cedars. In that cool spot, sitting on a mossy boulder, she had been overcome to the point of tears by awe and sorrow. Awe because she could feel the weight of ancient life emanating from every crevice of the cedar bark, from every damp stone, and from every gurgle of the creek as it swirled and twisted between cool, dark pools. And sorrow, too, for what we, humans, and specifically settlers, have done to defile this place. That experience realigned her life to the path she now walked.

If sasquatches exist, that would be their home, and Touley would be the place a young bigfoot might go to quench its curiosity about humans. And once it knew all it needed to know, it would likely retreat to the safety of its ancient trees, to its home.

Many of us don't realize it, but we are all seeking something: love, happiness, attachment, freedom, knowledge, community. It's the human condition to need; it's what drives us forward on this path we call life. Where it ends, I can't say because I have not reached its terminus. But what happens when that need is filled, when the path we're walking comes to an end and no side trail winds off into another forest?

The Buddhist have a concept called Nirvana, a state of enlightenment when earthly wants and ignorance have been extinguished. Only once this happens can you ascend beyond earthly suffering.

After losing his father, finding a sasquatch became the sole, driving need for Cortez Duclair, a goal that until recently I would have insisted was unobtainable. It matters not if I (or anyone else) believe this goal was unhealthy for Cort; it was his chosen path. And so, I wonder what happened when Cort came face-to-face with his bigfoot?

I showed Peggy a photo of Cort Duclair when I explained my reason for coming to Touley. "I'll tell you the same as I told the RCMP," she said. "A lot of folks come through Touley looking for something, so I can't say one way or the other if I saw that particular man." I received similar answers from the other Toulamites I interviewed, and I can find no fault in their sincerity. To a person, none believed Chuck would have harmed anyone, Cort Duclair included.

I would like to think, in that moment of truth for Cort, that neither man nor sasquatch (if that's what he was) did harm to the other. I'd like to fantasize that they met in some secluded grove of old-growth cedars, looked each other in the eyes, and, finding whatever it was that each of them was seeking, gained release from whatever might have tormented them. That afterwards, they peacefully parted ways, and continued on whatever path they now followed, forging new footprints through new forests.

Marianne King

Marianne King grew up in Port-de-Grave, Newfoundland & Labrador and spent most of her life living in the province.

King's short story "Open the Door" was published in "Paper Mill Press" (2022), a creative arts journal produced annually from Grenfell Campus in Corner Brook, NL.

In March 2019, King won the Kit Sora Flash Photography Fiction contest with the story "The Perils of the Sea," and again in January 2023 with "Pinpoints of Light."

They bring with them a story based on a cryptid that has occasionally been spotted on the west coast of the island, with the fuzzy video to go with the sightings.

Things Are Not What They Seem

The triangular silhouette of pine trees was barely visible against the twilight sky's backdrop. The darkness made the night sounds of the forest, the chirps, hoots, and rustles, seem even louder. At first, there was nothing else to see, then two large pale dots glowed brightly. They disappeared for a minute, then reappeared again about ten feet to the left. This continued, the reappearing and disappearing, for another few minutes, the dots moving back and forth in amongst the trees. A strange scream sounded, and then everything went black.

I closed my eyes and sighed. Another video, another assignment, another waste of time. "So, what do you think?"

Jess' chair squeaked as she shifted closer to the screen. Lifting her mug — the words, "Nessie is my Bestie" splashed across the front in a colourful, watery font — she took a sip of her coffee before replying. "I'm not sure. There's not much to go on."

This was true.

We sat in the cramped office area of Kraken Ink, a tabloid-style publication that dealt solely with reports of cryptid sightings around the world. Most of the articles were made up, based on whatever pictures or videos we were sent, especially if the sightings were too far away to travel to, such as another continent.

I'd started there straight out of college and had been there now for a decade. The pay was good, but it was starting to wear on me. All those articles on all those creatures, but there wasn't a single shred of evidence to prove any of it. I'd decided that, after this reported sighting, I was going to quit.

"Play it again."

I dragged my mouse back and clicked play. The video began again, the dots renewing their movements.

Jess was quiet when the video ended, staring at the screen. Finally: "Do you think it's a hoax?"

I did, but I replied with what she wanted to hear. "I've watched it numerous times, and while it's definitely possible, it's hard to say for sure."

"Where did it come from?"

"It was posted anonymously to the group with us tagged in it. It seems it was filmed near a small town in Newfoundland." The video disappeared as I opened up some other documents. "I did a bit of research on the area already to see if there were any other sightings. What I found was a bit more…concerning. It seems that while there has been another possible sighting or two, there've been a lot more reports of animals found viciously killed in the woods."

"So this cryptid could be dangerous?" Her swallow was loud in the room.

"With the assumption that it's the cryptid, and not

some random coyote. The island doesn't have any wolves anymore."

"And we're doing this?"

"I think so. The video seemed pretty convincing that there's something there."

"Newfoundland." Her voice was flat. "We're gonna have to take the ferry, aren't we?"

"Well, we could fly, but then we wouldn't have our own vehicle. We could rent one, but who knows what we'd get." I quickly showed her the map of the area that I had pulled up from the internet earlier. "Also, with the cost of airfare these days, we wouldn't be able to bring all of our gear."

"You know I'm afraid of deep water, therefore I hate boats, right?" The glow of the monitor made her face even paler.

"Yeah, I know. But, the bigger the boat, the less movement there is?"

Her sigh was explosive in its depth of feeling. "Well, I guess it'll be okay. Maybe."

I patted her on the back. "Get packed. Looks like we're going on a road trip."

The trip to the island had been uneventful, other than Jess' stress on the ferry ride over. The medication she had taken for the boat trip had given her a tired, yet giddy, demeanour. I'd been both concerned and quietly amused. Once we reached Newfoundland and started driving again, she was out like a light.

The mountains of the island's west coast slowly

changed to the hillier, forested central area. Early fall splashes of yellow and orange appeared amongst the trees, giving way to more pine filled forest the further east we drove.

Our plan was to stay in the nearby town overnight, giving us a chance to talk to the locals and get some eye-witness accounts of the creature. Then we would move on to the area where the video had been taken, camping there until we found what we'd come for.

The town was beautifully tiny, a cluster of houses at the end of a crater-filled road that was in dire need of maintenance. The houses were old but, ignoring the one or two houses that had too many painted ceramic figurines that seemed to be in every small town, clean and tidy. People's pride in their homes and town was clear.

The Airbnb that we had rented was small and boxlike, the pretty cream colour of the exterior complementing the mix of fall colours from the trees behind it. Jess, who had woken up when the roller coaster road to the town had started, softly muttered, "Ooooo…pretty," under her breath.

The sounds of birdcall and a chittering squirrel met us as we stepped out of the car. A small breeze blew, rustling the leaves in the trees. Other than that, peace. The silence of a small town. Even the sound of children playing in the distance seemed muted.

"We'll grab our gear from the car after we get settled." Hefting my bag over my shoulder, I headed for the house.

Jess huffed behind me as she did the same. She always packed too much for these assignments.

The door gave a small squeak as it opened, revealing even more charm inside. I inhaled, the smell of baked bread leading me to the small kitchen at the back. On the counter was a loaf of freshly baked bread, with a sweet little welcome note.

"I love small towns," Jess breathed as she came in behind me.

We put our bags in the upstairs rooms and then brought in the rest of the gear, setting some of it up in the living room. After this was done, we took some recording equipment and headed into town to get some food and talk to the locals.

We drove through the town, looking for a place to eat. As with most small towns, there were only a few places to eat, mostly deep-fried takeout. We finally settled on a small place that seemed to specialize in battered turkey and fries, with dressing and gravy, and some fish and wings available as well. Walking in the door, we were met with the smell of grease and an electronic chime letting the people in the back know we were there. There were a few other diners sitting at the rickety metal tables, and all eyes turned to us as we walked in. Old photos of the town and the people who lived in it covered the walls, framed by faded plastic. They stood out against the pale yellow of the walls.

We walked to the counter, ordered our food, and sat at one of the formica-topped tables. Leaning my elbows on the surface, the whole thing tilted, rocking on its uneven legs.

The server — a short, stout woman with dark curly hair, a contagious smile, and a name tag that said "Madonna" — came over to lay our paper placemats and cutlery on the table. "Your food'll be out shortly," then turned and walked away.

Cryptids seemed to show up near small towns, so by now Jess and I had done enough of these assignments that we knew how to start talking to the locals without them shutting us out. We chatted about this and that, intermittently studying the pictures on the wall above us and commenting on them. As we talked, we could sense the surrounding few diners studying and listening, trying to make sense of why we were in their small town.

"Now, me duckies." Madonna appeared, placing steaming plates piled high with greasy turkey and fries covered in dressing and gravy in front of us. My mouth watered as the smell hit my nose. "Careful, it's hot. Ye don't want to be burning da roofs a your mouths."

We murmured our thanks, and she asked, "Is dere anyting else I can get for ya?"

Jess and I looked and each other and paused, a practiced move we did without even thinking. I smiled at her shyly. "Well," I slowly replied, "we were hoping to talk to some of the people here in the town about any experiences they might have had lately in the woods. We'd heard that there have been some strange things happening lately?"

Her smile dropped from her face, concern replacing the sparkle in her eyes. "Yes, there's some goin's on. Everyone's right worried about it." Her eyes sharpened. "Now, there's no need of a couple a youngsters like you getting caught up in that business. It's awful, it is."

"So, there are people who've seen something?"

Lines appeared between her eyebrows. She glanced

around, then quietly said, "There've been talk of something in the woods. Something killing small animals, even getting bolder sometimes. Young Tom was out walking his little dog a few nights ago. The little dog got too close to the woods and before Tom could blink, it was gone. They never did find it. His little one is terrible upset about it. Loved that dog and doesn't understand where it's gone."

I put on my most charming smile. "Is there anyone here in the town that we'd be able to talk to about it. Someone who might have seen something? Young Tom, perhaps?"

Her eyes sharpened. "Most won't talk to you, even if they had seen something. It's best to leave it alone." Then she turned and walked back to the counter, disappearing through the kitchen's swinging door.

"Well, so much for that," I murmured to Jess. "Judging by her reaction, we might not find anyone willing to talk to us."

"Most likely," Jess agreed. Picking up her fork, she speared some fries and swirled them through the gravy, bringing the mess to her mouth. She chewed for a bit, then closed her eyes and said, "Mmmm, that is so good."

I starting eating too, skipping the fries and starting on the battered turkey. Little bits exploded from the crispy shell as I cut into it. As I chewed, the taste exploded over my tongue. I agreed with her declaration.

"So, what do we do now?" Jess asked around a mouthful of food.

"We'll have to ask around and see if there's anyone who'll talk to us. There's got to be someone." Shrugging, I continued, "If not, we'll just have to head out to the woods earlier than planned."

As we talked about our plans, we continued eating. More of the plate became visible as our food dwindled. A chair scraped across the floor, pulled from the table across from us, and a man sat down at our table. He was young, with a baseball cap pulled low over his short blond hair and wearing one of those thick plaid shirts that everyone seemed to wear in small towns. Bits of sawdust clung to the fabric. He glanced towards the kitchen where Madonna had disappeared, then turned back to us.

"You're looking for da creature?"

My fork paused, halfway to my open mouth, which I promptly closed. "You've seen it?"

"No, but I knows someone who might 'ave. And who might be willing ta talk to ya." Another glance towards the kitchen. "Cause by now, Madonna'll 'ave told em all not to say a word. When you're done here, head towards da edge of town, down towards da pond. You'll see a small house dere, looks a little rundown. In da back'll be a small shed. He'll be in dere, everyone 'round 'ere calls him Uncle Jim. I'll go and talk to 'im first, let 'im know you're coming."

With that, he got up and left.

"Well, that's interesting." I raised my eyebrows at Jess.

We finished our meal, cleaning our plates right down to the last drop of gravy. Standing up to leave, we gathered our things and headed for the door. I glanced back before I exited and caught Madonna's face looking through the kitchen doorway.

After a short drive in the direction the man had told us, we found the house that he'd mentioned. It was small, more of a cottage, with peeling white paint and faded black shutters. The front door looked like it would take a good push to get it open. Around the back was a small burgundy shed that was in much better condition than the house, with its windows glowing and smoke coming out of a small chimney in the roof.

The door to the shed was small, and it shook against its frame as I knocked. It creaked outward, a shaft of light falling across the ground, as it opened. Framed in the light was a small man.

"Yer lookin' for information about the creature." His voice was low and scratchy, the voice of someone who's spent many years either yelling or smoking.

I was suddenly wary. "Yes. Yes, we are."

Stepping back, he waved us inside. "Come on in. I'll put da kettle on."

Inside was warm, heated by a small woodstove in the corner. He shuffled over to it and, after tossing in some more logs from the woodpile next to the stove, put a small kettle on top. White light from an overhead fluorescent fixture lit the room, giving us a better view of him.

Short and wiry, his bald head looked like it barely reached my shoulder. The light from above shadowed his face, enhancing the grooves around his mouth and eyes.

I started talking.

"We were hoping you cou—"

"When da tea is ready." He nodded towards a small wooden table and chairs set along the wall.

We made our way over to the table and sat down next to each other on the creaky chairs.

Turning back to the stove, he pulled three mugs off

a shelf above him, along with a dented metal canister. Opening the canister, he dropped a teabag in each mug. Then he brought some powdered milk and sugar over and placed them in the centre of the table.

A shrill whistle announced that the kettle was boiled. He moved to the woodstove and picked up a small folded towel, using it to grip the handle of the kettle. He poured water into each mug, then brought them over to us. Once he'd gotten his own mug, he settled in the chair across from us. The aromatic smell of the tea mixed with freshly chopped wood and woodsmoke.

"Now den. What is it you'd like ta know?" he asked.

I rummaged through my bag, trying to find my audio recorder. "First off, sir, is it alright if we record the conversation?"

"Don't see why not. But what'll you be using it for?"

Finding the recorder, I laid it on the table. "We're journalists for a small magazine called Kraken Ink that deals with these sorts of incidents, so we'll just use it for our own records to write our article."

He shrugged, so I hit play and started.

"This is Charlie James and—" I paused and Jess provided her name, "questioning Mr..." I looked at the man sitting across from us.

"My name's Jim Whiffen."

"Mr. Jim Whiffen," I continued, "about the reports of a creature in the nearby woods that's killing animals." I leaned forward a bit. "Have you seen this creature, Mr. Whiffen?"

His chair gave a small creak as he leaned back. "I have yes, but not in the way you think."

I frowned. "And what does that mean, Mr. Whiffen? Have you seen it or not?"

Fire crackled in the silence as he paused, looking past us. After a few seconds, he focused on us and replied. "I've seen da evidence of it. Animals killed so violently that dere's barely anyting to identify it as an animal." His inhale was loud in the room. "And shadows in amongst da trees. Shadows where dere shouldn't be any, in da shape of an animal I've never seen in dese woods before."

Disappointment flooded me. Another person who thought they'd seen something that wasn't there. "So, you've never actually seen it?"

Now it was his turn to look disappointed. "I don't need ta see it. Da evidence shows dat it's dere."

"And how much time do you spend in the woods?"

His glare told me he knew where this line of questioning was going. "I've been in dere every day lately to cut wood for da winter. I knows it like da back of my hand." He shook his head. "Dis creature, it's dangerous. You shouldn't be going and looking for it."

"It's what we do. We get a report of something and we investigate it." My smile was slight.

"And what'll ya do wit da creature if ya finds it?"

I started in on the usual spiel that we gave anyone who asked what we do. "Usually, we just try to get some evidence, such as a photo or something a little more physical, like a cast of a print or even something from the creature's body."

"So how do you plan on getting this evidence?" he asked.

Jess answered: "Once we've spoken to anyone who

might give us more information, we plan on camping in the woods for a few days, to see if we can spot it, hopefully getting a picture."

Shock filled his face. "Camping? In da woods? With da creature?"

She gave him a stern look. "Mr. Whiffen, as Charlie has already stated, this is what we do. We have experience in this sort of thing, and we're confident in our abilities."

"Well, you won't find many who will talk to you, 'cause dere's very few who've actually seen anyting in da town. Most of what you'll hear is rumours from folks who likes to gossip."

She fixed him with a bright smile. "So you're the only one who can give us any information?"

"Other den Young Tom, poor ting, dere's no one. And he's still upset and not saying much about it."

"I understand." Her smile brightened even more. "Well, in that case, you seem to be the only one who can help us. And since you know the woods so well, where's the best place for us to camp?"

He blinked a few times. "You'll go in dere whether I helps you or not, won't ya?"

We nodded.

He heaved a sigh, then got to his feet. "I'm against you two going in dere. But I can't stop you, so da least I can do is show you da best place to set up. Let me get me maps." Heading for a book shelf in the corner, he grabbed some papers and started back to us.

Something skittered across the roof and he froze, looking up then looking at us. Giving a small chuckle, he continued toward us. "Damn squirrels. Always trying ta get in here."

Laying his maps on the table, he paused. "It's getting late and you two should be gettin' back. You're gonna be really busy over da next few days. Why don't you two go on now and I'll come over in da morning wit a camping spot for ya?"

It was an obvious ploy to get us to leave. Just like that, he no longer wanted to talk.

"Are you sure? We can wait." Jess, like me, wanted to get this information from him sooner rather than later. "We don't want to cause you to go out of your way in the morning."

He waved a wrinkled hand at us. "It's no problem at all."

"It's fine, Mr. Whiffen. Thank you so much for your time." Getting to my feet, I picked up the recorder and ended the recording.

Pulling Jess to her feet and grabbing her bag, I pushed her toward the door.

Mr. Whiffen waved. "Have a good night, now. I'll see ya in da morning."

As we exited the shed, he was right behind us, shutting the door. We both had to stop, blinded by the sudden, absolute darkness. Night had fallen while we'd been inside.

Our car doors sounded extra loud as we shut them, gunshots in the dark.

The lights from the dash cast a glow on Jess' face as I started the car. "Why'd you leave so quickly?" she hissed.

"He wanted us gone," I replied. But I knew that wasn't it. It was something else. Something I'd seen on Mr. Whiffen's face when the squirrel ran across the roof.

It hadn't been amusement. It had been worry.

Hoo hoo! Hoo hoo!

The soft flap of wings accompanying the owl's call made me look up, but there was nothing to see, just darkness. Sitting outside my tent, I watched the feed from the trail cameras on my computer. Vibrantly coloured by day, the green night vision video feed was eerie once the dark set in. Jess and I had been taking turns keeping watch during the night, so she was inside her tent sleeping.

Mr. Whiffen had been true to his word, arriving early the morning after our talk with a camping location that he thought would best suit our needs. He tried again to dissuade us, and in the end left us with warnings to be careful and smart.

We'd spent the rest of the morning getting more supplies, then headed for the woods.

The turnoff to the campsite was miniscule, almost missed because I was looking so hard for it. Just a small dirt road, a few branches reaching across it as if to protect it from view. Dust rose around the car as we slowly made our way as far as we could. Then we got out, taking as much equipment as we could carry, and followed a trail the rest of the way.

The campsite was a small clearing close to where Mr. Whiffen had sensed the creature. We could see it before we reached it. The sun warmed the area, a bright glow surrounded by shadowed forest. The trail cut through it, disappearing on the other side. Just past the line of trees, the gurgle of a stream could be heard.

We'd set up quickly. First the campsite, our tents and

campfire. Then we'd ventured further out, placing our cameras and setting our traps.

The cameras were set up along the trails, both high and low. Once night fell, we could switch them to night vision. There hadn't been much to see so far other than the occasional small animal, its eyes glowing white.

What we were relying on mostly was a simple setup, just some fishing line across the trail with some bells attached. It was more of a detection system than a trap. Any large animal coming along the trail would trip and alert us to its presence. These were placed near the cameras. We also set some snares, and even a few live traps.

That had been two days ago.

Since then, there'd been nothing other than a few instances where it could have been the creature, or it could have been the wind.

Late on the first evening, Jess had thought she'd seen some glowing dots in the trees, but by the time we'd hurried there, the branches were empty. We figured that it had been wishful thinking.

The next night, jingling bells had woken us at about 2am. Jess wanted to rush into the woods, but I, with my pulse racing, kept her back. We didn't know what was out there, and though it was probably already gone, I didn't want to go chasing a shadow through the woods in the middle of the night. Checking our camera feeds, one showed a blur going by.

As soon as the sun hit the clearing, we headed for the camera that had picked up the shadow. We knew there would be nothing there, but maybe there was something evidence left behind to give us a clue as to what we were looking for.

That early in the morning, before the sun had been able to warm up the trees, the woods were noticeably colder than the clearing. Jess shivered as she followed me along the trail. As we approached the camera we slowed, becoming more aware of our surroundings. The trees were quiet, even the birdsong seemed muted.

The fishing line had been broken, the bells lying on the ground beside the trail. Condensation had formed on them, beading along the brass. I set about repairing the line and attaching the bells again.

Once it was repaired, we continued on, checking the other lines to make sure they hadn't been disturbed. The rest were untouched, just the same variety of rodent prints around them.

"Small animals must be really interested in these lines. Do you think they're what rang the bells last night?" Jess was crouched by the final set of bells in question, taking pictures of the many prints below them.

I was further down the trail, looking at some broken twigs on one of the bushes. Something big had passed through this area.

As I was inspecting the bush, a fly flew around my head. A few seconds later, another one joined the first. Their buzzing seemed louder than two flies should be able to make, so I paused in my inspection of the twigs.

The buzzing wasn't coming from the two flies around me. It seemed to emanate from a spot to the left and just off the trail. I moved closer, parting the bushes.

"Crap!" Losing my balance, I fell back, then scrambled away.

Jess started, turning towards me. "What is it?"

"I don't know." I couldn't stop staring at the bushes.

"What do you mean, you don't know?" She stalked toward the bushes.

I reached out, saying, "Don't look!", but it was too late. She'd already pulled the bushes apart.

She stilled. "Oh." It was barely breathed.

Standing up, I approached the scene, as much as I wanted to run in the other direction.

It was a dead animal, but I couldn't tell what animal it had been. It was in pieces: some parts chewed on, some left intact. Iridescent flashes sparked as the flies buzzed around it. The blood-stained bushes were trampled all around, giving the impression that it had been more of a plaything than a meal.

It was then that the chittering exploded nearby. Quiet up until then, the aggravated sound disrupted the solitude of the trail. Jess shrieked. I was too numb to react. I looked up, but there was nothing in the trees, not even a twitchy silhouette.

Bushes rustled on the other side of the trail. I stepped toward the sound, pulling Jess with me.

As abruptly as it started, the chittering stopped. The flies were the only sound. All the other forest sounds had disappeared.

"Jess." Speaking low, I tried to get her attention as I stepped toward her.

"Yes."

I could tell she was in shock. "We need to leave, Jess." Feeling a sense of urgency, I gripped her arm, turning her toward me.

"What do you mea—"

"Listen."

She tilted her head to the side, a gesture people make when they're trying to hear better. Her eyes widening, she mouthed, "No sounds."

I nodded. It was like everything had stopped, frozen in place. A predator was nearby.

Dragging her with me, I started moving down the trail, back the way we'd come.

She pulled the tranquilizer gun off her shoulder, checked the chamber for a dart, then cocked it and trained it ahead of us as we walked backwards.

We moved slowly, placing our feet carefully and keep an ear to our surroundings. It could have been minutes or it could have been hours, but finally we heard birdsong again. The danger had passed.

Quickly travelling, we arrived at our campsite about mid afternoon. Neither of us was hungry, so we sat together, silently watching the forest as the sun began its descent. Towards dusk, we heard loud chittering coming from the nearby trees.

"That squirrel seems to be following us. I'm going to go see if I can spot it." Jess seemed to be recovering quicker than me, her pale face slowly regaining its colour. She got up and headed for the shade of the trees.

I had started to think about what we could eat for our supper, my stomach finally ready to eat again after what I'd seen that afternoon. I had just gotten to my feet to rummage through our food when I heard a sharp squeal.

"Charlie!" Jess's call seemed both panicked and excited. "Grab some gear and the tranq gun and get over here!"

All thoughts of food evaporated. Picking up our flash-lights and the gun, I ran over. "What is it?"

"The squirrel was here, chittering in the bushes, and then it went quiet again. A few seconds later, I heard the squeak." She moved a little further into the brush, point-ing at something a few feet in. "It sounded like it was in pain, so I tried to find it. Look."

Following her in, I looked where she directed. A few drops of blood were vibrant against some waxy green leaves. A little further in, I could see more drops, along with a path of broken bushes.

I suddenly had a bad feeling, like I was about to get coerced into a decision I was going to regret. "Jess, why did you ask me to bring the gun?"

Her eyes narrowed, assessing me. "The creature just grabbed something, which means it's close by. Obviously, we have to go after it!"

"Now? At dusk? We just spent a good part of our morn-ing trying to avoid this creature!" I hissed. My brain froze at the thought of going into the trees, unable to imagine following this thing as it got darker.

"Are you serious? This is why we're here!" she hissed back. "We're being paid to find evidence of this creature, so that's what we're going to do." Turning, she stalked into the trees.

"Jess!" I called her name in a stage whisper, the 's' lin-gering like an angry snake.

She turned, her face pale against the backdrop of the shadowed trunks. "Move it, Charlie! We're losing the light." Turning back to the trail, she started away into the cooling dusk, leaning down every now and again to look for the trail of blood and twigs. Heart hammering in my ears, I gripped the gun harder and followed her.

Night fell quickly under the canopy of branches, making the tiny drops of blood harder to see. After about ten minutes of following the trail, we had to turn on the flashlights to see the leaves.

I'd been so focused on the ground, trying to find signs of the creature in the dirt, when an unearthly scream echoed around us. My head came up just in time for my nose to smash into one of Jess's shoulder blades. She had stopped when the scream rang out. Excruciating pain bloomed outward across my face and fluorescent spots flashed across my vision.

"Ow!" Jess yelped, more startled than hurt.

My *ow* came out more as a squeal than a word. I wobbled on my feet, hiding my nose in my hand and blinking through the tears that smarted my eyes.

Jess held my shoulder to steady me. "I'm so sorry! Are you okay?"

"No. That really hurt!" Her startlingly pale face and wide eyes glowed in the light from my flashlight, framed by the slowly disappearing spots. The pain in my nose dulled to a throb after a minute and I moved my hand away, checking it for blood. Thankfully, my palm was clean.

"Are *you* okay? Your face is really pale."

Rubbing her arms, she glanced at the ground, then said, "I'm — okay. Whatever that scream was, it was terrifying."

Now it was my turn to hold her shoulders and look at her. "Do you want to continue? Because right now, I'm terrified, but I'll keep going if you do."

Her eyes wandered to the surrounding darkness, made more so by the beams from our flashlights. She nodded; the whites of her eyes gleaming. "Yeah, I do."

My stomach plummeted. I'd really hoped she'd say no. But, I'd given my word. "Then let's go."

We turned back to the trail, searching around until we found more blood. It glistened, dark in the artificial light from the flashlights. The surrounding branches shone white where they'd been broken. We spotted more blood and followed the trail until it disappeared into thicker bushes. I looked at Jess and though her eyes were still wide, she shrugged.

"It's what we're here for," she whispered.

I guessed we were going further.

Parting the leaves, I started into the brush, the branches pulling at my jeans. More rustling came behind me as Jess followed, her flashlight beam bouncing. The leaves blocked my view of the ground, making it harder to see where the blood was. Trying to be quiet had become much more difficult.

When we could no longer find any trail at all to follow, we stopped, looking around. The blood trail had already ended, and the fallen leaves and snapped brush ended at the base of a pine tree, claw marks running up the trunk.

Jess grabbed my hand and squeezed. Her swallow was audible in the silence.

It was then that we heard a slight rustle, a shift of something behind the tree. We both stiffened, waiting to see if anything appeared.

Nothing did.

After a minute or two, Jess inched forward, her beam low and sweeping the ground. As she disappeared behind the tree, I saw the beam halt, directed at something at the base. Her voice was low when she said, "You have to see this."

I stepped toward her, keeping my beam low like hers. As I rounded the tree, I paused to examine the claw marks. Lifting my hand, I laid it beside the marks, comparing the size. The marks came from a big paw, about six inches from the first claw to the fourth.

"Charlie." Jess's impatient voice interrupted my thoughts and I continued to where she stood and saw what she'd found.

It's a squirrel, I thought. But bigger than any squirrel I'd ever seen, about the size of a domestic cat. Black fur, more shadow than colour, covered its hide. Its large tail twitched and its body trembled, eyes shut tight.

Crouching, I asked Jess to move her light more to the side of the animal, closer to the tail. She did, and as the light moved away from its head, it illuminated the reason why there'd been a trail of blood to follow. Its back left leg had a long gash, white bone visible through shining red as the light passed over it.

"It couldn't climb the trees to get away. That's why it left a trail to follow."

As I spoke, the squirrel opened its eyes.

Jess gave a soft gasp. "It's the creature from the video."

And it was. It had to be. Its eyes, in comparison to the its head, were huge discs, glowing blue. There was no iris, no pupil. Just uninterrupted blue. The only description my numbed brain could think of was if a glowstick had been broken open and its liquid poured out on the ground. The colour perfectly matched the glowing dots in the video.

Light blinded me as Jess took a picture of the animal with her phone, the flash brilliant in the dark.

"Geez, Jess."

"Sorry. But I had to get a picture. We finally found the creature!"

I shook my head. "This can't be the creature that's been killing animals."

She spun toward me. "What? It has to be!"

"But it can't. Does this animal look big enough to do the damage that we saw earlier? It doesn't to me." I stood, then started to remove my jacket. Whatever it was, we couldn't leave the animal here to die. Moving slowly forward, I started to lower my jacket over it, hoping to wrap it up so it couldn't claw me. "This animal isn't big enough, nor is it equipped to do that sort of thing. There must be a bobcat or something around, and that's what attacked it earlier."

The squirrel didn't move as I put my jacket around it and picked it up. Shock must have made it immobile. To Jess I said, "I recognize where we are. One of the bell lines is just over in those bushes." I pointed a few feet away. "Let's get this guy back to camp so that we can get a better look at him."

Ding! Ding! Ding!

The bells chimed just as we turned to leave. One step ahead of Jess, her scream startled me. Spinning around, I saw her being dragged into the bushes, kicking and flailing. A giant cat, its eyes reflecting green, had its teeth sunk into her shoulder.

It was huge, a black void against the brush. A low growl, one I could feel in my chest, reverberated through the nearby trees as it started to disappear into the brush.

"JESS!" I grabbed for the gun slung over my shoulder, but the squirrel in my arms hindered my movements. I roughly placed it on the ground, then got the gun up to my shoulder, aiming at the shadow hauling my friend away.

BOOM!

A gun went off right by my ear. I grabbed the side of my head as I shook it, trying to get rid of the ringing. My yell of pain sounded muffled, as if I was underwater.

I looked toward the last place I'd seen Jess. She was lying on the ground, a large black mass next to her. I moved toward her.

Her shoulder was mauled, blood seeping through her torn jacket. Unconscious, her pale face was turned away from the dead creature beside her.

"Can ya hear me, son?" The familiar voice spoke in my good ear. I turned toward it.

"Mr. Whiffen!"

He was standing to the side of me, a look of concern on his face and a rifle slung over his shoulder. In his arms was the squirrel, still wrapped in my jacket.

"I knew I shouldn't 'ave let you two come in here alone." He glanced down at Jess as he said this.

Jess stirred, a painful whimper escaping her.

"Ya needs ta get her to a hospital. That wound looks bad." Laying his rifle down, he pulled his own jacket off. "Here, 'old this against it to stop the bleeding."

Accepting it, I pressed it to her shoulder, causing another whimper. "How will I get her out of here?"

Mr. Whiffen placed the squirrel back in my arms. "I'll carry her and show ya da quickest way to yer car. Don't worry, I'll come and take care of the other creature later."

It was then that I remembered the big black cat. Holding the squirrel with one arm, I took my flashlight and shone it toward the lump on ground.

The animal's fur was beautiful, a shining ebony that showed some barely visible spots in my light. Its head was huge, and its teeth were still bared with Jess's blood clinging to the tips of its canines. From its head to the tip of its tail, I would guess it was about seven or eight feet in length. In its side was a gaping hole, where Mr. Whiffen's bullet had hit it.

"We've got to go. She's losing blood." Mr. Whiffen turned and started walking away, Jess in his arms.

I followed, the squirrel still and quiet. Mr. Whiffen knew the woods, so we were much faster making it back to the campsite and then on to the car. When we reached it, Mr. Whiffen placed Jess in the backseat and took the squirrel, then directed me to drive to his house and call an ambulance from there. Then he turned and disappeared back into the night.

"So you have no evidence of the creature at all?"

Exasperation and disbelief tinged Jess's voice. She was sitting in a hospital bed, her shoulder stitched and wrapped up tightly. It had been two days since that night in the woods.

"I went back as soon as I knew you would be okay. There was nothing there." Spreading my hands, I shrugged. "Even the squirrel has disappeared."

Slumping back against the pillows, Jess sighed. "I didn't even get to see it. What do you think it was?"

"At a guess, I'd say it was an alien big cat. I did some research while I was waiting for you to wake up. It seems that there have been some reports of them on the west coast of the island, but never this far east."

"An ABC?! And I never got to see it!" Straightening, she reached for her phone on the nightstand. "Well, at least we got a picture of the squirrel." Jess's smile was small as she held up her phone, the injured squirrel filling the screen. Its black fur glinted white where the flash had struck it. "What do you think happened to it?"

"I don't know. But now that I think back, I do wonder about the scurrying creature on the roof of Mr. Whiffen's shed that night. I think he knew about that creature all along."

Alex Hickey

Alex Hickey has made it a lifelong passion to know the history, people, events and places of Fortune Bay. His Blog, All Things St. Jacques, chronicles and tells the stories of his home community.

As an arts educator Alex has previously published in professional education journals, magazines and edited collections. He is an avid community supporter and is currently engaged in a volunteer initiative to restore and preserve the light tower on St. Jacques Island.

In 2024 he released his first novel, *Misfortune Bay: The Loss of the Albatross* through Flanker Press.

Fortune Bay Monster

CPTV *Here and Now*, 6:14 pm May 10th, 1986

Host: Our next story may leave you shaking your head. Three fishermen recently reported seeing a mysterious creature in the waters off Long Harbour, Fortune Bay. John Hackett, Will Fewer, and Virg Saint of the neighbouring community of Trammer were all in the same dory hauling their lobster traps early last Monday. The day started out normally with fog hanging around the headlands and a light southerly breeze. The three men left their fishing stage and headed to the lobster grounds about twenty minutes away.

The morning progressed as usual. Early in the season the best catches occur in deep water. As Mr. Hackett told us, lobster remain in the deeper water until late May when they move closer to shore as the water warms. Like most lobstermen they set a few pots close to shore at the beginning of the season. When the catch rate in those pots begins to increase it is an indication that it's time to move all their traps into shallower water.

Fewer added new bait to the skewer in one of those pots, He looked along the shore to confirm his location, and eased it back into the water. Virg, who was manning the 65 horsepower Evinrude outboard motor, eased it in gear and moved towards the next buoy. John Fewer yelled STOP! That's where we pick up our story. Here's John Hackett—

John Hackett; We just froze in our boots. The adrenaline started rushing right through me. I was expecting the worst."

"Did either of you see that," Virg asked us.

"See what?" I said.

"In there, in the landwash. I swear I saw something watching us."

VIrg Saint: I cut the motor and allowed the dory to coast towards the shoreline. That's when we all seen it. It was the strangest thing I've ever seen out in the Bay in all the years I've been fishing, and I've been at this since I was fourteen. I'm sixty-two now. It was like two big eyes in this round head looking straight at us. There was no nose you could make out, not even a mouth, just a roundish opening below the eyes."

Will Fewer: That's right, two shiny, black eyes; and hairy. I thought it was a seal at first. You know how they slink along the shoreline waiting for you to heave away a bit of old bait. That's what I thought it was, until we got closer. Virg was right. It was hairy. Not like people hair, you know. It was matted, kind of thick, more like you see wet feathers on a dead seagull. All mussed up and sticking out at strange angles. And brown. It was brown.

The three men were standing at the edge of their wharf, their dory rising and falling on its mooring. The camera pulled back to reveal an array of single- and two-story houses and fishing stages strung along the shoreline of broken granite.

Host: Tune in next Monday night at 8:30 pm for more details on this story. Our *Land and Sea* crew, along with researchers from Memorial University, are in Long Harbour as we speak, investigating the appearance of that mysterious monster in Fortune Bay. We'll be right back after this break.

7:19 pm May 10th, 1986

Albert Dyett, a lifelong resident of Blanchard, ten miles further out Fortune Bay, hit the off button on his remote, uncrossed his legs, set both feet on the floor, and moved forward in his recliner until he was sitting on the edge of his seat in the sweet spot just before his two hundred pounds would tip the chair forward. "That's the same as what we seen years ago, Marge," he called to his wife who was standing at the kitchen sink washing the supper dishes.

"What did you see years ago, Albert?" she asked.

"One of those things, down among the kelp in St. John's Bay. The thing what was looking at me and Jim-Henry. I'm gonna call CPTV. Do you know the number?"

Land and Sea, 8:30 pm May 17th, 1986

A nylon stringed guitar played a mid-tempo melody as a montage of rural and urban Newfoundland and Labrador scenes floated across the television screen. Albert Dyett checked to see how much Dominion Ale was left in his glass as he squirmed his hips a little deeper into his soft chair.

"Turn it up a little bit, would you, Marge? Maybe a couple of notches. I don't want to miss anything."

"I suppose you don't. You're after calling everybody

you knows telling them you're going to be on. Heaven forbid that you'd be the one to miss seeing it."

"Ah, you're just jealous it's not you what's going to be on the TV. Hush now, they're about to start."

"Good evening. I'm your host Bill Kieley. Tonight, we bring you something unusual, something a little out of the ordinary for us here at *Land and Sea*. Tonight, we take you out to Fortune Bay on Newfoundland's south coast where we investigate a most unusual sighting by local fishermen. Join us as we travel to one of the frontiers of rural Newfoundland, one of the few places where men still fish from open dories to make their living in the harsh waters of the north Atlantic. You'll meet three fishermen from Trammer, a tiny settlement in the bottom of the Bay where this unusual sighting recently took place. Then we'll met Albert Dyett, a seasoned hand now retired, who had a similar experience several years ago. Our crew, accompanied by Dr. Ralph Linehan of Memorial University's Marine Sciences faculty, went to Fortune Bay last week. This is what we found."

Music swelled as the camera cut to the wake of an open boat as it passed a headland and entered the wider expanse of the open bay. Kieley's voice said, "Meet Virg Saint and his two fishing partners as they haul their lobster traps just as they were doing last week when they sighted this mysterious creature."

"Yes, b'y, it was something else, what we saw. As I said, I've never seen anything like it before. As we got closer, it started to duck under the water and come up again in the same place. John here, he says to me, 'Sure that's just a buoy or something that's all washed out into a funny shape. Or a toy someone threw away.' I told him, 'Johnny b'y, I don't think so. I think that's a mortal creature.' We was about ten feet away from it. All you could see was the head and them two big black eyes staring straight at us."

Kieley asked, "Could you see the rest of its body? How big was it? Could you tell if it was shaped like a fish or something else?"

"All we could see was the head, isn't that right, Will?"

Will Fewer joined in: "That's right. Just the head. And those eyes. I thought they were blinking, but John said it was the sun coming off the water, playing tricks."

"How long did you see this creature there in the water?" asked Kieley.

"I don't know for certain, but it must have been ten minutes or more that we watched it watching us. To tell you the truth, it began to feel a bit creepy. I mean, we didn't know if it meant any harm. It didn't seem to threaten us in any way. It just kept staring, and as Will says, blinking now and then. Yes, I'd say about ten minutes we sat there whispering back and forth. Then Johnny takes the oar and slaps the water. It didn't budge."

"I wish I'd brought me gun," said Will. "Most mornings I do in case we sees a saltwater duck."

"You would have fired a shot at it?" asked Kieley.

"You knows I would. What else could you do with something strange like that? I certainly wouldn't be trying to take it aboard the dory. God knows how big that thing was below the water."

The camera panned along the mountainous coastline and up the side of a precipitous cliff that rose out of the sea. Kieley's voice said, "When we come back, you'll meet someone else who claims to have seen this monster elsewhere in Fortune Bay."

Albert hit the mute button. "That's exactly what we saw, Marge. And we weren't the first." Dyett poured himself another beer. "Marge, do you know if I called Cousin George up in Lunenburg?"

"Yes, you did, Albert, but it was no good. That show is only on here in Newfoundland. They got their own *Land and Sea* in Nova Scotia."

"Just the same, I thought he should know. He seen that thing too. Are we recording this?"

A commercial for a St. John's funeral home faded into a shot of a sparkling morning ocean. Kieley's voice came in, saying, "It was a morning much the same as this when Uncle Albert Dyett of Blanchard, near Boxey in Fortune Bay, also saw something that didn't quite belong in the little cove where he launched his dory." Albert Dyett's face filled the screen.

"I've heard tell of men seeing them for years. You'd see them and then you wouldn't," said Albert.

"What do you mean?" asked Kieley.

"Sometimes you'd go for years and never see a sign, then one morning you could be sitting there jigging away and one would pop up right close to you. The funny thing is that they'd almost always come up between you and the sun so as you couldn't get a real close look at them."

"Did you ever feel threatened by one of them?"

"Not personally. But my cousin George, who lives upalong, he got quite a scare once."

"Tell me about it, Albert."

"The way he told me goes like this. He was steaming out towards Sagona Island to check his cod trap when all of a sudden something was thumping against the bottom of his boat. He cut the motor right away, thinking he had hit something. When he looked, he was surrounded by all of these little brown heads looking right at him. Well sir, he never hesitated. He started up and opened the throttle and never slowed down until he hit the bottom longer of his slipway. He never did go back to take that trap out of the water."

"He must have received quite a scare."

"Yes sir, and that he did. He gave up fishing after that and moved to Nova Scotia. He got a job at the Fisherman's Museum in Lunenburg as a storyteller."

"I bet he's told that story more than once."

"I don't think so, sir. No. It shook him up too much. That, and the stories what come out afterwards."

"What do you mean?"

"You knows how it is. You open a can of worms and you never knows what will crawl out. After we managed to get the story out of George years later, word got around and people stared telling what they and their grandfathers had seen. Before you knew it, almost everyone had seen at least one but was afraid to tell it."

"Why would they be afraid if it didn't hurt them?"

"It was a bad omen, sir. If you seen one of them strange heads coming out of the water, it was a sure sign that someone was going to die. The only way you could save a person from dying was to keep quiet about what you saw. I never told Marge about what I saw until last week when this come on the news. I figured after all these years there was none of them still around. The last one I saw was about twenty years ago."

"So, you've never seen the whole body?'

"They don't have a body, just a head."

"Just a head?"

"Yes, sir. And two big black eyes that stares at you."

"Have you known anyone who died after seeing one of them?"

"I expect the cemeteries are full of them. Whenever a

healthy man or woman suddenly drops dead, everyone knows that someone has seen one of them heads in the water. Nobody says anything about it but they knows. You've heard the saying that deaths will come in threes when there's a green Christmas, haven't you?"

"Yes, I have. How is that connected to these supposed creatures?"

"You see when there's a green Christmas the weather is usually civil which means it's a good time to be on the water bird hunting."

"You mean hunting for Turres?"

"Yes, Turres. And you can mark my word. It happens every single time. There'll be three deaths and everyone will say that's what you expects on a green Christmas. What they means is that someone has killed one of them heads after mistaking it for a Turre. If you kills one, three people will die. It has nothing to do with a lack of snow. But people can't say that so they says green Christmas."

The camera cuts to a row of staggered tombstones on a hillside overlooking the sea. A forlorn guitar interlude plays as the scene merges into a row of fishing stages in Trammer. The three fishermen are still standing on the wharf. Bill Kieley steps into the frame. "Gentlemen, I've spoken with other fishermen about seeing a similar creature as you've described seeing. They say there is a curse of sorts which befalls anyone telling that they've seen the creature. Are you aware of that?"

John Hackett looked directly into the camera. "Old wives tales," he said. "Old wives tales told by people with too much time on their hands. Back in the old days, people wanted an explanation for everything that happened around them, the same as today. The difference is we don't use superstition and myths to explain those things.

They did. No, I don't believe there's a curse. But I'm only one person. Others might think differently."

"What about Virg? What do you think?"

"I don't rightly know, Mr. Kieley. I know I felt something strange the morning we saw that face floating on the water. The more it looked at us, the worse the feeling got. Do I believe it means someone is going to die because we are talking to you? No. People are dying all around us. My great uncle died last week. One of my neighbour's sons died up in Fort McMurray last fall. We are all going to die one day. Some sooner than later."

"You are awfully quiet, Will," observed Kieley.

"I usually am, sir. The less I say, the less trouble I gets in."

"I can't imagine how much trouble you'd get in in if you talked as much as John," said Virg with a hearty laugh.

The camera remained close-up on Will's furrowed brow as if waiting for him to explode into a frenetic response. Instead, he shrugged his shoulders, lowered his bottom lip, and tilted his head to the left for a second.

The camera framed the three men staring out to sea then pulled back slowly and allowed the screen to fill with the water off Trammer, then panned across the water. Through the magic of editing, it carried on until a silhouette of Uncle Albert Dyett's face filled the frame. It then switched to the logo of Memorial University. Kieley's voice-over said, "We asked Dr. Linehan of Memorial University's Marine Sciences faculty to accompany us in the hopes that we might spot one of the creatures. Unfortunately, we did not.

"What do you think about all of this, Dr. Linehan? Is this a credible sighting?"

"I have nothing more to go on than the stories we

have just heard. People can draw compelling connections between two unrelated events sometimes and form quite strong and persistent beliefs about it. That is often the source of much folklore. However, there is usually a kernel of truth wrapped up in such stories. It might be a warning to stay away from unknown objects on the sea. It might be a way of coping with tragedy by attributing an event to a cause beyond their control. As a scientist, I never dismiss those stories for if you listen deeply enough you learn something new. They are usually born from experience and change with time as they are told and retold."

"So, you think this is simply a story?"

"No, not at all. John, Will, and Virg saw something. I don't know what they saw, but they did see something. Is it some undiscovered monster from the deep? There is always that possibility. We still don't know everything that lives in the ocean. Creatures that we long thought extinct have turned up living at great depths. It wasn't all that long ago that people believed in the Kraken which turned out to be real. It was a giant squid. Several of them have washed ashore here in Newfoundland. We have documented them alive in the ocean."

"I guess we may never know until someone captures one of them," said Kieley.

Linehan looked into the camera and said, "It's possible that someone has already done that and has never reported it or didn't know what they had found."

The camera switched to the host. He looks down at his hands as though reading notes, then back into the camera lens. After a short pause he said, "There's more to this story than Uncle Albert has told us. We've spoken with others throughout Fortune Bay. We asked if anyone had ever found one of these washed upon the beach, dead. No one could tell us of a specific instance except Uncle Albert Dyett. Here's what he had to say—"

"One time, more than a few years ago, Jim-Henry Smith and I were fishing out of St. John's Bay, just down the coast here a ways. We had all of our gear loaded aboard the dory and were about to push off when Jim-Henry spied something in the landwash. He said, 'Holy Smokes, Albert.' That's as close to uttering a curse that he ever came. Jim-Henry was a very religious and respectful man. 'Holy Smokes,' he said. I looked to where he was pointing his finger. There, partly hidden in the kelp was one of them heads. Both of its dark eyes were staring right through us. It gave me the creeps. Before I could say a word, he took the landing net from the dory and scooped the head up. We both saw it happen at the same time. The minute the head came completely out of the water, the eyes closed shut and never opened again. As much as we tried, we could not get those eyes to open. You couldn't even see where they were closed. It was as though they were never there. But… they were. We both seen them when they closed for the last time."

"What did you do with the head, Uncle Albert?"

"We tucked it under some bushes above the high-water mark and went fishing."

"Was there a body attached to it?"

"No sir, there was nothing but the head. We turned it over and over. but we couldn't see where there was a neck or fins or arms. It was a puzzle to us as to how it could possibly move through the water."

"What happened to the head after that? Did you show it to anyone? Tell anyone?"

"We believed we couldn't tell anyone, so we didn't. When we got back that afternoon, Jim-Henry said to me,

'I wants to know what that creature looks like on the inside.'

"It gave me shivers to think about splitting the head open. By then the hair was dry and had shrunk tight. It didn't look so big like that. Jim-Henry took it down to the water's edge, laid it on a flat rock and pulled out his splitting knife. Was that head ever tough. He cut and cut like a madman until he wore the edge of his knife. I said, 'Jim-Henry, you'll never split another fish with that knife, the way you've got the blade all mangled up.' Jim-Henry wasn't a wasteful man. When he realized he had ruined his knife he got angry; the only time in my life I ever seen him lose his temper. Well sir, he took that brown head and raised it above his shoulder with two hands and smashed it down on the rock. It split in two pieces and this runny, milky stuff spilled out. Jim-Henry drove his hands into the water and scrubbed them in the sand, out of fear of being poisoned. I'd never seen anything like it. Whatever happened to that creature when it died, I don't know. I do know that its insides liquefied and ran out like cloudy water when it broke open. We buried the remains and never spoke about it again, until now."

The screen faded to black and credits rolled. The voice of Bill Kieley said, "That, ladies and gentlemen, is our story of the *Fortune Bay Monster*. You judge for yourself. We'll be back again next week with a story you are all going to love. It's about a ten-year-old accordion player whose playing attracts more than listeners when he plays in his grandfather's boat. Join us next week, same channel, and same time. Good night."

Here and Now, 7:00 pm, May 18th 1986

"We have an update on a story we brought you earlier this week about the curious sighting by three fishermen in Fortune Bay. The same three men set out yesterday morning to haul their lobster traps but never returned. A search and rescue effort has been underway since yesterday evening when they failed to return home. At daylight this morning, a Coast Guard Cormorant helicopter spotted their overturned dory floating across the mouth of the Long Harbour Estuary.

"A story we are also following …

Albert Dyett lost all interest in the next story. He replayed the entire episode of *Land and Sea* in his mind. By the time he was finished, his body felt like jelly, a defeated lump of humanity slouched in a soft comfortable chair. He didn't have the strength to call out to Marge. The faces of the three men hung in the air before him. Then the telephone rang.

Marge answered and called out, "Albert, it's for you. It's Elsie, your Cousin George's wife."

Stacey Oakley

Stacey Oakley is an author originally from Moncton, New Brunswick who became a vibrant part of the local Newfoundland writing scene after the publication of "The Sorrows of War" in the 2016 edition of *Sci-Fi from the Rock*.

She has since gone on to independently publish her own novel, *Hunter's Soul*, its follow up *The Necromancer*, and in 2018 was crowned the winner of the 48 Hour Novel-Writing Marathon.

The Creature in the Well

"Are you sure it's safe?" Robyn asked, watching her cousin poke at the ice with a stick while she tied her skates. Normally Jaime's family visited hers. From what she could remember the last time she was here, they hadn't been allowed anywhere near the lake.

Jaime shrugged. "We had that cold snap last night, so the ice should still be thick enough for one last skate, right?"

Evan, his friend, frowned, but didn't stop putting on his own skates. "I don't think one cold night would be enough to make the ice thicker... doesn't there need to be rain or something?"

"Maybe we should call Uncle Tommy and ask?" Robyn suggested. "Could the arsenic affect how it freezes?"

Now Evan frowned at her for a moment, before nodding slowly. "You were told it was poisoned by the old mines, weren't you?"

"Wasn't it?" she asked.

"Well, there's something there, but it ain't arsenic," Evan replied.

Jaime rolled his eyes. "Not this crap again."

Evan shot him a glare. "It's not crap."

"What is it?" Robyn asked, stretching her feet to test how tight her skates were.

"There's a creature trapped in an old well in the lake that came from the mines," Jaime replied, kicking a rock across the ice before sitting on the same downed tree as Robyn to put on his own skates. "It's an old legend. Like Bigfoot or Mothman."

"Wouldn't it drown if it went from mines to the bottom of a well that's at the bottom of a lake?" Robyn asked.

"Exactly," Jaime said.

"You know there are bodies of water underground too, right?" Evan said. "Flooding is one of the reasons they gave for closing the mines years ago. Maybe they'd have the technology now to deal with the water, but they didn't then. And there are amphibians."

"What's the story?" Robyn asked before Jaime could continue the argument.

"They delved too deep and too greedily…" Jaime muttered in an ominous tone.

"Geek," Robyn said, but there was no malice. After all, she recognized the quote.

Evan snorted but started the story. "The miners found a system of caves underground, and a bunch of them led to small lakes and stuff. Anyway, there was a creature in one of them. No one knows how long it was there or how it got there. It started killing off the men; like, they'd find the mangled, bloody bodies of the last shift partly eaten, and there were a bunch of skeletons from small animals too."

"Did the survivors have to win a game of riddles to

Cryptids from the Rock

escape?" Robyn couldn't help it.

"Geek," Jaime said.

"You're both nerds," Evan said, and continued as if they hadn't interrupted. "Now, the owner of the mines thought they were full of it, right? So, one day they convince him to go down, and they actually see the thing. Or part of it. They only had lanterns and the thing ran off once the owner tried to shoot it. Now, the men were refusing to go down and he was losing money. So he comes up with this plan to lure the thing out of the caves. It works, but then the thing is loose in the forest and heads toward town and starts attacking people out at night and livestock."

"I think we technically live in a village," Jaime said.

"Whatever. The important thing is, they eventually come up with a plan to line the inside of an old well with sheet metal so it's too smooth for the thing to climb out and somehow get the creature into the well. Then they cover it up and figure that's that, it'll eventually starve or something. And things are fine for a long time, but the mine becomes too dangerous and has to close, and then the hydro project comes along. The whole village had to move out of the way of the flooding when they dammed up the river; like, if you went to the bottom of the lake, you could find foundations and root cellars and stuff. But anyway, the well was one of the things that ended up underwater."

"But isn't there a cover on the well?" Robyn asked.

"It's wood. I think cedar or something? Something with a smell the creature didn't like. But still, it's wood, and folks are worried the wood will rot and the creature will be free. Plus, having spent so long in the well, it's probably completely aquatic now."

"Okay..."

"And that's why they say the lake has lethally high levels of arsenic. To keep people out of the water. In the winter it's fine, because it's frozen over. Plus, Andy said his sister went scuba diving in the lake, for practice. She found the well and when she looked between a space in the boards, she saw eyes looking back at her."

"I can't be the only one to see the plot holes in that," Jaime said. "Also, Andy smokes a lot of weed and I think his sister was actually arrested for the scuba thing."

Evan shrugged. "I'm just telling you the story I know. If you'd grown up here, you would've heard ten different versions before you started school. I just gave you the details that don't change." He stood up. "But what I do know for sure is that my cousin, Alex, is doing chemistry at university, and tested the lake water for some project he's doing. It's safer to drink than tap water." Robyn looked over at Jaime, who shrugged and stood up, following Evan onto the ice. She was two steps behind them. The ice seemed solid enough, though spring was in the air. She couldn't see anything below the cloudy white surface. She could understand why it was dangerous if there were root cellars and foundations still there. Plus, all the plants that may or may not have continued to grow or not grow or rot or whatever. There would be plenty to pose problems for swimmers, especially kids and teens who had more confidence than wisdom and would get themselves into bad situations. How many people had drowned since they made the lake?

"Hey, guys!" Robyn turned toward the shore and waved back at Evan's girlfriend, Claire, who sat down to pull on her skates. She was one of the friendlier people Robyn had met and was helping to make the vacation in the middle of nowhere bearable. "What's up?"

"Your boyfriend was just telling us about the well creature in the lake," Robyn replied. "Or would it be the cave creature in the well in the lake? Does it have a name or anything?"

Claire shrugged as she wobbled onto the ice, less steady than the other three, but still capable enough. "Dunno. Most stories don't have a name. I think they used to be afraid it was one of those 'speak its name and summon it' kind of things, so they avoided anything like that."

Jaime skated around them, showing off a little as he moved backward across the ice. "Can it be summoned by a name given to it by someone else?"

"Technically no one names themselves," Claire pointed out. "You're summoned by the name your parents' gave you."

Jaime considered that for a moment. "Fair point."

Evan grinned and kissed Claire, making her blush. "That's my girl."

"Though it seems unfair she got the brains *and* the beauty in the relationship," Jaime teased, ducking Evan's playful punch.

"Don't worry, I have other skills," he said.

"I hope one of them is sparing us the details of the others," Robyn said. Evan blushed as red as his hair and Claire shook her head.

"Okay, you guys promised to teach me how to skate

backward before the season was over."

"Nice change of subject," Jaime said, but moved to her side so he could show her what to do. The lesson started out well, but between the four of them it eventually devolved into Jaime chasing Robyn and Evan across the ice while they all laughed.

Until they heard the first deep crack.

Everyone froze and looked at each other, trying to figure out who was in danger. A second crack followed and Robyn looked down. The ice under her feet was solid. She looked over at Claire, who was closest to the shore. The ice under her feet appeared solid.

There was a crash, and Evan vanished beneath the surface.

Claire screamed his name as Robyn and Jaime raced closer, freezing when there was another crack. Robyn dropped to her stomach and tried to spread out her weight as she got closer.

"Get a branch, or some rope!" she yelled. Jaime nodded and raced to shore, yelling at Claire to call for help. Evan surfaced, arms flailing to grab onto anything as he coughed and sputtered. Despite the danger, Robyn tried to grab him, digging the serrated toe of her skates into the ice in case he tried to pull her in. Evan reached for her, only to go back under. Robyn cursed and moved closer, and this time when he surfaced, she did manage to grab his hand and tried to haul him to the edge of the broken ice. "Hold on to me," she said. His grip on her wrist was painful, his eyes wide with fear.

"Robyn!" She looked over at Jaime, who slid a thick branch toward her, clearly weighing the risks of getting closer with the possibility his added weight would cause more damage to the ice.

"Help is on the way!" Claire yelled from the shore.

Robyn felt a yank on her arm and looked over. Evan was looking at her, eyes wide with terror. She was about to tell him it would be fine when he was dragged under again. She fought, but it was like something was pulling. And she was certain she saw black claws digging into his shoulder before he vanished below the surface, taking her with him.

Robyn didn't have time to scream as she plunged into the icy water. Evan still had her wrist in a death grip. She righted herself to try to kick her way to the surface, to the light she could see, but when she straightened her leg, she felt it break through something soft. A scream left her throat as bubbles rising to the surface. She looked down, and in the scant light saw that her foot had gone through wooden boards. She tried to push down with her other foot to free it, but her trapped leg sank deeper, the rotting edges still strong enough to hurt as they dug into her skin. Evan released her hand, so she reached down and managed to free herself. She swam for the surface and took a deep breath, ignoring Jaime and Claire's screams before diving down again, looking for Evan. He was sinking, but no longer moving. She grabbed the front of his coat and tried to pull him closer, but something else was holding him. Robyn reached around and froze when her hand wrapped around something that felt slimy even through her glove, and then she felt movement, like the shift of muscle under skin.

And then it grabbed her wrist.

Robyn barely held back a scream as she yanked her arm back. Long black fingers tipped with claws were wrapped around her wrist, followed by a dark arm and then a face mostly hidden by shadows, except for the brilliant yellow eyes that reflected the light like a cat's, and a mouth with far too many teeth. The eyes looked from her to Evan's body, and there was a strange intelligence to them. It seemed to decide to stick with the prey it had, and released Robyn, dragging Evan deeper into what Robyn realized was a well. Her vision started to go dark around the edges, and she struggled toward the surface, grabbing the long branch Jaime shoved at her.

"Evan..." she choked out as he dragged her out of the water and away from the weak ice. "I... he... I can't... it..." Her teeth started chattering and her body almost convulsed from shivering as it tried to get warm.

"You tried," Jaime said. "You... you did everything you could. I... I saw it..." In the distance she could hear Claire let out a wail of grief.

The next few hours were a blur. An ambulance arrived, and police. Robyn was rushed to the hospital to get warmed up and checked for injuries. She tried to tell them what happened to Evan, about the creature being real, but they told her she was in shock, or hallucinating because of the cold; never mind that both of her wrists had very different bruises, one from Evan and one from something entirely different.

There was a search for Evan's body, but all she could find out was that they found his coat. Jaime managed to find out that it was torn and bloody, but that knowledge wasn't made public. Every time she closed her eyes, she saw Evan's face frozen in a terrified death mask and the creature's eerily calculating gaze. She woke up screaming every night. Her parents stayed long enough for her to get cleared by the local doctor and let her go to Evan's funeral, with the empty casket, then they left quickly, with promises they would never make her go back. Jaime's parents weren't long in finding new jobs in another city, and from what she heard, Claire went to live with her grandparents in another province for a while.

Some days it felt like she was going crazy. She couldn't have seen what she thought she saw… right? It was just a stupid story, like Bigfoot or the Mothman…

They were just stories, right?

Sam Fletcher

Sam Fletcher is a journalist in the state of Washington, which has more Bigfoot sightings than anywhere else in the world. His short fiction can be found in Space Cowboy Books, Eerie River Publishing, Upstreet Magazine, and elsewhere.

His anthology, *Ike Papalua: Science Fiction & Fantasy Stories from the Hawaiian Islands*, is available through Mutual Publishing. See a full list of his work and appearances at Fletcherstories.com

U-44

Morning glowed against the treetops. Bram led Joey along the thin trail, placing his boots down slowly to not crack a stick. The two of them clutched their rifles, scouting in every direction for movement.

They ducked beneath long moss beards. By noon, they must have cleared miles. They'd seen a handful of does and a buck, a couple eagles. But not what they'd come for.

The last hour had been taken by steep incline, making up for the slope they followed earlier. When the two hunters reached the peak of the opposite canyon wall and the sun was directly overhead, Bram stopped and sat on a log. Joey joined him, rifle pointed upward, overlooking the ground they'd traversed.

"So, it's ten grand if we shoot this thing, but I'm the only one with a bear tag," Bram whispered. Though it was much warmer than when they started, steam still wafted from his heavy breath. "If you kill the wrong one, you're fined."

Joey chugged from his canteen, wiped the freezing water off his chin. "You just wanna say you're the one who brought in U-44."

"I'm not saying that at all," said Bram. "We split the prize fifty-fifty no matter who shoots. I'm just saying, there's no way to know if it's U-44 for sure."

"It's giant," said Joey, struggling to keep his voice down too. "Eight feet tall on its hind legs at least. All the accounts talk about its long arms, brown fur, glowing eyes. It killed eleven people in town, Bram. There's no mistaking it. They might as well have named the thing Goliath."

"They name 'em numbers so they don't feel bad when they get shot."

"You'd be crazy to feel bad for it."

"Still, if there's any question at all as to if it's the one, you better let me shoot first."

"Every hunter this side of the mountains is looking for it. I'd be happy if either of us shoots first," Joey said. "You know what my theory is?"

"Huh?"

"U-44 ain't a bear at all. Think about the reports — each and every witness described it the same way. It ain't a bear, Bram. It's a sasquatch."

Bram was too cold to give an animated response.

"I'm just sayin'," Joey continued. "Name a single black bear that fits that bill."

"It's a goliath, like you said," said Bram. "Could be a grizzly, too."

"There ain't grizzlies in these woods."

Bram cleared his throat and stood up off the log. He looked to where they were headed, then back down at Joey. "Better chance than Bigfoot though, right?"

In 1935 Hong Kong, paleontologist Gustav Heinrich Ralph von Koenigswald came across an old bone used for medicine in a drug store. The label called it a dragon tooth.

After a lifetime of paleontological education and exploration starting at just fifteen, as well as recently returning from an expedition throughout Java learning about several extinct primates, von Koenigswald identified the tooth immediately — claiming that it did not come from a dragon at all, but from an unknown species he then dubbed 'Gigantopithecus.'

In the years that followed, paleontologists found thousands of similar teeth — both molars and canines — across China, Thailand, Vietnam, and Indonesia. Gigantopithecus was first thought to be among the Hominini, a close relative of humans, but is now thought to be in the Ponginae subfamily, closer to the modern orangutan.

The gigantopithecus is thought to be bipedal, standing anywhere from eight to twelve feet tall and weighing upward of 600 pounds. It is thought to have been affected immensely by the lack of food during Late Pleistocene, being forced, like many megafauna at the time, to migrate or go extinct.

"Samples don't mean anything until they've identified the species, you know," Joey said. He'd return to this conversation of bigfoot anytime his mind wandered long enough. "Western scientists had hair samples, track castings, fecal matter, you name it of the giant panda before they knew what it was — I bet we have all that stuff for sasquatches sitting in a cupboard somewhere."

Bram paused on a cliff, overlooking the stretch of evergreens ending only by the horizon. He caught his breath.

"Think of how many times in history planes have crashed in the woods and not a single part was ever found," Joey continued. "Entire planes — just sitting there. You're telling me a halfway intelligent creature that can move around couldn't avoid humans if it wanted to?"

The sun was now dipping beneath those farthest trees. Neither men had fired a shot today.

"I'm hungry," Bram said. "Should we head back to camp?"

"Did you bring your headlamp?" Joey asked. "Almost half of all reported sasquatch sightings are at night. When you take in the number of people out and about at night versus day, it's safe to assume they're nocturnal. This is our edge against the other hunters. It might be the best time to catch a glimpse of U-44."

Bram continued to stare at the setting sun. "Eh, let's go," he said. "This place is starting to give me the creeps."

Before long, humans — at this point paleolithic hunter-gatherers — would too be affected by this cold world and be presented the same options as the animals around them. They started the trek that many species of the past millennium had to, traveling out of the Asias via Beringia — the glacial land bridge connecting present day Russia and Alaska — to the Americas.

Along this journey, they hunted mammoths, giant sloths, lions, bison, wolves, and many others that crossed their path. In passing, too, they came across a rarer species of primate. One that had developed over many centuries a thicker coat and an appetite for rodents and fish or anything at all that would sustain their kind.

In return for this compromised lifestyle, the gigantopithecus species dwindled by the year. Thus, human's sightings of this mysterious creature, the only one that walked like they did, became rarer and rarer.

At camp the two men boiled water over the camp stove and softened noodles. Not long after their bellies were full, eyeing the flames poking from the top of the old oil drum, did they pull the whiskey bottle out. The men passed it back and forth, enjoying the silence and starlight.

Joey fixed on his headlamp, turned on the beam. He hiccupped. "One more look?"

Bram didn't even humour the idea. "Hell no, tromping around half-drunk in the woods, not able to see nothin'. You wanna be U-44's twelfth kill, that's how."

"You're afraid of the dark? That's why we got lights."

"I'm afraid of what's in the dark," Bram said. "This place doesn't seem spooky to you?"

Joey took a swig of the bottle and looked around at their black surroundings. He looked up to the sky and howled at the full moon.

"Ass," Bram said. Joey passed him the bottle. "I'm just sayin'. It's a feeling, I guess."

"What, like a ghost?" Joey smiled.

"You can't say shit after all that bigfoot talk today," Bram said after a pull.

"Bigfoot can be proven."

"I don't even mean a ghost necessarily. It's just like… when you feel like someone's following you. Some places you can just — feel what happened there."

Joey didn't respond, so he continued. "Walking across a battlefield that's been vacated for a century, you can still feel that sadness. Same reason cemeteries have that eerie feeling. When something happens, especially over and over again, it lingers in the ether."

"And what happened here?" Joey's gaze was on the stars.

"U-44 ripping a lot of big mammals apart, that's what. But that's just a small part of it. This whole place is a battlefield of natural selection. Just think, if animals fought for their survival for centuries in one place, you'd start to sense it in the way they move about the place. In the sounds they make, where they nest. It's all based on years and years of history, and it all boils down to a feeling. An energy here. Like, the forest has a memory. Do you know what I mean?"

Joey took his last pull of the night. "No," he said. "I don't."

As generations progressed, some communities settled and others migrated. They formed tribes and languages, developed advanced hunting and fishing strategies, and told stories of the animals they came across. Oftentimes the people and the animals in these stories were hardly different from each other, even shifting their form throughout the tale.

They created art. They painted their cave walls with people and animals. They drew families of this mysterious primate they saw fewer and fewer of. They made masks and dressed as them. All of this would confuse Western researchers centuries later, as there was no other evidence to suggest any primate in North America.

As tribes drifted farther from each other, so did cultural norms and language structures. As each had its own name for the elk, beaver, eagle, and bear, each had its own name for the gigantopithecus.

First Nations people of present-day British Columbia called it "sésq̓əc," a Halkomelem word meaning "wild man."

Many years would pass before this would be Anglicized to sasquatch.

The two rustled from their cots before sunrise and drowned their headaches with their canteens. The morning air was brisker than memory.

They put on their layers, assembled their gear, and stuffed their pockets full of protein bars. Joey was able to stir some instant coffee into boiling water before they loaded into the pickup.

By shooting light, they were atop the mountain again. They got out, stretched, and proceeded once again down the steep canyon ledge.

Harvesting opportunities and natural disaster continued to break tribes and spread them apart. People grew in ways other species couldn't and watched over time as many of their animal contemporaries, who made the trek with them across Beringia, died off with the warming sun.

They lived on in humans' stories.

Many Coast Salish tribes practiced coming-of-age rituals, where members would partake in a solo trip to a location chosen by an elder. Youths would fast for days on end and meditate alone. In this space, animals could speak to them, guide them, and transcend from their physical bounds. When the tribal member returned home, they brought with them stories which would shape their actions moving forward.

Western anthropologists, upon researching this, would struggle to understand how in the same ancient reports of beavers, elk, and deer, were reports of two-headed serpents, thunderbirds, and sasquatches. They would struggle to learn that the dichotomy of physical and spiritual only exists within their culture.

The dense canopy of evergreens shielded all daylight. Neither man had eaten since morning, but the discovery of fresh bear tracks kept their minds focused. They were easily the largest prints either of them had seen. When they pressed their boots to it, the track stuck out on all sides. The hunters had lost the trail hours ago to the mossy floor, but they knew they were getting close.

Bram led the way still, holding his rifle tight. He couldn't think of anything but U-44 — how big it must be to leave tracks that size. He imagined its thick claws, its dense fur, its long teeth, its putrid smell. But he couldn't know any of this for sure, so after a while it was as if his mind was simply empty, creating a focused concentration on nothing at all.

Joey and Bram walked for miles this way. Not speaking to each other, just breathing, focusing, ready to pull the trigger.

Then, they saw movement. They stopped in their tracks.

It was almost nightfall when the being emerged, standing up from behind the tree to the left of them, well over their heads. A startling eight feet, at least.

There it was: U-44.

Long mats of light brown, almost reddish, fur dangled off its body. They could see its broad chest, meaty arms dangling almost to its kneecaps. Sharp teeth poked ever so slightly from its lips. Its head was round, with a large sagittal crest shaping its skull, common among apes.

After standing tall beside the hunters, the thing moved behind them and ducked behind a large shrub. As it tromped, all they saw was a wall of strawberry brown.

Bram jerked his head to Joey, whose adrenaline-fueled smile was wide.

I KNEW IT, Joey mouthed the words slowly with inflated eyes.

Bram put a finger to his lips, then the rifle to his shoulder and tiptoed in front of his partner. As he crept around the bush, a thousand thoughts entered his mind. How this thing could so impossibly exist; if he should even kill it at all... Bram put his boot down slowly, ready to curve around the brush.

He knew how strong the creature was, but he didn't know what awaited him on the other side. An entire state of hunters was after the beast, a war it was still winning. Bram knew well what was at stake. He remembered how many U-44 killed. How many it dragged into the woods and slaughtered. Its end was necessary. He held his gun out, put his eye to the scope, and brushed up against the trigger.

Then, he pounced.

What waited for him on the other side of the bush wasn't light brown, though, but black. It wasn't eight feet tall, but six. The thing stood up on its hind legs, stretching to eat the red berries off a twig before it. It wasn't a sasquatch, but a bear.

When it saw Bram, it fell back down on fours and fumbled its way on through the woods.

Matthew LeDrew

Matthew LeDrew has written over twenty-five novels, some of which have gone on to become Canadian and international bestsellers. They include: the ten book Coral Beach Casefiles series, *The Long Road,* The Xander Drew series, *Jacobi Street, Touch Your Nose, As Loved Our Fathers, Infinity, The Tourniquet Reprisal, Exodus of Angels, Garden of the Eighth Circle,* and *Rats of Refraction* the latter five of which with wife and co-author Ellen Curtis.

Since 2007 he has traveled all over Canada promoting his work as well as teaching seminars on writing and publishing. He currently holds a Canada Council for the Arts Research and Creation Grant and an ArtsNL Professional Projects Grant.

He holds an Honours Degree in English from the Memorial University of Newfoundland with a minor in Anthropology. He studied Journalism at College of the North Atlantic in Stephenville, Newfoundland. He has worked with Transcontinental Publishing as well as student-youth magazine The Troubadour.

He has been called "the face of Newfoundland Genre writing" and is one of the most successful authors working and living in his province today.

He lives in Chapel Arm, Newfoundland.

The Hunters

Recording on. 7:54PM, June 11th, 2024.
Copyright *Cryptid Hunters NLPT*, 2024.
Interview #8661-967-001
Why don't you just start at the beginning.
Well, it's hard to know where the beginning even *is*, you know. You could say the beginning was a very long time ago. In my twenties, when I started the hunt. In my teens, when Fadder, he gave me my first gun. When he took me out to shoot for the first time… well, he thought it was my first time. I told him it was my first time, but I'd snuck his rifle out three or four times and practiced acing bottles off of ol' Brian Gumtree's fence years before. It was getting so that I was right good at it too, so when Fadder brought me out, thinking I'd never shot before, man, he was some impressed, b'y. He clapped me on the back and gave me attay'boys and later that night he let me try my first sip of rum he was so impressed, yessir.

But I imagine you don't need me to go back that far?
No.

I'll just start. I know you can edit this down, I used to do some work in TV. I know how all this works.

They still call me *The Hunter*, you know. Even after the show went off the air, even after they stopped printing the trade books, there's still someone every day who calls me The Hunter. *The Newfoundland Sports Hunter* ran for twenty-one seasons! Can you believe that, sir? Twenty-one! Four-hundred and forty-one episodes of premium, Made-Right-Here content, and then all of a sudden? Bob's your Uncle, I guess. Gone. Pfft. Like nothing at all.

I was almost glad my dad didn't live to see it, I was. Shocking, b'y, the way they does you dirty. But there's some old timers, like I say, they still calls me The Hunter. I pass them on the street there off Smallwood or up at the Sobeys and they calls out to me, they says: "Hey, you're The Hunter!" and they says that they still turns on the TV to NLPT every Sunday at 2pm, just hoping I'll be back on. They never *really* cancelled us, you know. They're still calling it 'hiatus'.

But that's all well and good, right? That's the business, and twenty-one seasons is nothing to scoff at. When you two have been doing what you've been doing for twenty-one seasons, you'll know. How long have you had this on the air now, five? Six? Bah. Still wet behind the ears, sure.

I should have just retired, but I got *restless*. That's the thing that happens, right? That gets us old folk in trouble. You gets tired and you gets *restless*.

I tried to keep with the hunt. The government said we can't fish the cod no more, says they're almost gone. Well, they been almost gone for thirty years now, and they don't seem to be coming back. Maybe it'd be best to just let us have them. I tried the moose, but one year I didn't get selected in the license lotto, and the next when I did,

I swear, there wasn't a buck to be found. In my basement there's a set of antlers for every season I was on the air, twenty-one of them, and there was spots there for those two years too, but I didn't see one dang animal. And you knows now that every time I heard a shot off in the distance, you knows that made me right mad. Murderous I was by the end of that season. Murderous.

That was when I started staying home. Watching too much TV, that kind of bad TV, you know. Daytime TV where everyone's talking but nothing gets said. You know what I mean? And I'm watching the TV and I sees you two. There was some interview with you two, and you were talking about Cryptids. You were talking about these beasts, these things, that people say they saw and that people think exist, but there's no proof of. And you guys, you goes out with your camera and you tries to find them. To film them. So the wife — my first wife, that is — she showed me how to look up one of your episodes on YouTube. And by jibber, it really looked like an old episode of *The Newfoundland Sports Hunter*. Font was the same. Night-vision was the same, but there was more of it. Confessionals were the same. I said to myself, by jibbers, these young pups have gone and aped my whole style! You were even airing in my old timeslot!

But... no, calm down. That's not what I was trying to say here. That's not the point.

The episode, it was the one you did on the Bell Island Hag, you remember that one? Of course you do, what am I saying? You've only done a hundred and twenty-six episodes, you must remember them all. Talk to me when it's up over four-hundred and see how many you remember on a whim, eh? Anyway, you went out with the cameras, and it was at night and it was all night-vision mode, and you went looking for the Hag down in the caves of Bell Isle.

Only you didn't think it was a Hag. Mike, you had this wild hair that you thought it was a chupacabra. Goat Sucker, you called it, one of the beasts that's usually at home down South of the American border. But there had been reports, and by lord I looked them up, that there was one in Newfoundland, trapped on Bell Island. There were farms out on that island, and lo and behold, there were livestock killed. Neck injuries. Blood let. Enough to give you the creeps.

And maybe that was when the story started, when I saw your show. I saw your show and, I've got to say, I was excited again. Excited in a way I hadn't been since my first moose hunt. Since my first time reeling in a ten-pound-er. Since I hit that first glass bottle off of Brian Gumtree's fence.

But I don't think so.

Because I watched that episode, and I remembered a time, years ago. Ages. Long enough that I'd almost forgot-ten it. I was out hunting moose with my father and Sam. That's how long ago this was now, that'll tell you, me fad-der was still alive. We were hunting buck and we split up and I was creeping down this mucky, mossy old trike trail, trying to be as quiet as I could. Trying to be quiet, but you knows yourself it's impossible in terrain like that. Ev-ery step you takes sure, it's squelch, squelch, ssssquelch. Suction, as the mud tries to keep you.

I'm walking down this trail squelching my way along,

and it's getting dark, but the moon is bright. Big and bright, lighting up the evening like it was midday. The kind of weather you pray for, hunting or filming. You know. Good visibility, able to shoot at night without tinting everything green.

The moon is bright and so I see it, clearly.

There's a footprint in front of me, in the mulch. Not just one footprint, many. Something had stepped out of the brush to the side of the trail here and stepped down into the mud, and goddamn if it hadn't sunk down four feet. The hole it made was *deep*. The heel was deep, real deep, the kind of thing that happens when you're rolling on it, when you're walking upright on two legs; but to have sunk down that deep? Damn thing must have been five-hundred pounds. I was only a stone's throw over twenty stone and even I was only sinking six or seven inches.

And there were more of them, footprints, leading towards me down the path at first and then back into the brush. Like something had been coming down the trail towards me and then stepped off.

And then I realized something that still makes the hair on the back of my neck stand on end, even now, years later, thinking about it. I bent down to look at the track, thinking if it was a beast that made that how good it would look on my wall, when I see that the swamp water, it's filling back into the print. I should get a picture soon, I think, because it'll be gone. I look up further on the trail and sure enough, the tracks that were farthest from me, they're filling in. The furthest one is all filled in, you couldn't even tell where it had been now!

I didn't get my camera out, because it occurred to me,

then... it occurred to me that that meant the tracks were fresh, and that whatever made them? Whatever made them had stepped into the brush right alongside of me, and none too long ago. And when I realized that, I don't need to tell you, the blood ran from me a little. I could feel my face get cold from it, that feint feeling.

And right about the time I was putting two and two together, all the light from the moon at my back went dark. Like there was something between me and it, and there was a shadow over me on the trail. This massive shadow that I swear, must have been well over eight feet tall. I see that and I feel, on the back of my neck, I feel breath. Hot, humid breath. Stench of breath, that kind of rotted meat smell you only get from a carnivore's mouth.

I'm frozen. I don't know what to do, I don't know what I can do. And all of a sudden, the moonlight is back again, the shadow's gone. And then I hear that squelch... squelch... squelch as it's walking back away from me. Walking the same direction it had been before I'd interrupted it, made it step off into the brush. Before I'd bent down and looked at its prints and made it think that I knew it was there, before it had had to step out, beat its chest, show me what was what.

I think... I think that was the beginning. I've been on your site, seen some of your reference material. Some of the casts you've got, what people calls fake, from out in B.C.? The footprint casts? Yeah, they looks like what I saw that night. Sasquatch, you said you thinks it is. I don't know what it was. One name's as good as another.

Yeah. Yeah, I think that was the start.

So the old wife, me first wife, the ex-wife, you knows what I'm saying, she shows me more about the YouTube and shows me that you can upload to it yourself, too. No need for NLPT and their pocketbooks dictating everything. And she, the first wife, she shows me some of the channel numbers. Big viewership, more than we ever could have gotten on local cable, for some of it. And they're all getting brand deals and corporate sponsorships too... I'd been exited just from watching your show, just from the memory of having that thing come up behind me, but now the business brain was going. That's the thing about guys like us, it's one thing for an idea to turn us on *creatively*, but you also got to get the right-brain going, you know? You know.

The wife — the ex-wife now, you knows — she let me up with a channel *The Newfoundland Sports Hunter Hunts Cryptids*. Nice and simple. We had a few RED cameras in storage, a few lights. A few mics. No big setup, deal DIY kind of indie filmmaker style stuff. But where you and your lot was looking to catch one of these things on *film*, I was looking to take one down. I would have it on my wall, next to twenty-one sets of antlers, yes b'y I would.

We did a big press conference at The Rooms. I went up and stood in front of the giant squid they got pickled up there. I put my hand on the glass and reminded people — there was a time when they thought this thing wasn't real, either. Until they *caught one*. Until they had a corpse to cut open, test, prove that it was real and how exactly it fit into the ecological chain. And I was going to catch them all,

I said. I was going to start on the island, but I was going to catch them all. And people laughed, of course, and the channel sent over lawyers because of the name, but I had lawyers too, and mine was better.

So we started filming, and the first episode, we went over to Bell Isle, the same place you did in your episode. And we talked to people, but you might have noticed if you seen it — it's a little easier for me to get people to talk to me, what? Yes, that's *The Hunter* charm. Being beamed into everyone's rabbit-ears every Sunday after church for twenty-one years has its advantages, you know. You could learn a thing or two, both of you.

We made a show of it. If this thing was real, based on what evidence we have and how we would track the things it's like, how would we track these things? We didn't catch it, of course, but we found evidence. We found blood. Blood all over pine needles, blood that had come off of it while it was resting. It probably got spooked, I'd said, probably couldn't run of a full stomach. It probably had crouched there, blood dripping from the proboscis it drank from, waiting until it was left by its lonesome.

That was where I met my wife, on that first day shooting, and her daughter. My second wife, not the first one. Not the ex, the current, and her daughter. My stepdaughter, though she's too grown for me to call her that. They'd owned the farm where that thing had hunted, and we interviewed them on camera. That was the first time I met my wife, my new wife, interviewing her about some goat-sucking chupacabra hag that had been after her pigs.

Between the new wife and the new show and the new animals, I got to tell you, I was feeling real good. Feeling young again, let me tell you. Not that there was anything wrong with my first, but at a certain age you start to think every new experience you'll ever have is in the rearview mirror, and it's nice to be proven wrong about that every now and again.

The wife? The first one? She's fine. She was fine at first, then she got a bit panicked when the show started to take off. Then she went on a trip, the wife said. She said they talked and she decided to go on a trip, and she hasn't come back yet. The new wife said that, I mean. About the old.

The new wife, and the new daughter, they came on and helped out behind the show, like the old wife did. They came with me out on the boat with me when we went hunting for giant squid. We didn't call it a giant squid though, we called it *The Newfoundland Sports Hunter Hunts the Kraken*. Because you've got to know how to sell this stuff.

You know what gets me mad? They tells us stuff like this doesn't exist, and we says it do, and we goes out looking for proof. And if we don't find it, they says we're nuts. But if we *do* find it, they just goes, "oh yeah, I guess that would exist" and they give it some boring old name. 'Giant Squid' my arse. That's a Kraken! The suckers on those things, you seen them? They can take down a Killer Whale! That thing is a Kraken, and you do the people who believed when everyone else said they were stupid a disservice by calling it anything but. That thing *is a Kraken*.

The Kraken episode, we got in some trouble for that one. See you can't hunt giant squid. But we went out to international waters, paid someone a lot of money to bring us there. When we got back people said it was illegal, but it wasn't illegal. We went out to where their laws didn't matter none. Got my lawyers involved again, the good ones. We never would have gotten away with it on NLPT, no sir. But I was running my own show now, and they couldn't tell me no. No sir. And all the controversy? It didn't hurt the view counts, I'll tell you that for nothing.

We found one, you must have seen that! Caused a stir. We found a Mongolian Death Worm, but not in Mongolia. *Here.* There were reports and I tracked one and I killed it, the scientists have it now, but I'm told I'll have it back when they've sequenced it. And just like with Kraken, they're already fixing to call it something else. The Death Worm, they're calling it a 'large intestinal worm' now, because that's what it does. It gets up inside you when you've stopped to squat. Eats you from the bottom up.

Blood red when it's full, and it's always full. It eats moose mostly, and wolves. I imagine it'd eat just about anything that squat to relieve itself. And that wasn't a problem, until we started to encroach on its territory. Then! Then you've got yourself a right big problem. Then it starts finding a home in outhouses, curling up for the night where it's safe from predators. And then some hiker comes along, squats over the hole to relieve his bowels, and suddenly it's chow-time.

It spits poison, this thing. Spits it. If it doesn't get you, if it doesn't latch on, it spits it automatically. Gets its victim in the rear and they're running away, and before you know it, they're falling over and rotting from the arse up. They fall down, hard to run when you're burning up down south, and the worm, it can just slither up onto you at its leisure.

Roy Chapman Andrews wrote about it once. Said he interviewed Mongolian Prime Minister Damdinbazar. That was how it got its name, although it's not specific to that region. Damdinbazar had seen one and lived to tell the tale. He said it was "shaped like a sausage, about two feet long. No head nor legs, and is so poisonous that merely to touch it means instant death." And man, he was right.

I tracked it from a populated park area, knew it couldn't stay there. Used my dogs, tracked it out far into the woods. It must have been so fast, in life. It must have been so fast to travel that far. It's hunting radius was massive. Tens of kilometers from its nest. I think what happened was, I think we moved into the nearby area and scared away its food source, so it had to slither father for it. It went out so far it went to us, where it usually wouldn't go, right?

I follow it back to its nest and the new wife and new stepdaughter, they follow me, cameras in tow. They follow me and we're up on it and it's curled around these eggs and it's hurking up whatever it ate before it got there and it's covering the eggs with them, like a mother feeding baby birds, except they'ms eggs. I think it scoffs up on them to keep them warm.

And it occurred to me, it couldn't shoot the poison all the time, or it would be poisoning its young right now. So I rushed it, and it spat at me, but sure enough what it spat was bile. It wasn't spitting using its venom sacks, it only did that when it was eating. It wrapped itself around my arm and, by lord, Damdinbazar was right. It burned. And then I… well, you saw the episode, I'm sure.

They came with me on all my adventures, the new wife and the new daughter did. But they didn't want me going back to that farm on Bell Island what they come from. They didn't want me looking for that chupacabra hag. No sir. Scared, they were. Brave when they were out in their field, braver than any sportsman I ever came across, but they'd been terrorized on that farm and didn't want to go back to it, and I could honour that. Ayuh, that was something I could do.

And they were right to be scared, I tell you, because we got tales of people who'd experience the hag everywhere we went. The Old Hag, the Goat Sucker, some combination of the two. We'd see them everywhere, everywhere we went there'd be a fresh story about them. People with slits in their necks that didn't bleed where the proboscis had latched on, like a leech. It wasn't just Mexico and Bell Island the thing was on, that was for darn sure. These things were everywhere.

The stories were the same. Cattle falling ill, getting drained of all blood. Goats running scared until they were out of breath, found days later with their blood gone, that one wound on their neck it was all sucked through. And sometimes… sometimes there were human victims. Sometimes the goat-sucker story would get mixed in with the hag story, and we'd end up in a place where there weren't any goats to be had. And in those places, you'd get the stories of people waking up paralyzed, unable to move. Waking up with a weight on their chests, opening their eyes, realizing there was someone sitting on it, leaned forward, taking from them.

Something in the way they suckled, it made you calm. Complacent. Paralyzed.

We started to hear these stories everywhere we travelled. We'd be interviewing about an Ogopogo, but one of the talking heads, they'd mention the chupacabra. The hag. The goat-sucker. We wouldn't use those clips of course, but I'd keep them. I have them.

It became so prevalent, it started to put me in mind of a *season arc*. That was what was selling nowadays, right? Season-long storytelling. I could make another Bell Island story. I could go back there at the end of the season, a kind of close-by-return, you know? People eat that stuff up. And then I would have all this footage, from every place I went to all season, but I would show *more*. I could show that the people I interviewed about the Kraken? They'd also seen the hag. And the people I'd interviewed about the Mongolian Death Worm? They'd seen it, too. I could use those clips like flashbacks, add some nice music to it, and show me on the Bell Island ferry: going back to finish what I started.

It would be amazing. Screw NLPT! They'd have me on Netflix if I could pull that off. Or CBC! Or, bless, maybe even FOX.

You know the problem, though. I already said it. It was the wife. The new wife and the new daughter, they wanted nothing to do with going back to Bell Island or doing anything with the chupacabra hag. When we found people who talked about it, which we did often as I said, they got nervous. They asked me not to roll on it. I told them we wouldn't use it in the episode, and we didn't, but they thought it was destroyed, and it weren't. It was all edited together on my cloud, waiting.

We got back from our crossover episode with the

Haunted Hike people and I told them. I told them what I wanted to do and I told them how I wanted to do it. I told them that if we wanted to hit it big, this was how to do it.

And boys, they got *mad*. They got madder than I've ever seen them. I swear, their eyes turned red. I don't mean that figuratively. For a second, both of them, I swear their eyes. Turned. Red.

And then they were calm. It was like something just snapped, and they looked at each other, and they were calm. They just nodded and walked off, the both of them.

That was a month ago, and I've been working on the episode since. It has to be big. I've licensed some music, interviewed some celebrities what say they've seen the chupacabra hag. Alan Doyle. Ida Linehan Young. Vikki Barbour. You know, the ones you got to get quotes from if you want to make it big here. Linehan Young, she says she was attacked by it, even. Showed me a scar, right near her collar. Showed it on camera, too.

The new wife and daughter, they haven't been help-ing with these interviews. They want no part of it. It's been slower going without them... and if I'm honest, I've been slowing. At first I thought I was losing interest in the project, but no. If anything I'm more excited. I mean, come on. Netflix. You can have my 2PM timeslot if you want it, I'll be on streaming. On Demand, whenever people want me. But I was tired all the time, and it was slowing me right down.

And then last week, I was editing the footage from that interview with Linehan Young, and it was at the part where she was showing me her scar... and I felt myself scratching, and I was scratching at the same place. And I got that cold feeling in my face again, like the blood was gone out of me. Like there was something behind me, breathing down my neck with rotten meat on its tongue.

And I went into the bathroom and I looked in the mirror and sure enough, there it was. Just the same as what it had been on Linehan Young. A little sucker mark, a little bruise from the suction of it, and a little scar in the middle of it that looked like a starfish.

So that's... that's when I came to you. That's when I called you. Because even though I've been doing TV longer — and I *have* been doing it longer, and you'll be lucky to last half as long as I did — you've been doing *this* longer. The cryptids... thing. You've been doing it longer.

So I figure... I figure we do a crossover episode, or something, right? I give you the footage I have from all the people I interviewed about the chupacabra hag, you edit it together into a crossover episode of your show. "In this episode of *Cryptid Hunters NLPT, The Newfoundland Sports Hunter* becomes the hunted" and then you... help me find this thing. Stop it.

Save me.

You know, for the show. You save me.

Or just in general... please. Because I am in over my head and I don't rightly know how I got to be there, and I am really hoping you can help me see the other side of this.

End of transcript, Interview #8661-967-001

Copyright *Cryptid Hunters NLPT*, 2024.

9:01PM, June 11th, 2024.

He went home. The long way around.

When he got there the house was cold and empty. There was no food in the fridge. The clothes were gone from the closets. His guns were missing. It seemed like his new wife and stepdaughter had left, but he knew that was not the case. He knew because he could smell them, he didn't know how he hadn't before.

He ordered two moose burgers from the best place to eat them in the city, The Guv'nor, up at the top of Elizabeth Avenue. It cost an arm and leg to deliver it to him. They weren't even going to do it at first, but he'd told them who he was and they'd relented. The name of *The Newfoundland Sports Hunter* still had sway in this town. People used to tune their televisions to watch him every Sunday after church. You'd listen to God, you'd watch him while Momma cooked, and then you'd eat your Sunday supper. He was a part of that ritual for people, for a generation.

He ate them all, sopping with grease. When he was done, he took the soft bread they'd packed with the meal and soaked up the grease leftover in the paper plate with it, then ate that too.

It had been forever since he'd had a good moose burger. He remembered, suddenly, why hunters hunted. He remembered his dad, all those years ago, teaching him to shoot. And it hadn't been for fun or for ratings or for brand deals and sponsorships. It had been to put food on the table.

He patted his stomach full, took off his clothes, went to bed. Slept.

An hour later he woke up, but couldn't move. He struggled to open his eyes, but when he did, he saw that she was on him. His new wife sat on his chest, and his new stepdaughter sat on his legs, and he could not move. He couldn't move not because of their weight, but because he was paralyzed.

It was his wife, the new one, but he didn't know how he knew it was her. She was leaned over him, that stench he should have recognized that let him know she was still waiting in the walls with her brood. Her flesh was flaking, green skin that skittered, the texture of pine needles underneath. She had red eyes now, like when she was mad. The both of them did. Red multi-prismed eyes, like a fly's, and glowing red with retro-reflection. And there was a proboscis, hard and erect, come from her mouth and leading into the bruise on his neck that he had seen in the mirror.

And his new stepdaughter had one too, it lay flaccid against her chest, waiting for use.

And he tried to scream, but even his throat was paralyzed.

The Telegram

June 13th, 2024

Headline: Outdoor Enthusiast and Local Celebrity found dead in home.

The host of the popular NLPT series *The Newfoundland Sports Hunter* who entertained audiences all over the province with common-sense guides to hunting and fishing was found dead in his home late yesterday evening.

Police suspect foul play. He is survived by his ex-wife, Mary, and their two children, Clara and Peter.

Mary Hunter could not be reached for comment. Children Clara and Peter have filed a missing person's report to ascertain her whereabouts.

He is also survived by his second wife and stepdaughter. They could not be reached for comment. The police were unable to find records of them with the city. If seen, do not approach.

Tonight on NLPT, a special *Cryptid Hunters* tribute to *The Newfoundland Sports Hunter*, where Mike and Maria try to finish his final hunt and track down the chupacabra hag in a special episode: *The Hunters of Bell Island.*

Gregg Chamberlain

Gregg Chamberlain, a community newspaper reporter five decades in the trade, lives in rural Eastern Ontario, Canada with his missus, Anne, and their cats who allow their humans the run of the house. He writes speculative fiction for fun and zombie filk on a whim. Past fiction credits include Abyss & Apex, Daily Science Fiction, Apex, Pulp Literature, Mythic, and Weirdbook magazines, and various original anthologies.

Chamberlain says he "has not had the pleasure" of visiting Newfoundland or Labrador, but he and his Anne hope to retire to one of the Atlantic provinces soon and they both love the look of The Rock, being fans of Republic of Doyle.

Tee Time with Caddy

"So, this is where you go drinking?"

Gardy gestured with a thumb at the double-door entrance to The Tesseract. There's no lettering on the doors to indicate that it's a bar. On the building façade above the doors there is a rusted metal bracket. Hanging from that is a faded red-and-white wooden cube. Another smaller red-and-white cube is attached to one side of the larger cube.

My brother gave me a, *you gotta be kidding* look. I admit that it's not an impressive sight.

The doors of The Tesseract are sandwiched between Assad's, a hole-in-the-wall eatery with the best home-made samosas, soups, and sandwiches you could ever dream of, and the White Star Groceria, a mom-and-pop store owned and operated for three generations by the Kleins, a quiet Hassidic couple, with help after school and on weekends over many years from first their children and now their grandchildren. Old Mrs. Klein sits perched on a straight-backed stool behind the counter when it's her turn to manage the store during the day. Baby Sarai, the latest fourth-generation member of the Klein family, sleeps in an heirloom wooden trundle bed on the floor behind the counter, keeping her Nana Klein company.

An Arthur Murray's Dance Studio, which has existed there for decades so I am told, completes the small-business assembly for the block. The studio occupies the entire second floor of the building above The Tesseract. There's a walk-up stairway entrance, for dance students and aficionados of classic choreography, located around the corner where Robinson Street meets with Sprague Street.

I shrugged. "You know what they say, don't judge—"

"—a book by its cover," finished Gardy, grinning. "Yeah, well, you would know, brother."

I smiled in response. The family jokes about my ever-expanding 'personal library' were many and various. I reached out and opened one of the two doors. "Shall we?"

"Yeah, sure, why not?" answered Gardy. He stepped past me and into The Tesseract. I followed and, because I was expecting it, stopped at the same time he did, just inside the entrance of the bar. Standing behind him, I couldn't see his face. I still smiled, though, because I could imagine his expression as a first-time visitor to The Tesseract.

The common room opened out about ten metres each way on both sides of the door and stretched another ten metres ahead towards the bar at the far end. Slate stood behind the bar, wiping out a beer mug. Saw us standing in the doorway. Nodded a greeting and then hung the clean mug on one of the overhanging hooks above the bar.

Sunlight through the stained-glass mandala in the ceiling above shed a shifting pattern of lavender, aqua, emerald, citrine, amber, and rose on the floor. Over at a corner table, Nesbitt and Sky were engaged in their continuing chess challenge, with Harold the Hobbit sitting on one side and Rajeev on the other, serving as spectators, colour commentators, critics, and kibitzers. I saw McCrae and Adams at one of the pool tables. Murray bent over the table, lining up stick and cue ball for a difficult-looking shot while Tim stood at the far end, doing a slow skeptical headshake at McCrae's chance of success.

There was a scattering of other Tesseract patrons — both regulars and a few of the occasional drop-ins who were always discovering the place — sitting alone, in pairs or in groups at the other tables. Sonya waved at us as she passed by on her way to rejoin her husband at another corner booth. All the other booths and several of the tables were empty since it was still early afternoon. Even in Vancouver, the serious drinking for most of civilized society doesn't start until at least after six.

I edged my way around Gardy, who still stood in the doorway like a statue, silent and staring. "Yeah," I said. "There's a little bit more room inside."

He blinked. "Huh!" was his sole response as he followed me to the bar.

"Hey there, Slate!" I called out. "Meet my kid brother, G.T., or Gardy to his family and anyone who will still admit to being his friend."

I got a little smile from Slate and an elbow in the ribs from Gardy for that remark.

Slate took down a pair of mugs and started filling one from a tap. "Usual Wolfshead draft for you, Phil," he said as he kept a careful eye on the rising foam. "And for you?"

"Well, I like a good strong beer," Gardy replied.

Slate nodded as he handed me my mug after swiping a steel ruler across the foamy top. "Trollskin it is, then," he said, filling the second mug from a different tap.

Gardy's eyebrows lifted but he accepted the filled mug without a word, eyed its dark contents, and took an experimental sip. An expression of surprised delight replaced the look of cautious curiosity. He lifted his mug in salute to Slate before taking a good swig of his beer.

"That. Is. *Good*," he sighed.

Slate nodded in acknowledgement of the compliment. We drifted off towards the chess game just in time to hear Nesbitt exclaim, "Ha! *ZOT!*" and clack down a rook in the square right in front of Sky's king. Escape to either side for Sky's piece was not an option because of Nesbitt's bishop and knight standing guard. Taking out the rook was also impossible thanks to a lowly pawn acting as the rook's "squire" in a diagonal square behind.

Sky snorted in disgust and tipped his king over. "Another game," he said, looking at Nesbitt. He grinned in answer and began re-setting the pieces, then paused and, still smiling, glanced up at Sky. "Double or nothing?"

Sky shrugged. "Sure. You cain't win ever' time."

Nesbitt nodded in agreement. "I just have to win *this* time," he said, as he resumed setting the pieces back in place.

"What are they playing for this time?" I asked the Hobbit.

Eyes twinkled behind John Lennon-style glasses. "Green fees," he said.

Sky held up a finger without looking away from the

board as he considered his opening move. "Tee fees," he corrected.

"Pretty sure we said green fees," suggested Nesbitt, not looking up as he watched Sky make a traditional King's Pawn to King 4 opening move.

Sky held onto his pawn for a moment. "And I *know* we said tee fees." He looked at Nesbitt as he released the chess piece. "Tee fees at Putter's Paradise."

Nesbitt shrugged as he made the traditional responding move with his own King's Pawn to King 4. "Pitch 'n' putt is not real golf. It's almost miniature golf at best but without the windmills."

"Which always leave you spinning in circles," said Raj, grinning.

After introducing my brother to everyone at the table, what followed, as the chess match carried on, was a lively discussion and debate, mostly between Nesbitt and Gardy — with the Hobbit and Raj chiming in every so often — about the merits of various B.C. golf courses. Gardy and my other brothers were the golfers in the family. They inherited their love for the game from our dad (may he rest in peace), along with Dad's passion for hockey. Me? I'm the Canadian definition of an agnostic: I can take hockey or leave it, and most of the time I leave it. Kickboxing was my sport of choice, in my younger days.

As for golf, well, I once spent a day with Gardy back in the 'Stoke, wandering the 18 holes of the local course there. Nice sunny day and I managed not to lose my ball in the river, and that pretty much described my appreciation for golf. I did go with Sky once to one of his favourite pitch 'n' putts. After we were done, the management politely asked me to patronize another course in future. My 90-degree tee-offs seemed to upset the players on the adjacent greens.

At one point Nesbitt and Gardy began comparing their experiences on various golf courses in the Okanagan region. A three-way argument arose between Ernie and Harold, with Sky taking an interest in the subject, about whether an encounter with Ogopogo, the Okanagan's famous lake monster, would constitute a water hazard situation or a case of wildlife interference on the play.

Gardy kept silent during that discussion. He stood alongside me, working on his beer and listening until—

"Dunno about Ogopogo, but a sea serpent on the green is wildlife interference on the play for sure."

All heads turned towards Gardy. We all waited. He took another swallow of beer, then reached around and pulled a chair over from a nearby table, and sat down. I followed suit.

"A few years ago," Gardy said, "I was in Victoria, at a forestry conference. I stayed on for a few days after it was over, meeting with some potential company clients. There was this one day when I didn't have anywhere that I needed to be or anyone that I needed to see, so I took advantage of the situation and drove out in search of a place to shag a few balls.

"Victoria has some nice golf courses. Problem is that, like with most big city golf courses, you can't just drop in and expect to get on the links right away after registering and paying your green fee. Nowadays even club members sometimes have to reserve tee times at least two or three days in advance even if it means they have to get up before the crack of dawn to take their place on the fairway.

"So when I am away from home and don't want to settle for spending time on the driving range, I look for some little out-of-the-way community golf course. Like the one at Cadboro Bay."

I did a spit-take into my mug just as I was swallowing some beer. Everyone, except Gardy, looked at me with surprise. He just waited for me to stop choking. We exchanged looks. I shook my head "no" and he continued on with his story.

"I learned about the Cadboro Bay Golf Course during a meeting with one of my clients. He chuckled as he gave me directions on how to find it.

"'Maybe you'll see our Caddy while you're out there,' he said with a big grin.

"I just nodded and gave him my own 'no-clue-what-soever-but-the-customer-is-always-right' smile. I wrote down his directions, in case my car's GPS couldn't find the place. We shook hands on a proposed deal between his company and mine and went our own ways. The next morning, I was on the road, heading for Cadboro Bay.

"The village is one of those 'bedroom communities' in the Greater Victoria area. The UVic campus sits just up the hill from the bay itself and most days you'll see boats from the yachting club, along with canoes, kayaks, and other watercraft crisscrossing the bay.

"Driving through the village on my way in search of the golf course, I passed Cadboro-Gyro Park. Nice looking little community park I remember thinking at first glance. I caught a glimpse of kids climbing around on a stone octopus and what looked like a giant mutant snake.

Seeing the big stone snake reminded me then of that curious remark about 'seeing Caddy' so I pulled over, fished
my tablet out of the briefcase, and googled 'Caddy'. First
thing I got was the Wikipedia page on—"

"The Cadborosaurus," I interjected.

Gardy nodded. "Got it in one, bro."

Nesbitt, Sky, Raj, and the Hobbit looked at me. "Local
cryptid legend," I muttered. "Tell you later," and gestured
to Gardy to carry on with his story.

"Well, it was lucky — at least I thought so at the time
— that I wrote down those directions," he said, "because
I almost drove past Songhees Lane, which leads down to
the golf course, even with the GPS telling me to get ready
to turn. The laneway entry was half hidden with heavy
shrubbery. You couldn't really see the road sign, unless
you knew where to look for it, what with all the shrubs
and trees. The lane itself was a patchwork of old, cracked
asphalt with stretches of bare ground, sloping down towards the bay under a thick canopy of arching tree branches. Under the circumstances, I was pleasantly surprised at
what I found when I got to the end of the lane.

"The Cadboro Bay Golf Course is one of those nine-
hole community golf setups you often find in little vil-
lages. Proudly built and lovingly looked after by the local
golfers who can't always afford the cost in gas and green
fees to drive to the nearest big city eighteen-hole course.

"A double-wide trailer set up on blocks served as the
clubhouse and changing room for golfers. I didn't see any
cars or pickups in the gravelled parking lot, and no one
answered when I knocked on the clubhouse door. The
course operated on the honour system. A poster board

listed club rates for local and visiting players. If no one was there during the day to take the green fee, a note at the bottom of the board gave directions to a nearby gas station where you could stop and pay your money after you finished your game.

"A small wooden gazebo sat behind the trailer. A sign hanging from the cupola declared it was The 19th Hole. A smaller sign below that read 'BYOB & TYEP'."

Gardy paused to take a pull at his mug. "Bring your own beer and take your empties, please," he translated.

"Off to one side was a small pile of old cinder blocks, most of them with white scars and chipped edges. A sign stuck in the ground identified this as the 'Club Rock' where players could vent their frustrations on useless or offending clubs after a bad game.

"The fairways may not have been Kentucky blue grass or the greens as flat and smooth as they could be, but it was obvious to anyone that the Cadboro golf course offered wonderful views of the seaside along almost every hole, as well as the clean smell of the salt air across the fairways with every passing breeze from off of the bay. Any amateur or pro who loves the game of golf for itself would be happy to play a double-round any day at the Cadboro Bay course. I certainly felt that way on that day, or at least I did as I got ready to tee off for the first hole.

"That's when I almost thought I felt my arms break as my number one wood dug deep into the ground several inches in front of the tee, instead of hitting the ball. Shockwaves of pain ripped up both arms, forcing me to drop my club. I stood there, hugging my arms together and gasping at the throbbing ache beating its way up from my wrists to my shoulders and back down again.

"And that was just the start of what proved to be the most miserable game of golf I had ever had. Before it was over, I was glad, for more reasons than one, that I was the only person on the course at the time.

"I do not know what was wrong with my game that day. Whether I was always using the wrong wood or maybe the wrong iron or what else might have been the problem, but I just could not swing a single stroke without either hooking or slicing that ball into the bush alongside every fairway. And if I wasn't hunting for my ball in the brush, I was either fishing it out of the middle of the water traps or digging it out of each and every sand pit between me and the greens.

"A trail of divots followed me as I bogeyed my way from hole to hole. By the time I'd finished the ninth, I'd run out of curses and I'd given up keeping score on myself. I did not want to know how badly I'd been playing up to that point. I just knew it was going to be the absolute worst game that I would ever play."

Raj raised a hand in query. "So why didn't you quit?"

Gardy shook his head. "By then all I could think was that I planned to do the full eighteen holes. Call me stubborn ('you're stubborn,' I said), call me just plain mule-headed ('and mule-headed,' I agreed), but I was determined that this little nine-holer course was not going to make me say 'uncle'. It was me or the course and I swore it wasn't going to be me. By then I figured that I might end up throwing every club I had into the bay when I was done for the day, but I also knew that I was going to finish this game, one way or another.

"I returned to the first hole tee-off site to start the round over again. Before teeing up, though, I walked back to the car and retrieved a part roll of duct tape that I kept in the glove box and stuck it in my windbreaker pocket. I always have a roll of 'handyman's helper', just in case, and right about then I was thinking that broken club shafts or loose iron heads were good possibilities during this next round of the course.

"I teed up, and hooked the ball right into the bush. By then I had accepted that every shot would be shat, so I just shrugged, shouldered my bag, and marched off to beat through the brush again.

"The second round of nine holes went pretty much the same way as the first nine. Hook the ball, slice the ball, scour through the underbrush for the ball, dig through the sand traps for the ball, and go fishing with my reach in the ponds for the ball. Until I reached the sixth hole, which was the fifteenth hole for me on this second round.

"The sun was high in the sky when I arrived at the tee-off. I wiped the sweat away from my eyes, and considered my situation.

"Of all the holes in that little course, the sixth was the most devious of all. It looked like a simple and straight drive from the tee-off over a long open fairway to the green. The fairway was the hitch.

"Whoever had designed the sixth hole took advantage of a very shallow saucer-shaped curve in the slope of the terrain. If the ball didn't make it all the way across to the green on the first stroke, if it landed anywhere on the fairway itself, the ball rolled its long merry way downhill and shot off the edge of the slope onto the neighbouring beach, leaving any unfortunate duffer stuck in the biggest sand trap of them all. I'd had that pleasure on my first run-through of the course, and I did not plan on enjoying it a second time.

"I surveyed the terrain for a couple of minutes, calculating, then I teed up, took another look at the distant green, and slowly swung my club back. Eye on the ball, I paused a moment, then swung fast and hard.

"I hit that A-hole ball a good solid *crack!*, watched it arc high in the air and come down right smack on the damn edge of the green. It bounced up once in the wrong direction and rolled down the slope, following the curve towards the beach.

"I felt like whacking my head with the club. I tracked the course of my ball and saw it bounce off an invisible bump in the turf. Luckily, it seemed to me, instead of plunking down onto the sand, my ball fell short of the beach and landed instead on the end of a driftwood log resting on the edge of the fairway drop-off.

"I was just about to shoulder my bag and start making my way down towards the beach when a thought struck me. I didn't remember seeing any log the last time I was at this hole. I took another look and realized then that this log didn't really look that much like a log at all. I dropped my bag back onto the grass, fished out my mobile, and zoomed in with the camera setting.

"Well, I could see now that it wasn't a log. I wasn't sure right then what it was, but I knew it was not some huge piece of driftwood suddenly washed up onto the beach.

"From where I stood, and thanks to my camera zoom, I had a good clear view of the creature where it lay sprawled like a basking sea lion on the beach at the edge of the fairway.

"Dinosaur or dragon? To this day I still can't say which one the thing most reminded me of. The body stretched out on top of the sand looked slick in the glare of the sunlight, gleaming like the smooth skin of a dolphin, with just the faintest hint of scales where a few patches of tree shadow covered it. I could also see three sets of fair-sized flippers on either side of the body, and what looked like a flattened-out tail disappearing into the water of the rising tide.

"So, maybe not the Great Sea Serpent, but not some weird and unknown species of whale either. Especially not with that head attached to the long neck stretched out on top of the sand.

"Imagine if a goat mated with a sheep, and they had a kid, or a lamb-kid, and then that lamb-kid went a little 'wild child' with a camel, and their offspring had a relationship later on with a horse, and what came of that union then had an affair with a dog. Well, the final result of all that mixed-up mating would probably have a misshapen head that looked like what I was staring at, complete to a little pair of knobby horns sprouting from a thick clump of hair between what looked like alien ear flanges hanging loose and limp on either side of a mournful-looking face.

"Zooming my camera view in closer, I could see that thatch of hair between the horns had a feathery look. I remember thinking then that maybe there might also be an ostrich or an emu roosting on a branch of this thing's family tree. Of course, resting on top of the hair-feathers, like it was sitting on a tee, was my golf ball.

"I stood looking at that thing with my mobile zoom for a long time. And the only thought in my mind was 'How the hell do I play this lie?'

"Yeah, you heard me right. I was in the kind of mood by then that, monster or no monster, I was going to finish this hole. It was a 'go crazy Canuck or go home' situation, and I didn't feel like going home. The only question in my mind that needed an answer was how to do this? That's when I got an idea. Yes, it was an insane idea, but right just then insane just seemed the right way to play the game.

"Keeping an eye on the creature, I crouched down and slid the reach out of my golf bag. I spared a quick glance to make sure the little ball cup was clear of debris like wet weed or bits of grass.

"Satisfied the cup was clean, I fished the roll of duct tape out of my windbreaker pocket then, reach in one hand and duct tape in the other, I started to make my way around the curve of the fairway. I cut across between the edge of the fairway and the lip of the green to a little wooded section sitting between the beach front and the back of the green. All the time I kept glancing over at the thing sleeping on the sand. At least I hoped it was sleeping, because from where I was, creeping along between the edge of the woods and the fairway, and with the glaring sun overhead, I couldn't see its eyes well enough to tell if they were open or not.

"Slowly I slipped along the edge of the wood. Every so often I looked aside into the empty spaces between the thin trees and was glad to see that some volunteer groundskeeper had cleared out some of the underbrush. That was my escape route. Any sign of even the slightest stir of that scaly critter and I was hightailing into the woods. The hell with finishing the course, I wasn't *that* crazy.

"About halfway to where the edge of the fairway met the edge of the beach, I started extending the reach, one section at a time, as slowly and silently as I could. Section after section slid out, with just a short pause while I wrapped duct tape around each section joint to reinforce it, until I had the reach stretched out to its full twelve-foot length. By the time I got near the edge of the fairway and the little drop-off, I had a good sideways view of the creature where it lay. It looked almost as long as two canoes sitting end to end, say about ten metres, with its head and neck on the fairway grass and the rest of its body stretched out on the beach sand.

"And the one eye that I could see was closed! At least I couldn't see any sign of a pupil from where I stood, and I had a good view now. It was some kind of reptile — I was pretty sure of that — with scales that I could now clearly see outlined in the sunlight. Maybe it had some kind of special lizard eyelid for when its head was out of the water.

"I told myself to quit debating biology and get down to business.

"I came to a stop about two steps away from the edge of the fairway drop-off. Where I stood, I was just far enough away from the creature that its head and my ball were in clear sight. Slowly, hand-over-hand, I stretched out the reach until the cup was just hovering over top of that misshapen head.

"I was only going to have one shot at this. I took up a wide-legged stance to compensate for the balance of the reach, made sure my grip was tight, brought the cup down lower and just behind the ball. Slowly, I brought the reach back, then…SWUNG!

"The cup flashed over the hair-feathers, scooping up the ball. I finished my swing, let go of the reach and watched for a quick moment as it sailed up into the air.

"I spun around then and ran into the woods. I never looked back as I dodged around the trees, but I was listening for the sound of something crashing through the woods behind me. Except for my own noisy footsteps, though, it was all quiet.

"I stopped running and looked behind. Nothing but trees. No monster in hot pursuit. I crept back the way I'd run until I reached the edge of the woods, stepped out beyond the last couple of trees and looked around.

"The fairway and beach were both empty. Where the creature had been, was nothing but a gouged-up sandy hollow. A deep furrow led away from there through the sand and vanished at the edge of the waters of the bay. On either side of the furrow was a series of dents in the sand, which I figured were made by the thing's flippers as it dragged itself back towards the sea. Looking up and across the bay, I saw what might have been a large hump vanish beneath the water. Maybe it was the creature, or maybe it was just a piece of submerging driftwood.

"I found my reach about halfway up the slope of the fairway. My ball was sitting on the green, just at the edge of the hole. I toed it in, then collected it and the rest of my gear and went on to finish the remaining three holes, without suffering a single hook or slice on any of them."

Gardy took a long deep pull at his mug after finishing his story. Everyone waited politely until he'd finished. Then the comments flew fast and furious, most of them compliments, heavily tinged with scepticism, on his tall-tale-telling talent.

My brother just smiled, set his mug down on the table, and pulled out his mobile. Turning it on, he thumb-swiped a few times then handed the mobile to me. As I swiped at the screen, I watched a parade of photos pass by, a series of distance shots and close-ups of the creature Gardy had described, its head resting on a grassy shoreline and the rest of its body stretched out on a sandy beach with blue sea in the background. I handed off the mobile to Nesbitt and watched everyone's expressions of wonder as they viewed the photos while the phone made the round of the table before returning to Gardy.

He tucked his phone away but, instead of picking up his beer mug again, Gardy reached a hand inside his T-shirt and pulled out a neck chain with a little tube attached. It was one of those Plexiglas containers that seaside gift shops sell with tiny shark's teeth, bits of coral, or other marine life souvenirs sealed inside. Gardy handed me the tube. I took it and held it up close to see what it contained.

Inside the tube were several strands of what looked like hair but with tiny feathery frills running along the full thin length of each filament. I passed the tube on. There was complete silence around the table as everyone took a look at the tube's contents.

"Found those caught inside the ball cup of my reach," Gardy said, as he slipped the chain over his head and tucked the tube back under his T-shirt. "A guy at the office has a sister who works as a biologist at some lab. I gave him a few of these to pass on to her. About a week later, she phones him at home asking if he has any more samples that he can send her. Never seen anything like them, she tells him, and she's sure they're not from any animal that she knows about."

"Some story, brother," I said.

"Yep," Gardy replied. "Like I said, dunno about any lake monsters, but I figure a sea monster on the golf course counts as interference."

Nesbitt nodded. "So, did you ever go back there?"

"Nope, and don't plan to." Gardy took another swallow beer. "Not unless there's other people there," he added, setting his mug down. "I don't really fancy finding out if Caddy carries a grudge about me 'taking a bit off the top' of its head."

He paused for a moment, then smiled.

"Y'know, now that I think about it, that hole," Gardy declared proudly, "was rated a Par 4 and, even with all with weird circumstances, I still sunk my ball in two shots, if you don't count the toe-in. All things considered, that was the best bit of golfing that I'd had for the entire day or ever expect to have at any other course."

He held up his glass. We all lifted ours in response.

"Golf," said Gardy in a solemn tone. "The maddest and baddest and best game of them all!"

Jenn Coish

Jenn Coish is an early-career writer who came out of the gate running, winning the "Most Polished Pitch" award at the inaugural Pitch the Publisher event hosted by WritersNL in 2019.

Coish's first short story, *The Keeper of Knowledge*, was published in *Kit Sora: The Artobiography*.

She has an ingrained love of reading, and is a stage three melanoma survivor who is now working in cancer advocacy. She loves creating new things and up cycling vintage furniture.

She brings with her her short story *Looking for love in all the wrong places*.

Looking for love in all the wrong places

Yeti came in shaking off the snow from his fur like a dog getting out of the bath.

Snow and ice pinged off the cave walls, making little tinkling sounds as they hit. It had been another shitty night out there, he thought, as he plopped down in his custom-made lazy boy, designed to carry his weight.

Ever since he had been able to pick up a research satellite up here in the Himalayans, life had become much more refined. With the click of a button and a boatload of shipping charges, people will ship their stuff just about anywhere, really.

He sat back, thinking again of the day's adventures. He had been out doing his normal scouting of the mountain trails when he had come across a new group of hikers. Hoping to say hi and make a few new friends, he had run over to them, waving his large paws in the air and trying to shout over the whistling winds. He shook his head when he remembered the look on those faces of the hikers… pure horror as they saw his bestial form run towards them, snarling and growling. They ran away so fast that even he couldn't keep up.

He got up out of his chair and decided to warm the cave up a bit by starting a fire, hoping to melt away some the loneliness he felt. He brought his computer and chair close to it, snuggled in. It was a good life, a cozy life, but he longed to share it. *Maybe,* he thought, *maybe if I bought a bright fun shirt, it might make me more approachable.* He started flipping through ads on Amazon, trying to find something. When there was nothing even approaching his size, he got up, made some supper, then sat back down to watch the TV while not really paying attention to it as he flipped through the channels.

The phone on the table started to buzz. Even though he knew who it was, he still waited for the caller-ID to tell him. He hit the decline button as fast as he could. Not a minute later, the phone started to buzz again. He waited for the name to appear, growled low in his throat, and again punched the decline button.

Why on God's green earth did I ever give them my number? he thought, thinking back to the day, a little over a year ago, when they'd met.

He had received an invitation mysteriously one night when he had returned home to the cave. Attached to the door was a gold envelope, inviting him to a conference of 'beings who everyone thought did not exist.' At first he thought it was a crazy joke and ripped it up and threw it away. But night after night he would come home to the same gold envelope stuck to his door. For the first couple nights he would just rip it up and throw it away, not bothering to look at it, but on the third night he decided, against his better judgment, to see what it was.

Welcome to your paradise, it said at the top of the letter.

Dear Mr. Yeti,

Do you ever feel as if you are invisible? That the world has forgotten that you even exist?

Do you wish that there were more like you to connect with on a deeper level?

Then you have come to the right place! We here at Magic Exists have created a small original conference built of creatures like yourself, where you can be around others of your kind and meet other creatures from around the world that feel the same way you do. Those that struggle to connect and find connections.

We will have two days of fun-filled activities that will bring you closer and form bonds with others that can last for centuries. I do hope that you will join us for a one-of-a-kind experience. All you need to do is pack a few things and be ready to go on the 13th of October by 3AM; we will handle the rest. Feel free to bring along some clothing option for the fancier night but know that if your kind has fur, that clothing is optional.

Kindest Regards,

The magical team of Higgs and Clark

Please be advised that tiny children will not be available on the banquets menu during this event; if your kind requires this for a healthy and rounded diet option, please let us know in advance so we can have something set up in your accommodations for you.

also please make sure that you keep this invite away from any facial hair or beards as it will self-destruct in 5.4.3.2.1

The yeti had just enough time to wrench it away from his face before it burst into a golden flame, gone in a puff.

He frowned, scoffed, but found himself looking over at the Whiskeys of the World calendar that hung on the cave wall for the month in question. He knew full well that he had nothing listed for that day, or any other, but he checked nonetheless, the same way he checked his caller ID. Fooling himself, and no one else, for there was no one else there *to* fool. *Hell, why not,* he thought, adding the first thing to the calendar in over a century. It might be nice to try something different.

Oh, how very wrong he was, looking back at it.

The day finally came and, as he stepped outside, he was whisked away in a cloud-like shape and dropped off promptly at a large golden door to a grand entrance.

All around him were other beings who were also being plucked from the sky, dropping oh-so-gracefully on their feet.

The door opened with a slow creek until it was wide.

"Welcome one, welcome all," said a small horse-like creature that came trotting out to greet them all. "We are so happy to see so many of you here! Come in and make yourselves at home. Welcome again to the first ever magical ball!"

The Yeti walked in, looking around hoping to find himself in a grand ball room or something but no: they had been transported to what looked to be a hotel six-conference banquet room from the 1970s, with commercial carpet that had seen better days and a sad-looking bar covered in red quilted leather. Chairs were set up over on one side like they were here to get a talk on how time-shares could really maximize their vacation options.

Before he could turn and run out the way he came, he smacked right in to a body that was about an inch taller, and so much hairier than himself.

"Oh, sorry about that," the Yeti said, looking up at the creature.

"Brah, no worries, man it's all good," came the voice, much like his own. It had been the only voice like his own he had ever heard.

Yeti took a step back and sized up what he saw in front of him. It was like he was staring at a distant cousin. The stranger had a lot of the same features, but all brown in colour instead of his own bluish-white. And somehow, he looked *healthier*, as his fur glistened and looked as smooth as silk.

"H-hi," Yeti said, a little self-conscious that he was staring at this creature as intently has he was.

"Heyyyyy, man, how's it going? My name is Bigfoot, but everyone calls me Squash." Squash was holding out his hand in what looked to be a closed fist.

The Yeti, more refined in his interactions with others, did not know what kind of handshake this was until Squash grabbed his hand by the wrist, curled it into a fist, then bumped it against his. He made a sound with his mouth when their knuckles connected, like a POW, but less.

"Is this cool or what, brah?" Squash replied, smiling while nodding his head at a bit of an angle.

"Uh... I guess," Yeti said, not quite knowing what else

to say. "I am The Yeti, and people call me Yeti."

"Mannn, that is such a cool name, dude," Squash replied. "I was totally hoping to meet some cool people here at this shindig."

Over the course of the weekend, they became better acquainted. Squash was happy to have met his 'Brudder from Anudder Mudder,' as he called it. The Yeti thought that he had met someone who he could send a possible Christmas card too, or the occasional funny text if he was ever that bored. He gave Squash his number, hoping that he would lose it on the way back to the Appalachian Mountains.

The phone rang again, pulling Yeti back from the memory of one of his biggest mistakes in recent memory. He let out an exhausted sigh, knowing that Squash was going to keep calling until he picked up, like he did every damn night since they had met.

He hit the accept button and put the phone to his ear.

"Hello, Bigfoot," Yeti said.

"Brah, I thought you were never going to pick up, brah! And man, how many times do I have to tell ya', call me *Squash*."

"Sure, what did you want?" Yeti replied, knowing full well that he would rather freeze his tongue on a pole than call The Bigfoot *Squash*.

"Just checking in, man! Seeing how life is up in the artic, you know, man?"

"It's fine, thanks. Cold and snowing, just like it was last night when you called. And the night before that." He did not even bother to tell him, for at least the third time, that he did not live in the Artic. "How about yourself?"

"Man, it's sickkkkkk down here, you know, living my best life ever. Hashtag van-life, hashtag the-forest-gives-me-life. I just got the rain catcher for my morning showers, dude, it's like the only way to wake up, you know."

The Yeti looked over at his state-of-the-art steam shower with more nozzles than most high-tech car washes. "Cool," he said. He queued up his news app and started to scroll through *The New Yorker*. He remembered, absently, that he had yet to complete last week's Sunday Crossword.

Squash made a sucking sound, like he had inhaled something harsh. "So man, like, any luck in the lady department today? Meet any snow bunnies out on the slopes?"

"Same as last time you asked," Yeti said hating the fact that he ever confided, over one too many whiskeys, about his increasing loneliness.

"Ah man, chin up, dude. You are being way too hard on yourself. You should pop on over here sometime! Man, the chicks would totally dig your shiny white locks. For real, man. For real. It's got that look, what's the word? Distinguished, man. *Distinguished.*" Before Yeti could even reply, Squash continued: "Hey, are you at least using the leave-in all-natural beard oil that I sent you? It'll totally make that coat of yours pop. "

Yeti looked over at the bottle, still sitting on the counter in its original packaging. "Oh yeah, it's great. Thank you so much for that kind gift."

"Oh, awesome, man! Hey no worries, I got you, bro.

I'll add some more in with my next care package. Also, this cool, really natural fiber brush I handmade for you. You're going to love it, bruh. For real, you'll love it. I got to tell ya, I think I might start like an Etsy business or something, selling some of those things. You know, you got to stay current. Maybe we can do, like, a collab on Tiktok or something, showing off how good the product works?"

There was a migraine building at the bridge of Yeti's nose, and he pinched it between his thumb and forefinger. "Yeah... *maybe*. Listen, I am kind of busy over here right now, you know, mapping out the new trail system that the hikers want to put in place. Was there a reason you called?"

"Yeah, duh, I almost forgot did you ever think of putting yourself on a dating app?"

"What like EHarmony or something?" Yeti said looking down at the open tabs on his computer. Match.com, Bumble, OKcupid. "Nah, I don't think that those are a right fit for me," he said, closing his computer slowly, as if he thought one of The Bigfoot's many cryptid powers was to see through the phone line, even though he knew that was impossible.

"HAHA man they are so lame. No, you need to get on Tinder; that's where all the ladies hang out."

"Like I said, I really don't think that those sites are for me."

"Well, I think you're a stick in the mud, man, and bro to bro I am doing you a favor. Check your inbox, man."

His irritation hit maximum levels. "What the lord thundering did you go and do now?!" Yeti yelled. He opened his laptop with such force that he almost snapped the screen right off it hinges. He frantically logged in to his email looking for what carnage Bigfoot has created.

A *Thanks for signing up with TINDER, you have come to the right place* welcome email popped up on the top of his emails. He clicked on it and looked down through. "WHAT is this?"

"It's your gateway to finding a chick, man! The best thing is that you don't even need to say anything; just swipe your paw right or left and let them come to you."

"I... I don't even..."

"No thanks needed, man! Like I said, I got you! I even went as far as to add us as friends so we can see each other's profile and get notifications! Cool, right? I'll see if we have matches in common! Got to watch out for Furry-Chasers, man. Got to watch the hell out. You'll get the itchy scratchy head-to-toe, man, for real."

"Jesus, Mary and Joseph in the garden tonight, I do not know what to say right now," Yeti said growling into the phone.

"Listen, man, I know you're super busy, but you really should check it out! I started your profile, but no one knows you are well as you do. I have to head off as I have a cute little thing that swiped right popping by for a hike! Chicks love to hike man, it's in all their profiles. Talk! To! You! *Laters.*"

Yeti heard the click of the phone but did not take it away from his ear. He was too busy staring, mystified, at the screen.

What am I supposed to do with this? he thought to himself.

Days went by. Every time he walked past his desk, he saw emails: Add to your profile today! *Add a picture to get more hits! Sign up for our free web tutorial to help get you started!!*

Finally he decided: what's the worst that could happen? If Bigfoot was having luck, maybe he could. He sat down and went down the rabbit hole of answering all the basic questions. Height: 7'9. Weight: 350lbs. Hair colour: White… all over. Eye colour: blue. Favourite pastime: hanging out in the mountains.

What is your favourite movie: *Rudolf* — sorry I know it's cheesy, but it's a classic.

If you could plan the perfect date, what would it be: Taking you on the best hiking trails and then creating a huge campfire making s'mores watching the stars (will have to bring own marshmallows as they are hard to ship here).

Last but not least: what are you looking for in a partner: I want someone to see me for me.

He looked back at his profile and thought, *well done, old man; I think that looks great*. He then tried to upload a pic but every pic he took when he smiled, he looked like he was about to eat the camera. He finally picked one of the least cringe ones and hit submit. *Now we wait*, he thought.

Every other day, he would pop in to swipe on a few people that said they loved the outdoors, or that were big into adventure in the cold. He tried to reach out to a few people, but no luck. One day, someone asked for a picture and when he took a fresh one and sent it, she said that he was not being serious and if he didn't want to show his face why be on the site. *I am showing my face*, he thought.

He popped over to Bigfoot's profile and saw the basics of him as well as talking all about his van life and his castle in the forest. He saw more hashtags than there was actual sentences on his profile and thought to himself, *Huh, if he can get ladies, I should be able to.*

A week in, the phone rang at the usual time again. Yeti prayed that it was anyone, even a tele marker asking if he had time for a survey would be more welcoming.

"DUDE! How's it going, man?"

"Fine. Thank you. How have you been?" Yeti replied politely, hoping for a short conversation.

"Man, just wait till I tell you all about this week I have had! Back-to-back dates, bruh, it's been slamming down here."

"Oh really," the Yeti said, not believing half of what he was saying. "How is it that you are having a better time at this than me?"

"Bro, what do you mean? You shouldn't be having any problems! Do I need to send you up some more beard oil?" Bigfoot said, surprised that he was having such a hard time of it.

"No, I am still good, thanks," Yeti said, looking over at the dam oil that now started to collect dust on the lid.

"Okay, listen, bro-to-bro let me pop in and have a look at your profile right quick," Bigfoot said, keys clicking away. "Dude! That's the profile pic you are going with? No wondering chicks are swiping left." Bigfoot let out a hardy laugh. "You need a better pic; maybe try not snarling at the camera."

"I was smiling," Yeti said, his eyebrows knitting together.

"Okay, so maybe don't smile in the picture next time," Bigfoot replied. "Hey wait, we took some pictures while we were at that conference, maybe I got one," he said, running to his phone and opening up the camera roll.

"Sweet dude, I found one that makes you look good," he said.

Before Yeti could even say anything, a new message popped up on his email: *your new profile pic has been added.*

Yeti logged on and saw the most ridiculous pic of him dressed up for the costume dance at the conference.

"That's the one you decided was a good fit?" Yeti yelled into the phone, wishing with all of his might that he could go through the phone at him.

"What! You have a cute suit on, and your hair is all done up; the blue makes your eyes pop. I think it's a great one," Bigfoot replied casually.

"I was dressed up as the Freaking Beast from Beauty and the Beast; how do I look respectable in that that nonsense,' Yeti said, flopping back into his chair.

"It shows you can have fun. Chicks will dig it," Bigfoot said.

Yeti didn't even say anything, he just hit the end button on the phone all of a sudden, too tired by all of this to even care. He slinked off to his bed waiting for morning to come.

When he woke, he happened to walk by his open laptop sitting aimlessly on the side of his desk. As soon as he came near, it popped to life. *You have 46 new notifications,* it said. "What the…" Yeti said, logging in. They were all from Tinder; it seems like there was a bunch of hearts on his profile pic with a few comments:

"*Omg how cute,*" wrote one.

"*Hello big boy, I would love to cuddle with him,*" said another.

Well hell, maybe Fuzzy was right; I need to put a bit more effort in to this, he thought. He grabbed his camera and with a pep in his step, he decided to take some more pictures for his profile. He took the next few days to go outside and grab as many cool pictures as he could, of the perfect icicle hanging off the branches of the trees with the sun hitting it just right, of a snowman that he made next to a beautiful trail. He posted the pics which were gaining more and more likes.

When he came back the next day, he say a message: *Bigfoot has updated their profile.* Yeti was interested, so he popped over to check. His eyes could not believe what he saw: there was so many pictures of him out in the river, chopping wood, the perfect sunset, the list went on and on.

Okay, he thought, *that's nothing big.* He scrolled back to his profile, maybe to add a few words flesh it out a bit.

Favourite pastime: hanging out in the mountains; I love how there is such beauty in the simple minimalist here. Where I live with the snow cap mountains and the deep glaciers, it's a magical frozen in time place; Yeti wrote feeling better about it.

Bing! Your friend Bigfoot is online and has updated his profile:

Ladies, if you are looking for some outdoor fun and adventure look no further than me! I live in the most magical, lush place in the world: trees taller than most skyscrapers, and the forest floor like a mossy bed that you can just lie down on and take a nap as the sounds of the forest take all your cares away.

Yeti could not believe what he was looking at. *That copycat can't even use his own thoughts*, he thought.

This went on for weeks, back and forth; anytime Yeti posted something, before he could even get his account logged off, he would get that damn *Bing! Bigfoot has updated his profile* notification. One night just as Yeti was trying to add a few more pictures and try to convince the hiker that he had been talking to for the past week and a half to come visit him, the phone rang.

"What is it that I can help you with?" Yeti answered the phone abruptly.

"Oh, hey man; what's got you so riled up? Just calling to see if you check out my newest pic, the girls love the new 'do," Bigfoot replied.

Yeti took a look and had no words for the pic that stared back at him: Bigfoot back on to the camera shitless looking at his precious van with… was that a freaking man bun?

"What did you do to your hair? Did something decided to make a nest in it?" Yeti replied, not knowing what else to say.

"Nah man, it's a bun; they are on the rage here! Dope, don't you think?"

Yeti decided to bite his lipon what he really thought and just answered politely: "It's a different look. If you like it, that's all that matters, I guess."

"Yeah, I wanted to be more, you know, relatable and,

like, down to earth, you know," Bigfoot replied, not getting the sarcasm dripping from Yeti's voice.

They talked for a few more minutes before they decided to go. Yeti had to jump on a FaceTime call with the cute hiker hopping that if he could just talk to her, he could seal the deal for the date.

"Hi," he said when she popped up on his screen. "You look more beautiful in real time," he said shyly into the camera.

"O-M-G, that is *such* a cute filter you have on! You look just like that creature in that Christmas movie I love," she replied.

"What do you mean filter?" Yeti asked.

"Ha, ha you have such a sense of humour. I know that that's not you; take it off so I can see your real face," she said.

"Well, this is my real face… there is no filter on" Yeti replied.

There was another two rounds of this before finally: "Wait… so… O-M-G, the horror stories are true!" the girl shrieked before she slammed down her computer ending the call.

Yeti sat for a minute staring at the face that now looked back at him. *That did not go as I expected. Or maybe it did; how could I think anyone was ever going to want to date a freak like me?* He got up and decided to head out on the trails to clear his head a bit.

The wind was whipping up the beginnings of a good storm that night, matching his current mood perfectly. He was just about to head back home when he saw something flapping in the wind about a mile outside of the closest hiking base camp. He moved in closer to take a look: there was someone out in the storm trying to nail down what looked to be a tent to get out of this weather.

"Base camp is not far from here; you won't make it in this storm!" Yeti called out, but the wind took his words the other way so they were unable to hear what he was trying to say.

Screw it, I have to go warn them, he thought, moving closer again.

It was only when he got up closer did he see that it was a girl that was out here by herself. He was struck by the only thing that he could see as her scarf had fallen down under her eyes.

"Oh, hi," the girl said, looking directly at Yeti. "Are you stuck out in this too?"

"No, I was out for a walk — never mind, you won't survive the night out here in this tent," he said.

"I just need to ride out the worst of it; I know these storms better than anyone. I grew up on these mountains, and me and my tent have faced much worse." she replied, tacking down the last peg. "You can come ride out the storm with me," she said, holding out her hand.

"I... I mean, you do see me right? You're not delirious from being out in the elements or have snow blindness, do you?" Yeti replied.

The girl let out the cutest little giggle. "No, I know what you are. You're the Yeti, right? I've seen you out on the hikes here trying to help people when you can and just trying to say hi."

The yeti stepped back a step, surprised that she knew all of this and did not seem scared. As if she read his mind, she came over and said, "Sorry, I didn't mean to scare you. My name is Alina."

Yeti was taken aback by her kindness, so when she held out her hand again, motioning to the tent to get out the storm that was coming up even faster than he expected around them, he didn't think — just acted. He headed in to the tent with her to ride out the worst of it before he could bring her back safely to her base camp. They talked and laughed for hours in the tent, even making little shadow puppets on the side of the tent with the beam of the flashlight.

After a while though, he could see that Alaina was getting tired.

"Hey, why don't you try and get some rest? This storm will end soon and I will help you get back to your base camp," Yeti said softly.

Before she could reply, a small shiver escaped her body. Yeti saw how cold she was getting here now that she was not moving around. He did the only thing he could think of which was to move closer and wrap his big hairy body around her to keep her nice and warm. Before long, she was fast asleep in his arms.

As the sun came up the next morning, he could not believe the perfect night he'd had with this beautiful little creature. He helped her pack up and carried her bag and tent back to camp as she waited for the next load of hikers to check in. She popped in to the big supply tent for a minute and while she was in there, he snuck off back to his cave knowing that at least if nothing else, he did get to have at least one magical night knowing that someone saw him for him.

Months went by and things for Yeti went back to normal with the weekly call from Bigfoot that was getting harder and harder to stomach, but he was missing his very brief connection with Alina so much he took the distraction.

"You need to really go all in, man, I feel like you are holding back from your potential to be a trueladies's man," Bigfoot was saying one night on the phone.

"I think that my time on the dating scene is over. I am not like you, Bigfoot, and I don't think I ever really will be," Yeti replied.

"Nah, man, don't say things like that. Bro, give it another go." Yeti heard the *Bing!* on the other side of the line and knew what was going to come next.

"Man, you are such a chicken shit; you deleted your profile after all the help I gave you! hat sucks, brah," Bigfoot said, getting more worked up as he spoke. "I knew you'd give up; that's what losers do! I thought you were different than that."

Before Yeti could reply with all the things that he held back all this time — that he never wanted to be a brah and that Bigfoot needed to grow up and take that ridiculous bird's nest out of the back of his head — there was a knock on the door. He set down the phone, with Bigfoot's voice echoing distantly though the cave. He walked over, confused, but when he opened the door, there was Alaina smiling and holding up a bag of marshmallows. "Sorry it took me a bit to track you down, but I hope you're still up for some s'mores."

Yeti opened the door wider for her, letting her come in. As they stepped further inside, heremembered that he still had Bigfoot on the line going off. He walked back over, picked up the phone, hit the end button, and then deleted the contact.

"I'll get the chocolate," he said.

Dwain Campbell

Dwain Campbell is originally from Sussex, New Brunswick, Canada. After his university years in Nova Scotia, he journeyed farther east to begin a teaching career in Newfoundland. Thirty-eight years later, he is semi-retired in St. John's.

Contemporary fantasy is his genre of choice, and Atlantic Canada is a rich source of inspiration.

He is author of *Tales from the Frozen Ocean* (Jesperson Press, 1999), and has contributed stories to *Canadian Tales of the Fantastic, Tesseracts 17*, and *Fantastic Trains*.

Neil Gaiman is his hero of the moment, though he will admit to a lifelong fascination with Stephen King.

His collection of shorts *Strange Duty,* was released in 2023 from Engen Books.

Archie Mudd

In the days of the hard old line, people killed for a dollar. A job that delivered a buck a day plus eats was manna from Heaven.

Every red cent counted on a hardscrabble Newfoundland farm. Both of my older brothers signed on to fight Hitler, and my dad's hip, broken when an axed spruce bounced the wrong way, never did heal right. So, at age fourteen, I ditched school to cut mill logs, raise sheep, and haul lobster pots, all in the hopes of a dismal profit to pay taxes. Sadly, on that note, we were arrears.

That job? In 1940, Newfoundland Light and Power hired rugged youngsters to patrol electricity lines that crossed the wilds. Armed with long sticks, we knocked down crow, eagle, and osprey nests built atop poles. See, straw-and-twig nests catch fire and disrupt service. Important work, but really it was a lark for a Bayman. My kind spent dawn to dusk out of doors. We were sunbaked, wind-seared, mosquito-bitten tough.

"Nothing to fear out there in the deep woods, Jimmy," Dad assured, rum happy. "Wolves are long gone, sure. Worst you got to worry about is a moose walking on you at night. Sleep in a thicket, and even them stupid old plod-ders won't be a problem." I then fretted on black bears and asked the lend of a rifle. No go. Hunting was a reli-gion in the hungry years, and if I lost a gun, it would be the end of the world.

Light and Power didn't fork over a weapon either. Mr. Moffat, my boss, explained it this way. "Lawyers say if we give you a firearm and you trip over a tree stump and blow your head off, we're liable. You go to shoot a caribou and nail some guy's horse, we're liable. Bad enough we supply an axe, lest you chop your foot off by accident." Seems like lawyers regulated me right down to the last bean and cracker in my grub sack.

I met Mr. Moffat on the shingle beach at Bay de l'Eau where a fisherman pal dropped me off. I climbed in the company Ford pick-up and the boss handed me a Coca-Cola, an out and out treat. Though Moffat got on all crusty, he was a softy inside, and his wife even more kindly. Bet there were cakes or short bread cookies in my food sack, no small thing since wartime food rationing became strict-er by the month.

"Been hot as old blazes, Jimmy," Moffat reported un-necessarily. Only mid-May and I was brown as nutmeg. "Good news is the boggy stretches will be dry, less rubber boot slogging through mud. Bad news is you'll go through drinking water like nobody's business. I got two canteens so you can double up at streams. And a straw hat." Grin-ning, I put the hat on my dark brown curls and hammed in the rearview. Huck Finn grinned back at me.

I took his point on water, but wasn't worried. New-foundland has more lakes than *HMS Hood* has rivets. No matter how blistering hot, I wouldn't have to pull a Moses and get water from a rock.

Raising a billowing cloud of powdery dust, we motored up the bumpy gravel road to Pierre's Brook, site of the new power station that fed electricity to the Bell Island mines. Mr. Moffat stopped by the power line cut that proceeded northeast on a ruler straight bearing. There I hoisted the hundred-pound company pack on shoulders axe handle wide. Barely into my teens, I sported size twelve feet and had to dip my head under door frames. Big-boned and brawny, that was Jimmy Quin. Still filling out, but maybe in a year I could fib my way into the army. Anyway, the weighty pack was mostly food: cans of molasses beans, biscuits hard as hockey pucks, and a slab of bacon salty as the Dead Sea. Tied to various loops on the pack were a kettle, frying pan, a small axe, rubber boots, rain slicker, and a bedroll. I looked like a frigging tinker.

Lastly, three pole lengths that screwed together to offer a tool for demolishing nests.

Not quite lastly. Mr. Moffat tucked a bill into my front shirt pocket. "That's for Mrs. McAllister, to feed you one supper, one toast and tea breakfast, and a bunk in the shed. Ain't we generous?" I nodded vigorously. Mrs. McAllister served one helluva hunter's stew.

"Then git, kid. Wait for me in Goobies and we'll settle up."

Off I went on a dusty path well-trod by blueberry pickers. It had been a while since the cut, twenty yard wide, was cleared, so alders, young fir, and long grass choked my route. To either side was an endless dark and deep Boreal Forest. About ninety percent of the colony is tree covered, with the rest caprock and bog

Boy, that first morning I felt like a snowflake on a skillet. The pitiless sun blazed away in its China blue sky, and I blessed the wide brimmed straw hat which I no longer thought silly. That hat also came in handy for swatting off blood-hungry horseflies and dragonflies as big as Spitfires. This being high spring, sparrows and chickees sang merrily, and were accompanied by croaking bullfrogs immersed in the few sloughs that survived this hellish dry spell. Saucy crows, of course, don't sing, they scold, and I got an angry earful from them.

It being flat country I made good time, only having to pause once to join my poles and wreck a raven's nest. A shame about eggs or chicks, but I didn't lose sleep over it.

By and by, I came to a fair dip that had collected water to form a modest, insect-ridden swamp. I slipped on rubber boots to negotiate the muck. In I went, boots noisily sucking mud. Looking down, I saw cloven hoof prints. Stupendous tracks, the dimension of a round-pointed spade blade. If this was a moose — what else could it be? — it was as large as a locomotive. I walked alongside the strange trail, and therefore noticed an even more peculiar fact: its stride was like mine, two-legged.

That was impossible. I've walked behind cows and horses all my life. Four legged creatures leave a much different trail than people. I didn't like mysteries, and itched to solve them. So, I swanned about trying to make heads or tails of it. Finally, cursing under my breath, I gave it up for a bad thing. Once the other side of the tiny wetland, I shifted back into my scuffed work boots, greedily guzzled water, and pondered the problem.

Forest creatures don't sashay on two legs. Therefore,

I could either ignore my eyes, or just conclude there was an explanation that eluded me. Maybe a prankster. Whatever, it was no skin off my nose.

Young minds are easily distracted. I discovered Mrs. Moffat stashed yummy Queen Anne squares in my pack. I gobbled them in one go and killed sugary thirst by upending my second canteen. Only then did I realize I had used most of my water, and it was miles to Jack Jack Pond. No, I didn't stutter, that's what it's called by loggers. Nothing for it but to risk a marathon march and camp by the pond tonight. I courted sun stroke, but that was it. There were consequences to being a greedy moron.

I set a brisk pace, and my long-legged stride ate up the miles. Now that I knew what to look for, I occasionally spotted the Goliath hoof mark in gravel and hard-packed sand. The immense animal was ahead of me and staying to the cut. All afternoon, and into the humid evening, I squinted through heat haze, worried I might come upon the critter from behind. Mostly, moose just trot off on seeing a man, but some are notoriously stupid and skittery. Best I saw him before he saw me.

Twice more I stopped to destroy nests dangerously built upon poles bearing wires that hummed with high voltage electricity.

Hours passed. The burning sun crowned tall pines in angry scarlet and orange. Inky black shadows lengthened. It was a hot, muggy evening, more suited to August than May, and I sweated like a Trojan hauling the wooden horse. It was foolish to carry on in the half-light, for a twisted ankle, or God forbid, a broken leg, would have been the end of me out here. However, my Guardian

Angel walked with me, for about 10:00 pm, I made it to the pond safe and sound.

I drank like a hog and washed sweat and dirt off me, for nothing is worse than prickly heat rash. Too bushed to make a fire, I ate cold beans from a can, then cut fir boughs to make a spongy, sweet-smelling mattress which I positioned in a tight stand of birch trees. It was too darned warm to use a blanket, so I just laid my head on the backpack and put my hatchet and butcher knife close to hand.

I slept like the dead — exercise, fresh air, all of that — and woke to the sound of a beaver tail splashing on the tranquil pond. Groaning to my feet, I stretched out aches and pains then knelt on soft sand to throw water on my face.

Then I saw it, emerging out of soft mists hugging the pond.

A creature, its hairy head as big as the stern of a schooner, or so it seemed in the tricky half-light, swam across the pond. The head angled way up out of the water, such that a coarse beard dangling from the chin was dry. I was stunned and distracted by an incredible antler rack. They were thrice the size of caribou horns, and must have carried two dozen points on each antler — crazy! I've seen lots of racks nailed above shed doors; none held a candle to these babies. Aware of me, it turned my way. Jeez Louise, the thing sported a black and leathery gorilla face and burning ruby eyes! It was... no way... impossible. As I frantically grabbed my axe, the monster slipped behind a beaver lodge the size of the Great Pyramid. I did not see the thing leave the pond and enter the woods, but I sure heard it. Sounded like a Panzer tank smashing through the bush. Headed south, which suited me perfectly fine for I was bound northeast by east.

Forget breakfast, by God. Terrified, I scrambled to pack up and fill canteens. The weird encounter put wings on my heels, and I covered ground at greyhound speed. This pace would safely see me safely to the McAllister cabin round about supper time. A great sighting to relate at Saturday night card games, but otherwise I didn't want to mess with that hairy giant. Those Titanic horns could toss me into next week.

By now I was way into the back country. These woods saw little of man, save the odd hermit-trapper like McAllister and the occasional sportsmen who owned walk-in fishing cabins.

Within an hour I came across a savaged moose carcass, quite a fresh kill. Dad said wolves were nigh gone in Newfoundland, but a score of large canine tracks spoke otherwise. I was not a happy camper. First a freak beast, now wolves? Suddenly, this easy job was spooky anddanger fraught.

Saucy grey jays followed me that morning until the merciless sun drove them away. A wiser kid, I drank judiciously as the heat mounted to intolerable levels. I felt like a chicken roasting in the oven. The dry forest tartly smelled of parched pine needles. Woodland animals lay low in deep shade, and I considered a siesta but nixed the thought upon remembering the troll. I stayed on the trail and on the job, only pausing to wreck a nest or catch wind on an inviting rock. During one such break, I felt more than harsh sunbeams upon me.

I felt piercing eyes.

Without being obvious, I did a slow turnabout. Impenetrable bush on either side; an entire horde of cannibals could be thirty feet away and I wouldn't have a clue. I was at the top of a modest rise, having just crossed a shallow depression about half a mile long. Behind me, on the power line cut and opposite rise, loomed the colossal ape-with-horns. It stood in a thicket of seven-foot-high evergreens. The grotesque head rose well above those treetops. I blamed shimmering heat haze for the optical illusion. You know, like a desert explorer seeing an oasis floating in the air. Seemed the strange head was impossibly off the ground, fifteen feet maybe. Lordy, PT Barnum would love to show this towering brute in his circus.

This ogre, he was on the move. Following me. That thought sparked panic, I can tell you.

I upped my pace to a half-jog and told myself it was good training for army camp. *Yeah, if you plan to fight Italians on the scorching sands of Libya.*

Feathered bandits cooperated. Hours passed and no nests appeared on the wires. So it was that as old Apollo descended in the western sky, I came to a spot where the forest gave way to a large natural meadow livened by daisies, buttercups, and yarrow. On the other side sat the McAllister place, a frontier log cabin surrounded by crab-apple trees and a few tacked together outbuildings. I beelined straight over to discover the mister and missus rocking on their primitive verandah, fanning themselves with yellowed newspaper.

Here's the deal on this pair. Twenty-five years ago, Mr. McAllister left a rural classroom to be an officer with the Royal Newfoundland Regiment. The war broke him, jaundiced his faith in humanity. On coming home, he married a Plain Jane radical Baptist and moved out here in the middle of nowhere to trap and hunt. I suppose they went to town about once a year for flour and tea, but otherwise they socialized with lynx, pine martin, and the rare passerby like me.

"See, Mrs. M., I was on the money. Knew a Power man would come by this month, and it's none other than Jimmy Quin." Not a smile from the missus, for she was as sour as her husband was agreeable. Not yet forty, she sat there wizened and grey. Hard life out here. Her husband was a cross between Santa Claus and Daniel Boone; I doubt he'd cut his ash gray mop since the Depression started. I never saw him without a cracked and grease-staired hard hat; maybe he slept wearing it.

I grinned and held out the two dollars. "Courtesy of Mr. Moffat. Room and board for a night."

"Eyuh," grunted McAllister amiably. "That's the arrangement. Too hot for a fire in the stove, but you sit down here and Mabel will fix you a cold plate fit for King George." He wasn't kidding. I gulled thick slices of pork dabbed with mustard, potato salad, hard-boiled eggs, ginger snap cookies, and two wicked big slices of bread liberally smothered with homemade butter, all washed down with milk kept cool in their spring. It was a backwoods feast.

"You got hollow legs, Jimbo, to store away that much grub. Seconds, if you are of a mind." Not wanting to eat them out of house and home, I politely declined. Mr. McAllister continued, "What's all the news, this hot as

Hades May?"

Could have told him a rollicking battle raged in France. Or about Tommy Dorsey's new number *I'll Never Smile Again* that played on the radio every night. Instead, I babbled on about two-legged moose tracks, and of the ape as big as a mammoth — probably bigger! —and his weird million-dollar rack of antlers. I related my sightings breathlessly, but mister and missus M. never battered an eyelash.

"Eyuh," pronounced McAllister soberly. "We know this creature, call it Archie Mud. Likely been out here since the beginning of time, his kind."

My jaw dropped. His words riled Mabel. "No," she admonished severely. "All things derive from the Bible. My way of thinking, your ugly Archie was spawned by a Fallen Angel and a Daughter of Man in Genesis days. These wicked unions produced demons and trolls. Solomon the Magician chased many out of Israel, and this fellow swam the ocean to be exiled here." Baptists had a particular balefire gleam in their eyes when bandying the Word.

An educated man, McAllister smiled indulgently. "A fine theory, Mabel. But my dear, these trackless forests existed long before even the Indians came. Good chance a creature of yore could still exist here, completely hidden from folks." His hooded eyes, surrounded by a leathery tangle of wrinkles, returned to me. "That strange track you reported, Jimmy? That wasn't your imagination. Archie's hoofed, yet walks bipedal like us humans. The extinct Beothuk Indians called him Aich-mud-yim, the Dark Man, and were mightily leery of him. I shorten the

Beothuk moniker to Archie Mud."

"Bipedal," I echoed weakly. *I frigging well knew that hoof track was unnatural!* "Is it dangerous?"

McAllister pursed lips. "Not to our knowing. Matter of fact, it's somewhat intelligent. If we leave a pail of apples out on the cut, next day we find the fruit gone and the pail full of eatable mushrooms or berries. It understands barter, and cooperation, which is more than I can say for most people." He did not conceal bitterness from his voice, and unconsciously massaged a pale scar on his forehead courtesy of Hun shrapnel.

Dark Man stories continued as full dark descended. The upshot was the creature was live-and-let-live. If I minded my Ps and Qs, it would leave me be as I hiked further east. Mightily relieved, I washed off the day's sweat with heavenly cool spring water and tried to sleep on the verandah.

Tried, because my money-hungry brain teased a greedy plan. What if I wrote the St. John's *Daily News* and offered to sell the sensational Dark Man story? Worth ten bucks? Twenty? What would a big bwana game hunter pay to be guided into this country to bag that stupendous antler rack for his English castle or Texas mansion? A hundred smackeroos? I fell asleep with dollar signs dancing under my eyelids.

Next morning, I dipped toast in tea strong enough to strip bark off an oak tree. Mr. McAllister helpfully filled my canteens and saw me across the wild meadow to the power line. He handed me butcher paper wrapped about peeled carrots as large as Churchill's cigars. "From Mabel, for the trail," he offered. Looking east, he added, "Another forge hot day. Better water-up at Salmon Stream. From there, it's a dry fifteen miles to Bobby Lake." He studied the sky intently. "And mind a pack of wild dogs on the go, killing young moose and farm stock. Nothing meaner than hounds gone feral." That explained the mauled and half-eaten carcass. "And don't ruffle Archie, keep your distance."

"Will do on all counts, Mr. McAllister." I waved and started out. The only witness to my passage was a sleepy hare nibbling clover. That was not to last long.

About mid-day, I spied Archie Mud a quarter mile behind me. This sighting was from the waist up, and lordy, McAllister fibbed not. That wow-wee ape head sat atop a hairy human torso sprouting solidly muscled arms. What freak of nature created an orangutang and caribou cross? Once, in a school book, I saw a picture of a — darn, what was it called? Minnow-tar? A man and bull monster combination. That picture powerfully reminded me of Archie.

It curiously trailed me. Thinking to get on its good side, I deposited the carrots on a flat rock as a peace offering. Then, surprising myself, I waved to it. It did not wave back, but its heavily lidded eyes never wavered from my position.

Guiltily, I continued on. The plan to lead trophy hunters back here still flitted in my mind. In that light, the carrots were not so much a gift as bait. Win his trust, then boom, down him with an elephant gun. I winced at my dark-hearted, money-grubbing thoughts. However, they did not go away.

When you grow up with next to nothing, money is

the number one concern. Kind of made me feel like a heel, though, for Achie seemed peaceable.

This was the hottest day yet. Daniel must have exited the furnace and left the door open. Though I was super alert to the creature trailing me from a distance — my neck developed a crick from looking back so much — I felt drowsy in the hammering heat. At Salmon Stream, I emptied canteens and filled them in a shallow pool where lazy and languid trout cooled. I waded the ford that usually came to my waist, but today scarcely wetted my knees. Not liking to hike in wet pants, I stripped off and hung them on a dogberry tree for a quick-dry. I swear, wisps of vapor rose from them.

As I sat in maple shade, Archie Mud ponderously approached the southern bank. For a panicky second, I thought to run, for he was only about thirty yards from me. Now I clearly saw devilish cloven hooves. However, his main frame was great-ape flesh and bone covered in course, raven black hair. He lowered to his stomach with surprising grace and slurped water with a purple tongue. He took in enough to ballast a steamship. All the while he watched me with unnaturally bright eyes. I concluded his mind was more man than monster.

Wish I had a bloody camera. Pictures would fetch a pretty penny with a London newspaper. Then I wouldn't have to lead hunters back here to bag Archie. Maybe that should be my new Plan A. Less bloody and murderous.

One only murders people. I just caught myself regarding the thing across the stream as more person than animal. Maybe it was an Indian magician. The Conne River tribe talked of miracle workers, powerful wizard-giants.

Maybe I was looking one straight in the blood-red eye.

Having drunk his fill, Archie retreated to a stand of pine and treated himself to cones like I would gobble jellybeans.

Right, clearly not belligerent. Yet, I made no sudden moves as I dressed, strapped on my backpack, and resumed my long walk through the empty forest. Before, I was in the middle of nowhere. This new stretch was a million miles beyond nowhere.

I walked under a changing sky.

To the west, periwinkle blue gradually thickened to a grainy cobalt, a hard, angry hue very like burnished metal. Worrisome, for I have seen such flat cloud turn electric awful quickly. Lightning just loves to hit power poles. In a storm it is best to fade into the woods, away from the line.

According to my pocket watch, it was 2:00 pm in the afternoon when the rumbling started, a faraway sound like a turnip cart jouncing over a stony road. Harsh glimmers played along the horizon. Sheet lightning, which was mildly comforting because my teachers claimed such electricity danced between clouds and never came to earth. Even a tinhorn kid like me knows fork lightning and bone-dry forests add up to serious trouble.

An hour later, I swallowed hard as the first brilliant lance of lightning crackled straight down. Licking lips nervously, I counted seconds between the flash and rippling thunder. Maybe five miles off, not good. A breeze started, lightly tossing branches that beckoned for rain. However, this electrical storm begrudged moisture. Not a drop in the air.

Better get clear of the power transmission wires. Chop-chop.

Bobby Lake was too far away. However, just to the east, maybe a five-minute rough hike off the power line, was a modest hill of bare rock that loomed just above the treetops. A few boulders crowned the rise. Maybe a lean-to shelter just shy of the top would see me through the advancing tempest.

Ahead, a caribou cow and calf loped across the cut, followed by a pair of decidedly skittish red foxes. They smelled it before I did. Woodsmoke.

Then I heard the baying of hounds. *Nothing meaner than dogs gone feral.*

Rising wind brought a faint crackling sound. An ox-blood aura shimmered in the treetops. I muttered a prayer. Forest fires are hell on earth.

Two lithe bodies bolted across the cut ahead of me. German Shepherds, ferocious from forest living.

Crashing and whuffing came from behind. Shocked senseless, I beheld Archie Mud galloping up the trail. For a terrifying second, I thought he might trample me with lethal hooves. But he clomped past, locking his scarlet eyes with mine and gesturing with a hand the size of a serving platter. *Follow me.* He then smashed into the woods toward the hillock I just sized up.

Rock doesn't burn. This troll was canny. And it understood human gestures, maybe learned from McAllister.

When a guy grows up in a tar paper shack with candles, kerosene lamps and woodstoves, fear of fire is drilled into him. Not hesitating, I ran into the trail created by the behemoth. Strong as Hercules, Archie simply shoved aside close standing saplings and threw over deadfall obstructions. Never once he did catch his monumental horns in branches. Bulldozing a trail by main strength, Archie then clambered up the rockslide and into boulders. Drifting clouds of smoke, now thick and choking, swirled around us.

I was at the bottom of the slope when the first dog seized my ankle. Slavering teeth ripped off half my boot. Wolf jaws would have crushed my bones, but this mongrel wasn't of great size. Nearly had him beat off with my pole when a godawful big Shepherd landed on my back. I fell hard on jagged stones, twisting to protect my neck and guts. In seconds, four of them latched on to me, and all I could think of was the gory moose carcass. I tried to get my axe, but in the desperate tangle merely found a rock in my hand. I hit out, knowing I couldn't whip a frenzied pack.

Then a startled squeal. One of the big Shepherds launched into the air like a Messerschmitt on takeoff. Archie also kicked the mongrel, and from the sickening crunch I knew its hunting days were over. A hundred-pound mastiff lunged for him, but one flick of unbelievable antlers sent the canine rolling, a livid gash on his hind quarter. The attack melted away as flames raced closer.

Archie whuffed and made for the hilltop. Gagging on harsh smoke, I grabbed my gear and scrabbled after.

Not a great strongpoint. As wildfire leapt the power line cut, I frantically gathered rocks and constructed a bare firewall, coughing up a lung as I did so. Catching on, Archie Mud used his Charles Atlas muscles to roll the larger boulders together. A desperate minute was all we had, then the inferno lapped our hill and a whirling cloud of burning flinders sailed over us.

Gasping for air, I dropped flat. Imitating, Archie did likewise. We wheezed for oxygen, even as the raging firestorm sucked every molecule from the air. The stone around us glowed hot, like rocks circling an evening cookfire. A burning branch fell on Archie's back, and he reared in pain. Thinking quick, I covered my face with the straw hat and smothered burning hide with my blanket. This I did several times in the horrific hour that followed as hateful hellfire besieged our crude fort. Thus, we teamed against the conflagration, and in the fight, I lost every bit of fear toward him.

Exhausted, singed, completely unnerved, I passed out. On coming to in the night, the land to all sides twinkled with red embers as fires burned low. The main wildfire had passed like a lava flow from Vesuvius. The Dark Man was gone, for good I thought. However, at dawn he returned, bearing an armload of moss and slimy water plants. These he mashed into my burns, soothing the hurt, and turnabout I did the same to his blackened hide. I suppose we doctored each other until noon, when he suddenly upped and departed. At the bottom of the hill, he turned to squint at me through the haze of lingering smoke.

A day later, I met Mr. Moffat and a Light and Power Company repair crew hurrying a pony train laden with wire and tools. No surprise; the sudden forest fire destroyed a section of line and interrupted power transmission.

"Some good to see you alive and kicking, Jimmy. Though, you look like Stukas just bombed you." As the repair crew passed, he whistled at Archie Mud's first aid effort. "Pretty sharp woods medicine, Jim, but let me patch you up proper." He washed off moss and applied Noxzema cream and bandaged over the worse burns. As he worked, he asked, "Aside from surviving an up-in-smoke disaster, any adventures?"

"Well," I said hesitantly, arriving at a weighty decision. "Matter of fact, yeah. Saw a tall woods hermit wearing a fur coat and antler crown." To which he chuckled and immediately changed the subject to the war in France which was now hot and heavy.

Mr. Moffat and party hurried on, leaving me to slowly hobble for Goobies. I neared the settlement when I spied Archie Mud one last time, on the path behind me.

I waved. This time, Archie waved back. Then I realized money isn't everything.

Daniel Windeler

Born and raised in Happy Valley Goose Bay, **Daniel Windeler** is a wildlife Biologist who has worked deep in the woods of Labrador and across the island, as well as offshore in the Atlantic.

His previous publications with Engen have been "Freeson's Leap" and "Wave Bound". The newest tale takes us to the woods of the west coast in "Brittany and the Panther"

Brittany and the Panther

"I've been here in Deer Lake for almost an hour and I haven't seen a single deer!" Brittany Saf-fron huffs in the front of the airport. The influencer pulled out her phone from her large purse to check the signal. This was the first time she'd been this far east and didn't know how great the towers would be in the rural town. The sun glittered on her pink, bejeweled phone as it gauged the respective towers. She looked over the bright screen, satisfied to see that she had almost full bars outside the airport. Before opening her recording app, she pulled out a pocket mirror to check her makeup one last time before opening the feed.

"Good morning, Brittologists! I've finally made it to Newfoundland and am ready to start the hunt!" Brittany spoke enthusiastically as she flipped the camera around. She slowly panned it across the cluttered parking lot. "Far into the deep, rural woods of Deer Lake. The island doesn't even have Ubers!" Turning the camera back to her, she said, "But that's all right, Brittologists. There's no roads where we're going. This is just the first step to finding the elusive Newfoundland Panther!"

Brittany smiled as she heard the echoing pings of her followers liking and quoting her live feed. She spent half of her flight looking over the script for this trip. Brittany was better known for "Britt and Crypts", her online channel for hunting down cryptids across the country. Her whole career was investigating strange beasts all across Canada — that and plugging her sponsors every moment she could.

"As I brought up at the end of the Furry Trout episode, my plan is to venture with a local guide into the Newfoundland wilderness. For over a decade, there have been random sightings of this elusive panther around Deer Lake!" Was it an escaped circus animal from the 80's like the original story, or something else entirely?!" Brittany wiggled her fingers in front of the camera as she let out a campy ghost "Ooo!." The chat was filled with responses like "So Silly!", "Britt being cute!", and "Boo Britt!<3". She was eating up the attention and the views for her channel.

As she basked in the praise of her audience, a vehicle pulled up to the entrance. The rusty old car creaked as it went into park. The door screeched open as a scruffy young man in overalls stepped out of the vehicle. He walked around the vehicle with bent shoulders and a squirrelly look in his eyes. He spotted the phone and took a step back. Brittany spun around on the spot, pointing the phone in the man's face.

"And you must be my guide! You look like your profile picture. Though, I suggest a bit of a shave." Brittany flipped the camera back to herself. "I would like to introduce Anthony Woodland to all you Brittologists! A

Corner Brook man and fellow cryptid hunter who will get us all the deets on the panther. Say hi to the fans, Anthony!" Brittany leaned over her bags to push the phone into Anthony's face. The man stepped even further away, eyes bulging as he listened to the chat ding away on the phone.

"Can you put that away! I didn't say I could be recorded!" Anthony cursed as he pulled his ball cap further down his face. Brittany rolled her eyes and turned the camera back.

"It seems our guide is a little camera shy, Brittologists. Be right back! We'll start the video once we're in the woods." Her bright smile faded the moment she turned off the feed. "Actually you did agree to the recording. The contract my assistant sent over had a clause for the right to record every part of this hike. If you didn't read it properly, that's on you." Anthony looked about to say something but stopped when he locked eyes with her. "Do you want to get paid or not?"

Anthony didn't say anything else.

"That's what I thought. Now let's drop off my stuff at the hotel and we can get ready for the hunt." The guide grumbled under his breath but said nothing against her. Brittany gave him a cheeky grin as she threw her baggage in the back seat.

They both climbed into the rusted car and drove off. Brittany spent the entire ride explaining the plan and what was expected of a guide on her show. Anthony took it all in quietly. Occasionally he looked to be about to question her plans, but he never spoke up to interrupt her.

"So, we'll drop off my bags and head right into the

field. I want to scout out your little hiding spot before nightfall and set up the cameras. I need to film the planning stage of the hunt and the prep. I'll need you to show me the best spots for the motion sensor and the night vision cameras," Brittany trilled on as she answered emails on her phone.

"No. We can't put up the cameras at this spot," Anthony mumbled as he turned off the highway into Deer Lake.

Brittany looked up incredulous. "What do you mean no?! I always put out cameras and film. That's a third of my specials. Have you not paid attention to my show or just watched for the eye candy?!"

At that remark, Anthony turned to look at her, a faint blush rising in his cheeks. He stammered and looked to be about to argue more before turning back at the road. The car veered hard as Anthony almost drove into the opposite lane just to keep eye contact as he argued. When he spoke next, he kept his gaze on the road but the rose in his cheeks stayed, now more from frustration.

"Of course I watch your show! That's why I contacted you! And that's not the reason. If we are out there near the den too early, then it's going to smell us and not come back. We have to be very careful and sneak up on it while it heads back into its den, or we'll be caught. That's when you can record it for your show. I sent you the photo, didn't I?"

"Yes, yes. That blurry shot is the only reason I'm here." Out of habit, Brittany's fingers ran over her touch screen, opening up her photos to Favourites. In the wall of selfies and party pics were small windows of work photos.

The most recent shot was a blur of some kind of large cat. The flash and the creature's speed had significantly obscured what could be seen. But comparing it to the trees surrounding it, the cat was big. But a blurry photo wasn't going to cut it for Brittany. "Like, you couldn't get a better shot? What did you even take this with, a flip phone?"

"My phone was a hand-me-down…"

"Looking at this car, you seem to get a lot of those," Brittany sneered, running a manicured fin-ger over the torn leather seats. Anthony hunched over the wheel as his lips moved with silent insults. But for once Brittany thought better than to antagonize one of her guides. Crummy or not, it was a new photo of a unique cryptid. Her subscribers were tired of the same old Sasquatch shot that'd been plastered across the world for the last few decades. Anything other than the Big-Foot trio or Nessie gets attention. Her last special on the supposed Furry Trout increased her viewership by ten percent, and they didn't even see the bloody thing. This Newfoundland Panther though? With real shots of it, it would raise her viewership into the millions.

Brittany grinned as she thought about the retweet numbers. If she had to put up with more disagreeable standards than usual, she would.

"Well, if that's the case, then there's time for me to pick up a non-fat mocha."

"Um, sure, but we still have the hike to the spot. And about the payment…"

"I had my accountant send you the upfront payment an hour ago." Anthony took his hand off the wheel and fished for his phone from his jeans. But before he could unlock the screen, Brittany grabbed his hand and pushed it to the seat. "UMMM, NOT WHILE YOU'RE DRIVING! I'm not missing this shot because you got us in an accident. It's two hundred bucks."

"Two hundred?! You promised me three thousand!" Anthony slammed on the brakes so hard that Brittany almost dropped her phone from the force. Fire was behind his brown eyes as he bared his teeth at her. He looked like he was ready to throttle her; it was the first real emotion he had shown on the trip, and it almost impressed her. But Brittany just met his rage with the same indignant smile she had for the whole drive.

"Looks like you *really* didn't read that contract." Brittany let out a demeaning chuckle, which only seemed to fuel his rage. "What? You thought I was going to give you the full three thousand before we even get into the field? Don't be an idiot. Two hundred is for the pickup and drive. Three hundred for the initial interview, a thousand for the guide and set up, and the rest at the end of the night. I came here because you promised me a shot of the panther. I won't be paying another cent until I see results." Brittany leaned in as she tore down the guide. With every inch she gained, he pulled back. "Now, if you're finished with your tantrum, how about you stop holding up traffic and do your job!"

That was the last of their arguments. Anthony didn't put up much of a fight now that he knew his payment was on the line. When Brittany asked him questions, he answered curtly. When she took out her phone to do the interview, he spoke calmly. When the recording was running, her bubbly online persona was in full view. It wasn't a long reading. There wasn't much actual information on the Newfoundland Panther but rumours and a few sightings. Anthony explained what he had heard before coming upon the beast's nest a few years back.

"There was always talk about a circus. But I don't think it was from one. It lived too long to match up with the animal circuses that came through the island. Besides, I don't think it's really a pan-ther." Anthony was solemn on the recording. Brittany wasn't expecting her guide to be camera shy, but looking at his hunched shoulders and woodsman's attire, she should have known better.

"Not a real panther? What do you mean by that?" Brittany asked with false interest. Anthony's eyes darted up to glare at her for a split second. Clearly, he had soured to her happy online persona now that he had dealt with the real Brittany. But the glare was gone when he spoke — the desire for payment outweighed his annoyance.

"From a distance, it looks like some big, black panther. But even at night, if you get close enough, you can see it's something else. I don't know what it is, but I know it's not a panther. I think it's been around longer than any circus." Anthony shrugged, not looking at the camera as he answered.

"If it's as big as you say, what has it been feeding on?"

"Moose. The island is maggoty with them. We shot all the wolves on the island so there's noth-ing big enough to keep the numbers down. Well, nothing but the panther." Anthony shrugged again. "So it's not like anyone would notice a few missing moose deep in the woods. And it's not like it doesn't clean up after itself."

"So how did you find this panther-like creature?"

"One hunting season, I was out looking for my moose. I went deeper than I was expecting, and before I knew it, the sun was down. I looked for a place to set up my tent when I found this small valley. There was an outcrop of rocks at the bottom, so I went down to get out of the wind. Before I could make a fire, I saw it." Anthony paused in his retelling; his eyes almost glazed over as the memories hit him. "It was dragging a bull moose down to the rocks like it was nothing. I hid behind some trees and watched as it ate the moose. That time I didn't bring my phone. But when I came back a week later, it was there by the rocks. I believe its den in hidden inside."

"Have you told anyone else of the creature?"

"Of course!" His voice rose for the first time in the interview, the same anger lighting up his face. "But I couldn't convince anyone. They thought I saw a big coyote or a bear. Even when I went back and took a photo, they didn't believe me!" His voice was almost a plea. Brittany just nodded but said nothing. She wasn't surprised. Many of her guides were loners or social pariahs. Nothing in her time with Anthony told her he was any different. Brittany reached out and place a hand gently on his shoulder. The tender contact almost made Anthony jump. He gawked at her hand with an open mouth.

"I believe you, Anthony." Brittany's words were almost sweet whispers but loud enough to be picked up by the camera. "And tonight we are going to prove them wrong." Anthony didn't speak. But he gave an awkward smile as she kept her hand on his shoulder.

Their interview ended there. Anthony never spoke

much after that. His mind was still trying to comprehend the two very different Brittanys. He waited outside of her Airbnb as she dropped off her bags and changed into her hiking clothes, which consisted of matching pink camo pants and ball-cap, a dual headlamp and camera, and a small backpack to hold her night vision camera. Brittany climbed back into the car as she sent off another instalment of Anthony's pay. His phone dinged again as he threw his cigarette out onto the road.

The drive to the hiking spot was just as quiet. When they finally pulled off the road and parked down a dirt path, the sun was setting. Putting the vehicle in park, Anthony climbed out and made his way to the edge of the woods. Brittany lagged a little behind so she could take a few screenshots and recordings of the woods around them. In the editing process, she would get her assistant to play over her recordings of the brief history of the panther and add maybe an ad or two. Anthony marched on ahead, giving her a wide berth even in the thick growth of the trail. But Brittany didn't care; she didn't want to spend the hike making small talk. As long as she got her photos, what did she care if he liked her or not? It was only over an hour into the hike that Brittany finally spoke up.

"Oh my God, why can't I get any bars?!" Brittany lifted her phone into the air, spinning around, hoping to get any kind of signal. Her narrow face was illuminated in the dark forest. "I thought you said the island had coverage?"

"We do... but we're deep in the wilderness now. There's no towers out in the woods. What did you expect?"

"I expect Newfoundland to be living in 2023 like the rest of the country, not the 1900's!" Brittany mashed the cellular data button over and over, hoping the reset would strengthen the signal. But no matter what she did, the bars did not move. "It's a good thing I can still record this or I would be livid!" Brittany let out a flustered groan. She wanted to livestream the panther for everyone to see. Uploading the shots when she made it back tonight would have to do. Brittany took a moment to compose herself, doing the breathing exercises her assistant practiced before speaking again, but her words still came out as a snap. "How much longer until we reach this den!"

"We're almost there. We should be entering its territory on the other side of this hill. So from here on out, we should be quiet unless we want to scare it off." Anthony emphasized this by placing a finger to his lips. Brittany wondered if that was true or if he was just trying to shut her up. She mumbled under her breath but didn't take it any further.

The pair climbed over the hill to look down into a shrouded ravine. Sure enough, before them was the rock formation that Anthony described. Brittany let out a satisfied snort as she slung her back-pack down. Anthony jumped at the noise, but Brittany didn't notice. She rummaged through the bag, looking for her camera. The view screen illuminated, and Brittany smiled. She pointed the camera to herself and blew it a kiss as the recording started.

"Alright Brittologists, our fearless guide has brought us to the den. Let's see if all our hard hiking paid off!" Brittany gave the camera an exaggerated wink before standing up, pointing the camera at Anthony. Through the camera's night vision, she could see Anthony's annoyance in his face and stance.

"You done?"

"It's a good thing we can cut out this part in editing or that sass would cost you a hundred bucks," Brittany threatened as she marched down into the ravine. The rock formation was quite large down below. She was surprised that the jutting stones weren't noticeable from higher ground, but the moss camouflaging it might be the reason. Whatever it was, this little hiding hole was a perfect den for a big predator.

"If we don't see the panther then at least I'll get some cool shots of a black bear," Brittany mused. "Here we are, Brittologists, in the heart of the panther's territory! No telling how long it's kept hidden from humanity. Let's try to look into the den before it-"

Before Brittany could finish, she was pulled off her feet. She let out a yelp as the camera slipped from her fingers. Anthony had a hold of her arm and was pulling her backwards off her feet. But she ripped herself out of his grasp just in time to catch the camera before it hit the ground.

"Do you know how much that camera costs?!" Brittany's voice rose in pitch before Anthony grabbed her again. His clammy fingers tightened on her face as he silenced her. Brittany was about to scream out when, through her rage, she saw his other hand waving erratically.

"Shhhhhh! It's here!" he whispered frantically. That snapped Brittany out of her anger. When he released his grip on her, she slowly turned her head back to the ravine.

Anthony was correct. The panther was there.

From between the boulders, a shadow lumbered out of the darkness. It moved on all fours, weaving through the rocks as if its body was made of liquid. Large orbs reflected the moonlight as the front half of its body turned. Brittany assumed that was its head, but its body was still too obscured in shadows to make it out. All she could tell was whatever it was, it was gigantic!

Both guide and influencer crouched in the grass, slowly stepping backwards to hide themselves within the trees at the edge of the ravine. Once they were behind cover, Brittany leaned out to get a better look at the beast with the camera. The night vision zoomed in on the shadow in the rocks and slowly came into focus.

"Oh my God..." Brittany whispered. At first glance, she could see why people would call it a panther. But the longer she recorded it, was very clear that this was not a panther! Its body was gaunt but rippled with rigid muscle as it moved; the flank of the beast twisted at strange angles as it ventured out of the den. A striped tuff of fur ran down its back towards the tail, which bobbed and flicked against the boulders. Paws with strange, elongated toes scraped against the moss covered rock. Ears twisted and flicked sporadically, but its snout was elongated like a canine. The eyes glowed unnaturally in the camera's lens. Once its body was out in the ravine, it sat on its hind legs and opened its mouth wide. It was probably trying to figure out the new smells in its territory, similar to a cat. Nothing about this creature matched either a panther, wolf, or tiger! Even at a distance, Brittany gauged its size. Sitting like that, it would meet her face at eye level. "This is fantastic! I can't believe it's real!"

"What do you mean, you can't believe? I said it was real. What did you think we'd find?"

But Brittany ignored Anthony's questions. None of that mattered now. She had photo and video evidence of a unique and real-life cryptid! Evidence she could bring to the media and the Department of Environmental Affairs. Some abnormal creature would be made public by Brittany Saffron. Her viewership would be in the millions! Talk shows would want to interview her. Her online store would be sold-out. With this one discovery, everything in Brittany's career would turn for the better!

But before she became an internet celebrity, she needed to take a selfie.

While she was still recording, Brittany pulled out her phone and put in the password without looking. Without asking, she handed the camera over to Anthony, motioning him to keep it pointed at the "panther". Even in the darkness, she could see the confusion on his face. But that didn't matter; she was getting the new cover photo for her channel.

Turning her back to the ravine, she pulled out a pink selfie stick from her backpack. As it ex-tended, Anthony's eyes bulged. His mouth opened in a silent warning as Brittany pressed the button.

The flash breached the darkness, bathing the ravine in light. Brittany's eyes glittered as the phone screen lit up. The picture was perfect. Brittany was just off centre so as to make room for the panther. Her make up was immaculate even after the long hike. Her lips were perky with a shine from the flash. The panther was in full view, its whole body just fitting in the frame. Its fur was a deep black and had a strange, blue shimmer from the flash. Brittany noticed that it looked like the creature's fur had a spotted pattern.

But what finally wiped the smile off her face was when Brittany realized the panther was looking directly at the camera.

"Get down!" Anthony screamed, shoving Brittany behind the tree. As she turned, the panther rushed up the ravine with frightening speed. It jaws opened wide to release a hellish shriek that echoed through the silence. Brittany scrambled to her feat, and the two ran into the trees. Behind her, the panther continued to howl into the night. Anthony was a few paces ahead of her. He was hopping over bushes and ducking under branches, not caring if they swung back and hit Brittany. "Why the hell did you do that!"

"It seemed like a good idea at the time!" Brittany screamed as she stuffed her phone into her pocket. Behind her, the panther smashed through the undergrowth. She couldn't tell how close it was but was too afraid to look back. "You still have my camera?"

"What? I dropped it! Who cares!" Anthony hopped over another bush, swearing as his head broke through the low canopy of a tree. Brittany slipped to the side but continued to chase after her guide.

"I care! I need that recording or this was for nothing!" Brittany screamed in anger. In the moonlight, she caught sight of an overgrown brush in between some evergreens. Instead of following her guide, she dove into the bushes. Brittany slammed hard against the roots of the bush but pressed herself against the undergrowth. If the panther noticed she flung herself into the bushes, then she would be dead. She didn't move; she couldn't risk looking back to see if the creature noticed.

The thundering echoes of the panther's steps rumbled past her hiding spot. Brittany held her breath as she felt the creature smash through the undergrowth. It didn't notice her. It was still chasing after Anthony.

It was only after Brittany was sure that the panther was off into the forest that she climbed out of the bushes. The screeching howls of the beast were far away. Brittany let out a shuddering breath she didn't realize she was holding. But after taking a moment to stabilize herself, she snuck back to towards the panther's den.

At some point in the chase, Brittany had lost her ball cap and head lamp. Luckily for her, it wasn't hard to make her way back to the ravine. The path of destruction made by the stampeding creature made a small walking trail in the forest. And with her phone's flashlight, she jogged back at a nice pace.

As the trees opened up to the ravine, a scream echoed through the forest. Brittany turned quickly to look into the darkness. A chill ran down her spine as she recognized Anthony's voice in the howls of pain. Her muscles tightened as her guide's scream were instantly cut short. Nothing but silence followed.

"I need to be fast," was all Brittany could muster as the silence weighed on her.

In a frantic search for her camera, Brittany scampered around their hiding place. Her phone light waved around as she looked through the grass, occasionally jumping as she believed every dancing shadow to be the panther. The panther hadn't screeched out since it reached Anthony. There was no way to know if it was on its way back or playing with its 'food'.

As the phone's light scoured the ravine's floor, something silver shone back by a tree trunk. Brittany's heart leapt as she rushed to the side of the tree. She dropped to her knees as she grabbed for the abandoned camera. But as she lifted her camera, her hope sank as it fell apart in her hands.

"Oh no," Brittany groaned as the front of the camera bounced off of the tree trunk. Anthony must have thrown the camera when he ran from the ravine. The screen was completely cracked. The only hope was the memory card was intact. Brittany cursed as she fiddled with the broken camera. The compartment must have jammed when it fell. She pushed her fingernail into the compartment and wiggled it wildly, hoping to shimmy it in. "Come on, come on!"

A snapped twig pulled Brittany's attention away from the camera. Almost dropping it, she turned her phone's light towards the sound, only to meet the giant eyes of the panther.

The panther's head peered out from behind the tree, looking down at the kneeling woman. The creature's snout pulled back to bare sharp teeth. A low, dangerous growl rumbled from its throat. Being so close, Brittany still couldn't tell if the creature was more feline or canid. Even as she feared for her life, moments away from death, she noticed an odd pattern of bluer fur around the beast's snout. *What even are you?* was the only sane thought that echoed in her mind amongst a storm of internal screams.

But kneeling on the grass with a phone in hand, Brittany sat a few feet away from this great predator. Her fear kept her nailed to the ground. It was too close anyway; running now would just be a quicker death. While still keeping eye contact with her, the beast extended one giant paw. Brittany tried to lean back away from the panther, watching the paw slowly come towards her, but her back pressed against the tree. She couldn't move any further, but the paw closed the gap.

But instead of wrapping the gargantuan paw around her head, Brittany watched the panther reach for her phone. The panther's paw wrapped over the top of the phone case. Her mouth gaped as she watched two long claws extend from the creature's toes and push into the screen. With very little force, her phone crumpled in its grip. And with a degree of controlled delicacy, the claws receded.

The panther pulled away and stood in front of Brittany. She still held what was left of her phone as sparks fizzled from the broken chip board inside. Without realizing it, she dropped the broken camera that was still in her other hand. Just as it hit the ground, the panther's claw swung out. Before Brittany could blink, it struck the broken camera, sending it flying across the ravine. She didn't take her eyes off of the panther's face but heard the camera smash against a tree.

The panther's bright yellow eyes looked her over with a meaningful gaze. The large black pupils darted from her hands to her waist, up to her collar. If Brittany didn't know any better, it was as if the creature was assessing her. Its canid nose flared, letting out a deep snort as it came to a decision.

Letting out one last deep snarl, the panther turned. It made its way back into the trees. Brittany just gawked at it. She was still holding the scrap metal that was her phone, only letting it fall to the ground when the panther's long tail brushed against her fingers. When it was about to slip into the undergrowth, the dread keeping Brittany quiet waned enough for her to speak. But the words only came out in a whisper.

"Is… is that it?" It was a plea, a wish that she wasn't making a mistake. She didn't know why she spoke to the cryptid, but only moments ago, it had killed her guide. This strange act of mercy just made her ask. To her surprise, the creature stopped in its tracks. Brittany thought that it would turn around and take it back. But what happened next somehow shook her to the core.

"I-GaVE-hiM-a-cHAncE." The voice was deep, with a twisting lilt, as if it came from a tongue not used to the English language. Brittany throat tightened, her eyes bulged. *"DOn't-mAKe-hIS-mIStakE. BESide-S…"*

No no no no no!!! Brittany's mind screamed as she listened to the voice. Her fingers dung into the bark of the tree behind her. If it was possible for her to sink into the trunk, she would have tried. Her lips shuddered as she looked on. The panther's head turned, looking over its shoulder back at her. The long jaw split in a sickening snarl. No. Not a snarl. The knowing look in its golden eye as she failed to contain her fear. The flews of its snout twisted upwards.

The panther was grinning back towards Brittany.

"NO-onE-WilL-BElieVe-YOu-anYWay." The panther's toothy grin widened even more. It was as if a silent laugh was seeping out between its fangs. It continued to watch Brittany as it slipped between the trees. The golden orb of its eye still glowed as the body was swallowed by the shadows. Brittany didn't move as she watched the Newfoundland panther fade into the night.

Brittany didn't know how long she sat under the tree alone just staring at the empty space where the panther stood moments ago. Some irrational fear told her it was going to change its mind and come rushing back to finish the job. Her hands still rested on the trunk, but she loosened her grip on the bark. It was only when she was certain that it wasn't coming back that she stood up.

Her eyes wandered to the smashed phone and camera. She didn't even bother checking for the memory card. Brittany walked to the edge of the ravine. There was nothing in the forest ahead of her. No sounds. Nothing skirting across her vision. She thought about the last scream Anthony made before the panther caught him. Would she come upon his body in the woods? She didn't even know how far he made it or what direction he went in for that matter.

What direction….

"Huh." Brittany spoke out loud as she still worked on processing the events of the night. Finding the panther, whatever it was. The death of her guide.

Her guide.

"What direction did I come from?" she spoke to herself. A new fear bubbling up inside her. Or maybe she spoke to the panther. For all she knew, it was watching her from a hiding spot. *WhO's-tO-SAy?* She imagined it saying.

Who's to say….

Amy Sheppard

Amy Sheppard was born and raised in Newfoundland and Labrador. While Amy has published numerous non-fiction articles related to her work with criminalized women, this is her first published work of fiction.

The Bigfoot Widow

So, I suppose I could call myself a "bigfoot widow," as ridiculous as that sounds. You know those women whose partners leave them behind in pursuit of their manly passions? For some men, it's golf, or hockey or hunting. A friend of a friend's husband missed the birth of their child because he had to get his moose. He knew the baby was due, and still, he went on. Selfish. Some men are like that. I guess I didn't think mine was. When we were dating and as newlyweds we spent lots of time together. We would go for a nice dinner, for hikes and camping, on Saturdays we'd spend time at the farmer's market, and in the evening, cuddled together watching Netflix. Normal couple stuff.

But things have changed after a few years of marriage.

For me, and this is embarrassing, my man goes off in pursuit of a mythical creature: Bigfoot. Now, to him, it's not mythical. Bigfoot is very real, and he is determined to find the evidence to prove it. He has a group of buddies he goes off with. They load up their gear — cameras and various contraptions designed to call a Bigfoot — and off they go for the night. A couple of times a year, during Bigfoot season, they go for a whole weekend.

Bigfoot season. Have you ever heard of anything so ridiculous? Like moose season, I guess? The best time to catch a Bigfoot. But who the hell knows when Bigfoot season really is?! No one has actually been able to study these things and learn their habits. Christ. But I guess that's what my husband thinks he is doing.

I didn't mind at first. It was nice he had a hobby and a group of friends to spend time with. I have my own hobbies too, and I like to get away with the girls a couple of times a year. But my hobbies are normal and real. I like to paint. I watch YouTube tutorials. I take an occasional class on painting, sometimes the serious ones and sometimes those paint-and-sip nights where you get a little drunk while exploring your creative side. I like to hike and be outdoors. We used to do that together. We used to go camping together, for goodness' sake! Now he can't be bothered to go into the woods with me. He has "scientific experiments" and I get in the way. I also like to bake; I make cookies and cakes. Often I have too much and bring it into work where people are delighted with my hobby.

My hobbies are the normal ones.

Not traipsing through the woods looking for a goddam Bigfoot.

But yeah, I didn't mind at first. He and his buddies would go off for an evening or an afternoon every couple of months. More like hiking really. And I would pack a little lunch for him to take. It was great. He would go off for a few hours and leave me in peace. I could putter around the house a bit, have a nice bath and read. I might go out with the girls. Couples don't need to spend every minute together. It's good to have separate interests and hobbies, right? I wouldn't tell the girls where he had gone. Their men were off playing hockey every Friday night. They complained that it was every Friday night, but at least that was normal. They weren't out trying to track down something that doesn't exist.

A puck is very real, even if it is a stupid thing to be chasing after.

I couldn't tell them that he was off in the woods with this homemade Bigfoot caller. It's like a moose caller. You can buy those, for hunting moose. They make a noise that sounds like another moose? And then the moose come to you? I don't know, but it seems legit, I guess. But a Bigfoot caller? How the hell do you even know what a Bigfoot sounds like?

So, like I said, at first, it was fine. Once every couple of months. But then it started to get more frequent: every month, and a couple of overnights. And now it even takes over at home. He spends time on the internet "researching" and talking to other Bigfoot hunters. And my YouTube feed is crawling with BigFoot videos and other bullshit. Did you know how many variations of Bigfoot there are? I do. Because my YouTube recommends videos about ApeSkunk, GrassMonster, and the goddam Muddy Monster of Southern Illinois.

So now he is gone most weekends searching for a Bigfoot. And I'm left home alone. And when he is home, the house is filled with his Bigfoot equipment. I am not joking. Bigfoot equipment! Heat-seeking video cameras. Night vision binoculars. Audio-recording equipment. He has a boom mic! This stuff is everywhere in my house, taking up space. He must have spent a fortune on this shit .

So now I am getting fed up. This year, instead of taking his holidays so we could go on a little vacation, he took his annual leave from work and went on a week-long Bigfoot hunting expedition. So I am done. It's me or the Bigfoot. He needs to stop the nonsense.

I am going to pack up my stuff and I'm out. I am going to stay with a friend for a bit until I get my own place. But I have no idea what to say to people. How can I tell people I left my husband because he is obsessed with Bigfoot? It is mortifying.

I will miss the house. I love it. I spent so much time making it lovely… only for it to be filled with Bigfoot paraphernalia and Bigfoot "hunting" equipment. The irony is that we live in the woods, sort of. I mean, we are in town, but we are lucky that our property backs onto the woods. We are on the outskirts, close enough to all major amenities but if you look towards the backyard, you can pretend that we are in an isolated cabin. We have neighbours, but you can barely see them through the trees. It really is beautiful. I spend a lot of time in the garden. I will miss it.

He is gone for the long weekend. He won't be back now until Monday. Lots of time for me to get my stuff organized and packed up. Maybe I will ask one of the girls to come over to help and I'll tell her what's going on, why I'm leaving. I am sad and angry that it has come to this. But I can't live like this anymore.

I invite my friend Sarah to come over. She knows a little about what's going on, but I haven't told her everything and I haven't told her I am leaving. She is coming over with a bottle of wine and is going to stay the night.

When she finally arrives, I tell her everything. All the Bigfoot nonsense and why my husband is out of town so much. She is bewildered and laughs a little. And it is ridiculous. How can you not laugh? My marriage is over because of Bigfoot. We spend a little time organizing and packing my stuff. She has a lead on an apartment for me. I have to figure out how to split up all the stuff. I know he won't care if he is left a single chair as long as he has his Bigfoot equipment, but it's cruel to leave him with absolutely nothing.

I am soon tired of the packing and want to commence with the drinking. Sarah opens the wine and we chat. I put together a little tray of food and we head outside and I light up the little propane fire pit in the backyard as it begins to get dark. We get comfy on the chairs around the fire. Chairs that I picked out in anticipation of cozy evenings with my husband. But, I don't want to think about my husband or Bigfoot anymore. I want to just forget it all. The wine starts to relax me and Sarah, and I carry on and reminisce, laughing about memories of nothing important. We are scrolling through our phones, looking at memories provided by Facebook. I go way back, before I met my husband, to remember happier times when Sarah and I traveled. Memories from university days. Memories with family. Memories that do not include Bigfoot.

We are laughing and showing each other our phones, each giggling "remember that…" when I hear a rustling in the trees just beyond the fire pit. Sarah alerts, hearing it too. Probably the neighbour's cat I say as I bravely pour more wine. The cats are always out around. We settle again, but with a slight wariness, feeling like something is watching us.

"How far away are your neighbours?" Sarah asks.

"Just on the other side of those trees," I reply. But we can't see their house. It does feel really isolated. A feature I usually like. We hear more rustling and branches breaking. I grab my phone and turn on the flashlight, pointing it at the woods. I see nothing.

"We are freaking ourselves out over nothing. There are rabbits and foxes in the woods. I see them all the time. Or it's a cat or something." I turn on the music on my phone to drown out the creepy noises and Sarah and I sit back, relaxing, watching the fire. Moments later, we are deep in our gossip, Sarah telling me all about the antics of one of her co-workers. The co-worker in question is always up to something and is a great source of gossip material. This time, she is sleeping with a married man. And the wife of the married man. The wife knows she is sleeping with the husband, but the husband doesn't know she is sleeping with the wife. A deliciously detailed and complicated story, I am no longer thinking about my husband, Bigfoot or the sounds from the woods.

Suddenly, Sarah stops her story. Mouth agape, she is staring beyond the fire into the woods as out walks a large, humanoid hairy creature.

We are frozen as Bigfoot sits in one of the chairs around the fire. He helps himself to a glass of wine and some cheese from the tray. He is much more cosmopolitan than my husband gives him credit. In fact, Bigfoot is delightful company. While he doesn't speak English, he is excellent at communication through hand and facial gestures. Sarah and I spend a pleasant evening in the glow of the fire with Bigfoot sitting amicably in a chair slightly too small for him. He is indeed big, but he doesn't smell as bad as all those Bigfoot hunters claim.

Monday evening, my husband returns from his Bigfoot expedition to find a mostly empty house. I left a note telling him I was leaving on the kitchen table. On the fridge, under an "I want to believe" souvenir fridge magnet, I place a printout of the selfie of Sarah, me, and Bigfoot.

Dave Hangman

Dave Hangman is Spanish writer David Verdugo's pseudonym, born in Madrid. He has published stories in the Redwood Press anthology "Superstition," and in The Lorelei Signal, East of the Web, Space and Time Magazine, Twenty-two Twenty-eight, Hyphen Punk, Havok, The Sprawl Mag, History Through Fiction, Tales from the Moonlit Path, and Bright Flash Literary Review.

His story "Eternal Fall" was nominated for the Push-cart Prize 2022.

He has received four honorable mentions in L. Ron Hubbard's Writers of the Future contests for 4Q2021, 1Q2022, 3Q2022, and 1Q2023.

The Mokèle-mbèmbé

Swampy area of the Likouala-aux-Herbes River. Congo. 1980.

Mackal and Powell stared in awe at the mangled carcass of a huge hippopotamus. Their chief scout, Hans Schomburgk, walked cautiously across the waterlogged ground with his back to the animal's remains. He had his ear to the ground and his rifle pointed deep into the jungle.

"It attacks hippos, but it doesn't devour them completely," Powell commented, bending down to study the carcass. He was a burly forty-year-old man who covered his bald head with a colonial pith helmet. "Look, Roy," he pointed to his biologist colleague, "bites from a huge jaw with long, sharp, triangular-shaped teeth that have torn and ripped chunks of flesh without gobbling them up. These other deeper incisions on the neck are from two fangs that remind me of those of a sabre-toothed tiger, with which it kills its prey."

"The carcass is also bruised from being struck by a muscular tail," observed Roy Mackal, "like that of a gigantic crocodile, but much longer."

"The elephant we saw three days ago bled to death," said Powell. "Its belly had been ripped open from underneath, pierced with a sharp horn."

"Yes, that's a very different way of behaving from what we have here," agreed the Welsh biologist, who took off his wide-brimmed cotton safari hat to wipe the sweat from his forehead with a handkerchief and also to dry his beard and neck.

"I would say these are two different animals," said the reptile expert. "The *emela-ntouka*, the elephant killer, which from the natives' description must be a ceratopsid that survived the Cretaceous extinction. This other one must be the one they call *mokèle-mbèmbé*, the one who stops the flow of rivers in Lingala language, a huge amphibious sauropod."

"I think this one is an aggressive herbivore that defends its territory from other large herbivores, such as hippos," said Mackal, putting his khaki hat back on.

"Schomburgk warned us about the curious absence of hippos in this area," Powell agreed.

Both men looked up and saw the scout crouched down inspecting what must have been a track. They looked at each other in intrigue and, without a word, hurried towards him.

"It's a webbed footprint," explained the scout when they reached his side. "Much larger than a hippo's, with three toes, not four, and pointed claws."

"Definitely a sauropod footprint," Powell hastened to confirm enthusiastically.

"The *Aka* call it a water lion," said Schomburgk, standing up. An authoritative aura seemed to surround him.

"They also call it a hippo-eating dragon."

"It's not a carnivore," Mackal disagreed. "I think that like hippos it must leave its resting waters at dusk, forage during the night and return to the water early in the morning. It's just defending his grazing territory."

"Mackal and I believe we are dealing with two different animals. The one that gutted the elephant and the one that killed the hippo, with two very different fighting techniques."

"Or maybe we are dealing with a single beast, with a prominent horn and tusks, which knows how to use its different weapons depending on the opponent it is facing."

The biologist and the herpetologist looked at each other in puzzlement, unable to come up with a convincing answer to support their hypotheses.

"But that would mean it's a very clever animal," protested Mackal.

"I'm afraid so," said the explorer without further explanation. "Over there, coming out of the swamp, through the undergrowth, is a trail. It must be five or six feet wide. It must have been made by a huge animal."

"Excellent! We'll be able to follow it." Powell was anxious to find his beast.

Suddenly there was a strange squawking sound. Like a good big game hunter, Schomburgk immediately raised his gun. Beside the hippo carcass, the pygmy porters stood petrified. Mackal and Powell looked at each other in bewilderment.

"It was just a bird," Powell assured them.

The squawk was repeated, now louder and longer, as if the animal had heard the reptile expert's comment. Now it came from a different direction than the previous one.

"It sounds like a frog croaking," said Mackal in a low voice. "To make a sound like it must have a vocal sac under the throat similar to amphibians of the *Anura* order."

"It's stalking us," said Schomburgk in complete tension. His eyes were scanning the jungle closely. "That beast is not a bloody herbivore."

All the forest creatures had stopped making sounds. After a few seconds of intense silence, the rustling of something moving cautiously through the vegetation was heard until it finally broke into a fast run and was lost in the distance.

"It's gone," said Schomburgk. "It's very clever. It's inviting us to go after it."

"Well, let's not waste a moment if we don't want to lose its trail."

"Don't worry, we'll have to persuade our pygmies to come with us first."

The three men looked at the porters. They were terrified, staring into the thick jungle.

Schomburgk spent a long time talking to them in Lingala. Many of them were fussing and tugging excitedly at their companions with the intention of taking them back. After a while, the scout said something that made them calm down and change their minds. They piled up the loads they were carrying and began to sharpen their weapons.

"What did you tell them?" Powell wanted to know.

"They say that after the monsoon the waters are high and the *mokèle-mbèmbé* is out hunting."

"But it's an herbivore," protested Mackal once again.

"Herbivorous or not, it kills hippos, elephants, and even humans if they get in its way. When it has satisfied its hunger, it returns to its home in Lake Télé."

"Lake Télé," Powell enthusiastically realized. "So that's where it's hiding."

"It's a desolate and inhospitable place, virtually unexplored. It is surrounded by vast, almost impassable swamp forests. It is only possible to get there after a long and difficult walk through the swamps."

"Will they take us there?"

"I've convinced them, but we'll have to give them the animal's head as proof of killing it."

"The head? We don't want to kill it, we want to study it," protested Mackal.

"You see, about twenty years ago, the Bangombe tribe lived in the Lake Télé region's forests. They fished daily in the lake by accessing it through the *malibos* or channels that connect the lake to the swamps. The *mokèle-mbèmbé* used these same waterways to enter and leave the lake in search of food, which interfered with the pygmies' fishing activities. So, they decided to build a series of dams to prevent the animals from returning to the lake. One of them tried to break through the barriers so they opened an access for it and trapped it between two of the palisades. The pygmies then attacked it with their spears and killed it after a bloody fight. To celebrate their triumph, they cut the animal into pieces and feasted by cooking and eating it for several days."

"We need to talk to that tribe's pygmies!" Powell exclaimed enthusiastically.

"That's the problem. Within a few days, everyone who ate the meat died. We don't know whether it was natural causes, some kind of intoxication, or because the meat of the *mokèle-mbèmbé* is poisonous. The tribe practically disappeared. That has made the lake cursed."

"That doesn't mean anything. Life expectancy in the region is very low," Mackal assured. "Pygmies rarely live more than thirty-five years. Their stomachs may not have been able to digest so much meat."

"As far as I have understood you, there was more than one animal," Powell observed.

"That's right, there were two young specimens. The other one has grown up and is huge; it has become very cautious and kills every other life form that might pose a threat to it. That's the beast we're dealing with."

"And how did you convince them to go and capture it?"

"They are not going to capture it; they are going to kill it with the help of our weapons."

"They want us to hunt it with our rifles?"

"That's what I've promised them. The *Aka* will thus be left with all this territory and can boast that they have wiped out the last *mokèle-mbèmbé*."

"I won't take part in a murder," said Mackal emphatically.

"You can turn back, but I'm afraid you'll have to do it alone."

"Roy, if that beast doesn't have a mate, it will die one someday and the species will become extinct," reasoned Powell pragmatically. "What difference does it make whether we kill it or not? We have a unique opportunity before us."

Mackal looked at him in bewilderment. This infamous plan went against his most elementary moral principles as a biologist. But the thought of returning alone through the swampy Likouala jungle made him realize that he had no choice but to go ahead.

Two days later, they were exhausted. They didn't know if they were closer to the damned lake or if they were just wandering around, lost in the boggy swamp. Every day they had heard the shuddering squawk several times, each time in a different direction. At no time had they seen any trace of the beast. Schomburgk, however, claimed that it was stalking them.

"It is it that follows us, not the other way round," he said. "It studies our movements."

Powell and Mackal could not quite believe their increasingly alarming observations.

Shortly before dusk they heard a terrifying roar that silenced the jungle. Everyone was petrified. Then they heard the sound of a large animal approaching through the forest at a rapid pace. The sound of branches snapping brought the men to their guard. The ground trembled under their feet.

Suddenly a mottled brownish-green mass appeared before them, perfectly camouflaged in the vegetation. With a terrifying scream, one of the pygmies disappeared with a bite between its jaws. Another was crushed by its huge body. Schomburgk fired his gun, but the bullet barely made a dent in its tough hide.

What came next was a catastrophe.

The beast was moving with its huge tail fully outstretched, but as it passed the group, it made a double zigzagging motion with it, sweeping the entire expedition with a mighty lash. In its wake, it had left a trail cut like a gash in the jungle and a clearing of shattered trees and mangled men. The monster had passed right through the middle of the group, making sure that its mighty lash did maximum damage.

When Mackal got up, all bruised, he could see Powell's burly body blown apart. He had been crushed against the trunk of a felled tree. His bald skull was bloodied and his handsome colonial helmet was sinking sadly into the mud.

The bodies of several pygmies were also torn to pieces. Some had internal fractures and others had a broken arm or leg and were barely crawling. Only a couple of porters seemed to have escaped almost unscathed. When he looked into their faces, he saw the terror written all over them. Without a moment's thought, they both fled without stopping to help their companions.

Mackal sleepwalked through so much destruction hearing the cries of pain from the few men left alive. To his surprise, he saw Schomburgk standing there, loading his rifle with fresh bullets. He seemed determined to kill the beast and to bathe even in its blood.

"We have to help these men," he said.

"They are already dead," replied the scout dryly, his eyes fixed on the jungle.

"There are several wounded," Mackal explained as if Schomburgk had not noticed. "We must help them before that beast returns."

"Have you noticed where we are? In a swampy jungle hundreds of miles from the nearest inhabited place. There is nothing we can do for them. They'll all be dead before dawn. Carrying them will only kill us too, and the beast knows it."

Mackal was dumbfounded. "And what are you going to do?" he asked.

A new squawk was heard that chilled their blood, much closer than they could have imagined.

"I have a dozen armour-piercing bullets. I'm going to hunt that beast down. You'd better make a run for it. You might have a chance." He finished loading his rifle and cocked the gun. "Good luck!" he wished him and walked into the jungle.

It was almost dark.

Mackal tried to help one of the pygmies but when he pulled him up, the wounded man began to vomit blood. He knew Schomburgk was right. He had to get out of there as soon as possible. In the darkness, he could find neither his rifle nor his rucksack. So, he ran at a trot back the way he knew they had come.

All the creatures in the forest remained in tense silence. The only sound Mackal heard was the sound of their mad dash through the forest's thick foliage, and it frightened him. His heart was pounding so hard that it seemed to want to burst out of his chest.

Half an hour later, a terrifying roar flooded the jungle. Mackal stopped dead in his tracks for an instant. It had sounded so close. Then he heard a gunshot and what he thought was a piercing scream. His blood ran cold. Then the ground began to shake under his feet. In the darkness, he saw the jungle thicket shaking violently and heard the sound of branches snapping. Panicked, he ran at full speed. He could be the next prey.

He ran terrified all night long. Then he walked all the next day and for another night without stopping, until, exhausted, he found at dawn the bed of a river he thought was the Likouala-aux-Herbes. He followed its meandering course. The days followed one after the other, all of them full of terror, tiredness, and hunger, and a fever that made him suffer from hallucinations.

Every evening he heard the roar of the *mokèle-mbèmbé* and felt the jungle trembled in its wake. The terror didn't allow him to sleep. During the night, his body shivered with fear and even his teeth gnashed. He didn't know how long he had been walking. It seemed like an eternity.

Some Congolese natives found him near Mosembe and took him to the small health center in Bouenela, consumed by fever.

When, days later, he told them his story and what had happened to his expedition, they thought he had lost his mind. The Congolese explained to him that the *mokèle-mbèmbé* was a myth invented by the Pygmies to scare other tribes away from their hunting grounds. His friends, they told him, had got uselessly lost in the impassable swampy jungle of Likouala in search of a chimera.

He insisted that the monster was not imaginary, but a very intelligent beast that had been able to wipe out such a seasoned hunter as Schomburgk. By day he wandered around lost like a ghost with a blank mind. In the evening, his fever would return, and he would huddle in a panic in a corner all night long, suffering from intense chills. No doctor could find a remedy for his illness.

Even years later, back in Wales, every evening Mackal still heard the roar of the *mokèle-mbèmbé* and, at night, a cold fever would rise as he felt the ground tremble under his feet.

Josh Schlossberg

Josh Schlossberg's short fiction has been published in numerous magazines and anthologies.

He's the author of the Horror Authors Guild award-winning, cosmic horror novella, MALINAE, editor of the multi-award-winning THE JEWISH BOOK OF HORROR, lead editor of the award-winning, Denver Post bestselling TERROR AT 5280', co-founding member of Denver Horror Collective, and creator of Josh's Worst Nightmare, where he surveys the dark landscape of biological horror fiction.

Josh's eco Jewish folk horror novel, CHARWOOD, will be published by Madness Heart Press in August 2023.

Fishers of Men

Cursing, Guy slapped the back of his sweaty neck. Hand smeared with drops of blood and flecks of smashed mosquito, he once again wiped the mess off on the thigh of his wool pants.

"One down, 'nother million to go," he mumbled to the swarm buzzing around his head. Low in the sky, the burnt orange sun cast spiky shadows through tall reeds on the stinking banks of the slough. Dusk was only a couple of hours away; this would make five days in a row he'd be heading home empty-handed.

Shifting his sore, damp rump on the cypress roots, he pulled out his pipe and matchbook from a pocket. He lit the tobacco, took a deep draw, and blew out the sweet smoke, the cloud of bugs clearing for mere seconds before crowding in again.

Guy's wooden canoe lay empty on the muddy banks. Twenty years ago, when he'd first moved down to the 'glades, hardly a day passed when he hadn't filled its bottom. Yet every season since then, game had gotten more and more scarce, where entire weeks went by without bagging a single bird. And 1901 was by far the worst.

Guy gazed down the clear flowing water, the narrow miles of channels mazing out to the estuaries of the Gulf. "They'll come back," he muttered over the pipestem. Which was, of course, what every plume hunter up and down the Atlantic seaboard had been saying for years. Except these days Guy wasn't so sure, haunted by old timers' stories of how, when *they* were young, the flocks were so vast they'd blot out the sky.

Guy drew on his pipe, but it had gone out. Sighing, he shoved it back in his pocket. Word was over five million were taken last year, though that had to be an exaggeration, just more gossip from those Audubon Society prigs. What was a fact, though, was no more good hunting was to be found anywhere on the north coast within range of the cities. And as of late, even in the wild southern swamps they'd become few and far between. But how else was a man without schooling to support himself, much less a wife and daughter?

A splash sounded not far upstream. Leaping to his feet, he snatched up the small-bore rifle propped against the cypress. And, as he'd done ten thousand times before, he sighted down the barrel up the lazy waterway, trigger finger ready.

It was a bird, all right, stalking along muddy banks on stilt-like legs. But feathers pink as the shrimp on which it gorged, only a darned flamingo. For years, they and the red-splotched spoonbills had been all the rage for decorating the hats of rich city ladies. But since trends sent pink feathers out of style, plucking the whole bird bare would barely put a meal on the table. And he needed more than that.

Just that morning his wife Mabel had reminded him how the roof needed fixing before the rains. And his daughter Henrietta, about to graduate high school and a true genius in the ciphering, had vowed to be the first in the family to go to college. Which meant he couldn't scare off every other bird in the area for such small potatoes. No, he had to hold out for the jackpot.

With a frustrated growl, he leaned the rifle back against the trunk and pulled out a flask from his pocket. He typically only took a nip here and there to forget about the bugs or ease his aching joints, but today in his misery he polished off half of it, if only to wash down the rotten taste of swamp from the back of his throat.

The flamingo stabbed at the water with its curved black beak, throwing back its head on a long S-shaped neck to swallow its prey, most likely a frog. Unlike most plume hunters, Guy had at least some love for nature, birds in particular. Indeed, he got a kick out of how that Chuck Darwin fella Mabel was always going on about thought they were modern day dinosaurs, a theory probably more science-fiction than fact. One thing for sure, they were beauteous creatures coming in a rainbow of colour, which he understood as the male's way to catch the eye of a mate. But what he liked most was how, if things weren't working out where they were, they'd wing off at a moment's notice — something Guy could only do in his dreams.

The flamingo strode out of sight around the bend, the sun sinking just above the reeds, about an hour from setting. A pang of regret as Guy wondered if maybe he should've cut his losses and bagged the lesser bird, while another part of him wondered if this wasn't his just desserts.

More and more those days, he'd been pondering on that three-day trip out to the Key West rookeries back in '85, one of a dozen men hired on by a well-heeled trader. A few weeks into hatching season, the wild swamps were full of spoonbill, egret, heron, ibis, duck, geese, and swan. Not having seen many humans before, the birds didn't fly off as they should've. So, it was a bloodbath, the air filled with gunfire, terrified squawks, and floating feathers.

They spent the rest of the day plucking their trophies clean on the spot — nigh on 1,400 birds from thirty-six different breeds — heaving corpses onto piles to rot in the hot tropical sun. One image Guy still couldn't shake was all the limp heads and necks dangling from their nests.

Guy took a long swallow of the buttery whisky and then another. It was a job, like any other. And what man, if he looked hard enough, wouldn't find something wrong with how he made a living?

Telling himself he'd wait another half-hour before giving up for the day, Guy stepped into the reeds to urinate. Soon as he was done, movement down by his boots: three feet of dark brown oozing coils patched in yellow. He stopped short as the snake unhinged its jaws on that wicked wedge-shaped head, the threat display that gave it its name — Florida cottonmouth — the inside of its gaping maw pure white.

Guy stepped back a few feet, but he wasn't panicked. Because, as with gators, crocs, and snappers, if you left them alone, they did the same for you. Usually. Indeed, with the safe distance between them, the reptile shut its mouth and slithered off into the shadows of the swamp.

Over the next few minutes, the sun setting like a blood smear, Guy drained the flask. Though drunk, the hour-long paddle home would clear most of the fumes in time for whatever hearty meal Mabel had cooked up.

As he slipped the bowline from the jutting root, a light spot caught his eye a few dozen feet down the middle of the slough. Squinting bleary eyes, Guy expected a gator or maybe even a bold and curious sea cow. Instead, his breath caught.

Only a couple of feet tall — unlike its larger cousin — with a long slender neck white as an elephant's tusk, a "little snowy," or snowy egret, stood on a rock staring down at the water. The whole reason he'd come out to that reeking, godforsaken patch of muck.

Best of all, it being late March, its lacy crest of feathers — "nuptial plumes" — spread tall in all their glory. The very ornaments rich society ladies killed for. Or, more accurately, dished out handsome fees to shop owners who paid hunters like him.

Heart knocking against his ribs, Guy snatched the rifle and eased it up to his eye in a single fluid motion. With feathers selling in town for almost $100 an ounce, more than the price of gold, bagging this one would take care of the roof, a year of college for Henrietta, and living expenses for the next couple of months.

If he weren't drunk and the light so bad, he might've taken the shot from where he stood, as the bird hadn't moved an inch. But when it came to little snowies, he had hit to dead centre or he'd risk spoiling the delicate plumage. So, he crept along the spongy shore, walking toe-heel, toe-heel, the way he'd once seen a buckskin-clad Seminole do. Luckily, the bird was still as the rock upon which it stood.

Guy drew in a deep slow breath and, smooth as aged sour mash, lifted the rifle and aimed at the bird's breast. As he hissed air between his lips, he squeezed the trigger. His aim, per usual, was dead on, and the snowie plopped over face-first into the water. Wasting no time in case he'd only stunned the critter, Guy leapt into his canoe, hurtled down the bank, and paddled over, the adrenalin of victory singing in his blood.

As he reached over the gunwales for the animal bobbing on the surface, there was lightning-fast movement from below. Guy yanked back his hand as a pair of massive jaws snapped over the little snowie, barely missing his left wrist. His first angry thought was, *Croc!* But the mouth, barely jutting out of the water, was too large and wide for that: almost five feet across, prongs hanging from yellow lips more like a hawk's talons than teeth.

Guy gaped at the thing, trying to make sense of it all. A slick mottled hump where eyes and nose should be, it seemed more plant than animal. The closest image his mind could settle on was a child's drawing of a Venus fly trap — but one twice as big as Guy.

The commotion having stirred up the bottom of the slough, the clear water around the boat was muddy. Except the mud was red. Reeling as if in a dream, Guy found his left hand clean gone, blood spurting from the stump over the edge of the canoe into the water. Stomach lurching, he almost vomited. Whatever the thing was, it had taken his goddamned hand along with his snowie. And he was floating back towards its spiky mouth.

Panic thinning the alcohol, Guy grabbed a paddle with his right hand, and, in a frenzy, slashed at the water until he was several yards upstream. Peeking back in dread, he half-expected to see the thing swimming after him. But it hadn't moved; it seemed rooted to the spot.

Though safe for the moment, Guy had to stop the bleeding or he'd die. He stripped off his belt and lashed it tight around his forearm above the wrist, then fastened the buckle. His numb hands felt ten feet away from him — pretty sure what the fancy doctors called "shock." To his relief, the blood soon slowed from a gush to a stream to a trickle. Small solace, as help was miles away.

And the thing's jaws were creaking open again. Incredibly, the little snowie stood upright and whole in its yellow mouth. Except, now that he was closer, Guy was stunned to see it had no eyes or bill, while its "feathers" were smooth as rubber. Because it wasn't a bird at all but part of the creature. A tongue? Or a lure.

Like a deck of shuffled cards, the faces of fellow hunters who'd disappeared in the 'glades over the years flashed through Guy's mind. Everyone, including himself, blamed crocs and gators or simple drownings after one too many swigs from the bottle. But now he knew. And strangely — though he hadn't been to church since he was a boy — a snippet of a Bible verse came to him, something to do with "fishers of men."

In a hot flurry of rage, Guy scooped up the rifle and brought its butt to his shoulder. Animal or plant, he couldn't let this thing live. But black stars swirled, and, lightheaded, he pitched forward into the bottom of the canoe, tipping the boat and almost falling over its edge.

Luckily, he was able to roll back to the centre, though not before the rifle slipped from his grip and plopped into the water.

Time to get out of there. In a daze, head fuzzy, Guy drew on the last of his energy to J-stroke the canoe downstream with his one hand. As he snaked around the bend, he braved a last look behind as the thing slowly sunk bubbling beneath the surface.

The maze of narrow channels through the shadowy reeds would've gotten most people lost. And in his weakened, groggy state, Guy did run up against a few dead ends. But years of swamp travel had etched a pretty good map in his brain, and, as full darkness fell, he floated out into the wide main channel of the slough with a feeble cry of joy.

Dizzy, shivering with cold, his good arm cramping, it was all he could do to keep paddling, but soon the lights of town flickered. Strength giving out as he slid into the jetty, Guy felt himself slip towards unconsciousness, like something dragging him down into the murky depths.

Six Months Later

Rain sheeting from a slate-grey sky, Guy hurried along the crowded sidewalk on his way to the general store. As he came upon the diner, a large man in worn leather jacket and pants strode out. Guy couldn't remember Charlie's last name but knew that rough red face all too well from the Key West hunting trip where they'd slaughtered over a thousand birds. Guy strode out into the street, ankle-deep in the cold gushing gutter, to get away from him.

"Guy!" the deep voice bellowed.

Too late. Guy stopped, and, with a sigh, turned around to step back onto the sidewalk.

"Heard about the accident." Charlie yanked Guy's empty coat sleeve.

"These things happen," Guy said nonchalantly. The truth was, he still hadn't gotten used to it. More than once a day, he'd reach for something in vain. And, at least a few times a week, be tortured by a terrible itch where his left hand had been.

"D'ya ever find the old croc what done it?" Charlie asked with a grin, a chunk of meat between two yellow front teeth.

Guy shook his head. Of course, he'd lied to everyone, Mabel included, about what had really gone after him. How he'd been snared by a creature that — crazy as the thought was — seemed to be using greed as a lure. What would old Chuck Darwin say about that?

While his stump healed, he'd vowed to head back out there to kill it. He wasn't sure if it could move around, but regardless, knew he'd find it if he really wanted to. Alas, a moot point, as he never mustered the courage.

"What're you doing for work these days?" Charlie asked.

It would've been the easiest thing in the world for Guy to keep lying. Except telling the truth might actually save them both a bit of trouble down the line.

"I'm a warden," Guy blurted and braced for the reaction. Which came exactly as he expected, the older man's mouth drawing up like a miser's coin purse, dark eyes squinting and hard. And could Guy really blame him?

"Don't tell me —" Charlie grumbled. And then louder, "Don't tell me you've got something to do with that blasted Auto-*bum* preserve?"

Guy cast down his eyes to the dirty water rushing along the gutter. In truth, he'd had no part in setting it up — that had been entirely Audubon Society volunteers. Including sweet Mabel, who, unbeknownst to him, had for years been raising money from wealthy donors to buy up over a dozen miles of shoreline.

Maybe it should've felt like betrayal, his own wife undercutting the very work that put bread on their table… but it didn't. Plus, she'd been wise enough to wait until the accident to tell him she'd found him another job — if he'd take it. One that might not make them rich but paid a steady wage. So steady that, despite the day's heavy rains, not a drop leaked through their new roof, with four years of college for Henrietta well within reach.

Finding his backbone again, Guy leaned forward and whispered in Charlie's hairy ear, "Picking up a box of rifle shells right now." Though not fully there yet, Guy knew in time he'd make peace with his new role as a "fisher of men." Especially since he wasn't alone in the task.

Charlie's red face turned even redder, and he spat on the streaming sidewalk at Guy's feet before stomping off into the street.

Chuckling, Guy moseyed on to the store, going over his list of provisions for the weekend he'd be out in the 'glades with his feathered friends. Not looking where he was going, he bumped into a slight figure under an umbrella in a lacy pastel pink dress. As Guy stepped aside, a shriek of outrage from the pretty young society woman, stabbing a white-gloved finger at the puddle into which Guy had knocked her hat.

Apologizing, Guy reached over and grabbed the sodden thing. On its white silk base an entire small bird was pinned. Its brilliant blue head, breast red as a glowing coal, sun-gold back blending to mossy wings with black tips, made it a painted bunting, a chirping songbird Guy had spied many a time in the thickets at the edge of farmers' fields. He held the dripping hat out to the woman, who looked sneering down her nose at him.

Before she could snatch it — and just before Guy, with a muffled cry, dropped it into the streaming gutter — the stuffed bird's black eyes rolled to pin onto his.

Erin Vance

Erin Vance is an editor and award-winning, bestselling author from Newfoundland, Canada.

In 2007 she won the Newfoundland & Labrador Arts and Letters competition with her short story "Something White." Since 2016, she has co-helmed the bestselling *From the Rock* series through all eleven of its volumes.

Her poem, *Rough Draft*, is featured in the Nelson Literacy 7 Homegrown (Newfoundland Edition).

She is creative, spiritual, and loves reading, writing, and anything to do with words. She currently serves as Editor-In-Chief of Engen Books.

Her first novel, *Exposure,* was published in 2020.

To Binky or Not to Binky

Thunk.

I paused from my typing, my ears registering the sound as important. I waited, because if it was what I thought it was...

Thunk.

...then Sarsaparilla would try again because I swear that they had rocks for brains.

I pushed myself off of my stool with a low groan of annoyance. I still had a dozen forms to fill out — government funding took a lot of manhours, hours that I simply didn't have — and hadn't had lunch yet because my fridge was full of herbs, greens, and vegetables; and quite frankly, I really wanted a burger. With bacon. And cheese — really greasy cheese that would melt off the patty and mix with the mayo and ketchup and drip onto my already ruined jeans... Yum.

At the end of the hallway was an open doorframe. And in the middle of the doorframe, was Sarasparilla, hopping once again into the frame with a low *thunk*.

"Sass," I called, with the long-suffering patience I had cultivated in the three weeks since I had moved here. "You don't fit."

Sass, my nickname for the very dim-witted Sarsaparilla, tilted their head up to stare at me. They struggled with the motion because the antlers on their head were overgrown, easily two feet tall and almost four feet across, and honestly were even bigger than their twelve-pound body. They blinked at me, and then tried to hop through the doorway towards me *again*.

Thunk went the antlers against the edges of the frame.

"Oh, for Pete's sake!" I groaned, striding across towards them. They saw me coming, hopped once like they'd been electrocuted, and then turned tail and bolted back into the large back porch that led to the yard.

"Oy!" I snapped, picking up speed. "Come back — hey!" I followed them all the way to the yard where, immediately, I became the centre of attention as roughly a dozen rabbit-freakazoids turned to look at me. There was a stillness in the air as they all registered my presence and then, as if one of them had whistled an alarm, they all scattered to the wind: some flapping their wings, some tripping over their own feet, some almost goring another with their antlers, and little Marakeet charging right between my legs, hop-screaming into the house with her single unicorn-like horn.

I dropped my face into my hands and did my best not to scream.

So, funny story: I'm named after *my* grandmother. Lots of people are — not named after my grandmother, but named after grandmothers and grandfathers and even aunts and uncles; and do you ever stop and think about the history of names?

No? Me neither... or at least I didn't until I inherited Gran's Funny Farm.

I always wondered about the name, Delma. I hate it, actually, which is why I've gone by my middle name, Anna, since I was six. I guess Gran wasn't fussy on it either since she went by Delly her whole life. Apparently, it means, like, "a noble protector", which is cool, I guess. I mean, it's better than this girl I knew in college whose name was Anona, which means "resembling a pineapple" — and, you know? When she was facedown in a toilet, puking her guts up because she did too much pre-gaming? She kind of did.

Anyways: I never really knew Gran. She didn't like to leave her home and had a lot of family that lived all over the world, so once she started visiting them, she would need to take, like, the full year to hit every single one of them, and then she'd just have to start all over again; and I like travelling as much as the next person, but even that's a little much, y'know? You think I'm exaggerating? I've got sooooooo many cousins. I'm serious: there's like thirty of them, easily. Gran had six children *herself* and then each of them popped out kids like...

Well. I guess like rabbits. Ha. Ha ha. Ha.

I mean, we talked on the phone, and did the Facetime thing — Gran was actually really good at the technology thing. Picked it up a lot faster than Aunt Heather, that's for sure — so I knew her. We had a relationship of sorts. She always remembered my birthday (I have since found a giant calendar on the fridge that has every family member's birthday on it (the calendar is from 2005, but dates don't change), and it even made my tiny heart feel warm with her efforts to remember all of us), and kept tabs on what was happening in my life. Never asked me if I was going to settle down and get married, which is more than I can say for my grandma on my dad's side...

But! Of all those thirty-odd grandchildren, I was the only one named Delma.

Yay. How lucky for me.

Except, maybe it was luck, because when she passed away last month, it turned out she had left me her, quote-unquote, "estate and all the inhabitants within".

No, seriously, that's how she worded it. My brother started making jokes about ghosts, and my sister thought maybe she meant the staff —

But no. She meant the rabbits. Or, well, not rabbits. Skvaders, and jackalopes, and wolpertingers. Yeah, try saying that five times fast.

It turns out that Gran's Estate includes a small house perfect for a single or a co-dependent couple, and then five sprawling acres of land. There's roughly a half-acre of lawn, another half-acre of gardens, and then a surprisingly well-kept forest for the rest of it. And all of this land is for her dozens and dozens of... really *really* freaky rabbits.

And, look, it wasn't easy being in your early 30s, okay? Buying a house was *expensive*, and rent was ludicrous, and, yeah, I had a job, but I didn't enjoy it. I mean, I worked from home, and answered phones and dealt with customer complaints and tried to understand accents and dialects, and got cursed out; and sure, I could stay in my pyjamas, but for what purpose, you know? What kind of life was that? I didn't like dating — I was actually crap at dating; people were really boring, and I was including myself in that, don't worry, I wasn't that narcissistic — and I didn't have a dream job, and my hobbies mostly included puzzles and binging the latest crime drama.

So, yeah; when I learned I had inherited a home with land, I just accepted it. Packed all of my things (more than I thought there was: why did I have fifteen pairs of shoes? I didn't leave the house?), rented a U-Haul, and drove to this new estate.

(I am not allowed to tell you where it is. No, seriously, I can't. That was one of the conditions; and I signed a contract, okay, and I can't afford a lawyer.)

But as soon as I arrived, I realized that there was a catch. There's always a catch, you know? It's just that, well, this catch was a little more cryptic than I was expecting.

(Did you catch that wordplay? I know; I'm hilarious.)

Gran's Funny Farm, her Safe Haven, her Sanctuary, is home to dozens and dozens of wolpertingers and the like. What, you may ask, is a wolpertinger? That's an excellent question because I have been here for three weeks *and I'm still not sure.*

They're rabbits… Mostly. But they're… more than rabbits. They're rabbits with antlers, or horns, or wings???? Or all three??? There's this group that lives on the west side of the woods that have *fangs* (I'm serious; they scared the crap out of me last week), and there's this singular one that lives in a shoddily man-made pond that has an *actual duck's beak* that Gran apparently named Howard.

If nothing else, she had a sense of humour.

And yeah, I'll admit it: when I saw the first one, I yelped. It was one of the wild ones on the east side, with a small cluster of antlers, white fur, and bright red eyes (albinos, I swear) — and it screamed back. Have you ever heard a rabbit scream? It's heart-chilling. The jackalope bolted for its warren and I thought maybe the couple of times I'd gotten bad weed in college had come back to haunt me, but no. No. I was surrounded by things that shouldn't exist.

According to Gran's notes — and she had lots of notes. She researched these guys; my grandfather was a biologist, and I found this one book with a bunch of autopsy notes and sketches that I closed immediately because, nope. No way. Not today — there were several different subspecies of these rabbit-hybrid creatures. Unlike most hybrids, who are sterile, rabbits are so good at reproducing that it doesn't matter what freaky things they are, they will have bunnies. Not as many as normal rabbits — these hybrids rarely have more than five in a litter — but more than you would think. And, like most creatures, as long as they are happy and safe, they populate quite well.

So Gran and Gramps (who died before I was born, by the way), did a lot of travelling in their youth, and I guess they came across these wolpertingers, skvaders, and jackalopes in their European tours. Whether it was curiosity and or the goodness of their hearts, I'll never know, but they took them and brought them to this estate and gave them a peaceful, secretive place to live. And in the decades of her life, they had flourished.

And now... They were mine.

The problem was... I didn't know anything about rabbits. My brother had a severe dander allergy, and when I moved out, all my apartments forbade us from having pets. The only thing I've ever taken care of was plants — and that *I* can do. I'm actually super excited about the gardens on the west side of the house... The soil is really rich... Could that be all the animal droppings?

Huh. There's a thought.

Of the dozens and dozens of these rabbit-freaks, there were a handful that Gran had domesticated. There was Howard, the creepy duck-one in the pond who flapped his wings at me whenever I came too close, and Marakeet who was roughly five pounds and liked to sit in my lap with a four-inch horn that wouldn't be out of place on a unicorn sprouting out of her head. There were Basil and Parsley, two rabbits with pheasant wings, each roughly ten pounds, and who could muster enough strength to get their bodies roughly three feet above the ground, which was just enough for them to see what food was on the table.

And then there was Sass. I was pretty sure they needed their antlers trimmed, but I had no idea how I was supposed to do that. I'd been trying to read up on deer and moose and how they dealt with their antlers, but they used trees, and they also dropped them every winter and grew them back in the spring; and I didn't know if it was the same for jackalopes. Sass wanted so badly to come inside, but their antlers didn't fit in the doorway unless they turned sideways, and they were... very, very foolish and wouldn't let me grab them because they didn't know me. They were skittish. I didn't blame them; I hadn't figured out the various creaks and groans of this house either.

So I spent my mornings taking care of the yard, my afternoons reading Gran's notes and struggling with the various forms Gran had bookmarked for funding, and my evenings with little furry freaks in my living room while I watched first responders deal with natural disasters. Marakeet was very sweet now that I'd stopped accidentally stabbing myself with her horn.

It's... I'd adapt. It was better than people cursing me out because their warranty's run out, right?

I got my first visitor four weeks after moving into the estate.

I'd gone out into town — there was a town about half-an-hour's drive away, and I'd made the trip several times already. That wasn't the issue. The issue was that there wasn't really a fence or boundary around my property. Of course, there also wasn't a lot of people living around me — I passed two houses before I hit the highway, but they were much closer to the highway than my place was. There was this very long gravel driveway that you had to go down for almost a full minute before you hit the actual road, and I wasn't looking forward to dealing with that once the winter hit, let me tell you.

What this meant was that people had to know where they were going to find my house. It also meant that there was a decent amount of forest between the road and my house, and that forest was home to lots of animals.

Not, thankfully, a lot of my rabbits. You would think, since there were dozens of rabbits, that there would be bunnies going to and fro all over the place, but it turned out that rabbits didn't travel very far if they don't have to. They had their warren, and that was their home, and they were very happy with that. As long as they had food — and since we were in late spring, that wasn't an issue — they stuck close to home. Birds came and went, squirrels and other small creatures leapt from tree to tree, and occasionally rodents darted through the woods, but the rabbits stayed in the woods behind the house as far as I could tell.

So when there was a knock at my front door, I only had a minor heart attack. I dropped the journal I was reading — I had found the one on jackalopes and was trying to find something on antlers and trimming them back for poor Sass — and almost spilled the mug of coffee I was drinking, and poor Marakeet leapt from my lap in a feat of horned-bunny panic. I looked at the front door, which I had used a handful of times when I first moved here and had since exclusively used the back door, and the incredibly cluttered entryway into my small house.

I winced. I wasn't one for cleaning on a good day, and I was still feeling overwhelmed by the new property.

There was another knock and then a, "Hello?" It sounded like a man's voice, and I made sure the journal and coffee were safe on the table before I pushed myself up to my feet and headed for the door. I kicked aside a pair of slippers, a shopping bag full of shopping bags, and shoved a three-quarters full bag of sawdust I had bought before I realized I didn't need to change any cages off to the side, and then turned the doorknob and opened the door, feeling like some weird lumberjack hermit.

I mean, my leggings were covered in rabbit fur and my sweater was my ex-boyfriend's with the name of his favourite hockey team scrawled in calligraphy, but that was basically the uniform of an urban lumberjack, right?

On my doorstep was a man and a boy. The man looked a little older than me, that age when men's hair starts getting thinner, but no one says anything about it, and very awkward. The boy looked elementary school age — one of my cousins had a kid that had just turned nine that was roughly the same size as this guy, so I made an educated guess. The boy had dirty blond hair, the man darker blond hair, and they had the same nose.

I made another educated guess: father and son.

"Hell…o?" I said, squinting at them. "Can I… help you?"

The man just stared at me, like I was a ghost or something. A few seconds passed before the boy looked up at his dad and hissed, "Da-ad!"

The man cleared his throat and said, "Uh. Hi. My name is Caleb, and this is my son, Jackson. I, uh." He pressed his lips together and the awkwardness settled over his shoulder like an ill-fitting jacket.

"Um. Well. My name is Anna," I said, because my parents taught me manners.

"Da-ad," Jackson whispered, tugging hard at the back of his shirt. "Ask her!"

"…Is this like the Girl Guide cookies?" I asked. "Do Boy Scouts sell cookies too? Because, like, I think I've only got a fifty on me, and I'm pretty sure that's too many cookies just for me—"

"No no!" Caleb said, jolting forward a little. "Uh. No. I, uh."

I let him stammer for another several seconds, before I looked at Jackson. He looked back at me and made a face like, *My dad is so embarrassing.*

I nodded at him. I got it. Family was embarrassing.

"I'm a paramedic," Caleb finally spat out, the words finally forming. "I... I was here a few weeks ago for an elderly lady."

"Oh. My gran." I nodded past the slight twinge of grief. "She's, uh. Not here. Anymore. Obviously."

He winced back and said, "Yeah, uh. I'm... sorry for your loss."

I shrugged back. "Thanks. She was cool."

He nodded again, and there was silence until Jackson groaned, "Da-ad!"

Caleb jolted again. "Right. Uh. Okay, I know this sounds crazy, but my son loves rabbits." I glanced down at Jackson, who nodded like his head was about to fall off. "And... I couldn't help but notice when I was here that there were, uh. Rabbit warrens? In the backyard? And we were just wondering if it might be possible—"

"Can I play with your rabbits?!" Jackson burst out, his scrawny little body almost shaking. "Please!"

I blinked. I blinked again. I said: "I don't have rabbits."

The thing is, I hadn't spoken to anyone for, like, four days. And I hadn't used my customer service voice in weeks. So... My voice wasn't exactly the most confident.

They faltered, probably because of the sound that

croaked out of my mouth. Jackson looked up at his dad, who looked down at him, they exchanged a series of facial expressions, and then they both looked back at me.

"Are... you sure?" Caleb asked finally.

"Yup," I said.

Jackson pointed at my leggings. "But you're covered in animal hair."

I looked down at my knees and my thighs liberally coated in light brown and white hairs. I thought hard for several seconds before: "Those are mine. I shed. A lot. It's why I'm single." I looked up in time to see Caleb grin a goofy smile before he did his best to compose himself. I squinted my eyes at him, and he looked away, mouth twitching madly.

Jackson did not look convinced. "Your hair is red."

"And?" Damn, the kid was smart.

Which is, of course, when there was a low *thunk* behind me. All three of us stilled.

"What... was that?" Caleb asked, rising on his toes to peer over my head.

"I dunno. Maybe a bird? They fly into windows sometimes—"

Thunk.

I cursed madly in the safety of my own mind.

"Twice?" Jackson asked, squinting at me from behind his glasses.

"They're very dumb?" I tried.

Thunk.

"Look," I said, waving a hand. "I swear, I don't have bunny rabbits here. Just a lot of trees and journals and surprisingly good wi-fi—"

And that's when Jackson's face lit up and Caleb's jaw dropped, and I heard the sound of rabbit paws on hardwood floor.

I pressed my lips together and slowly turned on my heel to see Sass hopping towards us, antlers proud and fur brown and gleaming in the sunlight streaming through the windows.

"Oh, *now* you learn to turn sideways!" I snapped.

"Dad!" Jackson whisper-shouted. "It has antlers!"

"Oh. My. G—" Caleb breathed.

Sass came to a stop about three feet away from me and tilted their head to the side... And then kept tilting, gravity catching hold of their antlers.

"Oh for—" I stomped over, grabbed their antlers and steadied them. "We really need to do something about this, because this can't be normal."

"I... That's a jackalope," I heard Caleb say behind me.

"Yup," I agreed, keeping a hold on Sass' antlers. "And they're very dumb; aren't you?" I addressed the question to Sass, who just sat there, apparently happy now that they had exposed themselves. "Yes, you're really, very stupid."

"Can I pet it?" Jackson asked, and I glanced over my shoulder to see him take a step forward.

"Wait, Jack—" Caleb said as I also said, "Uh, one sec—" and released Sass' antlers. As soon as I did, they turned on their heel and bounced back into the house. I took a half step towards them, and then heard another low *thunk.*

I dropped my head in my hands. "So stupid."

There was a long silence before I lifted my head out of my hands. I looked these two guests straight in the eye and said, "Well. Now you know my secret."

Caleb swallowed a little and then actually pulled Jackson behind him. He straightened his shoulders and looked me dead in the eye, suddenly more confident in this moment than he'd been this entire time. "You can't hurt him."

I frowned at him. "What? Dude, this isn't a *'and now I must kill you'* kind of a thing. I faint at the sign of blood. I'm wearing *leggings*."

"And fuzzy socks," Jackson added, poking his head from around his dad's legs.

"They're very comfy," I informed him. "No, I mean, you literally know my secret. I don't have rabbits. I have wolpertingers."

Caleb frowned at me. "Gesundheit?"

"And skvaders, and jackalopes," I continued, shrugging a little. "And they're not mine; they just live here. With me. They're not, like, pets."

"Jackalopes aren't real," Caleb said, still frowning, but looking more confused than anything else.

I pointed down the hall where Sass had hopped down. "Tell that to them. And their friends."

Jackson leaned all the way around his dad's legs. "Can I see them? Please?"

I squinted down at him and then crouched down to look him dead in the eye. "How do I know you won't tell anyone?"

He shook his head so wildly his glasses almost fell off. "I won't! I won't, I promise!"

I glanced up at his dad, who still look shellshocked.

The thing was, I needed the help. I was trying to learn about rabbits, but there was a lot to learn, and house repairs and bills, and I still hadn't figured out what job I was going to do to feed myself. Plus, the fact that Sass hadn't freaked out when they saw these two gave me the sense that they were probably good people. I mean, Caleb was a paramedic.

Caleb was a paramedic.

I pushed myself up to my feet and straightened myself up to my full height of 5'3. Caleb frowned down at me as I said, "Paramedics take a vow, right? Of, like, confidentiality and do no harm?"

"Uh. No, we—"

"Well, *you do now,*" I informed him very strongly, poking him in the chest. "Alright then, into the back."

I turned on my heel and heard a low *thunk* coming from the library. Caleb, behind me, said, "Are you gonna—"

"Nope. If I checked on Sass every time they walked into something, I wouldn't get anything else done."

I led them briskly through the house, a straight line all the way to the back porch and then the backyard. It was empty, which didn't surprise me. The rabbit-hybrids had probably heard the car and new voices and hid. Smarter animals than me, that's for sure.

"Welcome to the Sanctuary," I said, dropping my voice down an octave.

Jackson came to a stop right at my heels, almost running into me. "...where are they?" he asked, his voice hushed.

"They're shy."

Which is when Howard, the skvader with a duck bill, let out something that was a cross between a rabbit's oink (no, seriously, that's what it sounds like), and a duck's quack. I could not mimic that sound for you if you paid me; and I was getting short enough on cash that I would have if I could.

Caleb's head whipped towards the pond and then: "What. The. Hell."

"Yeah, he's a freaky little grump," I agreed, nodding. "Very territorial."

"That's... a rabbit... crossed with a duck?!"

"Yeeeeup." When he met my eyes, I shrugged. "Hey, man, I just inherited this place. I ain't no Dr. Frankenstein."

Jackson took this moment to walk out into the middle of the yard and sit himself right down in a patch of sunlight and heather. I mentally applauded his choice.

"I don't... But where did they come from?"

"Gran has a whole library of journals, but I haven't gotten that far through them. I've been trying to figure out how to feed them and how the security system works, and whether the generator in the garage still works."

He gave a begrudging nod. "Yeah, okay, priorities." And then: "Is that a garden?"

"Yup. I was thinking about getting a chicken wire fence; some of these dudes have fangs and I don't wanna deal with them."

He was very silent for several seconds. "Fangs?"

I pointed down into the forest. "I mean, they live way over there and don't come up here much, but fresh veggies might be too tempting for them, y'know? And while I don't *think* they eat flesh, I also don't wanna chance, like, rabies."

"Uh… huh."

This was, of course, the moment that Basil and Parsley hopped out from the bushes. Jackson gasped with delight as Basil, the brave one, bounded right over to him and prodded his shoe with his little bunny nose, his wings fluttering like a bird trying to nest.

"That's…"

"Adorable, I know. They're not great at flying. Kinda like chickens."

Jackson reached out and Basil sniffed his fingers and then hopped over to settle by his knee. Parsley apparently decided enough was enough and joined his brother, bouncing over to settle by Jackson's foot.

Within five minutes, Jackson was surrounded by about five other skvaders and Caleb was locked in a staring contest with Howard.

"Anna?" Jackson asked. I was trying to help Sass through the doors again.

"Uh huh?"

"You should build a bunny obstacle course so they can binky around."

With a grunt, Sass was free and bouncing across the yard, heading towards Caleb. "What's a binky?"

"It's the bunny version of zoomies!" He grinned, and that's when I noticed he was missing a bottom tooth. "We could make one for the winged bunnies too! Let them fly!"

"Kid," I said, rolling my shoulders. "You bring me

plans, and we'll see what we can do."

And thus, the summer of renovations and research began. Jackson and Caleb designed an entire obstacle course that brought a lot of skvaders and jackalopes into the lawn, and even some of the fanged wolpertingers came to the edge of the forest, checking things out. The security cameras caught them exploring late at night, which made me wonder about nocturnal rabbits.

I focused on the library and the garden, and soon had greens poking their heads out of the soil. With the help of a couple of journals, I started to trim Sass' antlers with a pair of pruning sheers, a centimetre twice a week, and by August, they could bounce happily through the house. Marakeet followed me everywhere and even took to sleeping on my pillow, leaving me with scratches at least once a week.

The funding came through and soon I didn't need to work, which was good because the forest was overgrown and suddenly, I was a real lumberjack with a colony of rabbit-hybrids following me like I was their captain.

"I'm a little worried about hunting season next month," Caleb said, sitting on a lawn chair and petting Sass who had decided Caleb was their best friend.

"Eh," I said, squinting at Jackson who had created a tent and was making shadow puppet on the canvas wall to entertain the rabbit-hybrids. "We have fences all around and security cameras, and I'm prepared to hit people with a baseball bat."

"That's assault. You can be charged for that;" but by

this point, Caleb had gotten pretty used to me.

"They'd be trespassing; I can charge them for that."

He snorted, and Sass let out a happy rabbit purr. "I'll check with my cousin; he works in the RCMP, figure out what your rights are."

"Thanks, man. I appreciate it."

He glanced over at me. "I still can't believe you just let us in your house. We could've been anyone."

"Sass chose you. And you did try to save Gran's life. And, you know... Who's gonna believe you? It took you a week before you believed it wasn't a really freaky trip."

"I mean, it still could be. I don't trust your herbs."

I grinned but didn't say anything. There may have been a few cooking incidents over the summer, but we all had to learn somehow.

"Dad!" Jackson hollered. "I need an assistant!"

"Coming," he called back. He lifted Sass into his arms and then plopped them down onto my lap. "Duty calls," he grumbled, before he pushed himself up and walked over to help with the puppet show.

Sass oinked once and then settled again. I scratched along the base of their antlers, letting them purr happily, and enjoyed the moment. It was good to have friends and a house and a fat jackalope, and a moon shining from above.

But maybe I should have paid a little more attention to Caleb's words because not even two weeks later, I was sitting outside with Sass in my lap, Marakeet at my feet, one of Gran's journals (this one about Howard specifically) in my hands, and, oddly, a faint beeping in my ears.

Oh. The security system.

I scooped Sass out of my arms and dropped them onto the ground, scrambling up to my feet and running for the house. There was an ancient monitor in the kitchen that ran 24/7, monitoring the boundaries of the woods. There was a wire that ran across the ground floor of the property that set off an alarm when a certain weight stepped on it. I flicked through the various video feeds of the many sectors until the picture landed on two men in the western edges. I couldn't quite see what they were carrying — I made a mental note that next year I needed to update the cameras, get clearer pictures — but they *were* still trespassing, and it *was* hunting season as of yesterday.

I shoved my feet into my boots, grabbed Gran's walking stick, shoved my phone in my back pocket, and took off to the west. I scared a couple of my friends as I took off, sending them hopping away into the bushes, wings fluttering and long feet thumping.

The good thing about my many weekly walks through the woods through the summer was that I had a pretty good mental map of my land. The bad thing was that there was four acres of land and no way to trek through the land besides my own two feet. Now, I wasn't out of shape but I wasn't exactly *in shape* either, and I could only run so far before I couldn't breathe. Normally I would have stuck to a fast walk, but panic made me scramble, and soon I was panting and slipping on the dirt beneath my feet.

Several minutes later, I finally hit the sector where they had tripped the alarm, and I leaned against a tree and gasped and gulped for air. I heard a flutter several feet away from me and caught a glimpse of tawny wings disappearing behind a tree. My heart clenched in my chest, and I pushed myself up and forced myself forward. My rabbit-freaks needed me.

I wasn't quiet; I didn't want to be quiet. I was just going to find these men and tell them firmly that they were trespassing on private property. And then, if they wouldn't leave, I was going to call Caleb's cousin, the RCMP officer, and report them. My land was considered a sanctuary for local fauna and wildlife, and hunting would cost them a major fine. But because I wasn't being quiet, and they were, I was surprised when there was a gruff, "Hold up!" and a clicking sound behind me.

I spun on my heel, using the walking stick to balance myself, and came eye to eye with an older man, probably in his late fifties. He had messy grey-brown hair and a hunting rifle aimed right at me. My hand flinched on my walking stick — I'd never actually seen a gun in person before — and then I swallowed my fear down.

"Are you seriously aiming that at me?" I asked; and if my voice shook, I had just run across three acres of forest. "This is private property. You can't hunt here."

He lifted his chin and lowered his gun a couple of inches. "There's monsters in these woods," he informed me, his voice rough.

I tried to keep my face composed. "Sir, I don't know what you're talking about. This is private, protected property, and you need to leave. If I have to tell you again, I'm calling the RCMP."

He pushed himself up to his feet and glared at me. "Didn't you hear me?" he snapped. "There's monsters in here! I've seen them before — they've killed people—"

"You mean trespassers?" I interrupted. "Which, again,

you are. You and your gun—"

"They killed that lady that lived here!" he insisted, taking a step towards me.

I frowned. "My gran died from a heart attack," I corrected him. "She was in her early 90s and had a weakness for bacon. It happens."

"No, it was them creatures," he insisted, taking another step towards me. I took a hasty step backwards, and then cursed myself mentally. "They give off these pheromones, see, and it messes with your mind—"

I squinted at him. "Sir, what the hell are you talking about?"

"And then you start hearing things!" he continued, waving the gun around. "Things like growls and bones snapping and—"

"Hey, Dad!" came a shout from behind my shoulder. "I found something!"

Right. There was two of them. Stupid Anna.

I spun on my heel and bolted towards the voice, with the crazy man right behind me. Within seconds we pushed past several thick branches to see another man, roughly my age with a thick beard, kneeling down next to a warren entrance.

My heart tripped up along with my feet.

"See, Dad!" the bearded man said, teeth white and gleaming. "This must be their home."

I straightened myself up. "This is *my* home," I snapped, stomping the walking stick into the ground. "And you both need to leave right now—"

"You don't understand," the Paul-Bunyan-wanna-be said, getting to his feet. "These animals are crazy! They tore into my brother's dog last year—"

"Was your brother trespassing?" I asked, now past fear and straight into full-fledged annoyance. "Because, look, I'm sorry about his dog, but this is *my land*—"

"They're dangerous!" Old Man Kenobi said, waving the gun again. "You don't under—" And then he stilled, eyes landing on something behind me. There was a moment's pause, and then he was shifting his gun into a ready position.

I turned around, and there, at the top of the warren, was Vader.

I had called him that several weeks ago; my gran had affectionately and respectfully named him The Big Boy. He must have been thirty pounds; if he stood up on his hind legs, his front paws would reach my ribcage. He was almost black, with large wings that made me think of geese as opposed to the pheasant wings of the skvaders. Atop his head, between his floppy, lopped ears was a Medusa-like tangle of antlers — not spreading like Sass' did, but knotted and twisted together like a briar patch. His eyes had a shine to them, almost like a cat's, and when he opened his mouth, fangs sprouted and bared at us in warning.

I typically kept my distance, giving him a respectful nod, and then continued on my way, keeping an eye on him but not approaching. Just the other week, we had gone through this same meeting, and he had laid down and I had caught a glimpse of much smaller wolpertingers binkying around past the hill.

This was *his* warren, and this was *his* colony, and now there were two men with guns aimed at him.

I did the smartest thing I could: I scrambled backwards and ducked behind a tree. I was not trained for violence.

A gunshot sang out just as Vader moved — he leapt down the hill and the bullet whistled above his head. He charged, fangs bared; and just as another gunshot blasted forth, another four wolpertingers emerged from various holes on the hill and pounced upon the Bearded One.

Vader went for the old man, landing right on his chest and taking him down.

There was a lot of yelling and yelping for several seconds, and I won't lie: I closed my eyes. But then my stupid heart got the better of me, and I opened my eyes to see Vader ripping a strip of skin off the old man's arm, and the bearded one sobbing in terror as four fanged and winged rabbits beat upon his limbs.

I gathered my courage and swallowed down the bile in my mouth. I *hated* blood. "Alright, alright, *enough!*" I snapped, stepping around the tree. "Vader, that's enough!"

The wolpertinger lifted his head, and with skin still in his mouth, he bared his teeth at me.

I waved Gran's stick at him and ignored my nauseous stomach. "Enough. If you kill these men, the police will show up, and then there'll be reporters and news vans, and the next thing you know, we're on National TV *and* YouTube. Or, even worse, TikTok."

His ears flopped down and he stilled. Beneath him, the old man whimpered, but didn't say anything. Vader drummed his back foot twice on the old man's stomach, and the four wolpertingers behind him (each roughly half his size) all stopped their biting and beating.

Vader squinted at me. I squinted back. "TikTok," I said again. "C'mon. Have some dignity."

Vader huffed, gave the old man another sound thump of his back foot (which, honestly, I didn't blame him for), and then made a weird sound. The other four all leapt off the younger man with nary a care for comfort (I was pretty sure one of them purposely bounced off his groin) and then darted for their warren. Vader's bouncing was far more dignified and purposeful, but I suppose when you're the Patriarch of twenty-odd wolpertingers, that's just how you hopped.

I waited until they were gone and then stepped forward. Both men were bleeding from various wounds and bitemarks and had tears leaking from their eyes. I averted my eyes, feeling my head spin at the sight of all that blood, reached down and gingerly grabbed both of their guns and then set them aside by the tree I had hid behind. Then I called Caleb.

"Hey. So... I need a paramedic. And probably your cousin. A couple of crazies trespassed on my land, and I'm *really* bad with blood."

Since Caleb was a friend, the questioning of the whole event was minimal. It was obvious that the hunters had trespassed and it was obvious they were hunting on protected land. While I did my best First Aid, guided over the phone by Caleb, taking a lot of breaks to just breath through my panic, I told these men that if they said anything about my rabbits, I would just leave them for dead right now, and let the wolpertingers eat them.

It helped a lot that when they got to the hospital, it turned out they were both high. Driving while impaired was another mark on their record. Win for Anna.

It was another week before I felt safe again though. I kept the walking stick in my hand anytime I went outside and caught myself counting my rabbits over and over again. I walked through the woods, checking for any bodies or blood, wondering if someone else had gotten in. I checked on the warren, but no fanged bunnies came out to greet me. It would probably be a while before I earned their trust again. Oh well. It couldn't be helped.

And then it was harvesting time, and my vegetable garden was finally ready. I spent hours there, with skvaders, jackalopes, and even a couple of the north-side wolpertingers (blond bunnies roughly ten pounds each with striped wings and baby fangs) watching my every move, waiting for when I would pass out their portion of the harvest.

In another few weeks, winter would be upon us, and I still didn't know what to do about that gravel road and my inappropriate car. I had a to-do list as long as my arm for winter preparation and was still unsure about Howard and his pond. Was I going to have to break the ice every morning for him?

The thing though, about living on your own in the midst of a Cryptid Sanctuary, is you could only take it one day at a time. So I would wash the dirt off my hands, try to keep the greens away from a dozen happy, hungry rabbit-hybrids, and ask Caleb how to run a generator. I'd check with Jackson on his ideas for winterizing the obstacle course and where the best snowmobile trails were, and call my mom, let her know I was still alive. I'd probably suffocate under Sass and Marakeet tonight while we watched TV, and then fall asleep on the way too comfortable couch.

And tomorrow? The sun would rise, the bunnies would binky, I would cross a couple things off my list, and life would move along.

Not too bad for an urban lumberjack named Delma Anna.

Jai-Lynn Francis

Francis is a behavioural neuroscience student at MUN. In his free time, he draws, writes, studies languages, and hangs out with his pet rats.

In 2021 he won the Mount Pearl Focus on Youth Literary Arts Award. In 2022 his short story, *Say Goodbye Before You Go*, was featured in *Sea Stories from the Rock*.

Verdigris

My name is John White and I have a story for you. Maybe you'll believe it, but maybe not. You might want to sit down.

I'm from Verdigris, a little town on the southern shore that used to be home to a booming copper mine. When the mine shut down in the year 2000, many of us turned to fishing and farming to make a living. I myself fished for a while, on my cousin's boat, but I could never get past how my stomach rolled with the waves, and the all-consuming fear of the dangers that hid beneath them. I mean, God knows what's down there. When I was young, the older folks would say all kinds of things. I'll never forget the day I learned the tale of the giant eel — sixty feet long they say he was! There's a lot of strange legends around here.

That being said, I retired from the fishing industry at my first opportunity. Now, I spend my days blissfully in Verdigris, with my two feet on solid ground. My time is spent with my family and friends, doing odd jobs here and there, and tending to my precious vegetable garden.

It started as a hobby, about ten years ago. Just a way to pass the time. It was much smaller then — just a few beds of potatoes, a bed of turnips, and a bed of carrots. But as my yield grew better, the more excited I got about it, and the more curiosity I had regarding what I could grow and how it could turn out. Now, it takes up the majority of the land behind my house, with only about ten feet of lawn separating it from my shed, and far less than that separating it from the greenhouse in the back.

I've now got potatoes, turnips, carrots, cabbage, lettuce, green, red, and yellow onion, pumpkins, beets, parsnips, and rhubarb. In the greenhouse I got bell peppers, roma tomatoes, cucumber and zucchini. Oh — and I got an apple tree. But that was planted by my uncle, many years ago.

But what do I do with all this? It's just my wife and I here, after all. Neither of us even eat cucumber or zucchini. Well, I keep some, give some away to the people I like, and sell some to others. The cucumbers and zucchini are for one of my daughters, who persuaded me to try growing them for her this year. I've been enjoying watching them grow though, I must say. I think they might become a yearly fixture.

The odd fruit or vegetable gets stolen, an example of such you'll hear shortly.

Over the years, I haven't had too many big problems with my garden. In its second year, an unseasonal bout of frost laid waste to the works of it. As disheartening as that was, I continued. Five years or so ago my crops got ravaged by grubs, but with some advice from better farmers than I, I was able to bring them back from the brink. I think these hurdles made me better at my craft, and now I feel I'm able to tackle *most* issues that come my way.

This summer, my big problem had been the crows. I shooed them away time and time again, but they just didn't get the hint. I wasted one of my own shirts and hats to build a scarecrow. It looms menacingly, arms out, staring in all directions from his post in the centre of the garden. But they use it as a perch, from where they look at the selection in my beds below, deciding what to maul next.

It was a nice hat too. A yellow-ish straw hat with a wide brim. It made me look the part of a farmer. It's ruined now.

I also heard somewhere that crows don't like reflective things, so Mr. Scarecrow was given a chain of CDs hanging from each of his arms and a tinfoil cap atop the hat he already had on. When that proved ineffective, I screwed aluminum pans to each fencepost, and scattered a few of them around the garden. They just avoided them when they're going about their business.

I wouldn't mind them so much if they just took care of the bugs — but no. They'd taken a liking to the crops. I was almost flattered.

I felt kind of hopeless. There wasn't much else I could do. Some people use a net over their garden, but mine was too big for that to be feasible. Well, maybe it was. But it'd look so messy. I went and talked to a few people around to see if they'd been having the same issue. Maybe they'd have found a solution.

They hadn't, and they didn't. Some of them had the odd crow here or there, like any other year in any other garden, but nothing what like what I was describing — which they had all greatly underestimated. I explained myself several times, but nobody seemed to believe me when I told them crows were the cause of all the damage. It was disappointing.

The fourth person I spoke to about it was my first cousin, Tom. I hadn't intended to bring it up actually. The whole thing was making me quite frustrated. But, just as to be expected in a small community, word of my crow issue got around.

He had the same initial reaction as everybody else. "John, crows wouldn't do all that."

I huffed. "They did. I'm telling you, they did."

"I dunno, b'y. You must got grubs or something."

I was tired of all the skepticism. I needed confirmation that my wife and I weren't losing our minds. I promptly told him to get into my rig. He was going to see for himself.

"I suppose I have seen a lot of crows flying around," he reasoned, following a moment of thought. I glanced over at him before pulling out of his driveway. His bushy eyebrows were downturned in a contemplative positon. "But why are they only goin' after your garden?"

"I'd love to know." I scowled benignly. "S'pose my vegetables are better than the rest of ye'res. Hopefully they won't ruin them all and I'll get to taste 'em for myself."

He laughed heartily. "We'll see."

And that was about all we had time to say, because we were already at the house. I fixed my eyes downward as I stepped out of my blue SUV.

The front window was open. The lacy white curtains rippled with the breeze. I could hear Lydia talking to someone, laughing. There were no other cars in the driveway, so she had to be on the phone.

We walked around the side of the house, and I could see a few of the winged beasts perched on the fence. I looked to Tom for his reaction but he hadn't seemed to form one yet.

We walked along the short, cobblestone path that started at the back patio and ended at the dark brown garden fence.

Many people I knew had questioned why I wanted to build a fence around my garden, when I set out to build it about seven years ago. Well, back then I'd had a dog, and while I loved him to bits, he was most definitely a terror. I didn't want him trampling the beds. Even though that had since changed, I liked the fence. I don't know why. I liked how tidy and put-together it made the garden look.

I unlatched the gate and opened it with a wide sweep of my arm, giving the crows a grand reveal. I quickly counted ten before stomping into the garden and making more big gestures to try and scare them away, while shouting, and using expletives. They were persistent. It took me running up to the last one to get it to fly off.

I sighed with vitriol. "See?"

"Mm... yeah. That's a lot of crows." He swallowed.

"Ten. That was ten crows just that time. See the leaves?" My eyes swept the scene around me. The tops of many of my vegetables were shredded. Bits of green were scattered all over the beds and the spaces between them. It was so disheartening.

I'd finally gotten my validation, at least. Tom's eyes were wider now; his lips parsed in a thin line. "Christ, b'y. That's pretty bad."

I nodded my head. It could be worse, granted. Most of my vegetables weren't touched. Their leaves being strewn about made for a shocking sight. However, it was getting worse each day, and I needed to find a way to stop the birds before they attacked all my crops.

"I just..." Tom looked about as flabbergasted as I'd ever seen him. He raked his lower lip through his upper teeth. "Why is it only yours? I haven't seen 'em, Perry up the road hasn't had 'em, and Bill and Ida put up a scarecrow and haven't seen 'em since."

I took my blue baseball cap off my head, smoothed back my hair, and put it on again. "That's what I've been wondering for the last few weeks." I thought back to all the suggestions of using a net and discovered another reason against putting one up. "If I did put a net up, if they're this determined, they'd probably just tear through it." It may have been a slightly biased opinion, but that didn't mean I didn't think it was likely.

Tom produced an "mm" of affirmation, his eyes studying the garden with an intensity that didn't correspond to the rest of his features.

How long did the silence between us last? And most importantly, why was it so tense? The whole thing was peculiar, but it was just birds and vegetables. I crouched down again with a wince to examine some more of the carrots. Some of their tops were notably shorter, and one other carrot had an unquestionably triangular gouge taken out of it, this one also being diagonal in the bed.

I noted his eyes again, just as intense. He was mumbling soundlessly, like he wanted to say something but had reservations about it, or like he couldn't find the right words.

"What is it, Tom?" I looked back at the carrots, aiming to confirm my hopes that only two had been targeted.

"B'y, I don't suppose this is the work of the Crow Man."

I blinked. I straightened up so I could look at him. I blinked again. I was trying to read his face but I couldn't. Was I supposed to laugh? "You don't believe in that old foolishness, do you?" It didn't come out as flippant as intended.

He shrugged. "I dunno." He swallowed. "This is definitely not what crows normally do."

"I know but... The Crow Man, Tom. Really?"

He grinned. "I mean, it'd make sense, wouldn't it?"

"But — that's not *real*."

"John b'y, you look a bit too frightened to be sayin' that." He laughed.

I frowned. I opened my mouth to make a snide remark but all that I produced was a choked noise, followed by a quiet, "I'm not *frightened*."

"Come on. You were — even on the boat when we'd talk about the eel."

"Yeah, I just... I don't know. I don't like thinking of how these big ol' scary things can be out there and none of us can really agree on if they exist or what they're like." I grimaced. "So I try not to think about it."

"Frightened."

"*Fine*. Maybe I am. Just at the thought, though. I don't think any of it's actually real."

"Mm."

If the Crow Man did exist, that could be an explanation

for my here problem. Some say he controls all the crows. But I didn't think I believed the stories. If they were real, surely I would have saw something at some point. I've lived in Verdigris my whole life. I've worked in the mines, on the water, and have lived and worked on the land.

Silence befell us again, though less awkward this time. Idly, both of us began scrutinizing the garden once more. I walked over to the turnips, watching my footing as I navigated the narrow paths speckled with green.

The turnips — not their leaves — but the turnips, what could be seen above the ground, seemed untouched for the time being.

The cabbages though, they looked great! I hated that "not being bitten or shredded" was my new top standard for my vegetables, but I smiled nonetheless. These green, leafy orbs gave me some hope.

Except one of them wasn't round. Well, it was round, but it wasn't a sphere. It was nearly two-dimensional. "Tom, c'mere."

The two of us stood over the remains of the head of cabbage, peering over it.

"Lydia cut off a head of cabbage?" Tom proposed.

"She didn't. And if she did you think she'd take the works of it up." It didn't really look like it had been cut *off*, more so like it had been cut *up*. It was like someone took a big knife and had jabbed at it until the top four-fifths of it had fallen off.

I doubted that the crows would have collectively decided to desecrate one single head of cabbage. I would have to have noticed them at it. But that would just be another bizarre happening explained by my equally as bizarre issue, so maybe it was their work after all.

Begrudgingly, I hauled the remains of the mauled plant out of the bed. Holding it in my hands, I got a closer look at the cuts made to it.

The leaves weren't torn off in pieces, like what I would expect if the birds had been tearing at them. The jagged spikes of cabbage weren't haphazard. Some parts almost looked like short blades of grass.

"It's not... torn off." I analyzed it with a grave countenance.

"It's torn *through*." Tom sounded almost weary.

We both knew a person with a knife or a bird with a beak couldn't achieve this particular form of destruction. We looked at each other with puzzlement and uneasiness. If not a bird or a human, then what? What could've gotten in and done *that*?

The nipping breeze of approaching autumn passed through my bones and for an instant it felt like my skeleton had been replaced with ice. I shivered.

"Looks like someone took a chainsaw to it."

It somewhat did, but we both knew that that wasn't the case. It would be less of a head of cabbage and more a pile.

I closed my eyes, not wanting to look at Tom, the cabbage, or the garden. Another pleasant thought came to mind. "If it was the crows... we'd *see* leaves around. There's no torn-up cabbage anywhere."

Worrying his lip with his teeth again, Tom turned around, doing a scan of the area. "You're right."

A few nights and one found-shredded head of lettuce later, I was sat at the kitchen table reading my book. This one was about wildflowers that grew around Newfoundland and Labrador. I was never much interested in flowers, but I'd been enjoying applying the information I was learning to plants I could remember seeing before, and ones I've seen since reading about them. Did you know that touching a Lady's-slipper's leaves can cause a terrible skin rash? I'd have to tell Lydia that when she got back home. She was out in town for the weekend, for our grandson's girlfriend's baby shower. I was told that I wasn't expected to go to that. She'd be home the day after next.

The crow situation hadn't gotten worse or better, meaning that they'd been causing the same amount of damage, but cumulatively the damage has increased. I was beginning to seriously consider putting up a net.

But right now, it was nighttime, and I was reading my book. The detailed illustrations and unpronounceable scientific names were a welcome distraction from my frustrations. Before I knew it, it was quarter to twelve! I smiled, satisfied. Sometimes it was nice to let time just disappear.

I stood up and stretched. A backache had crept up on me from being in the same hunched position for several hours. I pushed in the light brown, wooden chair to the similarly coloured rectangular table and took off my black reading glasses and laid them on its surface.

It was time for bed I supposed, as much as I was compelled to read more. I walked over to the cupboard and opened it, taking out a glass. I turned on the tap and put my fingers under the water. When it was sufficiently cold,

I filled up my glass and took a sip, as *I watched something big and green climb the garden fence through the kitchen window.*

I watched something big and green climb the garden fence through the kitchen window.

I dropped my glass in the sink. It hit it with a dull *clink.*

What — who was that? Who was wearing all green and climbing my fence quarter to twelve at night? Why couldn't I see their face? Why couldn't their face be seen? Why did they look like they were covered in leaves? Why were they covered in leaves?

Holy God.

It was the Moss Man of the Marsh.

No, no, no. This could *not* be happening. This creature was not real. It was just a story made up by the old folk to keep us kids from wandering off onto the marsh alone. Something like this could *not* exist.

Yet, here it was, getting its other leg over the fence, tripping on an aluminum pan, and falling on what appeared to be its face.

I was dreaming. I had fallen asleep at the table, reading my book. I pinched the wrist of my other hand. I definitely felt it.

I wasn't asleep, was I?

No, I wasn't. I quickly forced myself to accept that I was awake.

I ran as fast as I could up the stairs in the dining room to our bedroom, which overlooked the back of the house.

Time became fluid, and my logical reasoning evaporated, as I spied on the green monster in the lamplight through a small gap in the white curtains. It crawled on its hands and knees from the spot where it fell over to the cabbages, where it sat cross-legged in front of them. It opened its mouth inhumanly wide to reveal long, thin teeth that glinted under the moon. It leaned forward and took a bite of what looked to be a third of the head of cabbage.

They all questioned why I'd built that fence. I now questioned why I didn't make it taller.

I felt weak. Why did this have to happen while Lydia was gone? How was I supposed to explain this?

Seconds or minutes later when it had chewed and/or swallowed the bite it took, it took another bite of comparable magnitude.

I was trying to process this while simultaneously attempting to assure myself that I was losing my mind. Evidently, this was the not-human, not-bird that ate the other spherical victims. If it was contributing to the fall of my garden, I was going to have to take action. But what? What could I do to scare or attack this *thing*? I could barely see it from up here. I could see it and what it was doing but I couldn't make out some of the important details, like just how sharp those teeth were.

Sharp enough to cleave dense heads of cabbage, which I realized was sharp enough.

I needed to be brave, but I feared that I was not.

You need to do it, John. For the garden. And if I didn't do something while I had the chance, what if Lydia encountered it while outside? What if it hurt her? What if it went after one of the grandkids while they were out? The youngest was only six-years-old...

I took a deep, shuddering breath. I needed to think.

What did I know about this thing? Well, judging by how it got over the fence with relative ease, it was around six-foot tall. That gave it a few inches on me. It was clearly much more agile too. My chances weren't looking good.

Hands shaking, I took the flashlight out of the top drawer of the bedside table and put it in the back pocket of my old jeans.

What if something bad happened...? No. I couldn't think of that. I had to do this. For my family and for my crops.

I took one last look at the garden, grateful that I listened to my wife when she told me I should put those outdoor, solar lights in and around it. The scant pole lights just wouldn't have been enough.

The big, green biped was poking one of the chains of old CDs that I'd drilled holes in and strung together with a mossy hand. It seemed transfixed, its head tilted to one side.

Thinking of my family, I set out into the night.

I kept a wide distance from the back of the house, moving as hurriedly and silently as I could. Following the perimeter of my land, I made it to the side of my shed, the tall, green building keeping me out of sight from the beast.

I opened the shed door and reached in to grab my shovel which was just next to it inside. The creature appeared to still be incapacitated by the gleaming discs. I needed to take this chance.

Crouched over to conceal myself as best I could, with the shovel in one hand, I crept over to the gate. If I survived this, I was going to be sore in the morning.

It hadn't noticed me yet. Perfect.

I unlatched the gate. It came to attention. I burst in, wielding my weapon in both hands. I swung it back, threatening to strike. The monster took several wide, fast steps backwards before it fell to the ground, tripping over another tray. It scuttled backwards, kicking its feet until its back hit the fence. I approached it, ready to attack. It covered its face with its arms.

It was in that moment that I was finally able to get a good look at it. It was shaped like a human, but covered in a thick layer of moss, leaves, and the scattered flower bud, so thick that its head looked like a globular shrub. Its round, black eyes peeked out from within the foliage: big, with a ring of green inside. Its greyish skin could only be seen on the palms of its hands. Otherwise, its exterior was an assortment of varying shades of green and textures of plants.

The creature was visibly shaking. Its knees were up to its chest. It looked so small on the ground before me. Its breathing was heavy and ragged. I saw fear in those dark eyes.

My heart swelled with guilt. I found my arms returning to my sides. Look what I had done to this poor creature. He was so scared, fearing for his life.

Why was my first reaction to assume he was dangerous? He just wanted to eat some vegetables. Why would I treat him this way just because he wasn't like me? Or because he was something I hadn't seen before. It didn't feel good to be ostracized for your eccentricities.

I threw the shovel behind me. The thud it produced

made the creature jump. It became even smaller some-how. It covered its eyes with its verdant hands.

What could I do to fix this? Maybe he had the poten-tial to be dangerous, but so did I to him. But he needed to steal from gardens at night to eat. Throwing all caution to one side, I slowly approached him.

"Hey, I'm sorry, little fella." Little he was not, but in this light, he seemed that way. I spoke with the gentlest voice I could muster, making an effort to keep it level in spite of my own shakiness. Could he even understand me? I'd talk to him regardless, to ease my own mind if nothing else.

"I thought you were dangerous, I'm sorry." I could hear him whimpering. It broke my heart in two, as much as I knew I definitely wouldn't have been able to hit him with the shovel. He thought I would. That's what mat-tered.

"You're alright... but... you can't steal, you know? Stealing is bad." He finally put down his hands to look at me, but his trembling persisted. I pointed at the veg-etables and then shook my head "no". "They aren't done growing yet."

I glanced down at his unfinished meal and sighed. There was a third of the cabbage left. It was a wide, trian-gular spike. I gripped the vegetable from underneath and pulled it out of the soil. I brushed the dirt off of it. I took two more steps toward him and extended my hand.

He looked suspicious of me. I can't blame him. After a few seconds of staring, he leaned forward and took the cabbage. He opened his mouth wide, not breaking eye contact, and finished it in one large bite, aside from the hard part with the roots at the bottom. He laid this on the ground beside him.

"But that's it, okay? The crows are already taking my vegetables."

He still looked so pitiful, afraid to move. What could I do? I glanced around. *Ah*. I unhooked a chain of CDs from the nail in the scarecrow's horizontal piece of wood. I knelt down on the ground to be at his level. I handed it to him.

He held one end of it in each hand, bringing his hands together and apart, enamoured by how the lights caught the discs. After twenty seconds or so, he looked up at me and bared his pointed teeth in a gesture I hoped was a smile.

It appeared the tinfoil cap on my scarecrow had attracted an alien.

I smiled (back?). What now? I could feel a headache setting in as this event was finding its place in the organization of all my other memories and thoughts. Did I just kick him out now? I was still wavering on the thin line between existential terror and intrigue, and it wasn't even because of the green man himself.

If he existed, what else did? I've never thought myself to be extraordinarily intelligent, or the most well-read, but now I felt like I knew nothing. The world, even Verdigris, felt a thousand times bigger and deeper.

I tried to stand, but I wobbled. Curse getting old. I put my hand on the ground in front of me to try and steady myself. I saw movement in my peripheral.

Looking up, I saw the green man stood before me with his hand outstretched in my direction. Confused, I took it.

With a bit of struggling from the two of us, he helped me up.

"Thank you. You're very kind. I'm still sorry about earlier."

He smiled again.

He seemed pretty smart. "Can you talk?"

He made a funny gurgling sound in his throat that I perceived as jovial.

"Not English, then. Okay." I pondered this for a moment. He seemed responsive to my words, like he understood that I was trying to communicate with him. I'd assume that he could make sense of some of what I was saying. "Well, it was nice to meet you, Mr. Green Man, but I should be heading to bed there now."

He blinked.

I walked over to the garden gate, knees inflexible and aching from their contact with the chilly earth. With an upturned palm, I gestured for him to join me outside the fence. I felt kind of bad for wanting him to leave. He was trespassing in my garden and eating my vegetables right from the beds, but somehow he had endeared himself to me. I wondered where he normally lurked. On the marsh I suppose.

"I need you to leave now, sorry. I got to close up the garden for the night." I smiled despite my guilt.

He seemed to take no offense to this. He walked toward me with what appeared to be a skip in his step. Now outside the garden's walls, he presented me the CDs with both hands.

"Oh — no! They're for you, my son. I want you to have 'em." I shook my head, waving my hands in front of my chest.

He protracted his arms further, eyes larger.

"No, I'm sure! We don't use them. You'll enjoy 'em more than we do." I smiled once more. He was polite for a giant plant.

He regarded them with wonder, then hugged them close to himself, flattening the greeneries of his chest.

"Goodbye, Moss Man." I waved.

After a short delay, he mimicked the gesture with great enthusiasm before running off into the woods.

The next morning came too soon. I wasn't accustomed to staying up so late. I was usually in bed by eleven o'clock. It wasn't until quarter to one until I got to bed — and I didn't get to sleep until a long while after that. But regardless, I had a garden to take care of.

My intention today was to haul up all the weeds, and I wanted to do it early as it was forecasted to be hot in the afternoon. By eight o'clock I had finished my breakfast. I put on my cap and my brown boots. I retrieved an old plastic grocery bag from the front porch and left the house.

I was correct in my predictions. I woke up feeling like I'd been pelted with rocks. I really should have stayed in bed longer, but it wouldn't have been possible for me to fall asleep again. My mind was swimming.

Having accepted the previous night as something that had actually happened, I was experiencing a convoluted mixture of emotions. I felt wonder, warmth, curiosity, and a heavy solemnity when I considered what other enigmas could possibly be sneaking through the trees around my property at night.

But all that was out of my hands, was it not? I supposed I could convince myself to find some peace in that.

Now was not the time to panic. Now was the time to be a farmer.

The first thing I did was put the shovel back in the shed. I then got to work. There weren't too many weeds, but that was only because I kept on top of them. It wasn't the most enjoyable task, but it was a beautiful day! I pondered what I could go at once I got this done.

The beds didn't need watering, as it had rained just a few days ago. But the plants in the greenhouse probably needed watering. I'd have to check. That also wouldn't take very long, if it needed to be done. What could I do after that...?

My contemplation was interrupted by a tall shrub with sharp teeth peeking over the fence.

Instinctually, I jumped, dropping the bag.

"Oh J— oh, hello there. Beautiful day."

It gurgled happily and showed me the CDs, not once putting its teeth away.

"B'y, you know I said you could have those." I laughed.

He sped around the perimeter of the garden to the gate. He put a hand on it and stared me down, smiling still.

He was waiting to come in. What did he want?

Reluctantly, I approached. I unlatched the gate.

He bounded into the garden just to sit on the ground cross-legged on the other side of the bed I was tending to. He moved his hand along the carrot tops, watching them ripple. He didn't show any intentions of eating them, so why was he here?

Had I accidentally befriended a man-shaped plant? A plant-shaped man? Would I be upset if I had?

I had heard a few positive stories about the Moss Man, but those stories were drowned out with all the ones that depicted him as a villain. In this moment, with him poking his head through the carrot tops to smile at me, I decided that he wasn't a villain. He was just misunderstood.

I gave him a grin before returning to my work, yanking another dandelion out of the carrot bed.

He took up a carrot.

"No no no." I spoke calmly, shaking my head and waggling my finger. "These ones." I held up the dandelion, pointed to it, and showed him the inside of the bag.

He inspected the bed with a focused gaze. With care, he laid the CDs to one side and pulled a weed up. Eagerly, he handed it to me.

Be he man, be he animal, or be he plant, he seemed like a good soul. He had good intentions.

Before I could congratulate him, I became aware of the presence of unwanted guests. "Go! Shoo!"

Sensing that I wasn't talking to him, the green man looked over his shoulder.

The crows eyed me from the fence with amusement.

"If any of ye come down here I swear to—"

One descended upon the turnips, another upon the beets.

"No!" I shouted, as they began ripping leaves.

I didn't make it over to them as the Moss Man did first. It happened so fast. One minute, he was sat down, observing. The next, he was on all fours, scampering out of the garden with a crow in his mouth. The others scattered.

He returned a moment later with a pile of feathers in his hands and an innocent smile on his face.

A lot of things changed that day. Firstly, I'd made a new buddy! If I was a farmer, he was now my farmhand. Lydia just about died the first time she saw him, sitting down on the ground inside the greenhouse. But once she got over the initial fright, she grew fond of the green man too. He came around most days, and his presence was always welcome. He was a good hand to help! He knew which plants were weeds and which were to stay in the ground, and he knew how to water the plants in the greenhouse. Eager to learn too. I tried teaching him how to use the hose to water the garden, but he was a bit too clumsy. The soil got the least of the water.

Also, my crow issue seemed to have resolved! Lydia and I were delighted. She was very grateful to our new friend for keeping the birds away. I just left out the detail where he ate one.

Mr. Green — as we'd taken to calling him — was becoming a well-adjusted feature of our lives. And we'd only known him for a week at this point. This particular afternoon, Tom and his wife Irene dropped up to our house for a visit. Lydia boiled the kettle and got us all cups of tea.

Well, Mr. Green wasn't drinking tea. We'd offered it to him but he refused, shaking his head. Would he even have been able to drink out of a teacup? Maybe one day I'd find out.

Sat around the kitchen table, we talked about this and that. One of Tom and Irene's sons was coming down from Alberta to visit soon. Our grandson and his girlfriend hadn't picked out any names for the baby yet. Lydia had given several suggestions, but to her amusement, Kelsey wasn't too keen on any of them.

We heard the front door open and all of us in the room collectively stiffened. Mr. Green, who was previously content stood up next to the table, squeezed past my chair to stand in the corner of the room, back to the wall.

The person took off their shoes while in the front porch and as they turned the corner into the kitchen, the familiar sound of a cane making contact with the floor gave me a clue as to who it was.

"Hello!" Uncle George gave a big smile as he made his way over. He sat down at the head of the table furthest from the wall, furthest from Mr. Green, whom none of us had yet to address.

I was glad it was Uncle George. His story of the Moss Man was the only positive one I could remember hearing as a youngster.

Before we could, Uncle George took off his salt and pepper cap and regarded him. "Luh! A Moss Man! Where'd you find him?"

I laughed. "Found him in me garden, eating the cabbages."

"Ah, God love 'im." Uncle George's timeworn eyes creased with fondness. "When I was only young, a Moss Man like yourself helped me find me way back home when I got lost in the woods." He took the cup of tea Lydia had made for him in hand. "But that was a long time ago, and 'e looked different. He must've been your grandfadder."

Mr. Green made a noise between a purr and a chirp.

This prompted Uncle John to tell some more old stories, ones he was never reluctant to tell. Though I'd heard many of them before, I listened. Even if the story wasn't new to you, his zeal kept you entertained. During one of these stories, Mr. Green slipped away, back into the garden. I let him go, trusting him to know what he was doing at this point.

I wouldn't be able to say how much time had passed when I looked out the window and saw the Moss Man on the ground, shielding his face. More crows were behind the house than I had ever seen. They spectated from the fence, the patio railing, and the grass.

Before Mr. Green, roughly ten feet away, was a tall black creature wearing a long cloak that obscured its form. What I could see though, was the lustrous beak and the fearsome wings that jutted out from its sides through openings in the fabric.

Oh no!

I stood with a jolt, I turned to my family. "Stay here." Without a second thought I burst through the back door that was to take in the scene from the patio. I could now see that Mr. Green had a triangular dent in the leaves and moss on the top of his head. I could see red.

"No! Leave him alone!" I shouted, my heartbeat rattling my bones.

Slowly, the Crow Man turned its head toward me. "Be gone, hominid. This is between me and the Terrestrial." It spoke with a deep, rumbling voice without moving its beak.

"Well, you're on my property and he's my friend!

What do you want from him!?" I wasn't aware of this conviction I had, but I hoped that it didn't make chances worse for my friend.

It took two slow steps toward him. I panicked. He looked like he wanted to eat him. *Oh.*

"'E was just hungry!" A sad plea which was almost certainly not the truth, and not only that, it was one of the most incriminating things I could have said. I wish my mind had considered the consequences for a second or so longer before delivering the message to my mouth.

"He *ate* one of my brethren, hominid. I must exact my revenge."

Its foreboding tone had developed a tinge of melancholy. There was something else going on here, and I needed to figure it out for the sake of Mr. Green.

"I know, and I'm… very sorry for your loss. But he didn't mean any harm. He's a good young fella. You can see that, right?"

"Goodness is irrelevant. The Aquatic inhabits the sea, the Subterranean inhabits under the town, the Terrestrial inhabits the land, and the Avian have the sky as our domain." He turned to face me, and pale yellow eyes glared from under the hood. "But the sky cannot be inhabited, and therefore we do not inhabit anything. I intend to change that."

I swallowed, making an effort to still my quivering form. "I know it must be hard. Humans can be mean, but there's no need for all this. There's plenty of land here in Verdigris for all of us." Was this creature also just misunderstood?

"The assault on your garden is just the beginning of a full-scale attack on the town. One day, it will be ours."

"You… were trying to get me to leave by… destroying all the vegetables?"

"Yes." His poise and firmness had not wavered, and neither had his gaze.

I briefly glanced at Mr. Green, who was still on the ground, but sat up now. I tried to show compassion. "I understand that it must be hard. Feeling like you've got nowhere to call home, but this is our home too, alright? We can all share."

"Sharing requires having another individual to share with."

I thought. "Well… you're welcome around here. Just leave the gardens alone, please. Unless the crows want to take the bugs."

"Very well." He lowered his head. "But please remove the aluminum. It's *disorienting*."

And with that, all of the crows and their leader rose in tandem and flew off past the trees. Wasting not a second, I rushed over to Mr. Green and helped him up. Lydia and Tom came quickly down the cobblestone path.

"Let me see your head." Lydia lightly touched the back of Mr. Green's head so that he would tilt it downward. The grey skin of his scalp had just barely been scraped by a beak. He was okay, just shook up. "Ah, you'll be alright. But we'll need to clean it."

Crisis averted, I supposed. The three of us laughed at the absurdity of it all while walking back to the house with Mr. Green. I anticipated drinking the rest of my cup of tea, while trying not to acknowledge that the existence of the sixty-foot eel had all but been confirmed, and that there was some other kind of creature living underneath the town.

Adam Dwyer

Adam Dwyer has had a passion for writing for many years but is new to publishing fiction. After living most of his adult life in Toronto, he recently moved back to Conception Bay South, Newfoundland where he grew up.

In his spare time, he loves reading and spending time in nature. Also, with his nephew, he enjoys hunting for the cryptid featured in his story.

Incident On and Off a Blueberry Patch

"We should leave."

If it wasn't for the fact that she was in territory unfamiliar to her, Catherine Newhook could have enjoyed the low hanging fog permeating the blueberry field in which she stood. She always thought fog was a miraculous weather phenomenon. It brought with it a coziness as well as a sense of awe. While out here picking berries with her sister, Stephanie, the fog somehow silently crept in over this valley without detection from either of them. From where she stood, she could barely see Stephanie, who was still crouched down picking away, through the greyness halfway across the field.

"Soon," she heard Stephanie say.

Cathy realized that having her focus narrowed to a repetitive, close-at-hand task for a long period allowed her mind to wander and forget about her surroundings. Time itself seemed to have melted away with the view of the woodland scenery. Cathy unzipped her jacket pocket and pulled out her cell phone to check the time. But the first bit of business she looked at was the little number three buttoned to her WhatsApp icon. She knew all three were from the same person. She wasn't going to response now because she knew that it would turn into a conversation — one she didn't want to have in front of Stephanie. Also, it would keep her planted here in the damp air longer than she wanted to be. Presently her phone displayed a connection strength of two out of four bars. Next to that, the time indicated that they had been out here for close to an hour and a half. About thirty minutes longer than she figured.

She looked down at the plastic yogurt tub of freshly plucked berries at her feet. It was three-quarters full. She had already filled another tub earlier and stashed it in a reusable, canvas grocery bag, which was with her sister.

"Wow," Stephanie said, standing. A ghostly figure in the mist. "That fog moved in fast."

"Let's go. Before we can't find our way out."

"The highway is just over there," Stephanie said, pointing north.

Or what Cathy thought was north.

"The path is that way," Cathy said, pointing in a direction ninety degrees to Stephanie's north. "I don't even see it anymore."

Stephanie snapped the lid on her tub, then she bent down to fetch the grocery bag from the ground. Cathy walked over, stepping over the damp bushes, and handed her tub of berries.

"Awesome," Stephanie said, and secured a lid on the tub and placed it the bag with the other containers. "Thanks, Cathy."

"This was fun."

The day went better than Cathy expected since she

had wanted to kill her sister for the last couple of weeks. But she managed to put that aside today and joined her on this outing.

She was glad her sister was happy with their haul. Stephanie had voiced her fear yesterday that the blueberry fields might be well-picked over this late in the season. So, she'd chosen this patch because it wasn't a popular one due to its middle-of-nowhere location and the fact that you couldn't see it from the highway. Cathy didn't know of this spot before today.

Stephannie was the baker in the family. She made a lemon-blueberry scone that was to-die-for. Which was their mother's favourite, and what inspired this trip, with tomorrow being her birthday. And what do you get the woman who has everything (or, doesn't want anything, more accurately)? Her favourite dessert would go some ways to putting a smile on her face. As for Cathy's idea of a special gift for *mudder*: a gift card for her favourite store, Bed Bath and Beyond.

"Alright, let's get out of here," Stephanie said, throwing the grocery bag's long straps over one should and heading north.

"Shouldn't we go this way?" Cathy said. "The path should be straight down here."

"The path is too windy. This way will be quicker."

"Today is not the day to explore a new path ..."

"I've gone this way before."

Cathy wanted to ask her when that was because she'd never heard about any such a trip. As far as she knew, Stephanie hadn't been berry picking probably since that last time she had been, which was years ago. When they were kids, they would hardly miss a season. Into their teenage years, they largely opted out of such excursions. Now in adulthood — Stephanie, thirty, and Cathy, twenty-seven — the interest in local produce and homemade goods was rekindled. But these years demanded more time for work obligations and social engagements ("entanglements" might be the better word, Cathy would agree).

"C'mon," Stephanie said. "It's getting late."

She watched her confidently trot off northward with bag in tow. She was already half-devoured by the fog before Cathy started to follow her.

There was no clear trail to guide them through the knee-high scrubs. Leave it to Stephanie to beat down her own path out here. Cathy caught up to her and followed directly behind her. The bottom of the bag hanging from her sister's shoulder was brushing off the tops of some of the tallest bushes as she trudged through the thicket. Aside from that, the only other sounds were their footfalls on the soft ground, their legs kicking past the bushes, and the soft brushing of Cathy's own ponytail brushing back and forth on the hood of her jacket. It was as if the fog had smothered any surrounding noises from the woods.

They walked in silence.

Finally, Cathy said, "It's so quiet out here."

"Yeah, it's nice," Stephanie said.

"I don't even hear a bird. I don't hear the highway, either."

"Who would be driving out in this mess?"

"Us. When we get to the car."

"We'll have the road to ourselves, then."

Stephanie sounded a little out of breath. The trek was turning into a real slog, navigating their way around and over the bushy terrain on uneven ground. Cathy offered to take the bag, but Stephanie declined and said she was fine with it. She seemed determined to carry their prized ingredient all the way, from plucked to plated. Cathy figured that her newly single sister needed this. A new mission, however small. It's the small goals that'll get you through the tough times, she recalled reading in some self-improvement book. Not that being single was so tough. Cathy had enjoyed being a bachelorette for long stretches at a time. The trick was to make it look like it was by choice.

"How can you see where you're going?" Cathy said.

"Oh, it's not that bad."

From memory was the answer Cathy wanted to hear. Now she really wanted to press her about the last time she trekked through these parts. But she didn't for fear of sounding doubtful of her ability to get them out of here safely. She trusted her sister. But, as they marched on, that trust was being tested.

Tomb quiet again. A soft breeze was detectable only by the moving mist.

Stephanie stopped. Cathy nearly bumped into her. *What is it?* she wanted to ask but instead took a moment to register the look on her face. Was it frustration or confusion? She watched Stephanie staring at a cluster of taller, thicker torn brushes ahead. Barely visible beyond them, the branches of a fir tree, with its thick needle-studded fingers piercing the mist, reaching out for them. Cathy waited for Stephanie to question her own decision to go this way, which would be her cue to express her dissatisfaction about it.

But Steph said, "This way," and walked right.

"But shouldn't we go ..." Cathy trailed off, pointing to the left as she watched Stephanie get slowly swallowed up by the fog again. Between the reduced visibility, the damp air, and her sister's stubbornness, she was getting annoyed.

"C'mon, my dear," she heard Stephanie call out from the fog in a cadence mocking their mother's baymen accent.

She sighed, then followed her along the thorn bushes and into what felt like bumpier terrain underfoot. And onto a steeper incline.

She found Stephanie standing atop the short summit. She was looking back out the way they came, as if she could see the wild landscape past the fog that blanketed it.

"Look," she said.

The mist slowly floated by like a white cotton veil sliding across a pale grey, bottomless ocean suspended upside down in air. It was as if the world ended beyond the blueberry patch before them. The mouth of the path that brought them here didn't exist anymore. The only thing thicker than the fog was the silence. Stephanie was marvelling at this. The tranquility of it.

"It's like we're in a cloud," Stephanie said.

"Yeah. A cold one. We should really get going. It gets darker earlier these days."

And their way out was still unclear, at least for Cathy.

"It's not a good day fer some tings — but it's a grand day fer udder tings," Stephanie said in her baymen accent. Then in her normal voice: "C'mon. Just through these trees."

Once again, Stephanie led the way. They were headed northward, as far as Cathy could gather. Which felt like the right direction at least.

Upon entering the woods, there was a soft crunch to their steps as they walked over the tiny, dry twigs littering the ground. Here, it instantly seemed like night. Tall, wide trees provided a canopy. Overhead their many black branches made lattice work of the encircling fog, backlit by the last of the day's light.

"Shit! I can't see shit!" Stephanie murmured, humourlessly.

"We can't go this way," Cathy said. "Let's go back."

"C'mon — it'll be fun. This is the worst of it."

"Steph! This is stupid. We've never gone this way before."

"I have."

Cathy thought that she might be lying. But she kept her rebuttal practical: "Not in this mess. Not in the dark."

"The highway is on the other side of this …"

"Are you sure?"

"Yes."

Stephanie didn't sound convincing. But Cathy wanted her to be right badly enough that she continued to follow her.

They walked around an old birch tree. Its exposed root system sloped down into the ground and became a tripping hazard. They ducked beneath its long branches and pushed back on the thin, lower branches of a neigh-bouring tree. As Stephanie plowed through these bushy, flexible bows, Cathy slowed her pace to avoid getting whipped by them. On the other side of this, they walked into a small clearing, one with no obvious path forward, but Stephanie continued straight ahead, nonetheless.

They were surrounded by thick, black trunks disap-pearing up into mist. It was dreamlike. Perhaps, Cathy thought, a fairy would come out of the woods and lead them out of here. Then she remembered the folklore she'd heard of fairies in Newfoundland were about fiendish, little tricksters that did just the opposite — they lured people out into the woods and left them to be hopelessly lost. She also recalled her grandmother saying that there weren't more stories of fairies because most of those who encountered them were never found again. She started imagining if they never made it back to civilization what legend would be made of them...

Stephanie stumbled halfway across the clearing and cursed the ground.

"What the ...?!" she said, looking down at a red-slicked, brown hiking boot.

Then she realized that she had accidentally kicked the carcass of a small, dead animal. It was half-buried in loose dirt and dead leaves.

"Oh my God!" Cathy exclaimed.

"Gross!" Stephanie said, trying to wipe her boot off on the black, mulchy soil.

"What is it? A rabbit?"

A closer look confirmed that. The only characteristic that identified the type of animal was its head: its long ears lay flat to the ground like wet leaves. Its body had been gutted. Ribbons of torn innards were strung out on the ground from a shattered rib cage. Pale pink flesh at the wound curled back into grey fur, caked with gore and dirt.

Cathy murmured, "What did this?"

Stephanie set down the grocery bag, reached into her inside coat pocket for a packet of facial tissues, and knelt to wipe off as much of the blood from her boot as she could.

"A cat?" she speculated. "There are feral cats every-where."

"Must've been a big cat," Cathy said. "Maybe it was a coyote."

"There's no coyotes on this part of the island."

"Oh, I've heard of it."

"Maybe it was an eagle. Swooped down, tore into it, and dropped it here."

"In this fog? Because that looks fresh."

Unvoiced guesses included a wild fox, a rabid dog, a lynx, a black bear (although, the last two were highly un-likely)... Cathy didn't want to spend too much time think-ing about what could be lurking around here.

"I'm not going any farther," she said. "Not in there. Let's go back the way we came. It might take longer, but it'll be easier to find our way out."

Stephanie's frustration boiled over as she threw a third reddened tissue on the ground. "You know, we wouldn't be in this mess if we got out here earlier — like a month ago — when I wanted to do this. You had to push it to the last minute. The day before—"

"How did I know—?"

"—we needed these berries. No, no — you do this all the time. I just don't know what your excuse is these days. Before it was Paul but since you two—"

"This time is no different," Cathy stopped her.

"What? You're seeing someone?"

Cathy nodded, yes, looking down at her Timberlands.

"Who?" her sister asked.

"Paul."

Cathy found the whites of Stephanie's eyes in the gloominess and watched them widen upon hearing the answer. This wasn't the best time or place to have this conversation, nor was she presently in the best mood to deal with what fallout may come of it.

"How long?"

"About six weeks," Cathy said, knowing it has been six and a half weeks. She watched Stephanie doing the math in her head. Then she added: "We're getting married."

She studied Stephanie's reaction. Her mouth was agape as she searched for words.

That was telling enough for Cathy. She turned to walk out of the woods.

Finally, Stephanie said: "… engaged? When did this happen?"

"A week ago," Cathy said, disappearing back around the old birch tree.

"Why didn't you tell me?" Stephanie asked, and snatched up the canvas bag of containers and followed her.

On the other side of the tree, continuing back through

the thicket, Cathy said, "I was waiting until I had a ring." It wasn't the whole truth but believable enough.

Stephanie caught up to her. "You didn't tell me because you knew I'd have something to say about it."

"Why would you have any objections about this?" Cathy said, keeping her sister behind her on this walk. "Because you don't like him? Or because you want him for yourself?"

Cathy let a branch swing back on her.

Whap!

"God, no!" Stephanie said. "It's just that you two never seem to stay together for more than …"

Cathy stopped walking, turned toward her sister, and said, "You know how I know it's different this time? Because he told me about the two of you." She let that hang between them for a moment. Then she continued: "No one is hiding anything anymore. We're good — never better — Paul and me." She turned away and resumed retracing their path back to the blueberry patch through the mist.

"Cathy, I didn't know you were still talking to him," Stephanie said, defending the unsaid accusation, as she chased her.

Reaching the edge of the field, Cathy stopped again to recite a line from memory. "'She doesn't deserve you!' Was that what the text said?"

Stephanie looked pallid when she stopped next to her. "Yeah, as in, you don't deserve a scumbag like him."

"That's not—" Cathy caught herself from falling into what she knew would become one of their circular arguments where they got nowhere. "I'm sick of your bullshit! You always have an answer for everything. You'll never admit to being wrong or that you were ever wrong. Like now, you know this isn't best way for us to go. We're not familiar with this area. The smart thing to do would have been to—"

"We were almost there," Stephanie interrupted.

"Doesn't feel like it. Going straight through the bushes, Steph? I'm friggin' soaked!"

"Sorry for trying to get us outta here before dark. I'm sorry you saw a dead bunny rabbit…."

"I'm sorry you have to live in your little sister's shadow. That I figured out my shit before you did. That must be tough for you. What other course of action could you take than try to blow it all up?"

"Really?"

"If you change your attitude, I would love for you to be a bridesmaid."

Stephanie squinted her green eyes, trying to read her countenance for sincerity.

"Don't let a guy come between us," she said, and started shaking her head, no. "Not him. Not Paul."

Cathy drew a deep breath to shout, but let it out in a long, slow exhale. Then, pointing back the way they came, she said, "I'm going this way." She headed back into the field.

"Cathy, don't be stubborn. We'll talk about this later. C'mon…" Stephanie waved for her to come back.

But Cathy was already walking away into the mist. "You go that way and let's see who gets back to the car first."

Cathy wanted to walk faster but the fog kept her pace at a careful stroll. She listened for Stephanie's footsteps behind her. But there was nothing.

Then Stephanie called out: "We'll talk later!" After a beat, she added: "Congratulations!" It sounded like a plea.

Then there was the faint swish of bows off Stephanie's nylon jacket. She really was going to cut through those woods. *Good luck with the feral cats*, Cathy thought.

She had a lot of time to think while out here picking berries. Earlier it had been mostly about her future with Paul: when they would get married, where they would live, when to start having children, do they even want children… When to tell her sister, her mother, and the rest of the world about her engagement was not among the questions running through her mind. She had convinced herself over the last few weeks that she didn't really care what her family — specifically her sister — thought of her romantic relationships. But the truth was she just got proficient at blocking that noise out; she became a master of deflection when it came to personal matters. Working as an assistant property manager for a set of three apartment complexes gave her great education in the art of the political answer — that is, the ability to address a question without answering it. The skill enabled her to buy time on an issue — to kick it down the road, as the saying went. Sometimes that time was long enough for the complainant to lose their steam on the matter. Any objections her family may have of her choice of a mate would in time, she figured, become less about *who* and more about *when*. On the topic of settling down, she was twenty-one when she first heard her mother say, *You're not gettin' any younger*, suggesting she was running out of time before she was unsuitable for marriage or motherhood. She knew the pressure on getting hitched from Stephanie would be pulling in the opposite direction *(Don't rush into this ... Are you sure you're ready to make this commitment? ... Marriage is not for everyone)*. She could only imagine what discourse Stephanie would come up with on the forty-five-minute drive back to her house.

She was in no rush to get back to the car. She was happy that her sister chose not to follow her back through the blueberry field. It was a much needed break from her after that argument. It had stirred up images of her older sister with Paul and it was a reminder of the fact that those hookups occurred not too long ago. During a time when she was still with him; albeit, not happily, but they were working on it. The peace and quiet now on her stroll across the field would do her some good to clear her mind of those thoughts again.

She had been walking long enough now in the silence that she felt alone out here. The featureless fog before her offered no direction or safety. Her confidence in that this was the better way out of here was starting to crack as well. The comfort knowing that the path she chose provided more daylight than the woods was lost in the atmosphere. Moreover, the blueberry shrubs scuffing her feet all seemed indistinguishable from each other. The unmarked geography as well as the poor visibility conspired to slow her pace even further. While she treaded carefully, she still stumbled on the uneven, weed-studded ground from time to time. She wanted to make a turn but forced herself to stay the course. She tried to walk the straightest line she could for fear of walking in circles. She wasn't in a hurry but the thought of getting lost in the woods was as much embarrassing as it was terrifying.

Put one foot in front of the other and sooner or later you'll hit the edge of the woods and find the original path, Cathy thought. *Girl, you got this!*

Although, she felt like she should have reached the bottom of the valley by now. She was still drifting through the white-grey mist with no sense of an end to this walk. It was disorienting.

She had a frightening thought: because she could barely see beyond two body lengths in front of her, she could very easily walk off a cliff or into a large body of water if she had to come to the edge of either one of those. The thought of falling brought her to a halt. She took a beat to tell herself she was letting her imagination get the better of reason. Of course, she was nowhere near a pond or a cliff; she wasn't that far off the path on which they journeyed here. She was just moving slower than she desired, which was contributing to her frustration. She wanted to go home and for this day to end.

The light was changing: the sun was creeping down behind the treeline. Not that she could see it, but the signifier was the golden haze that was filtering through the fog. It was beautiful, she had to note, in spite the circumstances.

Snap!

A branch cracked.

It came from her left.

It didn't sound like it was that far away, either. How

close was she to the adjacent patch of woods along which she traveling? Had she gone that far off course? She should be closer to the group of trees to the west, not the south. Perhaps she got turned around amidst the fog and her daydreaming and that this was indeed the westward direction.

But her bigger concern now was: what had made that branch break? It didn't sound like a tiny, dry stick, either. What kind of animal was roaming the nearby woods? The rabbit killer? The elusive coyote? But she quickly dismissed that creature as the "snapper" because it seemed too dainty for such force. Any birds were also crossed off as suspects. She came to the idea that this could be another human being. Surely, it was not Stephanie; she would still be on the other side of this field. If she was correct after all, she might be as far as the road by now. Perhaps there was another lost forager out here. Better yet, a hunter. Was it hunting season? Were these even hunting grounds? She didn't know. She was just hoping to a meet trusty guide to help her exit this place.

But her fight-or-flight instinct kicked in and told her to prepare for an unfriendly encounter. Whether man or beast, what did she have with which to defend yourself? Nothing more than her fists. And her legs. Perhaps she could outrun a man but something on more than two legs? Not a chance. She could find a rock and conceal it in her coat pocket and use it to bash a head in, if it came to that. She crouched down to search the ground before her for a suitable weapon. This field offered little in the way of palm-sized rocks. Her hands felt over pebbles — suitable for throwing but with her aim and force it would be a terrible defensive plan — and a boulder embedded in the earth. She heard some rustling ahead and shot her head up to look ahead and discovered that the visibility low to the ground allowed her to see much farther than eye level. She could see the edge of the woods — a thin wall of trees separating this valley from the one beyond. The trunks of the trees looked like black posts against the white fog beyond them, randomly placed and of various sizes.

Then one of the trunks shifted.

Cathy realized that it was a part of a set of two legs. Someone very tall was standing there. In wide-legged pants, possibly.

She heard a deep, hoarse huffing sound from the man. Which caused to her question if this thing was a bear, reaching up into a tree on its hind legs. But the legs were too long for a bear.

Then she saw a hand drop down to its side. A hand, not a paw. This should be a relief to her. A fellow human nearby — however friendly — instead of the unpredictability of a large, wild animal. But she stared hard through the haze and concluded that the hand did not look human. As hard as it was to believe in this part of the world, the hand looked ape-like.

Gorillas in the Mist, she joked to herself. She didn't dare giggle aloud. Although, it would have been a welcomed tension-breaker, but she still didn't know what she was dealing with here: friend or foe.

The hand indeed was furry. Attached to a furrier arm. No jacket or shirt sleeve. She was certain now she was not dealing with a man.

So much for finding help.

Just stay perfectly still and silent.

She tried to get herself even lower to the ground, using the shrubs around her as cover in addition to the fog cloaking the field. The most difficult part of staying hidden was trying to keep her breathing controlled and heartbeat steady. The latter was a soft thundering in her ears as she tried to listen closely for any movements.

Her curiosity matched her terror. She raised her head to peek over the bush in front of her to get a look at the creature and determine its kind. She quickly realized the fog wasn't going to let her see the upper part of this thing. Maybe it would make a distinctive sound. She continued to watch and listen.

The thing was still reaching up into the tree and was preoccupied with a finding. It pulled down a branch — wood creaking, leaves rustling.

Then something fell out of the tree and hit the ground with a soft thud. Cathy figured it was a bird's nest.

How tall was this brute? she wondered.

She watched the thing crouch down to pick up its prize off the ground. The man-like creature was indeed completely covered in fur — medium-length, shaggy brown-black hair, like that of a mangy ape. Also, like a primate, the palms of its hand and around its mouth and eyes looked leathery and hairless. Moreover, its facial structure appeared flattened above a cleft chin and under a sloped forehead leading back to the bowl of its skull. The most remarkable characteristic about the ape-thing was its size. Even in a squat position, she could tell it was very tall — taller than any man she had ever seen in real life. Seven to eight feet tall, she guessed. Her heart was raced a little faster at the thought of getting caught by this thing. What would it do to her? Tear her up like the rabbit?!

Stop staring.

She lowered her head back down behind the bushes. She feared that the creature would feel her scrutiny and detect her hiding spot amid the shrubbery. All she could do now was pray that the creature didn't happen to walk her way.

She listened for footsteps.

Quiet.

A soft rustling.

A faint crunch.

The thing was still foraging in that spot.

A wild thought occurred to her: if only she could get a picture of this thing. Words alone would make her sound crazy no matter how convincing her performance. But a picture — or, better yet, a video — of it would go a long way to squashing any denial of her claims. She felt her iPhone in her jacket pocket, which she had zipped up for safe keeping while out here bending and crouching for berries. Normally, she kept it in her back pocket of her jeans, which would have granted much easier access now. She felt it was too quiet to covertly unzip her coat pocket.

She raised her head again to see if the creature had moved on …

It was still there. Apparently, the nest provided some protein for the ape-man to munch on. This animal was hungry — being in proximity to a berry patch, the freshly killed rabbit, raiding a bird's nest … She did not want to be added to the buffet today. She lowered back down to the ground.

"What is love?..."

The opening line and title of the song she used for Paul's ringtone sounded off in her coat pocket.

"Baby, don't hurt me..."

She frantically scrambled to zip open her pocket, pulled out her smartphone ...

"...don't hurt—"

And swiped the screen left to ignore the call and silence the ring. A shaky finger tapped the screen twice to put the phone on silent mode. She glanced at the picture of a smiling Paul before it faded to the home screen of icons.

Frightened, she spied over the bushes to see if the creature had heard it, too.

It was indeed looking in her direction, frozen in its crouched position.

Cathy was hoping it would retreat deeper into the woods after hearing the unfamiliar of sound of an electronic human voice singing to an up-tempo beat.

The creature stood up.

It started walking.

Toward her.

Instantly she had two thoughts: this beast was not about to pass up big game nearby, and that she needed to move — and fast.

Due to its height, the creature cruised over the berry bushes like un-mowed grass. She watched the long, furry legs and the dull outline of its upper body slandering across the field for the few racing heartbeats she took to plan her escape route. She begged that the atmospheric obscurity blinded it from seeing her low to the ground.

She also hoped that the noise of its own heavy footfalls masked her own strides as she started running in a low army-style sprint down toward the dark woods to the west.

She kept her eyes on the woods ahead as she heard the stomping and the bending and cracking of bushes behind her. It was moving to the middle of the field.

Has it spotted me yet?

In her panicked state, she wasn't going to look back. Not until she reached the woods which offered her better protection. The best chance of escaping through the path she knew was on the other side of this thicket or by fighting it off with whatever weapons in the way of sticks or rocks she might find there.

She ducked under a branch and entered the woods and halted behind a thick fir tree. Her laboured breathing, sucking in the cool, damp air, was loud in her ears. She peered back into the fog.

The bulk of the shadowy figure parted the fog like drapes as stalked toward her. She jumped back from the tree, faltered, caught herself, and started running. She dodged trunks and branches as she scampered over the black ground, which was blessedly flat. She felt the large presence behind her and heard its struggles getting its tall, board frame through the woods — dry branches snapping, bushy bows whipping, and the soft thuds of each advancing stomp.

She knew the beaten path she was looking for had to be to her right. If she could find that cut trail through the thicket, then she could motor out of here and get to the safety of the car. Hopefully, Stephanie would already be there in the driver's seat.

The hulking creature sidestepped a tree to slip through another opening. This created a little more distance between the hunter and the hunted.

But just for a moment. She could hear it to her right. *Dammit!*

She couldn't turn that way now, so she drove straight ahead into a thicker patch of woods. The branches of the cluster of thin trees there pushed back on her progress. It was as if the woods — the beast's natural habitat — had come alive to conspire to capture her with some of its long, spiky fingers. Furiously, she fought through it and broke free of the grabbing and stumbled into a small clearing. The enveloping fog robbed her of any directional support the light beyond the trees may have given her.

The thrashing through the foliage behind her was nearing.

With arms extended in front of her, she hastened forward. One arm deflected a branch but a second thin, boney stick from the neighbouring tree poked her in the left eye. She squeezed her eyes shut and ducked her head back and grunted a curse word but kept plowing through this patch of woods. The pain shot through her eye like a lit firecracker.

Nonetheless, that discomfort didn't affect her legs and she knew if she didn't keep them moving, she would be in a whole new world of pain. With one eye closed, she bobbed and dodged a network of the branches as she continued to run. She dipped so low that from time to time her hands would catch the ground, practically running on all fours — becoming an animal to escape one. The monster in pursuit of her didn't have the ability to tunnel through like she did. From what she could hear behind her, the big guy was struggling with the thick vegetation, and losing a step on her.

Again, she came out into an opening that disoriented her for a moment in the grey void. With both eyes, she looked down and saw stoney earth, like the kind on the path that brought her and Stephanie here.

She advanced and felt her steps dropping lower with each one. The earth was on a slope. She was descending a little and found the mist thinner at this level, which promoted a little more visibility of her surroundings.

She stepped in a puddle, soaking her left foot. She realized she was in a dry riverbed. *That's right — the path came up along the bend in the river!* She could see that turn in the distance to her right.

Snap!

Snap!

Crunch …

A snarl.

A loud crack.

A shinny tree fell and crashed to the stoney ground, bouncing on its bushy bows. The act of brute force was a display of its strength and a testament to its persistence in its pursuit of her. Worse, it also meant it was no longer hampered by trees and bushes.

Over the flatness of the riverbed, she knew its long strides wouldn't take long for it to gain ground on her and finally get its large paws on her. She needed to cross the riverbed and climb to higher ground where she had the option of disappearing into the woods on the other side.

She ran and leapt on the bottom of the bank.

She heard rocks being kicked and a splash of a puddle and heavy, hoarse breathing.

Perhaps she could outrun this lumbering man-beast after all and let its exhaustion be its defeat in this chase.

The soil of the embankment was softer and looser, which prevented a swift incline with her steps sinking as she dug in and clay sticking to her wet boot.

The clack of rolling rocks behind her …

The deep huffing of its dogged pursuit …

Adrenaline lifted her energy to a new height and her legs kicked at the earth, but the loose foundation and the smooth water-beaten rocks denied her the speed needed in this moment.

She snatched one of those fist-sized rocks as a hand hit the bank in her struggle to ascend it, knowing her pursuer was only steps away.

As she turned back, her foot slipped on a rounded rock …

For a split second she watched a large, embedded rock in the embankment rush toward her face, and she surely would have smacked her skull off it, but gravity suddenly and miraculously changed directional velocity. She was pulled back upright to her feet and over, falling backward now, by a force clutching the upper back of her coat. She gasped, dropped the rock, arms flailing, grabbing at the mist for stability, but she fell back into a warm rug of wiry hair. She observed large hands holding her steady in this reclined position. She felt hot air on the top of her head. She looked straight up. The silhouette of the creature's head, outline with spiky hairs, against the grey, fog-shrouded sky, entered her view.

Her eyes didn't have time to adjust before the blood ran from her head and everything went black.

The Icelandic explorer Leif Erikson and his crew first landed in the New World in 986 A.D. During this trip, the Norsemen recorded sightings of tall, man-like beasts that were horribly ugly, hairy, swarthy, and with big, black eyes. They had gotten close enough to them to note the foul odour that they gave off. Also, they reported that they made a loud shrieking sound, which distinguished them from any native peoples known to be living in the region at the time. These are the earliest documented encounters with such a creature, whom the Vikings called *Skelling*, but is more commonly known today as *sasquatch* or *yeti*.

The next reported encounter in Newfoundland would come a day after sisters Stephanie and Catherine Ne-whook went blueberry picking and got separated in the fog. It would go down in Bigfoot lore as one of — if not —t he closest confrontation with the creature. Catherine Newhook's report would state that when she came to, she was in its lap.

Even before her eyes opened after regaining consciousness, her olfactory nerves were assaulted with the creature's putrid smell. The concern of the stench was superseded when the image of the creature's head, upside down against the grey sky, came into focus. She gasped deeply, seeing the shape of the furry, ape-like head and the gleam of the black marble eyes set in it looking back down at her. Instinctively, she moved to get up from its lap but a shooting pain in her neck kept her from making any sudden movements. She evidently had injured a vertebra in her upper neck when she fell back against its body. Quickly, she gathered her wits and thought staying still would be the best tactic right now. After all, if it wanted to kill and eat her, it could have done it by now.

What does it want with me? she thought.

It looked at her curiously. It was studying her, as her kind would do if it was him captured. She felt its body heat on her head, which slightly rose and fell on its belly with its breathing, and the pressure of one of its hands on her upper arm. Its other hand came into the edge of her view. She tensed up, which worsened the pain in her neck. Then one of its fingers gently touched her lips. Her mouth was slightly agape, then its finger pried it open a little more. She felt its fingertip on the upper row of her front teeth. When the finger gently moved to the bottom row, she could taste the dirt off its fingernail. She wanted to heave, but she mustered the intestinal strength to remain calm and still.

While it was giving her a dental checkup, she now felt the gender of the thing on her back. She tried not to panic. She took inventory of her surroundings. She gathered that she had not been unconscious for too long. The sky wasn't dark yet.

It removed its finger from her mouth. She closed her mouth and swallowed hard, lubricating her dry throat.

Then it occurred to her that it might explore other parts of her body.

Hurry, girl! What's your next move here?

"Hey …" she whispered. Maybe she could talk to it.

Tenderly. It would see she was not a threat, and it would let her walk away. Of course, it wouldn't know spoken language, but it would comprehend the body language behind it. She raised an arm with an open hand …

It touched her opened palm with the same exploratory finger …

"Get out of here!!" Cathy heard shouted.

Then the banging of rocks …

"Get away from her!!"

It was Stephanie.

To the rescue. But had she thought this battle plan out, which apparently consisted of making noise and throwing rocks. The first one thrown missed them both only by inches. But it got the big guy's full attention. It rolled Cathy off its lap with a surprising gentleness despite being under attack.

Another rock hit the creature in the back ribs, and it let out a grunt. It turned in the direction of the thrower.

Cathy knew its view of her sister would be more obscured by the mist than hers from the ground where she could see Stephanie's legs at the other side of the riverbank. She picked up another rock and threw it. Cathy heard it smack off the earth of the hill behind the creature. She prayed in that moment that the thing would retreat, get scared off by the unseen attacker in the fog.

But, no, it took steps toward Stephanie. Growling.

"Steph, it's coming for you! You have to run! Go back!"

Cathy tried to get to her feet as fast as she could but fell again. In addition to an injured neck, she had also suffered a twisted ankle.

"Cathy!?" Steph called.

"I'm okay. Go! Go!"

The man-beast stalked across the foggy riverbed, looking for his attacker.

"Run, Steph! I'm behind you!"

But her voice was drowned out by the loud shriek of the creature.

Followed by Stephanie's scream.

Her sister took off back into the woods across the river. The swooshing of branches and the snapping of twigs under frantic feet. A new chase was afoot.

But, unlike the last one, the prey had an ally. Maybe — just maybe — if she could catch up to them, she could save Stephanie from a worse treatment than she got from the monster. A wild shot but what other one did she have now? There was no time to call for the help.

A second scream from Stephanie.

One that sounded like it was cut short.

Did it get her?

By the time, she got across the riverbed and entered the wooded area, she could no longer hear the ruckus of the struggle between the two.

Maybe it had captured her and was holding her down and she was smart enough to stop screaming at it …

If they were still in this area, they would certainly be heard amid all the sticks and brush. But there were no noises.

Where were they?

She hobbled hastily through the woods, surveying the damage and debris around her. She saw no clues as to the whereabouts of neither Stephanie nor the beast.

She spotted an old stick, as thick as a beer mug and about two metres long, and picked it up out of the dirt. She held it in both hands, with the long end in front of her, and moved on like an ancestral hunter.

Upon reaching the edge of the field, she saw the canvas bag laying in the grass.

She scanned the foggy lowland and listened.

Nothing.

With weapon in hand, she walked as swiftly as she could back through the blueberry bushes and searched the field.

It was not long before she began finding her sister all over the valley.

Michael Paige

The work of **Michael Paige** has been included in a few literary magazines such as The Furious Gazelle, The Scarlet Leaf Review, MetaStellar as well as several printed anthologies for Savage Realms Press, Crimson Pinnacle Press, Ill-Advised Records, Gravelight Press, October Nights Press, Media Macabre, Little Red Bird Publishing, Chilling Tales for Dark Nights, and also a charity anthology for Great Lakes Horror Anthology (GLAHW).

Between the Groves

The phone on the passenger seat rang for the twentieth time.

I eyed it peripherally with partial attention to the road.

What number were we at now? Who cares? She'd see that none of the messages were being read, and the only thing stopping me from switching the phone to silent — or, lordy, lordy, *off* — was my desire to let it die on its own. She wouldn't be able to deny that her barrage of messages and voicemails had choked the battery to death. Regardless, she'd sure as hell check. Jen always had an impulse for misgivings.

Objection, Your Honour! The question calls for speculation!

I had *"explicitly"* promised that the kids would be home before nightfall. But time must have slipped to the inattentive crevice between my thoughts. It was still a great time with them, though. We had all so desperately needed the day at the lake. How long had it been since they'd gotten to fire off the old slingshot? Too damn long. Jen always hated it and considered me childish for even owning such a thing at my age — as if she were the absolute embodiment of it.

The boys and I spent the day zapping pellets at a few empty cans atop a fat rock and digging in the sand until we found a partially buried arrowhead. By the time the rippling bar of sunset had finished crossing the lake, I was already prepared to bleed for ignoring the clock.

Bzzzt! Another goddamn one. "Jesus, give it a rest already!" I blurted at the phone and then immediately twisted my head toward the back seat.

Dylan and Ajax weren't stirred awake by my sudden outburst, still slumped over and sleeping against their windows.

The vacant road was becoming progressively narrower, and dense tree canopies encompassed both sides of the worn asphalt. A pair of rabbit eyes reflected from within the thick foliage and fireflies fluttered across the headlights like shooting stars.

I slapped my cheek lightly. *Knock it off; you had a good day today. Don't let her ruin it, not yet.* The self-assurance didn't help much, as it was only the prickling reminder that I was happier away from home — away from her.

When had that paradigm become so backward for me? Home was supposed to feel like the refuge you could come back to after a bad day. A safe place. Why bother surviving the shark-infested waters when *this* was the harbor you reached?

Simple: I had no clue from the get-go. The woman I had bought a drink for at the bar, the woman I had loved to make laugh, the woman I had shared vows with twelve years ago was not the same woman who was waiting there for me. She was like a painting that I had carelessly grown fond of before realizing that if I'd just taken one step closer, I could see the violent strokes that made up her coating.

The first of the violent strokes had presented themselves when the stiletto was flung at my face — bruising my cheek. Despite this, I still gave her the benefit of the doubt. Maybe it had just been a bad day, a bad week. Wouldn't anyone consider something like that for someone they cared about? But unfortunately, it had become routine. Anytime she felt her argument become lopsided, and anytime she felt the need to intimidate, it resulted in shouting and shrapnel. She would scream that she'd lie and tell everyone that I was abusing her.

Your Honour, permission to treat the witness as hostile?

I couldn't help but think, would the version of myself twelve years ago tolerate this kind of treatment? Of course not. But what happened to me?

Again, simple: Too much time had passed, too many deposits put into a failed dream. That part of me was gone — beaten into submission and held underwater until the bubbles stopped popping.

I talked to my father about it last week that divorce was inevitably in the horizon. But, of course, nothing would come easy, especially in Jen's vengeful universe. Shared custody would imply that she'd lost in that all-or-nothing brain of hers. No, it wouldn't be enough for her. It was a cyclone that I very much wanted to avoid.

And to top it all off, I was not the only victim on board.

I looked dolefully in the rearview mirror. What parent

wants to put their kids through that mental anguish and tug-of-war?

One friend had warned me that custody cases primarily favor mothers in these circumstances, and false or not, Jen would use anything in her arsenal of sleazy, dishonest connections (and well-versed lying), to see to that. As much as it made me feel sick, she had already won in that respect. She had succeeded in turning herself into a chain and the kids into the attached iron balls. I was trapped.

"Given the circumstances," my father told me, "there's a snowball's chance in hell that you won't have some tough decisions to make. But if you want something — I mean *really* want it, Matt — you will have to be willing to fight tooth and nail for it. Maybe do some studying. Wouldn't hurt to get an idea how a court of law works." And that is what I'd been doing in secret for the past few weeks, reading online books and watching shows, including late-night courtroom dramas.

Then, in the span of a second, there was movement.

A vague shape bolted through the headlights. I cursed as my foot flattened the brake and watched as a pair of antlers sank beneath the grill. Too late; the loud crunch of bone impacting metal filled my ears. The vehicle lurched to a dead stop in the middle of the narrow road. As eight-year-old Ajax started to sob, his ten-year-old brother, Dylan, looked perplexedly at the thickets of tree silhouettes.

"Shit." I exhaled between clenched teeth. My heart shuddered rapidly and showed no signs of stopping. I squeezed the wrinkled leather of the steering wheel until my knuckles were white. "Everyone okay?" I called to the back seat.

"Daddy, what happened?" Dylan asked solemnly in between Ajax's wailing.

I sucked in a deep bitter breath and then sighed. "Nothing to worry about. I'll check it out. Just calm your little brother down." Behind the confident façade, I could only hope we weren't totaled out here; that would be fan-friggin'-tastic.

I stepped out of the driver's seat and approached the damage, swatting away a few fireflies as I did so. Sure enough, an elk lay dead and broken in the road. One of the headlights was shattered, and bits of glass crunched beneath my soles. The grill was reasonably dented and had speckles of blood and dangling chunks of fur. It reminded me of the time I'd accidentally hit that grey cat in the road.

Must've been a juvenile. Poor little guy, I thought as I leaned in to take a closer look at the animal.

I stopped.

My stiff shadow stretched across the pavement from the surviving light, and my rising pulse had vibrated the inside of my throat.

It wasn't an elk that I hit.

Poking out of the thick reddish pile of fur was a pair of small legs and bare feet. I stumbled toward them and fell to my knees. A young girl — maybe around nine or ten. She was wearing an elk pelt that encased her whole body, and the antlers that jutted from her hood were shedding their velvet strands. The depressions in her cheeks signified starvation. The lips on her extremely pallid face were an invisible white, and flakes of dried mud were caked over her tight skin.

I tapped her face lightly. "Hey." The unsteadiness in my voice evident. "Can you hear me? Come on, please. Please say you can hear me." My fingers checked her neck and then her wrist for signs of a pulse. Nothing. "No," I breathed, "No, no, no."

The phone! I realized in sheer panic. *Call for help!* After checking both pockets mindlessly, I stood up, launched myself to the passenger seat, and rummaged for the phone. It had flown to the foot of the seat.

Dylan looked distraught.

Ajax was no longer wailing. "I wanna go home. Can we please go home now?" he sniffled.

"We will. Just hold on a bit," I said, feigning even the slightest bit of confidence despite the crumbling demeanor. My hands seized the phone and tapped the screen relentlessly. No use; the battery was done for — killed by the woman I'd put up to it. Regretful knots fastened and choked my brain.

I returned to the girl, aiming to drive her to the closest hospital. Maybe there was still time, there had to still be time. But just as I walked a few paces towards her, I nearly jumped out of my skin.

Her eyelids were twitching, almost as if they were struggling to open.

I leaped to her side and attempted to gently lift them.

But admittedly, what I saw caused me to scream pitifully.

I clamored away from her, small pebbles digging into my palms.

The girls' sockets were vacant holes, and a lone firefly had crawled out from one of the craters and flown off.

I then heard a snapping sound resonate from the trees followed by a louder, even meatier snap, like someone were breaking a thick stick over their knee.

Without warning, the next loud snap shifted into a prolonged, creaking moan as one of the trees fell to the road — the one right above my truck! Its wide trunk plummeted over the hood in a fine spray of dust and white splinters. Broken limbs ricocheted off the asphalt. The surviving headlight dangled from its fixture, flickered a few times, and then died.

"No! No-oo-oo!" I bellowed, making a mad dash for the vehicle. Horrible thoughts and images flashed in my vision. I practically ripped the back door from its post. Both boys were crying hysterically but were otherwise unhurt, thank God.

"Home!" Ajax bellowed, using his small hands to cover his ears.

I uncurled my grip over the heap of flesh above my heart and embraced them. Luckily only the front of the truck had been pinned down by the fallen aspen. The windshield had held but was now a network of cracks that interweaved like cobwebs.

What the hell is going on? Why did this specific tree fall? Why did that girl have no eyes? No, I couldn't lose my wits to the pondering void. All that mattered right now was getting them home safely. With both headlights now retired, darkness blanketed us. I remembered the Coleman flashlight in the glove compartment.

As I crawled in through the driver's side and popped open the hinged door, Dylan pointed his finger. "Daddy," he sniffled again, "something is looking at us."

I whirled around to the spot he pointed at, both eyes trying to adjust to the dense black sheet around us. Then I caught them, the two yellow bulbs glowing uncannily from the undergrowth. "Just lightning bugs, that's all," I said with an artificial clarity more convincing myself than him. "Yup, just a sprinkle of them."

The bulbs then blinked and moved closer.

I slammed the car door shut and clicked the flashlight on to illuminate the area. Whatever had just been staring was gone. *Just an animal*, I assured myself lucidly. But how could they have shined without any reflecting light? *It was an animal. Drop it. Case dismissed.* I lowered the window a measly inch and listened carefully. Beyond any doubt, something was moving out there. I could hear rustling behind the tree covers: *thak thak thak* — Shrubs and dead leaf litters being crushed and brushed aside.

The yellow bulbs appeared again, but there were more of them now. I counted about five or six creeping behind the cover of dark vegetation, their candlelit eyes glinting. A few amorphous shapes crossed the street but were impossible to see past the trunk and damaged windshield. I reluctantly leaned my ear further out through the tiny space at the top of the window. In between the sounds of crackling plants and pounding footfalls was something else. Whispers. All far too soft and incoherent to make out.

I mentally juggled if this was a good or bad thing. Voices meant that they weren't a pack of animals, but that also meant that a bunch of strangers were hiding in the dark. Were they here for the girl I hit? Had I idiotically stumbled upon an unforgiving tribe of eyeless scalpers living in the wilderness?

Something else approached from the trees and every thought retracted back to the soft tissues of my skull, snapping shut like a clam. My eyes were locked against the passenger-side window. Faster than fear could inject me with hesitancy, I shone the flashlight over the sudden obscure thing.

The thing was tall — easily nine feet if not for a hunch that curved its back in a severe arch. At first glance, I actually thought its body was covered in hair, before realizing that the hair was not its own. It was wearing pelts — a whole assortment of them, each belonging to a different animal and crudely stretched across its broad chest. A few were matted with permanent clumps of bloodied hair. In between the chaotic mesh of diverse fur were gleaming sections of yellow, doughy skin. I had never seen blubber up close before, but this had to be the closest thing to it.

Its arms were a dark yellow tinge of ridiculous length that hung limply at its sides. They were pockmarked with gaping pores that resembled undeveloped mouths. Its slender, multi-jointed fingers rested against the dirt. What I'd first taken for its greenish-white face was actually a chunk of chalky bark wrapped over its skull. Two carved eyeholes signified it was some sort of mask that had been cut — or ripped — straight from a dying aspen. Large, callused folds of blackened bark were peeling off of it. Housed within each eyelet were twin rectangular pupils, both a dusty olive color.

And extending out from its monstrous shape, climbed the jagged bones of antlers.

As the flashlight trembled in my hand, I fought the

urge to shut it off and return the being to its mantle of darkness. But that would be insane. All of this was insane. *This is all a prank,* my inner denial presented to the jury in my head, *the defendants must have waited hours for a potential victim to drive by. When one rolled up, they threw a realistic — too damn realistic — dummy into the road. Then, when the dumb schmuck comes out thinking they'd killed a child, the defendants dropped a tree that was perfectly aligned with the point of collision. They'd pay for the repairs, don't worry! Got to avoid those legal fees after all. Then for the grand finale — out walks the most horrifying thing that poor soul would ever see in their life! I rest my case, Your Honour.*

Yes, that was the only explanation for all of this. Yet, I could not ignore the opposition: that this was horrifically real and actually happening. What would transpire if I stepped out of the car to test this theory? Either the laughter and cameras would come out or the arteries in my throat would.

Ajax started sobbing again. The thing's horizontal pupils turned toward the back seat.

"Be quiet." I pleaded, only to have the demand ignored as the waterworks continued. My already capsizing heart sank even deeper. "BE QUIET!" I screamed hoarsely. Dylan cupped his hands over his little brother's mouth.

The thing's rippling chest heaved. Black, tortuous veins bulged from the dark yellow bulk of its neck as low, guttural sounds came out in hastened spouts. A pronounced otherworldly ribcage swelled in its sternum. At first, I mistook the sound for rumbling growls, but it was too distinct — too defined. Flaps of a jaw bobbed beneath the dead bark strips as strands of thick saliva threaded off its translucent human-like teeth.

Good god, it was talking.

I felt my stomach curl into a tight ball. It was trying to speak, clearly making a straining effort to force even the slightest hint of coherence out of that craned throat. The varnished glowing eyes still stared eerily from the thicket, most of them now congregating near the tall being.

One of its grotesquely long arms rose from the cracked asphalt and pointed an ugly jointed finger toward the back seat.

"Jesus Christ," I breathed. The boys . . . It was pointing at the boys. A mixture of nausea and anger washed through me. Was that what it wanted? My children? *You have taken one of mine, now I will take two of yours.*

As if I'd just pop open the door and hand them over to spare myself. No, there was no way in the rotting intestines of hell that I'd ever allow that to happen.

Whatever this thing was, it would have to kill me first. Then another thought sprouted up — *why hadn't it done that exactly?*

It felt like nothing was stopping one of those pulsed-eyed things from breaking the window or even the large being itself from ripping the door clean off. *It's a power play, a vaguely recognizable voice sounded in my head, taking them from you isn't enough; it wants you to do it willingly. Save itself the trouble.* The voice was my father's, spoken to me just a week ago. *Are you going to let it, tough guy?*

"Hell no," I said unconsciously and rested my head against the steering wheel. Then what was the plan? Throw my dead cell phone at it?

An idea struck. My eyes found the glove compartment

where the slingshot was still tucked away. I reached over and pulled it out.

Any sort of ammunition would pose a problem, as we'd used all the remaining pellets at the beach. Technically I could fire off anything that could fit in the leather pouch, but that didn't automatically make for a good trajectory. Then it hit me: the arrowhead.

It was a difficult shot, but there was still a chance I could peg it in one of those large eyeholes. Maybe it was a ridiculous, farfetched, schoolboy idea, but at least it was better than throwing a dead cell phone.

"Dylan, Ajax," I said sternly to the two of them as I fiddled with the compartment and found the arrowhead, "unbuckle yourselves, and crawl up here to me." One after the other, they did as they were told and squirmed over the armrest into my lap.

I placed the side-notched thing into the centre of the leather pouch. "Hold the flashlight," I instructed Dylan, who took it and shone toward the beast. My pulse quickened as I visualized all the maddening what-if scenarios. I lowered the passenger window, letting an acrid, eggy smell waft in. Rotten curds mixed with spoiled milk and the overwhelming rot of carrion.

I raised the slingshot and pulled the tapered band straight back to my cheek. After finding the anchor point, I visualized the invisible line between the forks of the frame.

I could see fireflies within the fleshy orifices of its arms, crawling in and out like bees to a hive.

The deep, guttural breathing was drawing closer. It didn't appear to notice my actions yet. *But it soon will. Je-*

sus, it soon will.

After one last plea to the universe, I sucked in a bad-tasting breath and released the leather pouch. The rubber snapped forward, and the arrowhead sailed through the open window. It rang free and true before delivering itself squarely into one of the creature's eyes.

The creature flung back, letting out a reverberating shrill of pain.

With my sons in my arms, I clicked the door open, intending to run like hell.

But the efforts were thwarted as the yellow-eyed silhouettes erupted from the underbrush and collided with my car, their different-sized bodies pushing against the door in an animalistic scramble to get inside. Nails scraped against the windows. The roof was being pounded from above. A few skinny — but luckily short — arms reached fruitlessly through the gap in the passenger-side window.

I could see their faces: hollow, sunken cheeks; tight, bloodless lips; and eyeless sockets crawling with fireflies. *Is this what happens to the ones it takes?* I wondered mindlessly.

I shifted my body forcefully until my spine touched the armrest and then pushed at the door with both legs. It was slow-moving, but it was starting to budge! The beast's ululating scream pierced my eardrums. Dylan and Ajax buried their faces into my chest.

The dwindling strength in my legs combusted one more time and pushed hard against the door. It finally pried open, scattering the surrounding creatures. I gripped the boys tightly, leapt out of the seat, and burst into a run, heedlessly stomping over one of the small things that I'd knocked to the ground. Something, maybe an arm or a wrist, crunched beneath my shoe.

I pushed on, begging my out-of-shape legs not to cramp up or my lungs not to pop from the boys squeezing them. One of my soles skidded across the asphalt, nearly making me fall forward.

Sets of feet scurried behind me, close enough to hear their short, haggard breaths.

No, I couldn't allow myself to trip. Tripping meant the end of everything. I gained my footing back and re-covered my balance. *I'll fight for them*, I screamed at the jury inside of my head, their skulls all plastered with Jen's face. *I'll fight you, your sleazy friends, and even the goddamn DEVIL FOR THEM!*

One by one, the pursuing footsteps dwindled, the beast's angry, tortured shrieks fading with them.

I had a masochistic urge to look back, but the surviving speck of rationality stopped me. How far we'd have to go I had no idea, but I'd first let my legs give out under us before I stopped again.

Eventually as the slim road connected to the main one, I saw something that almost brought me to tears.

Coming down the way was two glorious balls of light, burning away the darkness as they drew closer. A car!

I used the last of my energy to meet them.

The small compact car they were attached to nearly swerved when it finally saw us.

The driver, a gentleman who looked to be in his fresh-man year of college wore a buzzed haircut with a var-sity jacket to match. He looked shocked; his jaw frozen in a what-the-hell gasp. The blonde woman next to him swung her arms in a frantic pinwheel. It looked as though they were in the midst of a peaceful night drive only to be interrupted by a crazy man in the woods.

As they came to check us out, I brought the boys in my arms closer and began to weep. Somewhere within the crippled recesses of my sanity, a sure sign of clarity remained:

No matter what would come next after this, I was ready to fight.

Ainsley Hawthorn

Ainsley Hawthorn, Ph.D., is a cultural historian, author, and multidisciplinary artist. Raised in Steady Brook, Newfoundland & Labrador, and now based in St. John's, she earned her doctorate in Near Eastern Languages and Civilizations at Yale University.

Hawthorn is passionate about using her academic knowledge to bring new ideas about culture, history, and religion to a general audience.

As a public scholar, she blogs for *Psychology Today*, writes for CBC, and has contributed to various other publications, including *The Globe and Mail*, the *National Post*, and the *Newfoundland Quarterly*.

She edited the anthology *Land of Many Shores: Stories from a Diverse Newfoundland and Labrador*, and is currently completing her first solo-authored non-fiction book, The Other Five Senses.

Previous From the Rock series credits include 'The Patchwork Skin' in *Mythology from the Rock* and 'Every Child a Changeling' from *Fairy Tales from the Rock*.

She brings with her her short story 'Big Cats of Newfoundland.'

Big Cats of Newfoundland

Gerard Penney March 22, 2016 - Pinned Post

Welcome to Big Cats of Newfoundland, a discussion group dedicated to tracking sightings of large wild cats on the island!

Officially, the government doesn't recognize the existence of cougars, mountain lions, pumas, or panthers in Newfoundland, but many of us have seen them with our own eyes. This group's purpose is to collect documentary evidence we can submit to Forestry and Wildlife to prove big cats are really here.

Group Rules:

1) No bullying or name-calling.

2) No promotions or spam.

3) No posts about lynx. We already know lynx are here, and lynx posts distract from the group's focus on unidentified big cats.

> **Jacob Mercer** October 15, 2018
>
> Just a note: the names "cougar," "mountain lion," "puma," and "panther" all refer to the same animal. The cougar actually holds the Guinness World Record for the animal with the widest

variety of names — it has over 40 in English alone!

> **Gerard Penney** October 15, 2018
> @Jacob Mercer Thanks, Jacob, but I'm going to leave all the different names up so everyone who joins understands what we're talking about.

Kaitlin Basha June 6, 2024

A few years ago my girlfriend and I were driving the highway between Daniel's Harbour and Port Saunders on the Northern Peninsula when a massive tan-coloured cat jumped right out into the middle of the road. It looked straight at us, and I thought my heart was just going to stop. I'll never forget its great big yellow eyes. Then one more jump and it ran off into the trees on the other side.

We see foxes up here all the time, but a fox can't cross the road in two hops! I've never seen anything like it before or since.

> **Gerard Penney** June 6, 2024
> I hear this a lot. People seeing cats so big they can cross a road in a jump or two. Thanks for sharing your story!
>
> **Jodi Peddle** June 9, 2024
> Nor Pen seems super active for big cats! Need to road trip up there sometime.

Brandon Pike May 21, 2024

Went camping w my buddies on the wknd out Terra Nova way. Seen a big blk cat cross the path in front of us. Went right into the brush. Too bad I never had my phone w me. Wondering what kind of animal I saw??

> **Meghan Hillier** May 21, 2024
>
> Could it have been a black lynx? They're rare but they exist. Someone photographed one in the Yukon in 2020.

>> **Brandon Pike** May 21, 2024
>>
>> @Meghan Hillier Not a lynx .Had a long tail.

>> **Meghan Hillier** May 21, 2024
>>
>> @Brandon Pike Maybe a Maine Coon? They can be black and get crazy big.

>> **Jacob Mercer** May 21, 2024
>>
>> @Meghan Hillier Maine Coons can grow up to 40" in length.

>> **Brandon Pike** May 21, 2024
>>
>> @Meghan Hillier Could of been I guess. Pretty far out in the woods for a housecat, tho.

>> **Gerard Penney** May 21, 2024
>>
>> @Meghan Hillier Banned.

> **Gerard Penney** May 21, 2024
>
> Hard to say what it was without more detail, Brandon. There are a number of black land mammals on the island, and I can tell you from experience that it's tough to gauge size from a quick sighting like this.

>> **Rowan Wareham** May 22, 2024
>>
>> @Gerard Penney May I see inside?

>> **Gerard Penney** May 22, 2024
>>
>> @Rowan Wareham If I get any further information on Brandon's sighting, I'll

let you know. I try to share as many of my files with the group as possible.

Philip Marche May 24, 2024

@Gerard Penney You run this group. I thought you believed in big cats. Why are you trying to debunk this guy's sighting?

Philip Marche May 24, 2024

@Rowan Wareham Inside what?

Gerard Penney May 24, 2024

@Philip Marche Hi Philip, I want to PROVE that big cats are here in Newfoundland and have been for decades. To do that we need credible evidence. It doesn't help the cause to take every sighting at face value.

Amy Lynn May 8, 2024

Hey, gang! What's the more common colour for big cats in NL? Black or tan? If you've had a sighting, what was the colour?

Greg Conway May 8, 2024

Black in Central in 2020

Dani Buckle May 8, 2024

tan

Brenda McCarthy May 8, 2024

Blk

Bassim Yacoub May 8, 2024

Black

Sean Partridge May 8, 2024

The one i seen in Makinsons was black!

Al Hynes May 8, 2024

1 black 1 tan

Amy Lynn May 8, 2024

@Al Hynes You've seen two?? whoa!!

Al Hynes May 8, 2024

@Amy Lynn Yep, sure have, unmistakeable. black near colliers in 2011, tan on the Burin peninsula in 2015.

Dave Lundrigan May 8, 2024

Black

Janet Alteen May 8, 2024

Black

Isaac Levitz May 8, 2024

Tan

Gerard Penney May 8, 2024

Reported sightings are black by a mile.

Lexie Mitchell May 10, 2024

@Gerard Penney But if people are seeing black cats, what are they?

Jaguars can be melanistic, but we're way out of their habitat. They're equatorial and prefer temperatures 20 degrees plus.

Cougars could survive in our climate, but there's never been a confirmed instance of a black cougar.

Gerard Penney May 10, 2024

@Lexie Mitchell They could be black leopards. About 10% of leopards are black, and leopards can survive the cold. Look at snow leopards.

Lexie Mitchell May 10, 2024

@Gerard Penney But snow leopards don't

come in black, either. Seems more likely people are either mistaking tan cats for black in the dark or just seeing housecats and overestimating the size.

Jacob Mercer May 10, 2024

@Lexie Mitchell Did you know black leopards and jaguars still have spots? They're just tough to "spot" (ha ha!) on a black coat. You can see them using an infrared camera.

Gerard Penney May 10, 2024

@Lexie Mitchell I hear ya. I'm not arguing, just repeating what people have told me and posted here.

Siobhan Kelly May 8, 2024

Tan

Mark Weir May 8, 2024

Black

Denise Ong May 8, 2024

black

Dave Lundrigan April 13, 2024

anyone ever been stalked by one of these bad boys? I have and it was the most freaking terrifying thing that's ever happened to me in my life. Was out trouting with a buddy in the woods all day and started back around nightfall walking up the trail home. All of a sudden I get this feeling like I'm being watched, hair standing up on the back of my neck kind of thing. I turn around and see this huge black cat, tail swishing... standing on the trail watching us from about 30ft behind. I can see its fur shining in the moonlight slick as oil.

I look at my buddy and he looks at me and we both start backing up real slow and calm. But the cat follows us. So we're backing up and the cat's coming along behind and now it's crouching low to the ground like when a cat's stalking a mouse and I start to think we've had it. We're not that far from a fork in the trail where one way goes to the community and the other goes in to a little soccer field and I whisper to my buddy that on the count of three we'll book it up the trail, take the fork for town, and hope the cat goes the other way.

I'm absolutely shit baked at this point thinking one of us is about to die and I'm smaller than my buddy so it'll probably go for me first. So I count to three and we take off and every second I think that cat is going to hit me like a brick between the shoulder blades and it'll all be over. Well we don't stop running until we get way down the highway to the first house and my lungs are on fire but when we look back the cat is gone. I call my mom and I'm so happy to still be alive I'm crying on the phone and scare the hell out of her. I felt what it was like to be prey that night and I take the wilderness out here seriously now I'll tell you that.

Gerard Penney April 13, 2024

What a story, Dave! Thanks for sharing!

Neil Jesso April 13, 2024

Sounds like a scary experience but might not have been predatory behaviour. Mountain lions usually ambush their prey — if one was stalking you, you wouldn't know it until it was too late. It sounds like this cat was trying to run you out of its territory. It could have been protecting cubs. Very rare for mountain lions to hunt humans. They see us as an injury risk, not as prey items.

Rowan Wareham April 13, 2024

I've had a feeling of being stalked by something lately when I'm out in the woods around my house. I haven't gotten a clear look at it, but when I go for a walk it's like something is keeping pace with me behind the trees, stepping when I step so I can't be sure if I'm hearing an animal or just my own echo. It used to seem far away, but it feels like it's gotten closer. It's making me nervous. I've tried the RCMP, but they said they only respond to calls about animals that "pose an immediate threat to human safety." Thoughts?

Meghan Hillier April 13, 2024

I think I was stalked by a lynx once. I was hiking Cook's Lookout Trail down on the Burin. It's a 4 k trail in and out, a mix of woods and barrens. It was a foggy spring day, and I was walking along one of the scrubby parts of the trail when my dog started barking. I followed his gaze and saw a brownish-grey figure about twenty yards away. The barking scared it off. I wouldn't have known it was a lynx except for the ear tufts. They're so distinctive!

> **Gerard Penney** April 13, 2024
>
> @Meghan Hillier No more lynx talk. Last warning.

Nicolette Semigak March 30, 2024

Hey everyone, I'm a sheep farmer up in Roddickton, and I've been having a hell of a time with some predator getting at my flock.

For the past couple of weeks, I've been waking up almost every other day to dead sheep. And I mean completely gutted. Split open from the base of the skull to the tail, their spines torn out and scraped almost clean on the inside. I can spot them now from across a field. They look like deflated balloons.

I've been farming for almost a decade, and I've never seen anything like it. I've had coyote attacks before, but they normally tear out the throat and eat the innards through the flank. Any chance it's a cougar? I haven't seen any big cats up here myself, but my brother-in-law swears he saw one in by Rocky Pond.

> **Gerard Penney** March 30, 2024
> Could be. Cougars go for the head and neck and sometimes crush the skull. Any claw marks? Parallel lines with sharp edges?

>> **Nicolette Semigak** March 30, 2024
>> @Gerard Penney Not that I can see. But the edges of the wound are always pretty neat, and there's never much blood.
>> **Cherrie Beaupre** March 30, 2024
>> @Gerard Penney Not a cougar if all the organs are missing. Cougars eat the heart, lungs, liver. Leave the stomach and intestines. Cats are clean. Would you want to eat a sheep's poop chute?
>> **Leanne&Donnie Fizzard** March 30, 2024
>> @Cherrie Beaupre Blessid Jesus. Me stomach's turnt.

Derek Seung-hyun Kim March 30, 2024
@Nicolette Semigak Black bear. Bears
attack from the top and eat the stomach.
Philip Marche March 30, 2024
@Derek Seung-hyun Kim Dude, I've never
heard of a black bear attacking anything.
They're shy as hell.
Derek Seung-hyun Kim March 30, 2024
@Philip Marche Sorry to disappoint
you 'dude' but there was literally a black
bear attack in Labrador in 2019.

Al Hynes March 31, 2024
What about a wolf/coyote mix like the Beast of
Botwood? No telling what them injuries would
look like

Nnamdi Onodugo April 8, 2024
I work with the Animal Health Division in
Pynn's Brook as a veterinary pathologist. Have
you preserved any of the animal remains? If so,
we would like to collect a carcass for necropsy.
We can also set up monitoring equipment on
your property to record any further predator
activity. Please call me at your convenience at
[redacted].

Gerard Penney April 8, 2024
@Nnamdi Onodugo Is this an official
statement??? Can you confirm that
government is investigating big cats on
the island???
Nnamdi Onodugo April 8, 2024
@Gerard Penney This should not be

construed as an official statement. We investigate all unexplained livestock predation and are tracking several similar incidents in the western region.

Rowan Wareham April 8, 2024

@Nnamdi Onodugo You mention other incidents. I'm near Main Brook — have you recorded any attacks up this way? I've been coming across dead animals, too.

At first, it was a hare skin here or there in the woods near my house. Always in one piece, not like a trapper would skin one with the hide in two pieces. I thought a fox must be getting at them.

Then yesterday morning I opened my door, and there was a whole caribou on the doorstep. A juvenile, I think, but big as I am, slit down the back and hollowed out just like Nicolette said. I hauled it into the woods so it doesn't attract anything else to my door.

Nnamdi Onodugo April 8, 2024

@Rowan Wareham I am unable to discuss the details of livestock losses currently under investigation, but a release will be published by the Department of Fisheries, Forestry and Agriculture as soon as our assessment is complete, within 60-90 days on average.

Rowan Wareham April 8, 2024

@Nnamdi Onodugo Can you send someone up here to see what's going on around my place? There's something I forgot to mention. The caribou's tongue was missing. Its mouth was lolling open, and I could see where the tongue had been torn out. Is that normal? What types of predators eat their prey this way?

Nnamdi Onodugo April 8, 2024

@Rowan Wareham Our department only documents attacks on livestock. The conservation office in Roddickton may be able to advise.

Rowan Wareham April 8, 2024

@Nnamdi Onodugo I called Roddickton conservation, but they just handle poaching and wildlife offenses.

Jodi Peddle April 8, 2024

@Rowan Wareham Typical government! Can't be bothered to help a farmer protect their sheep but out here fining hardworking people for trapping rabbits and catching cod.

God forbid we FEED OURSELVES. They want us to spend all our hard-earned money at the grocery store so they can collect our taxes and laugh all the way to the bank. People can't afford to live anymore and we can't even use our own resources???

Gerard Penney April 8, 2024

@Nnamdi Onodugo Sure sounds like some kind of statement to me. You're saying there have been several incidents of unexplained predation in western Newfoundland? It's only a matter of time before Wildlife will have to acknowledge what we've been saying all these years. Big cats are here, they're established, and they're reproducing.

Trent Quehe April 8, 2024

@Gerard Penney they're here! they're queer! they don't want any more bears!

Philip Marche April 8, 2024

@Treat Quehe No one wants any more bears. Haven't you heard? A little bitty black bear attacked someone in Labrador in 2019.

Derek Seung-hyun Kim April 8, 2024

@Philip Marche JFC

Justine Spracklin March 11, 2024

What's everyone's theory on how big cats got to the island?

Bassim Yacoub March 11, 2024

A circus truck crashed near Daniel's Harbour in 2010

Amy Lynn March 11, 2024

@Bassim Yacoub I've read about that, but the only animals involved were an elephant and two camels.

Bassim Yacoub March 11, 2024

@Amy Lynn unless the government's covering up a large predator escape to keep the public from panicking

Casey Pardy March 11, 2024

There's a book called The Quest for the Eastern Cougar that says cougars were brought to Newfoundland in the 1960s by a group of American hunters.

> **Gerard Penney** March 11, 2024
> @Casey Pardy Yes, Wildlife has records of this. Two doctors from Idaho allegedly flew in three cougars, two female and one male, and released them in the Main Brook area for hunting. Officers investigated and though they didn't find the cougars, they did find large cages and "strange tracks" around the doctors' camp.
>
> **Jacob Mercer** March 14, 2024
> @Casey Pardy Actually, cougars aren't technically Big Cats because they can't roar.
>
> **Hayden Reid** March 14, 2024
> @Jacob Mercer dude wtf, cougars r literraly big cats
>
> **Jacob Mercer** March 14, 2024
> @Hayden Reid Cougars are large felines, yes, but they are not Big Cats in the scientific sense because they have an ossified hyoid bone. Only lions, tigers, jaguars, and leopards are Big Cats because

their floating hyoid allows them to roar.

Casey Pardy March 14, 2024

@Jacob Mercer From Wikipedia: "The term 'big cat' is typically used to refer to any of the five living members of the genus Panthera, namely the tiger, lion, jaguar, leopard, and snow leopard, as well as the non-pantherine cheetah and cougar."

Jacob Mercer March 14, 2024

@Casey Pardy I guess Wikipedia trumps my biology degree then. That's how the term Big Cat is "typically used" by the general public but not by the scientific community.

Philip Marche March 14, 2024

@Casey Pardy What's the difference between a cougar and a leopard?
A leopard can drag something twice its weight up a tree. A cougar can drag someone half her age into bed.

Meghan Hillier March 14, 2024

@Jacob Mercer If cougars aren't big cats what the hell are lynx?

Casey Pardy March 14, 2024

@Meghan Hillier They're all big cats. This whole discussion is pointless semantics.

Jacob Mercer March 14, 2024

@Meghan Hillier Lynx are part of the subfamily Felinae, like domestic cats, cougars, and cheetahs.

Gerard Penney March 14, 2024

@Meghan Hillier Second warning. Stop with the lynxes.

Jodi Peddle March 11, 2024

Anyone else here the rumour that Johnny Cash brought them when he went hunting near Millertown in 1961?

Gerard Penney March 11, 2024

Every time this comes up, there are three main theories:

1) A circus truck crashed

2) Hunters flew them in

3) They came over on ice pans from Labrador

Personally, I think big cats have always been here. If they can come down on ice floes from the mainland now, why not a hundred years ago? Five hundred? Cats are elusive and most of the island is uninhabited. There could be lots of animals in the woods no one has ever seen, but as our population rises and we encroach on the wilderness there are bound to be more encounters. I'm optimistic we'll be able to prove the existence of big cats on the island very soon.

Rowan Wareham February 27, 2024

Can anyone help me identify some tracks I found in the snow? Yesterday evening something was scratching at my front door. Three or four scrapes at a time, followed by long pauses, like it was trying to get in or maybe trying to get me to let it in. I wasn't about to open my door to a wild animal, of course, so I ignored it, and when I woke up this morning I found fresh tracks all around my house. They're four-toed and about six or seven inches across.

Miranda Peddle February 27, 2024

Could they be bear tracks?

>**Rowan Wareham** February 27, 2024
>@Miranda Peddle No, I don't think so. Bear tracks have five toe impressions and these only have four.

Cherrie Beaupre February 27, 2024

Can't be a cougar at that size. It would have to be enormous.

>**Lexie Mitchell** February 27, 2024
>@Cherrie Beaupre Snow can melt, though, and make tracks look bigger than they are.

>**Cherrie Beaupre** February 27, 2024
>@Lexie Mitchell True girl.

>**Lexie Mitchell** February 27, 2024
>@Rowan Wareham Maybe coyote prints that have enlarged through snowmelt? Can you see claw marks?

>**Rowan Wareham** February 27, 2024
>@Lexie Mitchell I can't. Just the toes and the footpad.

>**Lexie Mitchell** February 27, 2024
>@Rowan Wareham That does sound like an animal with retractable claws, then. Maybe a lynx or even a domestic cat. Impossible to get a good read on print size in the snow.

Meghan Hillier February 3, 2024

Have any of you ever seen a lynx in the wild? I saw one once on the Burin peninsula, and of course I visited the captive ones at Salmonier Nature Park when I was a kid. What beautiful creatures. I'd love to hear about other experiences you've all had.

> **Gerard Penney** February 3, 2024
>
> This group is for sightings of cougars, mountain lions, panthers, and other big cats not known to be native to the island. We know lynx are here. Please reread the group rules.

An admin turned off commenting for this post.

Derek Seung-hyun Kim January 25, 2024

Why does no one ever have their phones on them when they see these cats? So many alleged sightings and can't get a single photo?

> **Philip Marche** January 25, 2024
>
> Brother, I've seen so much cool shit out in the woods and never ever been fast enough to snap a pic. Unless you've got a camera stuck to your face by the time you think to grab your phone whatever you saw is long gone. These are wild animals. If they posed for the perfect shot hunters would've got them by now.
>
> **Linda Whalen** January 25, 2024
>
> When I was a kid we were told there were no coyotes in Newfoundland, then they were discovered here in the 80s. We were told wolves were extinct too, then DNA testing proved they

were here in the 2010s. I don't care what's been captured on camera, I know there's more on this island than we think there is. As long as the snakes stay off it I'll be happy! Me nerves lol.
Luke Jesso January 26, 2024
My pop and two of his friends saw a mountain lion fifteen years ago in by Strickland Pond near Lethbridge. They're older and wouldn't have known how to use a smartphone to take a pic. But all three were experienced hunters and knew what they saw.

Rowan Wareham January 11, 2024
New member here! I'm wondering if anyone here can shed light on a weird experience I had last night.

I have a small house – a cabin, really – outside Main Brook. I'm from the Grand Falls area originally but left for university. During COVID I decided to move to rural and work remotely. It's beautiful here, but I don't have many connections in the local community I can go to for help.

I was sitting in my living room by the fire last night, when I started hearing these wailing sounds. First they were far off, but they got closer and closer until it seemed like they were coming from right outside my door. They circled the house, then eventually went away. The whole thing probably lasted about half an hour.

Whatever it was, it was moving too quickly and erratically to be a person, but the noises it was making sounded almost like speech. Wildcats make human-like sounds sometimes, right? Maybe what I heard was a combination of mewing and hissing.

Gerard Penney January 11, 2024

Yes, cougars have been known to make sounds like a woman screaming.

> **Justine Spracklin** January 11, 2024
>
> @Gerard Penney Thanks, I hate it.
>
> **Jacob Mercer** January 11, 2024
>
> @Gerard Penney Correct. That's because cougars are unable to roar like true big cats.
>
> **Matt Squires** January 11, 2024
>
> @Gerard Penney First time I ever heard a bobcat I near wet myself. Sounded like a cross between a baby crying and a woman screaming bloody murder.

Denise Ong January 11, 2024

I've read about margays (they're a small South American wildcat) luring monkeys out of trees by mimicking the sounds of their babies.

Philip Marche January 11, 2024

Yo, so if it sounded like speech, what was it saying?

> **Rowan Wareham** January 11, 2024
>
> @Philip Marche It sounded like it was saying, "May I see inside?"

Lily McCarthy

Lily McCarthy is an author originally from Tor's Cove, Newfoundland.

They enjoy reading, writing, and spending time with their brothers.

In 2021 her first novel, *Quick Bright Things* was published by Engen Books.

Everyone Liked Henry Reid

His house was in the opposite direction of mine, but I couldn't resist walking him home.

I had to ask him outside the party. I shouldn't have cared who saw. We weren't in high school anymore. But I'd chased him — half-drunk — out the front door when he announced he was leaving. I grabbed my coat and bundled myself up and slipped out the door behind him with my friends rolling their eyes at me as they watched me go. I was glad for the few beers I'd had, because they kept me from feeling embarrassed. I must've still had some shame, though. I made sure the door was shut behind me before I reached out and caught the end of his sleeve.

He turned to look at me. He'd been working on his pop's boat all summer, so he had a remarkable tan (remarkable where Newfoundland weather was concerned), but I could still make out the flush of his cheeks. I couldn't tell if it was my fault or just the alcohol. Either way, I released him the second our eyes met.

"Oh, Thomas," he said. It wasn't a greeting. I hadn't spoken a word to him at the party, but he was unphased to see me. He must've noticed I was there. He also didn't go on, which I couldn't exactly blame him for. I was the one scrambling after him. He was under no obligation to say anything.

I stuck my hands in my pockets, my shoulders instinctually rising to my ears. To the untrained eye, I may have looked cold, but in reality I was just terrified of him. I thought I'd be over this by now. But boys like him — the kind that could smile at a roomful of people and still make it seem like it was just for you — still made my hands shake.

"Reid." It was his last name — but it was what everyone called him. His first name was Henry, and I would've preferred to call him that. It suited him. It was handsome. But I didn't know how he'd react if I strayed from the way everyone else spoke to him. I sounded weird enough talking to him now. I had a relentless bubble in my throat. Likely my body working against me, trying to stop me from doing what I was doing. But I didn't listen. I just cleared my throat and tried again. "Uh, you're headed home?"

He'd said that. He'd announced that to the room, because he was the kind of guy whose absence you'd notice, and he knew that. I just didn't know what else to say.

He nodded, with nothing but amiability. As always. "Yeah, I gotta get home. My little sister's home alone, so I promised I wouldn't be out too long."

He always did that: explained himself. Said more than he had to. He was so self-assured. He could always trust that I'd — *that anyone* — would care what he had to say when he opened his mouth. And we did… every time.

"Oh, cool. That's nice of you."

"Yeah."

Lull. I suddenly wished I'd just stayed inside. He was swaying on his heels, obviously eager to go. I should've just left him alone. I resigned myself to the fact that I had made a stupid decision. He was *that guy*. Every town had one like him. One everyone loved. The guy that no one had anything bad to say about. The guy some people really put effort into hating, but inevitably would stop in the halls to compliment or smile at. The kind of guy that came home to help his parents over the summer for the *whole summer* and not just a week, that talked to everyone at every party — even dorks like me and my dorky friends.

Someone who was, inarguably, too good to be around all of us, who hurt each other regularly and got into petty, undeserved fights with our family and held resentment for one another.

I couldn't ask him anything. I gave him a polite smile and was ready to turn back in. "Well, bye th—"

"D'you want to walk with me?"

His words took me so off guard, I could've tipped over. I thought I misheard him.

I tried to act casual but I felt more like a casualty. "You want me to?"

He smiled at me then — playfully, incredulously — and I stumbled a step. He didn't react, so hope remained that he would see me as simply drunk. On the contrary (and unfortunately for both of us), I was beginning to sober up.

"Of course. I wouldn't ask if I didn't," he replied. Like everything else he did, he made it look easy.

"Okay, sure."

"Cool."

I glanced back at the house for half a second, wondering vaguely if everyone in there felt the world move the same time I did, before we descended the walkway. At the end, I expected him to turn right. The way to his house was to the right (I knew that because I'd been to his house for birthday parties when we were in elementary school.) But he confidently turned left.

Of course, neither direction was the way to my house. I followed him anyway.

It was dark out, and the street (if you could even call it that) only had two streetlamps to illuminate our path. Beyond that, we had to use the porch lights to guesstimate. I glanced over at him curiously.

He noticed my look immediately. "There's a trail through the woods, behind the houses. It's a bit longer, but a nicer walk," he explained, then quickly added, "Did you want to head straight home? I should've asked."

"No, no! It's fine. Lead the way." It was better than fine actually. The normal walk back to his house was ten minutes away, tops. But we were walking to the end of the road, then cutting through the woods, which was essentially like circling the whole neighbourhood. It would certainly prolong the night. I wasn't about to complain. Even though my parents' house was much farther away, since it was on the edge of the community, hugging the coastline. A thirty-minute walk away on a good day.

"Did you have fun tonight?" he asked. The end of the road had reflectors nailed to the trees. My dad had done that at the end of all of these roads we played on when we were kids. He'd told all of the kids scary stories to try and

divert us from playing in the woods where we could easily get lost, but, naturally, we never listened. There were
likely the remnants of our old forts in there, and trees with
dirty words carved into them.

I shrugged in response. "It was weird seeing everyone
again."

He glanced over at me curiously. "Why? It's only been
a few months."

I shrugged again. "I don't know. Feels different."

We ducked under a thick tree branch and into the
woods. The path was so dark — nearly pitch black — with
some moonlight peeking through the trees. He fumbled
for his phone and turned on the flashlight. He shined it
down by my feet just in time to catch my last, cautious,
clumsy step.

"You okay?" he asked.

"Not lost yet."

"You're a wilderness expert."

He pointed his flashlight down the path. It was overgrown, with brush and sting nettles overtaking the foot-
path and branches encroaching like partial gateways or
outstretched hands. The white of the flashlight turned the
trees a distorted grey, and I felt like we were stepping into
a found footage film.

Not the romantic walk in the woods I was picturing.
But it would have to do.

We started walking with his light to aid us, and he
went on, "Maybe you're just different now." I looked over
at him from where I was walking at his side, but he seemed
solely focused on the trail ahead. "It felt weird to me too,
honestly. But mostly because it was like nothing changed.

I guess I expected to feel how you feel. Different."

There was something grounding about knowing he felt weird, too. Everyone seemed as comfortable with each other as always at that party. But I couldn't move beyond our topics of conversation. The way everyone had something new, something I'd never seen or heard about through the grapevine of small-town gossip. Going to a tiny high school, with tiny class sizes, where every peer was at some point a childhood friend made you feel off-kilter the more estranged you became from them. Suddenly, we went from seeing each other every day and knowing every detail about one another (usually unintentionally), to having to fill one another in. It wasn't even like I was friends with them all. If I was honest, I wasn't friends with most of them. But they felt like my family in an odd way.

I had no frame of reference whether they felt the same way about me. Even among my close friends, I'd always been too embarrassed to ask, just in case the answer was no.

"Did you keep up with everyone after grad?"

He shook his head. "No one."

I couldn't believe what I was hearing. He was practically beloved in the town as a whole, let alone amongst our classmates. He was friends — or at least friendly — with everybody.

"No one?" I repeated, unable to mask my disbelief. "Not even Max or Dean?"

Reid, Max, and Dean were practically attached at the hip since kindergarten. Probably before then actually. Reid and Dean were neighbours, so they'd probably been playing together since they were born. And Max was Reid's cousin — their moms were sisters, and very close ones at that — so they were practically raised as brothers. I felt stupid even asking if he kept in contact with them — it felt like asking if he still talked to his parents. So, I was dumbfounded when he shook his head again.

"Not really."

It was a good thing he was paying attention to our surroundings, because I was too busy staring at him and nearly clothes-lined myself on a branch. He startled me when he reached over and held it up, just high enough for me to duck under.

"Careful." He chuckled, but he sounded far away. He seemed just as surprised as I was that he hadn't maintained his friendships, only his surprise sounded sad. Reserved. Still, he had his usual soft smile that I used to be certain was the permanent shape of his lips. Now, I realized it was intentional.

"Did something happen between you guys?"

He thought about it and blew out a breath as I resigned to at least try and keep my eyes forward. I didn't need to make an idiot of myself tonight by getting knocked out by a tree. I was sure I'd find a much more creative way of doing that.

"The cliché stuff, I guess," he said. "Everyone always said we'd fall out a bit after high school. We didn't believe it. We knew we were all doing different stuff, going in different directions, but I figured it didn't matter. We'd figure it out, we'd see each other anyway. MUN and I are so close to each other, it just made sense. And we tried for the first month or two. But we were all swamped with school, and they made new friends really easily and…"

I d'dn't want to say it, and yet… "You d'dn't?"

He sucked his bottom lip, flicked his phone on and off as if he was checking the time in that awkward gesture Gen Z tended to whenever there was an uncomfortable moment. Being that I did it too, I knew he didn't even glance at the time. In my experience, I usually just wanted a worthy distraction. Or for the screen to swallow me whole.

He peeked over at me for a moment, and I knew my face was more serious than he would've liked. He quickly grinned and shook his head at himself. "God, sorry to bring down the mood. I'm just feeling sorry for myself, I guess."

"No, it's okay," I said quickly. I had an urge to lay a hand on his shoulder, offer him more comfort than just a few sloppy words. But I maintained my distance. "I guess I'm just surprised. I always thought… I don't know."

"No, tell me," he said. He sounded hungry for my opinion. I swallowed the feeling that arose in my stomach.

"I guess I always thought stuff like that was effortless for you. The social stuff, I mean. Making friends, getting people to like you. It always just *happened*. It's like we can't help it. We just have to like you. Like you have your own orbit."

There was a moment of silence, save for the sound of our shoes crunching the brush and sticks underfoot. I risked a look over at him. I didn't know what to expect. My words could be taken a dozen ways: jealousy, bitterness, admiration — but in actuality, I was just being honest. The sky was blue, time went on no matter what we did about it, and everyone liked Henry Reid.

I couldn't really make out his face in the dark, but from the effort he made not to look at me and the slightest wash of flashlight that came back on him, I could almost call him *flustered*.

"We?" he repeated teasingly. He looked over at me and smirked, brow raised, and a smile slipped onto my face easily. "You like me, huh?"

He didn't mean it the way I felt it, so it was easy to roll my eyes at him. "I wouldn't say it if I didn't."

His smile widened, teeth peaking through his lips. The sadness I got a glimpse of evaporated, and all at once, it was as if it were never there at all. I couldn't unsee it. But we could move on.

"Enough about me," he said. "Tell me about you. How's—"

Before he could get the sentence out, there was a loud wooden crack behind us. It wasn't the snap of a stick, just subtle enough to be unsettling like in horror movies. Instead, it was a crack that thundered through the dense forest. It was loud and full, less like a branch and more like a partially hollow tree being crushed. We jumped when we heard it and knocked shoulders as we turned to look in its direction.

We waited, holding our breath and keeping perfectly still, for an explanation to show itself. Or a follow up sound, which (I couldn't speak for him but) I'd run from instantly.

After a long minute of quiet, we turned to look at each other.

"What was that?" I asked, knowing he knew as much as I did.

He glanced back down the path before meeting my eyes again and shrugging. "A moose, maybe?"

"That's one angry moose, then."

"Or just a clumsy one."

"The farther we get away from it, the better."

He nodded in agreement, and we kept walking, noticeably faster this time.

I remained unsettled as we went on. The quiet that followed was heavy. It reminded me of the quiet of a house full of children playing hide and seek. The silence of intentional quiet. If Reid felt the same way, he didn't let on. He carried on, having shaken off his fear.

"You moved away after grad, right, Thomas?" he asked. He said everyone's name liberally, like it belonged to him. I was surprised he knew I'd left the island for school. I posted a few photos of my university campus and new friends, but I never thought about him seeing them. I wasn't so desperate that I pined for him and made Instagram posts with his reaction in mind. I liked him. I hadn't stopped liking him. And every so often when I saw someone that vaguely looked like him, or a stranger was a little too kind to me, I thought of him.

It was an odd feeling — being a face in a yearbook to someone who'd occupied your thoughts for longer than you'd like to admit. Someone who taught you things about yourself that — at the time — you'd have rather not learned. I was never anything to him, really. We were just classmates. We'd kissed once when we were fifteen. I never knew why. I suspected he was feeling sorry for himself then too, and my feelings for him were not as expertly hidden as I thought. He seemed down the day it happened. Maybe he just needed the ego boost.

We led such different lives. To him, every kiss was a song of praises. To me, they were generally awkward.

But not when he kissed me. I couldn't put a finger on precisely what was different about it, but I walked away feeling like I was someone worth kissing.

"How are you finding life beyond the rock?"

"It's good." The answer came out too fast. I was trained for answering family members who were so proud of my decision, who bragged about how smart and adventurous I was. I always defaulted to calling it good. Exciting. Fun. That's not to say it wasn't any of those things. But... "It's far."

That was all I said because I knew he'd understand. The island had a certain feel to it. It was home, yes. But that wasn't it. It had a certain magic. You could go anywhere in the world, live there for as long as you want, but Newfoundland would always be a core piece of you. I knew I'd miss my friends and my family, but I didn't expect being away from the physical place to be so challenging.

"Are you happy there?"

I was asked that question a lot, but this was the first time I really thought about it. "Yeah, I think I am."

He smiled. "Good. I'm glad you went."

I looked over at him and was surprised to see that he was already looking at me. His expression was unreadable. Serene, but not much else. His words — though I knew they shouldn't — made me feel dejected.

"Why?" I asked, hiding my disappointment.

He shrugged. "You're too big for this place."

My cheeks and ears burned. I had an intense urge to look away and change the subject. But I felt trapped, with our eyes locked together. His chocolate brown and long lashed, and mine blue and round and lost.

My mouth opened before I could stop myself: "You know I like you, don't you?"

His lips parted immediately, before he quickly pressed them together again. He hesitated for a moment, and I realized that we'd stopped walking. I didn't know when or who initiated it, but we were standing, facing one another in the centre of the trail.

Slowly, he nodded.

When he didn't say anything, I took the hint. I felt the gut punch, the quick exhale through my lips and blinked at him. But I refused to wallow. I knew he didn't like me back. I never considered the possibility that he would. But the confirmation hurt all the same. I forced an understanding smile, knowing I wasn't convincing either of us before I couldn't stand the sight of him anymore. I hung my head to stare at my shoes.

I watched his open hand twitch at his side.

"Thomas—"

An otherworldly howl, hollow and echo-y like blowing into a conch, cut him off and rattled through my ribcage. My head shot up immediately. Birds fled the trees, rustling the leaves as they evacuated and Reid and I were staring, frozen, down the trail behind us. It remained empty but looked longer and narrower the longer we waited for something to emerge.

There was a short beat. The wind was cold.

Then, we felt the tremble underfoot. The distinct, unmistakable sound of a large animal stomping through the woods. For the life of me, I couldn't tell if they were getting closer or farther away.

"That doesn't sound like a moose," I muttered. I was afraid to raise my voice above a whisper. I'd been in the woods plenty. I'd been hunting with my dad since I was old enough to carry the rabbits or ducks he caught back to the bike in my arms. I'd been moose hunting, too. It was scary. However big a moose was when you pictured it in your mind, it was always double in real life. But I'd never been afraid like this. I wasn't one to be looking over my shoulder in these woods. I'd spent too much time in them.

Now, as I felt anticipation building in me, dense enough to split me in half, my bottom lip was trembling. I didn't even notice that Reid hadn't answered me.

We both flinched when the howl came again, this time guttural and rasping, from a gravelly throat. More like a roar than a howl, accompanied by the quickening of stomps that made my stomach drop.

Definitely *closer*.

Reid grabbed my arm, and we took off running in the opposite direction. His grip on my arm was ironclad, but he was faster than me and I had to take quick, long strides to keep up. My heart was thumping. His palm was sweaty.

"Do you think it's a bear?" I gasped at him over the buzz of our feet crushing branches, nettles, and leaves.

"What kind of a bear sounds like that?!" he retorted.

He jumped over a thick root, which I almost lost my footing to, but he pulled on my arm and I managed to keep up without dragging him down. I felt sweat on my brow — not from exertion.

"I don't know! I don't even think we have bears on this side of the island!"

"There was a polar bear once, I think!"

"Oh good, the deadliest of bears! I feel very reassured!"

He huffed — or winced, I couldn't tell. "I'm sorry!"

"If it's not a bear, what the hell is it?"

"I don't know! Your guess is as good as mine!"

We didn't slow down. The path weaved and we clumsily weaved with it. I couldn't tell where in town we were — I couldn't even tell if we were getting closer or farther from Reid's house. It didn't help that the woods in the Avalon were so furiously dense that every step risked a stray root or rock catching us off guard and tripping us up, and we were constantly ducking beneath tree limbs.

The stomping was still behind us, consistently fast — faster than something so heavy should be moving. If I wasn't so focused on getting away, I could've doubled over and thrown up.

We turned a blind corner, and I was looking desperately at the back of Reid's head. As he turned the corner, he risked a glance behind us.

I watched his face go pale, then green in a millisecond.

The breath caught in my throat.

He tugged my arm harder, and I almost toppled over. He was panting at this point, his stubby nails and calloused fingers digging into my arm.

"Come on, Thomas!" he barked.

"What is it?!" I demanded. "What did you see!"

I didn't even want an answer. I just wanted him to lie, say it was something I'd recognize so I could pry open my closing throat. But his only response was his gasping breaths.

The thing was gaining on us. The footsteps were getting closer, and so was the beastly, grunting noises it made with every stomp. My cheeks were wet and my vision was blurry, but I couldn't tell if I was crying or if sweat was dripping into my eyes.

We were approaching a fork in the road and Reid's head frantically looked side to side before he took a turn so sharp I could hardly tell where he was going until I was there with him.

He feigned taking the right path and instead ducked both of us in between two trees so lush their branches smacked into my face and the needles scraped against me as he pulled me beneath them on the opposite side of the trail. He'd forced me to crouch with him, with sticks and bushes digging into our legs and sides. Somewhere in our clatter, the hand on his arm became wrapped around my shoulders. His chest was heaving but he sucked in a breath and held it.

I could hardly see through the trees. I could just make out a glimpse of the trail we were on. My face felt wet and stung all over. I looked over at him. His skin was torn up from the branches, little scrapes that sprouted tiny spots of smudged blood with needles stuck in them. I imagined my face looked about the same.

He was staring blankly out at the trail, eyes darting around. It was as if I wasn't there.

In a hushed voice, I started, "Reid, what—"

He hissed, almost inaudibly, through his teeth and clamped a hand over my mouth. Huddled together, I could barely breathe from his hand covering most of my nose unintentionally and we were shaking so much the trees around us were likely shaking along with us.

The stomps got closer and closer until they were just to my left, hidden only by the thick trees. It stopped, sniffing and grunting. Then, it dragged itself — impossibly quiet. I could barely hear the ground being torn up when I caught my first glimpse of it.

Thick, gnarly antlers covered in a patchy brown velvet. As the thing turned its head, I could see the antlers were stained crimson and shedding in thin, bloody sheets that hung from the edges. It edged forward and the sight of its face very nearly forced a whimper from my lips if it weren't for Reid's hand.

It was mostly bone: bone that was yellowed, with stubborn bits of sheer flesh and fur clinging to it in random patches around its cheeks and forehead. Where its eyes should've been was just hollow skull, black inside from the shadows. The skull was massive, much like the skull of a moose, only longer, and where the muzzle should've been was replaced with two thick, sharp… teeth? Tusks? I couldn't say.

The thing continued to move, dipping the bone slits of its nose to the gravel. Its neck was coated in dark fur, as thick and long as a mane. It was unfathomably big, so long that it folded up its limbs — lean enough that

I could make out the lines of muscle through the spiky hairs — close to its body and took the steps by dragging the thick pad of its feet, adorned with claws the length of my arm, through the dirt. Silently. The body was as thick and furry as a bear's, but decaying, creating misshapen holes through which I could see the red of intestines that threatened to fall out and a partial bloody ribcage. They didn't look like wounds — I couldn't fathom a creature on earth that could hurt it. The body was *eating itself* from the outside in.

I wanted to squeeze my eyes shut, but I couldn't look away. Reid clutched me tighter, as if he could feel the yelp climbing up my throat.

I didn't know how long it took the thing to move away. It lingered for so long, taking its steps so slowly, I thought we'd live forever huddled beneath those trees. But it did keep going. And the further it got, the larger it seemed. Because no matter how far it got away, it never seemed to get smaller. It seemed to remain just as big as it was when it was right in front of me.

Even after it disappeared, releasing another earth moving, devastating howl, we didn't move. Reid's flashlight was still on, though he'd dropped his phone face up in the brush at some point. I was staring in the place where the thing had been. I hadn't blinked.

It wasn't until the sky started to brighten that my eyes focused again.

My eyes finally pried away in time to see Reid swallow heavily. He met my gaze and seemed to only then remember that he'd been holding my mouth shut all this time. He finally released me, wordlessly, and reached for his phone. The flash caused us both to flinch. He turned it off as quickly as he could and tucked it away. The blood on his face had dried. I suspected mine had, too. My skin felt tight.

He stood up, having to push the tree limbs away from him as he went. He moved slowly and silently. We both still felt like prey. He held the branches out of the way before reaching a hand up and helping me to my feet.

When I stood, my legs felt cramped and burned. My heart hadn't slowed for a second, not in the hours we lay in wait. We cautiously weaved between the trees and back onto the clear trail.

Reid was still prying himself free of stray branches as I stared at the earth underfoot, where it was tossed and torn up by the claws.

"Where…?" I couldn't finish the sentence. The words just withered and died on my tongue. But Reid understood, anyway. He nodded toward the left turn in the path, and we started to walk again.

We didn't say another word to each other.

Above us, the sky was still deep blue, no hint of red or pink of sunrise, but bright enough that we didn't need a flashlight. Not that we'd have dared one, anyway.

When I saw the end of the path, the opening that gave way to the side of a red shed and the back of a yellow house, I wasn't even relieved. Crossing the threshold of the woods wasn't freedom. It wasn't safe. It was just more space.

Still, breaching the other side meant that eventually I'd be able to lie down. Maybe even close my eyes. Though, I could already guess what I'd see on the other side of my lids. At least I didn't have to wait anymore.

I hurried up to get out. Not by much. I couldn't muster the energy to run. But I used the last of my strength to push myself to the end of the path and onto the green plush of the backyard.

Just as I let myself exhale, I heard the subtlest rustle of branches, and gravel being kicked up. I turned only to catch the dirt hitting the ground again.

Reid was gone. The only trace of him was a long claw mark and the print of a paw across the ground he was standing on.

CRYPTIDS FROM THE ROCK

EDITED BY ELLEN CURTIS AND ERIN VANCE

There are creatures in the dark we cannot explain. The fog rolls in and the light plays tricks, and all logic leaves us in the moment. Every culture has them, and they all exist on an island off the east coast of Canada.

From the editors of the From the Rock anthologies comes a new selection of twenty stories, carefully curated from some of Newfoundland and Labrador's favourite authors. Between these pages, revisit old legends and fresh new additions to the world of cryptids.

Including the work of Ali House (*The Hunters and the Hunted*), Ainsley Hawthorn (*Land of Many Shores*), Dwain Campbell (*Strange Duty*) and more!